MOCENDI'S GAMBIT

ALSO BY S.K. RANDOLPH

VARTERELS' UNIVERSE™

(as paperbacks)

Part I - UnFolding

1. DiMensioner's Revenge

5. ConDra's Fire

8. MasTer's Reach

10. Jaradee's Legacy

Agothany 1 (Companion Shorts 2, 3, 4, 6, 7, and 9)

Part II - CoaleScence

11. Incirrata Secret

13. Corps Stones

16. Mocendi's Gambit

19. Queen's Quest

Agothany 2 (Companion Shorts 12, 14, 15, 17, 18, and 20)

Part III - Quickening

(a work in process)

Told with words and art,

contained in novels and companion shorts,

available in print and eBooks.

MOCENDI'S GAMBIT

ILLUSTRATED BY THE AUTHOR

VARTERELS' UNIVERSE
BOOK SIXTEEN

S.K. RANDOLPH

Cover and Illustrations by
S.K. RANDOLPH

CheeTrann Creations LLC

Mocendi's Gambit: Illustrated by the Author (VarTerels' Universe Book 7) Second Edition

ISBN
Paperback 978-1-962777-19-3
eBook 978-1-962777-39-1

Self Published by S.K. Randolph
CheeTrann Creations LLC
Suite 316-160
1410 Valley View Drive
Delta, CO 81416

Web Site: www.skrandolph.com
Substack: skrandolph.substack.com
Facebook: http://facebook.com/S.K.Randolph11

VU-132-J VU-16 MG 260706-1033 | 240127 PIbtA VUPt-2 | 328 6X9 .vellum

To Charles H. Lawrence, an internationally recognized shaman, whose wizard-like presence in my life inspired the character of Wolloh Espyro, High DiMensioner od DerTah and VarTerel of the Inner Universe.

I first met Charles as a shy thirteen-year-old during a rehearsal for a ballet my mother had costumed at the City Hall Theatre in Hamilton, Bermuda. Draped in his grey wind costume, he whirled around the stage. A final spin brought him around to face me where I watched from the wings. His hazel eyes gleamed and his magic smile flashed. I was bewitched! Older than me by several years, he became my mentor, protector, and friend.

https://danceforallpeople.com/charles-lawrence-video/

VarTereis' Universe ™
SCIENCE FANTASY

MOCENDI'S GAMBIT

Prologue
TaSneach

Revenge is a game, one of life's breaking,
That causes more pain, not a remaking.
Those who unwind in their devious brewing
Most often create their personal undoing.

ocendi DiMensioner Vygel Vintrusie tensed as the transport shuttle landed on TaSneach, the planet of Soputto's ever-winter moon. He fastened his heavy winter jacket, yanked the hood lower over his knit cap, and pulled thick mittens over arthritis-crippled hands. Surrounded by six prison guards, he and Karlsut Sorda, his accomplice in stealing three Corps Stones from the Clenaba Rolas Solar System, disembarked. A snow rover braked to a stop. In silence, they climbed aboard. The engine revved, inching the rover forward into a blizzard of blustering flakes and howling winds.

Vygel grimaced and slumped in his seat. Next to him, Sorda scowled at the white nothingness. Both men headed for a lifetime of solitary confinement. Guards in front, behind, and beside them impeded their ability to converse about what lay ahead.

With a sideways glance at his fellow prisoner, the Mocendi sneered. *We've said everything, right, Karlsut Sorda?*

They had already played the blame game, accusing each other of the debacle in New York City, 1969. To himself, Vygel grudgingly admitted they were lucky not to be facing execution. *We almost destroyed an entire galaxy.*

He wiped his dripping nose on his jacket sleeve and stared straight ahead. The emptiness inside him matched the bleak, barren whiteness enshrouding them. Desolation sent his mind back to the recent trial. *The Galactic Tribunal let us live, but—*A shudder wracked his pain-ridden body. His jaw set hard as stone. Anger replaced self-pity. *They stripped me of my DiMensioner's power; they thought they left me defenseless.* His eyes narrowed. *I will make them sorry.*

Next to him, Karlsut muttered. Vygel caught the name of his half-brother, a man whom he despised, a man who had been the Governor of this Penal Colony for several sun cycles. *I wonder where you are, Skultar Rados. If you hadn't refused to help us steal the Corps Stones, we might have succeeded.* He swallowed a snarl. *The plan wasn't yours, so you wanted nothing to do with it.*

He ran his tongue over crooked, yellowed teeth. His large nostrils flared in disgust. A fellow Mocendi had warned him the plan would backfire. A scowl distorted his thin-lipped mouth. *Damn you, Thorlu Tangorra! Just this once, I should have been right, not you.*

Vygel massaged a throbbing knee and stared into the never-ending winter. His eyes closed. His chin dropped to his chest.

"Pay attention, idiot."

The telepathic words brought his head up. A mental image formed and focused. Despite the agony in his arthritic hands, he grabbed Karlsut Sorda's arm.

The snow rover, the soldiers, and the winter landscape vanished.

1
Myrrh

Brielle AsTar smoothed her long red curls and smiled at herself in the dressing-table mirror. As she studied her sprinkling of freckles, her alternate persona's dark hair and eyes flashed across the silvery surface and faded away. "Rayna Deejara, I miss you and ballet class and performance. I even miss New York City."

She reminisced about the weeks she and her friends had spent in the Earth year 1969, hunting for the missing Corps Stones. "What an adventure!"

Swiveling on the padded stool, she walked to the window. The beauty of the Guardian of Myrrh's garden and the freshness of the air made her smile. She had just returned to this time and dimension. The odors of the big city—smog, the smell of filthy humans, car exhaust, animal feces, and back-alley trash—lingered in her memory.

Laughter below refocused her attention on the garden. Torgin and Gar, tossing a flying disc, made her laugh. Gar's skin, several shades darker than his cousin's warm brown, gleamed. His curly black hair framed an impish face and highlighted the deep chestnut eyes, reflecting his delight in the game. He caught sight of her and waved. Spyglass, his small rat terrier, gave an excited bark.

Torgin waved, too, and with a wide grin at his young cousin, he yelled, "Garon, catch!"

The disc flew high overhead. Gar jumped and missed. He pivoted, searching the garden.

A flash of golden light flared by the pond. Chealim, the Galactic Guardian of the Fourth Galaxy, stepped free with a furry brown dog at his side and the flying disc in his hand. Spyglass dashed across the garden and met the big dog midway. They greeted each other with wagging tails and a nose-to-nose sniff.

Torgin, his grin expressing his pleasure, knelt and flung his arms around the shaggy brown neck. "Buster! It is you." He looked up at the Fourth Galaxy's Guardian. "How? Why?"

Chealim grinned. "This is a genome twin of our dear Buster, exact right down to his memories. Since Almiralyn has agreed to resume her role as Guardian of Myrrh, the Council determined Buster might be the perfect thank you gift."

Buster! Brie remembered how he had saved her life and Ari's four sun cycles earlier. A final peek out the window left her smiling. Chealim tossed the disc. Barks and laughter mingling, Gar, Buster, and Spyglass chased after it.

Chealim caught her eye. *Find Esán.*

The urgency in the telepathic message erased her delight and sent her in search of the man she loved.

A ri AsTar stared out the bedroom window at the sunflower field, camouflaging the portal to The Borderlands. Worry had kept her from sleeping. *What did I do wrong, Troms el Shiv?*

As though he had heard Elf, the man she had fallen in love with, appeared in her doorway. "May I come in?"

She folded her arms. "Only if you tell me why you have been avoiding me since I returned from New York City. Have I done something wrong?"

He looked away, then sighed. "I'm not going to El Stroma, Arienh. I can't make the trip." An unsteady hand rested on his throat. "When I was twelve and refused to become a Mocendi, and The MasTer ordered my vocal cords severed and erased my memories, something inside me broke. Your work with the healing knife Efillaeh and Brie's with the Stone of Remembering gave me back my voice and my early memories. As powerful as they are, they could not heal the damage to my psyche. All I want, Arienh, is a quiet life with Gregos, Marji, and Tamosh, working on the boat and living near the sea. El Stroma is of no interest to me." He hung his head.

She studied him in silence. His reluctance to look at her and the fatigue-painted circles under his eyes when he did sent gooseflesh racing. She shivered. "There's more, isn't there?"

A tremble of emotion shook his shoulders. "You will always be important to me..." His hand twitched.

"I could go with you, Elf. We could get a boat and sail together. We could—"

He shook his head. "Your destiny is on El Stroma. You have important things to do. I can't ask you to stay behind for me."

The bleak expression on his face made her flinch. "You don't love me?"

Stark pain filled his eyes and left her trembling. Her anger surged. "What did I do to make you hate me?"

He hesitated, reached out, then lowered his arm. "I don't hate you. I just can't spend my life with you. Don't you understand, Ari? I'm not the man you need. You need someone who will inspire you to be the best you can be." He made a choking sound. "I am broken. Something dark and unhappy hides inside me. Forget me. Find someone who can match your strengths with his." He moved to the door. "I'm leaving for DerTah."

The finality of it closing behind him left her gasping. Her anger sizzled and died. The pain of loss rushed through her. Tears threatened. A flash flood of emotions stripped her breath away. She gasped. *I need to be alone.* Gathering her power around her, she teleported to the loft in the barn and burrowed into the hay. The tears came, lava-hot tears that scorched her cheeks and left burning wounds in her heart.

Henrietta Avetlire sat on the window seat in her room, her lips pursed in thought. Restless fingers rearranged her silvery hair. Violet eyes narrowed. With a nod, she rose to her feet. Settling her new pale-blue, wide-brimmed hat on her curls, she tipped her head to see in the mirror, smiled at the white roses bedecking the brim, and slipped her spectacles into their special pocket. Back erect, she stepped into the hall. At the top of the stairs to the first floor of the Guardian of Myrrh's cottage, she gripped the wooden railing, descended the carpet-covered steps, and made her way to her niece, SparrowLyn AsTar's, art studio. A glance at a finished painting on the easel brought her to a standstill.

Sparrow's prophetic art had provided guidance to those fighting to save the VarTerels' Universe since The Unfolding began. Now, as the CoaleScent Cycle matured, her paintings continued to point the way.

Spectacles in hand, Henri studied the young man portrayed on the canvas. Tap, tap, tap. The amethyst-covered rim sounded a soft rhythm on her palm. "Just as I expected." Another tap, tap preceded their disappearance into their hiding place.

She exited the studio through a side door into a small, private garden and tottered along the stone inlaid path. As she skirted a lattice draped with flowering vines, she caught sight of her quarry. Esán Efre, Brie's true love, sat on a bench, twirling a leaf between his fingers. His shoulders drooped; his troubled gaze roamed from flower bed to flower bed. The leaf fluttered to the ground.

She stepped into view. "I'm here, Esán. You wish to speak with me?"

Relief brightened his eyes. He jumped up and hurried to meet her. "Thank you so much for coming, Henrietta. I wasn't certain you heard my message." He offered his arm. "Would you prefer to walk or to sit?"

"We should sit, don't you agree? What you wish to share is important." She rested her hand on his arm. "I don't want to be distracted."

When they had settled on the bench, she withdrew her lenses and perched them on her nose.

Esán studied his hands. He looked up and attempted a smile. "I'm uncertain how to begin, so I'll put my problem on the table. We can go from there."

Henri heard the slight tremor in his voice. "I'm listening."

His gaze darted away, then back. "I've just received word I cannot travel across the Décussate to the planet of El Stroma. Although my disease is in remission, if I were to go so far from my home planet, chances are it would not remain so. I might not make it back to Tao Spirian." He sighed. His stormy blue eyes sought hers. "I can visit closer planets, but periodic visits home are vital to ensure the disease doesn't reoccur."

Anguish flooded his features. "Brielle is excited to make the journey on the living ship *El Aperdisa*. I love her, Henri. I don't wish to hold her back, but..."

Henrietta removed her spectacles and tapped them on her knee. "I gather you and my great-niece haven't discussed this?"

He shook his head.

She offered the glowing lenses. "I recommend you formulate your most pressing question, then put these on."

He studied them for a long moment before resting them on the bridge of his nose. Tension squeezed his eyes shut. A held breath released in a quiet whisper. He peered through the lenses. Magnified eyes rounded. A slow inhale later, he removed them.

"Henri, I love your niece. Not being with her would destroy me." He stared at the shimmering frames. "These suggest a life filled with her. Do they always show what is true?"

"They show truth or nothing." She tucked them away. "Most people don't have the clarity of mind to see anything. I thought you might be the exception." She tipped her hat-bedecked head and smiled. "I suggest you prepare yourself. Your lady is on the way." She rose. "Come straight to the point, Esán. I imagine she's guessed more than you realize."

With an encouraging smile, she toddled along the path and reached the door as her niece stepped into the garden.

"Aunt Henri! I saw Mother's painting. Have you seen Esán?"

Henrietta bobbed her head. "He's waiting for you on the bench.

Brie kissed her cheek. "I'll find you later."

Henri watched her hurry along the path, then turned. A tall, imposing figure held open the white gate into the front garden.

She peered up at the serious face. "You need me, Chealim?"

E sán rose as Brie walked toward him. His heart skittered around his chest. *If she decides she can't Join with me, what then?*

"What ifs accomplish nothing, Esán Efre." Serious brown eyes searched his face. She sat down and patted the bench. "We'll deal with whatever's worrying you. Tell me so I can help."

He crossed to the lattice and then retraced his steps. "I think I need to move while I talk."

"I'll sit right here and listen." She rested an arm on the back of the bench.

While he paced the garden, he allowed the images he had seen through Henri's spectacles to bolster his courage. He paused in front of Brie, absorbed her natural tranquility, and shared his concerns.

A cocoon-like stillness cloaked her. His heart seemed to stop. He needed to express how much he loved her; how much he wanted her beside him always. A lump in his throat held him quiet.

A small smile played at the corners of her mouth. She rose and touched her lips to his. Tears glistening, she looked into his eyes. "Esán Efre, I love you. Our destinies are linked as surely as a Tirips Tree's roots reach deep beneath the Terces Wood. I need you healthy so we can accomplish what the Galactic Guardians require us to do. I am a VarTerel. You carry dual Seeds of Carsilem. There's plenty to do in the Fourth Galaxy. Going to El Stroma without you would break my heart. I would be of no value to anyone."

His arms enclosed her. "I love you, Brielle AsTar." Holding her at arm's length, he stroked her cheek. A tear dripped onto the tip of his finger. She caught one as it leaked from the corner of his eye. Fingertips touching, they watched two tears become one, kissed the spot where they merged, and moved into each other's arms.

Esán felt her heart, heard the rhythm of her breath match his, and gave her a lingering kiss he wished could last forever.

When they came up for air, she stepped away and blushed. "Relevart, how long have you been there?"

"Long enough to enjoy your delight." The Universal VarTerel's amber eyes twinkled. "When you catch your breath, I have something urgent to share." He took a seat.

Esán grinned at Brie, planted one more kiss, and drew her down on the bench. "What's the message?"

Relevart scratched his chin. "Congratulations on your upcoming Joining.

I understand you propose to announce your formal engagement to your friends this afternoon." He paused. "The Council asks that you keep your engagement to yourselves. Those who plot against the return of Eleo Predans to El Stroma and desire the rise of The MasTer covet your power. They already know you are in love. If they discover your plans, they will redouble their efforts to find and use you against each other and us. When you return to Tao Spirian, you may be Joined. Tell no one, not even your family and friends."

Brie fidgeted. "I planned to ask Ari to be my Witness. I don't wish to leave her out of something this important."

He frowned. "I gather your sister has not shared her news?"

The regret in his voice triggered a slight response from the Star of Truth on the nape of her neck. "I need to find her. Excuse me." She hurried toward the cottage.

Esán started to follow. Relevart stopped him with a look. "This is between Ari and Brie. She will share with you later. You and I have serious things to discuss."

Esán sank onto the bench and forced himself to pay attention to the Universal VarTerel.

2

Myrrh

Relevart ran a hand over his shoulder-length, white hair. A frown tugged his mouth into a downward curve. Amber eyes studied the face of the young man opposite him. He cleared his throat. "Brielle does not yet know what I am going to share."

Esán straightened. "You sound serious. How can I help?"

"The Council informed me Vygel Vintrusie and Karlsut Sorda never made it to the Penal Colony. Chealim believes Thorlu Tangorra and Skultar Rados organized their escape. We are certain they will make their way to El Stroma. Before that, however..." He pursed his lips, then shook his head. "The Guardians stripped Vintrusie of his DiMensioner's powers." His piercing gaze narrowed to gleaming golden slits. "He wants revenge, Esán."

The young man's face paled. A hand flew to his heart, then dropped to his thigh. "He wants Brielle, right?"

"He and his cohorts crave power. Brie is not the only target, but she is, for

Vygel, the most important. More than anything, he desires a protariflee child created from her eggs and his sperm. He hopes The MasTer's gene will pass to his son." He studied him in silence. "There's more, Esán."

Hands that had been gripping his thighs clenched into tight fists. Esán leaned forward. "More?"

Relevart came straight to the point. "Thorlu Tangorra has discovered a way to free The MasTer's gene to reclaim its masculine form. If they find her, Brie will face a fight for her very existence."

"Wait! Brie changed The MasTer's gene to feminine. Rayna's female and strong. How can The MasTer re-emerge?"

Relevart's frowned reappeared. The conversation he had had earlier with the Council flashed through his mind. "Chealim tells me there is only one way, but chose not to reveal more. As is the way of the Galactic Guardians, we must find our own solutions."

"Did he offer you a hint?"

Relevart shook his head. "He did not."

One determined motion brought Esán to standing. "I must take Brie somewhere safe. Tao Spirian isn't it and neither is Myrrh. What do you suggest?" Verbal questions transitioned to an expression filled with pleading.

Relevart forced a calm reply. "You and Brie must go to DerTah. Our enemies will expect you to travel to Shu Chenaro to confer with Wolloh. An alternate destination programed into Demrach Gateway will take you elsewhere. You will recognize it and realize who to go to for instructions on your next move. They aren't only after Brie. All those she loves and all those you and I love are at risk. In the morning, I plan to escort everyone but Almiralyn and Corvus to *El Aperdisa*."

Esán sank back onto the bench, his forehead a ladder of wrinkles. "Wait. If Sparrow leaves, what will Myrrh do without its Guardian?" His brows lifted. "Oh—"

A large, shaggy brown dog bounded down the path. Esán's tense expression transformed in to a delighted grin. "Buster! Is it really you?" He threw his arms around the big dog.

Relevart smiled. "The Council thought Buster's return would be the perfect gift for Almiralyn. She has agreed to resume her duties as the Guardian of Myrrh. It will give her time to heal from her imprisonment in Roween Rattori's crystal cage. Corvus and Buster will remain here with her. Sparrow's artistic talent is important to the success of El Stroma's resettlement, so she and Allynae will journey on *El Aperdisa*. Their relationship to Brie makes it necessary for them to leave Myrrh." He glanced toward the cottage. "Let's hope Brie and Ari have had time to share."

Esán came to his feet as Henri rounded the trellis, her violet eyes seeking her life-mate. The white flowers on her hat fluttered in the breeze. One hand held it in place as she stopped in front of them, gasping for breath. A long inhale seemed to steady her. "Relevart, Mira's gardener sighted interlopers in the Terces Wood." Her attention switched to Esán. "I can see Relevart has shared the news. You must take my great-niece and disappear, Esán Efre." She pressed a small, double-terminated crystal into his hand. "This is a herkimer diamond, the most powerful of the quartz crystals. Its name is Keersé. When it's time, you'll understand how to use it." She kissed his cheek. "Be safe."

Relevart clasped her hand. "Go, Esán. Take Brie to the gateway. Once you arrive on DerTah, I will return its destination point to the Desert of Fera Finnero. We will cover your departure."

"Can Brie say goodbye to her parents?"

"Tell no one. Do not use your powers until you are free of Myrrh." He caught Henri's eyes. "Information has been finding its way from here to our enemies."

Esán, frowned, pivoted, and sprinted for the cottage.

Buster lifted his nose and sniffed the air. Tail wagging, he trotted to a large bush at the back of the garden and gave a soft bark.

Relevart cleared his throat as Henri placed her glasses on her nose. "You can come out, Garon Anaru."

The bushes rustled. Gar stepped free, his expression a cross between stubborn and guilty.

👁　👁

Gar looked from Relevart to Henri. Spyglass, tail wagging, tagged after Buster along the path to the garden gate. Henri sank onto the bench and adjusted the tilt of her hat.

The Universal VarTerel studied him with a nerve-wracking intensity. "How much did you hear?"

"Everything you told Esán. Sir, Brie's in real trouble, right?"

Relevart glanced at Henri. She nodded.

Gar frowned. "You talking in each other's head?"

Ignoring the question, Relevart seemed to look deep inside him. "How brave are you, Garon?"

"Real brave, Sir, especially if someone I love's in trouble."

The VarTerel's amber eyes grew distant. "I must leave. Henri has something to share and something to ask." He kissed his life-mate's cheek and flashed from sight.

Henrietta patted the bench beside her. "Our time together is short, Gar. Sit with me, and I will explain our need." She perched her spectacles on her nose. Eyes the color of the amethysts on the rims scrutinized him with the full force of her VarTerel's power.

Gar squirmed. "Are them glasses magic?"

Her serious expression softened into a tiny smile. "They are very special, Garon." She pressed her palms together and whispered,

> *"Believing one's eyes is a masterful gift,*
> *One that can cause an improbable shift.*
> *Spectacles paired with the talent for sight*
> *Will help to bring forth what's true and what's right."*

Gar gasped. On her open palms were a pair of spectacles with round lenses framed in dark chestnut brown. "Where—" He shook his head.

Henri placed them on the bridge of his nose, checked the fit of the temples that rested on his ears, and sat back with a satisfied nod. "These are yours, Garon. Through them you will see the truth and the correct path to follow." Her serious expression kept him still. "They will help you achieve your destiny. I am giving them to you now because I require you to go with Esán and Brielle. Not only will they need your help, but you will need theirs."

Spyglass scampered along the path and sniffed her hand.

She placed it on his head. "Spyglass must stay with me for now. He will be on the ship, *El Aperdisa*, when you arrive. Take off the spectacles and hold them between your hands."

He took them off, folded the temples, and cupped his hands around the smooth rims. His gaze sought hers.

She nodded. "Good. To hide them whisper, Nehidd. Try it."

Gar swallowed. "Nehidd."

The spectacles vanished. Gar gasped and shook his head.

Henri smiled. "Good. To call them forth, repeat the word Repapa. Go ahead."

He cupped his hands together. "Repapa." The feel of the spectacles between his palms brought a sigh of relief and a gleeful grin.

Hands resting on his shoulders, the elder VarTerel commanded him to hide them.

He whispered and shook his head in awe. "Wow."

Henri looked him in the eye. "You must distract the men guarding the portal in the woods, the one Brie showed you yesterday. You go where Brie goes and if you can't, you stick close to Esán. Take care, Gar." She pointed at the back of the garden. "Those bushes hide a gate leading to a trail that will take you to the portal. Hurry!"

Gar hugged her and ran down the path, slipped through the gate, and sprinted without a sound toward the Demrach Gateway.

Ari's deep voice filtered through Brie's door as Esán made his way to the second floor of the cottage. "Elf is not going to El Stroma. Now, you're telling me neither you nor Esán are making the trip." Something hard hit the floor.

Esán dodged into his room and tuned his senses to listen to the soft murmurs penetrating the wall. While he tried to pay attention, riotous thoughts bombarded him. He shoved them away, only to have them return full force: Vygel Vintrusie—The MasTer's gene—Thorlu's discovery. Relevart's news had confirmed his worst fears. Danger stalked the woman he loved more than anyone in the galaxy. *I swear by the Seeds of Carsilem to keep you safe, Brielle AsTar.*

He opened the door a crack and peeked out. Before he could decide if he should interrupt the twins, Ari marched into the hall, headed for the stairs.

Brie ran after her. "Ari, wait. I have more to share."

Her sister swung around, anger sparking a fire in her eyes and a rush of blood to her fair-skinned cheeks. "I'm not speaking to you, Brielle AsTar." She pivoted, and, with a flip of her long red curls, stomped down the steps.

Shoulders slumped and tears glistening, Brie gripped the banister and stared after her twin.

Esán hurried to her side and guided her down the hall to her room. She threw her arms around him, accepted a hug, and stepped back; her brown eyes filled with questions. "You're worried. What's happened?"

"You and I must leave Myrrh as soon as possible. Grab whatever you might need. I doubt we'll be back."

Frustration palpitated the space between them. "Can you at least tell me why we're leaving?"

"I promise to explain everything once we are safe." He moved to the window. After a quick scan of the garden, he turned. "Ready?"

Lips pressed tight around the questions he knew she wanted to ask, she nodded.

He shouldered her pack, eased the door open, and scanned the hall. "No DiMensionery. Follow me."

Leading the way down the stairs, he avoided the squeaky fourth step from the bottom and darted into SparrowLyn's studio. The exit stood ajar, giving him a view of the empty garden. He motioned Brie behind him and surveyed the area a second time. When nothing triggered an alarm, he clasped her hand, hurried along the path to the hidden gate, and led her into the Terces Wood.

They were well beyond the Guardian's acreage when Brie pulled him to a halt. "Why are we running away? What did Relevart tell you?"

Esán kept his urgent response low. "You are in danger. We need to disappear right now. Relevart reprogrammed Demrach Gateway to take us to a secret destination. I promise to tell you everything he shared with me when we're safe."

He thought she might argue. Instead, she crossed to a thicket of bushes. "I know a shortcut. Stay close."

Senses alert for danger, he followed her along an overgrown trail. The murmur of voices not far ahead brought them to a halt.

"He said to stay put." The deep voice continued after a frustrated hiss. "He wants to know who uses the gateway, when, and where they go."

A second voice responded. "We've been here for two sun turnings. The only one we've seen near the portal is our sneaky little snitch. You can stay if you want to, but I'm going back to camp."

The snap of small twigs beneath heavy boots suggested the voice's owner was leaving.

"You sure you wanna anger the boss?" The first man growled. "He can be awful mean."

The soldier approaching their hiding place hesitated. Muttered cursing accompanied them back the way they had come. "Can we at least go eat something? No one's gonna leave the cottage or Myrrh without us knowing."

The first man remained silent. The shuffle of feet and a soft expletive suggested he fought with himself. "A meal and back at it. Right?"

"Got it. Let's go." The heavy tread headed their way. Lighter footsteps followed.

Esán pulled Brie lower behind the bush where they hid.

Two pairs of booted feet marched past. As the footsteps faded, Esán led Brie to a huge, dead tree at the edge of a small clearing. Demrach Gateway swirled into being, its golden light glowing in forest dimness.

"Hey, you! Stop!" Boots pounded back in their direction.

Gar broke cover and raced toward the whirling vortex, shouting over his shoulder. "Come on!"

Esán clasped Brie's hand. They darted into the open and leapt after Gar into the swirling golden mist. Suspended in a tunnel of streaking colors, they clung to each other, their eyes glued to the boy in front of them. Seconds before the vortex closed, the quake of another person's entry into the portal sent the trio cannoning through dimensional space. White light exploded, carrying them into a giant forest where trees and bushes towered above them and leaves the size of a man's torso littered the ground.

Brie scrambled over a huge root and grabbed Gar's hand. "The Tinga Forest! Stay close, Garon. This is the most dangerous forest on the planet of DerTah."

Ahead of them, Esán braked to a halt. An immense tree, its branches writhing overhead, blocked the way. "Oh no! A Ratee Tree. Look out!"

A muted thud and a low groan announced their stalker had made it through the portal. With boots pounding through the brush and heavy breathing, he pursued them, broke cover, and froze, his chest heaving. A purple-red scar running from the middle of his scalp, behind his ear to his chin, pulsed. Bug-eyed, he gaped. "Is that tree what I think it is?" Horror left him gasping.

Esán pulled Brie backward. Gar stumbled after them. A snake-like limb encircling the man's waist lifted him skyward. A howl of despair echoed through the Tinga's vastness.

Brie stopped and released a panted breath. "We can't allow the Ratee to devour him." She raised a hand. The lithe branch suspended motion, held the man above the ground, quivered, then let him fall. He landed in a breathless heap amongst the Ratee Tree's massive roots and struggled to right himself, his expression stunned; his entire body shaking.

The scythe-sharp roar of a large cat cut through the rainforest.

Esán spun around. "Run!"

Brie grabbed Gar's hand and sprinted after him along an enormous animal trail. A short distance ahead, he dodged behind a bush. Brie and Gar skidded to a halt next to him.

"I know where to go." He gripped their hands. "Hold on."

The forest shimmered and faded into a manicured estate garden, surrounding a huge, gray stone mansion. The High DiMensioner Seyes Nomed strode their direction, his intense gaze searching the grounds behind them.

"I see you lost your unwanted companion. Excellent. I'll take care of him as soon as you're gone."

Esán frowned. "Any ideas who he is?"

Seyes shook his head. "No time for small talk." He tapped Esán's temple. "I'm sending you back to the Tinga. Racholet, your friendly gothraw, will carry you to a portal on the far side of the forest near the TheDahan border. No matter what occurs, do not dismount until you reach it." He met Esán's questioning gaze. "When you get to the portal, the information I just placed in your mind will guide you to a safe destination. It's good to see you, nephew."

Brie put her hands on Gar's shoulder. "Seyes, this is Gar. Please see he gets back to the Guardian's cottage on Myrrh."

Stubbornness buzzing around him like a swarm of angry wasps, Gar pulled away. "I ain't going anywhere without you."

Nomed held out his hand to Gar. "VarTerel Henrietta let me know you were coming, Garon. It's good to meet you."

Brie's hands went to her hips. "Aunt Henri?"

His charming smile flashed. "I believe this young man is your personal guard, Brielle AsTar." He made eye-contact with each member of the trio. "Take care of each other." He raised a hand.

The garden vanished into giant trees and the dim light of the Tinga. A soft bellow accompanied the pounding of hooves on the mulchy ground. Racholet, a warthog-like animal the size of a horse, trotted between the trees. Her piggish snout sniffed the air. She slowed to a walk, her dual sets of ivory white tusks gleaming. *"I Cho, your friend."*

Brie stepped from behind a tree and responded to the telepathic message. *"I'm Brie, your friend."*

The gothraw snuffled the air. *"Hurry."* She lowered her huge, muscled body until her belly rested on the ground.

Esán helped Gar onto the broad back in front of Brie and scrambled up after her.

She wrapped her arms around her young guard. "Hold on to the gothraw's mane, Gar. Don't let go."

Esán encircled her waist with his arm and nudged Cho's tough hide with his heel.

The gothraw's strong legs heaved her to standing. She swept her head from one side to other, sniffing the air. *"Hold tight. I fast."*

A fearsome, rumbling roar thundered through the immenseness of the forest, shaking the leaves overhead, and leaving Cho straining to catch the owner's scent.

Gar's head whipped right, then left. "What the heck?"

"Ludoc Cat." Cho dodged down a narrow ravine and set off at a gallop, her muscles rippling beneath them.

Gar looked over his shoulder. "She talked in my mind. What's a Ludoc Cat?"

Esán groaned. Images of the largest feline in the Tinga crouched ready to spring, its hind legs tensed; its extra-long tail, with its tufted black tip, switching back and forth, brought terrifying memories rushing to the fore. "It's one of the fiercest animals you'll ever meet. Hold on and keep your eyes peeled." He suppressed an alarmed shudder.

Fear's not an option, Esán Efre. He focused on keeping himself, Brie, and Gar calm.

A ri entered her sister's room to find the closet door standing open, and clothes scattered everywhere. She had come back to apologize for her less than mature response to Brie's decision not to go to El Stoma. The chaos made her heart ache; her twin's absence inspired a wave of anxiety. *You didn't even tell me where you're going, Brielle.*

Vexation escorted her from the bedroom in search of the Universal VarTerel. He was nowhere to be found, but she discovered her Great Aunt Henrietta alone in the den, staring out the window through her amethyst-rimmed spectacles.

An internal fight to hold her temper in check fisted Ari's hands and clenched her teeth. A breath calmed her down. "Where's Relevart, Aunt Henri? I need him to tell me why he sent Brie away without me."

Warm violet eyes regarded her through crystal-clear lenses. "Esán removed Brielle from a dangerous situation to protect her. She said goodbye to no one, not even your parents."

Ari's fists pressed into her hips. Fear for her twin stiffened her spine. With a toss of her head, she sent her red hair flying around her. "I'm *not* just anyone, Aunt Henrietta. Brie is my sister, my identical twin. If she's in some kind of trouble, I should be there to help protect her."

A flash of white light left the Universal VarTerel standing next her great aunt.

Ari held her ground. "Where is Brielle, Relevart? How dare you send her away without me."

Aunt Henri cocked her head and peered from beneath the brim of her hat. Her delicate brow arched. Her soft pink lips pursed.

Relevart put an arm around his life-mate, a movement which added fuel to Ari's fire.

She glared harder. "You two have each other. Now that you've sent Brie elsewhere, I'm all alone." Turning her back, she blinked away tears. "Soon, we leave for *El Aperdisa*. My parents will stay here. Esán has taken Brie some unknown place, and—" A choked sob stopped her tirade and squeezed her eyes shut.

Relevart drew Henri down to the sofa beside him.

Ari faced them. "I apologize. You are not the reason for my anger. I didn't mean to be so rude."

Her aunt's expression softened. "Please sit with us, Arienh. We would like to share several important things."

The desire to leave the room evaporated as Ari smoothed her hair, sat down across from her aunt, and folded her hands in her lap.

Relevart turned to his life-mate. "You start, Henri."

She placed her hat on the coffee table, patted her silvery curls into place, then removed her specs. After a long moment, she nodded to herself and tucked them away. "Your parents have given us permission to share some news with you. The Galactic Council has asked Almiralyn to resume her role as Myrrh's Guardian along with Corvus, freeing SparrowLyn and Allynae to join the expedition to El Stroma."

A tiny, relieved smile unfroze Ari's gloomy expression. "What about you? Den and Penee mentioned you may not be on the ship."

Relevart rested his forearms on his knees and cleared his throat. "Henri and I have a job to do before we join you on El Aperdisa. With luck, we'll complete it by the time the ship reaches Roahymn, the nearest space port to the DéCussate and the magnetic bridge which will connect us to El Stroma's solar system." He straightened. "Tomorrow morning, we all depart for Treblaya. Henri and I will be there off and on until the ship leaves. Arienh, it is most important that you say nothing regarding Brie's departure until we reach *El Aperdisa*. Our plans keep finding their way to our enemies. The less we share with anyone, the better chance Brie and Esán have to escape unnoticed."

Ari frowned. "Are you saying someone here is a spy?"

Neither VarTerel answered. Their serious expressions and their silence told her all she needed to know.

3
Der Tah

The ludoc cat howled a second time. Gar's small body tensed. Brie pulled him closer, her gaze darting over the forest terrain.

In the distance, an answering wail sent a stab of fear shooting up her spine. Ludocs, the fastest, fiercest creatures in the Tinga, terrified her.

Esán spoke next to her ear. "Stay calm. Fear will bring it faster."

Although his heart pounding against her back belied his low-keyed message, she let his closeness soothe her and concentrated on staying alert and ready for anything.

Cho's steady pace did not falter. Zigzagging between trees, she navigated the moss-covered roots and forded the rushing streams traversing the woods. Another howl brought her to a standstill at the edge of a small clearing, her snout lifted, her ears alert. *"Ludoc close. No panic."*

Brie strained to find the approaching cat in the dense foliage between trees. Nothing moved. Not a breath of wind stirred; not a bird called. Then, across the clearing, the leaves near the bottom of an immense, flower-covered bush trembled. A triangular head half the height of a man appeared between its branches, its black-tufted ears twitching, its feline nostrils flaring. Mammoth gray paws edged forward. Powerful shoulders cleared the shaking bush. Pewter-gray eyes fixed on its prey glinted in a ray of sunlight. A low, rumbling growl widened the enormous jaw. Razor-sharp canines flashed.

Gar's alarm sent a shudder through his youthful body.

Brie grabbed a handful of mane and pulled him closer. Behind her, Esán held his breath, his arms tightening around her.

Cho held stone still.

Crouched and ready to spring, the ludoc's muscular body grew taut. Its long, black-tufted tail twitched back and forth, then extended over its head.

The Gothraw's second and most deadly pair of tusks shot into place. She lowered her head. A rumbling roar shook her. The ludoc pressed lower.

A second cat bound into the clearing and paused midway between them. A white-tufted tail and fur divided into pale gray patches outlined in white marked her as a female. Her charcoal eyes sought her male counterpart. Pointed gray ears topped with white tufts twitched, picking up sounds Brie knew were far out of human range. Huge nostrils closed. A low-pitched purr pulled the male's attention away from his quarry. The sensual odor of musk filled the air. The female's extra-long hind legs launched her into the trees. With a final, long, whining caterwaul, she sprinted from sight.

Its nose inhaling the aroma of female, the enormous male ludoc crept forward, gave a final threatening growl, and raced after her.

Cho's fighting tusks withdrew. She shook her head and trotted into the cover of the forest trees.

"That was one scary cat." Gar squeezed Brie's hand and grinned at her over his shoulder.

Esán relaxed behind her. "The female was Trinuge's protector, right?"

She nodded. "It was the Dreelas TheLise in shifted form."

He leaned nearer. "How did you know it was her?"

She laughed and shrugged. "It's a girl thing. I recognized her essence when she leapt into the clearing."

Gar wiggled and pointed. "Over there."

Esán's soft laugh rustled her hair. "We made it."

Through the trees, a portal shimmered in the late afternoon sun. Sparks of color glittered like gemstones, sending rainbow light arching above it. Cho sniffed the air, walked to the spinning gateway, and lowered her belly to the ground. Esán slid off her back and helped Brie down. Gar jumped, landing beside them.

The Gothraw pushed her hindquarters into the air, straightened her front legs, and touched her nose to Brie's extended hand.

"You go." She flicked her tail toward the swirling gateway.

Gar studied it, then looked at Esán. "Do you know where we're going?"

"Nope. Nomed put the destination in my mind." He reached for Brie's hand. "I suggest we go find out."

Cho's prancing grew more restless. She swung her head to look behind her. *"Hurry."*

Brie grasped Gar's arm.

Esán pulled them both after him into the swirling gateway. Colors streaked by. White light flared in the distance. They shot through the brightness and stood blinking at an unfamiliar world.

~ ReTaw au Qa ~

Brie, with Gar clinging to her hand, rotated, taking in the beautiful strangeness. Eerie fingers of light wove their way around massive tree trunks and filtered through the glowing wisteria-tinted mist hovering above the ground. A skirt-like curtain of grape-dark, man-high roots anchored the trees to the shoreline of a winding river tinted the color of red wine. The odors of damp moss and standing water scented the moisture-laden air. Mounds of earth covered with pale orchid grass and surrounded by murky, mulberry pools created a pock-marked effect on the land across the river. In the distance, bordering the immenseness of the mound-covered plain, more gigantic trees hid what lay beyond.

She glanced at Esán. "Are we on the planet of ReTaw au Qa?"

Gar gave a startled squeak and darted in front of her. "What the heck!"

A blue-scaled Pentharian half again as tall as Esán and smelling of swamp water stepped from behind a tree, his gold piercings glistening in the late-turning sun. The bulging muscles of his humanesque torso twitched, magnifying the warning in his gold reptilian eyes.

Brie choked back an exclamation of delight, gripped Gar's shoulders, and nudged him closer to Esán.

The Pentharian's long, scale-covered tail switching back and forth suggested agitation spiced with fear. His long tongue flicked out, tasted the air, and snapped back. "We have unwanted company." He examined Gar with intense interest. "I am Voer of the Clan Auqan. Relevart shared that you, young Garon, are Brie's guardian. Can you shift shape?"

Gar licked his lips and glanced at Esán, who mouthed the word friend.

With a fisted hand on his heart, the boy met the Pentharian's steady stare. "I am honored to meet you, Voer. Yes, I can shift."

Relief shone in Voer's lizard-like eyes. "It is good. All must shape a bird and follow me. Stay alert. Jeet, Stee, and Yuin are close. I have sent a message to Yaro. If we get separated, hide and one of us will find you."

A squeal of surprise escaped from Gar as a vulture materialized in Voer's place. Massive wings carried the Pentharian over the wine-red river and across the swamp on the opposite side.

Brie squeezed Gar's hand. "He is our good friend. Shape your raven, and we will follow him." She shifted to a small hawk.

Beside her, Esán became his favorite kestrel. In unison, the trio lifted into flight and shot after Voer's bearded vulture.

They were halfway across the wide, orchid-colored plain when a towering, vertical cloud rose above the distant horizon and grew more menacing by the second. Lightning striped the column from top to bottom. Thunder crashed. The clouds roiled and rolled higher. A saucer-shaped vessel separated from the top of the cylinder and sailed over the trees.

Brie pressed her wings harder. Ahead of her, vulture wings carried Voer in a wide curve. Esán landed in the forest, his kestrel coloring blending into the leaves and bark. A blast of air opening a hatch on the underside of the saucer sent her small hawk tumbling backward. A snake-like tentacle shot toward her. Voer snatched her from the air, swooped low over the swamp, and deposited her by the curtain-roots of a huge Ficus Fig tree. Gar touched down in human form as she shifted. He nudged her beneath the root system and squatted in the shadows beside her.

A high whistle ending in an explosion rocked the swamp world of ReTaw au Qa. A second and a third blast followed. The ground heaved. Smoke billowed, obscuring everything in sight. Brie pulled Gar further beneath the curtain of moss-covered roots, where they clung to each other and tensed with every explosion.

A shrill hum elicited memories of the robotic-wings and the Klutarse, who attempted to kill her on the Isle of Neul. More shrieks ignited fear for the Pentharian. *Can our friends survive this battle with the Brotico? Pheet Adolan trained killers are unknown to them.*

"Stay here, Gar. I'm going to look."

He sniffed. "I'll be right behind you."

She chose not to argue, crept closer to the outer edge of their hiding place, and squinted through thinning smoke. High above her, Brotico and Pentharian fought. Chaos reigned in the swamp. Torn earth intermingled with sprawled bodies, some motionless, some attempting to move.

No sign of Esán's body on the ground or his kestrel form in the air brought a moment of panic. Forcing herself to remain calm, she searched again. The vessel portal hovering high overhead blocked her view. Its rotation —opposite to any vortex she had ever seen—filled her with dread.

Behind her, she heard Gar fighting to breathe and shivered. Her attention fixed on the conflict above them, she watched six robotic-winged Klutarse and as many Pentharian engage in battle. The sharp repeat of weapon fire echoed over the swamp. A vulture jerked and plummeted. Another swooped from overhead, gripped the Brotico by the canisters secured to his back, and hurled him into the river.

A shudder of anger left Brie standing in the open, her heart fighting to escape her ribcage. A swell of anger deluged her. The MasTer's hatred seared her brain until she pressed her hands to her throbbing temples and moaned.

Strong hands gripped her shoulders. "Brielle AsTar, look at me."

Esán's stormy blue eyes fastened on her fanned The MasTer's anger into a throbbing heat that doubled her over and left her panting.

"Brie, shape Rayna." Esán's calm voice cooled her intensifying alarm.

She forced herself to focus on her alternate persona.

Rayna flashed into being. The inner anger faltered. She straightened. Power rippling through her lowered her racing heart rate. Air entered and exited her lungs in even steady breaths. The MasTer's masculine essence dissolved. She absorbed Esán's calm. "What just happened?"

He glanced up at the swirling vortex. "The MasTer's gene maintains a balance of masculine and feminine. The male aspect must have sensed help nearby."

Sounds of fighting grew silent. Esán's calm expression vanished. A warning flared in the depth of his eyes. Two Brotico flanked him; another gripped Gar by the arm.

Rayna swung around. The saucer now hovered above them. A caped figure descended in a radiant shaft of amber light. The hooded man raised his head. Blood-shot eyes bored through her with such self-indulgent triumph she wanted to scream. Instead, she kept a civil tongue in her head.

"Vygel Vintrusie, imagine meeting you on ReTaw au Qa."

"Tell the Pentharian to leave, Rayna."

She looked up at several Pentharian vultures circling at a safe distance. One swooped in for a landing. Voer materialized. His blue scales glowed. His unblinking gold eyes fastened on Vygel.

The MasTer's Mocendi looked him up and down with an air of disdain. "Leave with your fellow Pentharian, or Esán, Rayna, and the boy will suffer the price."

• •

While the adults waged a verbal battle, Gar summoned his spectacles, put them on, and regarded the ship and then the Mocendi. *"Rayna, Vygel is a hologram."*

Rayna caught Voer's eye. His sudden shift to a bat caused the Brotico on either side of Esán to go rigid. One yelped in pain and gripped his neck. The other blundered against the light shaft as he tried to dodge the Pentharian bat's poisonous bite.

Gar pulled free of his captor and ran into the trees as the hologram shimmered and reformed. The Brotico pressed a button on his vest, waited for his wings to close behind him, sprinted after him.

Esán shot forward. The palm of his hand rammed into the soldier's chin. A backward stumble sent the trained killer tripping over a mechanical wing. With a yelp of surprise, he fell. A loud crack echoed through the woods as the wing snapped beneath his sprawled body.

Rayna grabbed Esán, pulled him with her into the trees, and pressed the blue-velvet pouch containing the Remembering Stone into his hand. "Keep this for me."

Gar, his heart pounding, focused beyond them. "Run!"

Esán jerked around, grabbed Rayna, and pulled her to one side.

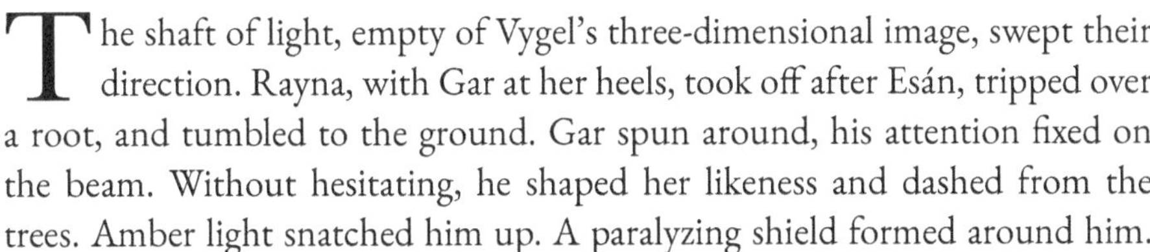

The shaft of light, empty of Vygel's three-dimensional image, swept their direction. Rayna, with Gar at her heels, took off after Esán, tripped over a root, and tumbled to the ground. Gar spun around, his attention fixed on the beam. Without hesitating, he shaped her likeness and dashed from the trees. Amber light snatched him up. A paralyzing shield formed around him. He heard Rayna scream, felt a cold unlike anything he had ever experienced, and fought to remain conscious. His spectacles humming on the bridge of his nose triggered an instinctive response. A picture formed. The next instant, he was free with the ground rushing up to meet him.

Rayna scrambled up, terror for Gar blinding her to her own danger. Esán pulled her back into the cover of curtain roots and vines. Voer flashed into vulture form, streaked toward the falling boy, extended his taloned-feet, and snatched him up seconds before he hit the ground. Soaring upward, he dodged the beam and swooped between two massive hardwood trees into the forest.

Rayna could have sobbed in relief. Instead, she watched as Esán fought to keep the last upright Brotico from reaching her. A golden bat shot between moss-covered branches and sunk its fangs into the soldier's neck. The quick acting poison left him immobile. Glazed eyes sought Rayna. Fear preceded his collapse to the forest floor.

Yaro, his gold scales glistening, materialized. "Follow me."

"Wait." Rayna searched the trees. "We have to find Gar."

Lizard eyes, in a humanesque face, peered down at her. "Voer will bring him to meet us. Hurry."

He led the way through the thick dampness of the forest to an enormous Ficus Fig. Ducking between the curtain roots, he descended a steep trail leading underground.

Esán urged Rayna ahead and followed. The deeper they went, the more surreal their surroundings. Intricately carved pillars defined a path that widened into a cathedral-like space. Rays of light from high overhead formed glowing patches on the polished wood floor. At the center of the room, an altar glistened with mystery.

Yaro stepped around a carved pillar and pushed aside a curtain of magenta vines. Rayna preceded Esán onto a staircase that took them into an area where a vaulted ceiling glowed with an ethereal light. At the far end, Voer rested on a bench and watched Gar pace.

"Garon—" Relief flooded her voice.

Gar jerked around. He held his spectacles up to his eyes. Relief flooded his "Rayna!" The specs vanished. He darted forward, hugged her, gave Esán a shaky smile, and gazed up at Yaro. His fisted hand touched his chest. "You are Yaro, my cousin Torgin's heart-brother." He bowed his head. "I am honored to meet you." Dark eyes focused on the Pentharian. "Thank you for saving Rayna and Esán."

Yaro remained serious, although Rayna noted the twinkle in his eyes. "It is my honor to serve you, cousin of my heart-brother."

Voer cleared his throat. "You can get acquainted another time. The ship remains in orbit around ReTaw au Qa. Our fellow warriors tell me a strange shield surrounds the planet." He sounded less than hopeful.

Rayna frowned. "Do you think we're trapped?"

He tugged at a long bluish braid. "A way through the shields has not yet been discovered.

G ar joined the adults in a circle. The worry on their faces and the edge of fear in their voices motivated him to cup his hands. *Repapa.* His spectacles appearing filled him with hope. Putting them on, he squared his shoulders and cleared his throat. "Excuse me, everyone."

His companions' attention darted to the spectacles perched on his nose.

He touched the frames. "Henrietta told me these see the truth and show the way. Bet they'll find us a safe path. A slow rotated search left him breathless. The space reminded him of St. Patrick's Cathedral in Midtown Manhattan. Gin had taken him there only once, but he had never forgotten the arched ceiling and beautiful, rich colors in the windows. A wave of homesickness brought a lump to his throat. *I miss you, Gin.*

A line of pale blue light caught his eye. He sucked in a breath and pointed. "Over there behind the altar. Look!"

Silence, the only answer to his excitement, made him glance at his companions. A frown furrowed his brow. "You see nothing, right?"

Yaro knelt beside him. "Describe what *you're* looking at."

Gar swallowed. "A tall, narrow crack filled with light." He squinted and looked closer. "I can't see any shields around it. My specs show a safe passage from here to..." He looked at Yaro. "I don't know where it will take us."

Yaro stood and offered a hand. "Guide me to it, Gar, and we'll do some exploring."

With his hand engulfed by the Pentharian's, Gar walked between ornately carved candles to the far side of the altar and stopped. He tugged Yaro's hand. "The crack's as tall as you and straight ahead." When the golden Pentharian shook his head, Gar removed his spectacles and offered them.

Yaro peered through the round lenses, his lizard eyes growing wider and wider. "Stay here." He stepped closer to the wall, ducked, and vanished from sight.

Rayna gasped. "Where did he go?" No one else made a sound.

A braid-covered head reappeared, followed by broad shoulders and scaled lizard legs as Yaro stepped back into the space and straightened, his long tail flicking back and forth.

The ground overhead trembled. Esán edged Rayna in front of him. Voer glanced up, then back at Yaro. "What did you discover?"

Yaro handed the spectacles to Gar. "From what I could tell, it is a safe passage. There are no shields or Brotico, but I don't know where it leads."

A deep rumble penetrated the space. Esán grabbed Rayna's hand. "Gar, put on the spectacles and take the lead. We need to go."

Voer frowned. "Yaro, go with them. We will deal with things—"

"Stay where you are, all of you!" The yell echoed through the cathedral-like space, cutting him off, and sending Esán and Rayna edging closer to the wall.

Gar donned his spectacles, grabbed Yaro's hand, and stepped into the glowing crack. Rayna and Esán scrambled after them. The edges of the crack merged, leaving a solid wall. The friends huddled together, staring in wonder.

4

Tao Spirian

Rayna shifted to Brie and clasped Esán's hand. A wall of glass separated them from an ocean world of sea anemone and coral-covered reefs, fish swimming in schools of rainbow colors, and plants moving to the rhythm of the water's ebb and flow.

Gar gaped as he pressed his nose to the glass and stared at the strange, undersea world. "Where are we?"

"Welcome to Tao Spirian, Garon."

Surprise turned Brie to face the speaker. "Somay?"

Esán's father crossed the room to a second exit. "Come with me."

Gar hesitated. "Who are you?"

Somay touched a hand to his heart. "I am Esán's father. When you are safe, we'll take some time to get to know each other."

He led the way along a steep corridor to a nondescript, shadow-colored door recessed in a wall of blackened brain coral. Whispering a quiet phrase, he pushed it wide and escorted his guests through.

Brie entered and stopped a short distance into a candlelit cavern. Rough stone walls shimmering like sunlight on the ocean encircled the rounded space. On the opposite wall, an archway framed the illusion of a night sky. Patterning the floor, geometric figures resembling those in Tumu Nnoci's gold encircled bow glowed a warm red. On one side, a comfortable sitting area provided a place to relax and converse.

Yaro ducked through the doorway and straightened. A slow smile transformed his alien features. "We have a Guardians' Cavern, much like this one on ReTaw au Qa." He placed a hand on Gar's shoulder. "We are safe here, young Garon."

His nose wrinkling, Gar examined the intriguing space, then looked from the Pentharian to Somay. "What's a Guardians' Cavern?"

Esán moved to his side. "You met Chealim. Guardians like him created this cavern, and, others like it throughout the solar system, to protect those who are in danger."

The boy reached for Yaro's hand. "Sure wish Torgin was here."

Yaro smiled down at him. "I do, too. The most important thing is that we remain sequestered in this unknown location until we decide what our options are."

Esán guided Brie to the sitting area and sat next to her on a large sofa. Somay took a seat opposite them, smoothed his dark blond hair behind his ears, and rested his forearms on his knees. "During his brief visit, Chealim did not explain what happened to you on ReTaw au Qa. He only warned me to hide you here the moment you arrived in Tao Spirian."

Brie scooted closer to Esán. "Vygel Vintrusie is seeking reprisal for being stripped of his DiMensioner's powers. He feels I am to blame." She laced her fingers through Esán's. "I'll let your son tell you the rest of the story."

Esán squeezed her hand and shared their adventures. Somay's brow lifted when he described the cloud tower and the saucer-shaped ship. His expression hardened as his son painted a vivid word picture of the battle and their ultimate escape from the Pentharian's home planet.

He shook his head. "Now I understand why the Guardians' Cavern is the safest place to hide you. Not even advanced technology can penetrate the shields in place around it. Any idea what your next step is? Even staying here too long makes you easier to find and easier to catch." He rose and paced to the arched sky, stood in silence, and then and paced back to his seat.

"I think right now you should rest. Tianna..." He smiled at Gar and Yaro. "Esán's mother has been working with researchers here to find a cure for his disease. They summoned her earlier this morning to discuss a breakthrough. Since I am certain we are on Vygel's list of targets, I must leave to find her and bring her here. She arranged for a meal to be served in less than a chron circle. Get some rest." With that, he strode from the space, closing the door behind him.

A quiet calm settled over the occupants of the Guardians' Cavern. Yaro sat with his lizard tail curled between his scaled legs and his long, golden braids hanging over his shoulders. Translucent membranes lubricated his golden eyes and retreated. He looked from Esán to Brie before fixing his attention on Gar.

"I must soon return to ReTaw au Qa. As the Venerat of my clan, my absence will create unrest. There are those who require my gifts of healing." He knelt in front of Gar. "You, young Garon, must continue to help Esán protect Brielle. To assist you, I would ask to become your heart-brother as I am Torgin's. When we share blood, we share our gifts, one with the other. I know Torgin would be happy to have you become our bother. What do you think?"

Gar's brow wrinkled. "What gifts would we share?"

Yaro offered his palm. "Touch your palm to mine, close your eyes, and allow yourself to feel what I am feeling."

Youthful eyes searched his face, then flickered over his own palm before he placed it on Yaro's. Lowering his eyelids, he slowed his breathing. "Oh. Now, I understand. Please, I would be honored it to be your heart-brother."

Yaro produced a small dagger. "You and I must share blood. I will make a cut on my finger and one on yours. Then we will press our fingers together, allowing our blood to flow into each other. Can you do that?"

Gar nodded and seemed to grow taller as he held out his hand.

Yaro made a cut on the boy's index finger. As his blood oozed, he cut his own and pressed it to Gar's. "Repeat after me," he directed. "Comrades of Heart."

"Comrades of Heart." Gar's youthful voice rang out with confidence.

"Share life and death." Yaro's golden eyes gleamed.

"Share life and death." Gar stared up at Yaro.

"Arg doo me teekay. Dio ordek od pier." The Pentharian touched his forehead to Gar's and sat back on his heels. "We are now pledged to be brothers, Garon Aureka Anaru." He stood up.

Gar studied the cut on his finger and grinned. "Can I hug ya?"

Yaro's eyes twinkled as he opened his arms, gathered the boy to his heart, and then held him at arm's length. "You must train your many talents, young Gar. Work with Esán and Brie to hone them to be the best they can be. Untrained, they will control you. It is vital you control them." He touched a long gold finger to his canine tooth. "Pentharian carry venom that can put a victim to sleep or can kill. You now have that ability, too. Use it with care."

The young boy swallowed. "How do I know which is which? I don't want to kill by accident."

Yaro lips pursed. "Do not worry, Gar. You can only put your enemy to sleep. As you mature in your gifts, the venom will mature with you and with it the knowledge you require to use it appropriately." He rose from his knee as Somay ushered Tianna into the room.

"Yaro, this is my life-mate, Tianna. She has a request, and then we will decide the best way to return you to your people."

Tianna smiled. "I have always wanted to meet a Pentharian." She touched her heart before withdrawing a small clay jar from her pocket. "The Tao Spirian researchers believe the waters on your home planet may contain an organism that can destroy Esán's disease. They have been in touch with your medicine clan. This jar contains a sample of the disease's morphological elements. We are hoping you can take it to them."

Yaro accepted the jar. "I will deliver this to our medicine clan. If they discover anything of value, I will get word to you."

A flash of pale blue light left a young woman facing the group. Royal blue eyes glowed as she studied each one of them. A slight smile gave her features an impish look as she regarded Yaro. "My name is E-annai. The Guardians sent me to escort you, Yaro, to your home planet. The enemy's ship has left its orbit around ReTaw au Qa and travels this way." She turned to Somay. "We believe you and Tianna may be targets. All of you must vanish and soon. Chealim says to follow your instincts. You know where to go next."

She moved to Yaro's side. "We must go." A small hand touched his. Before he could say goodbye, pale blue light enveloped them.

Esán hugged his mother. "It is good to see you, Maman." He beckoned Gar forward. "This is Garon Anaru. And..." His arm encircled Brie's waist. "This is Brielle, my life-mate to be."

Tianna's beautiful face, brightening with delight, turned to Brie. "I have wanted to meet you for a very long time." Her smile broadened. "You are even lovelier than Esán's description of you. I wish we had more time, but we must act quickly."

Brie returned her smile. "It is wonderful to meet you, Tianna."

Somay cleared his throat. "Tianna and I will leave first."

Esán felt a jolt of concern. "I thought you might stay with us."

Tianna kissed his cheek. "We are all powerful individuals. As a group, we're a beacon for our enemies to home in on. Your father and I have places to disappear to that will distract Vygel's attention from you."

Gar looked at his companions. "Do we know where we're going?"

Somay shook his head. "Don't discuss your destination until we're gone. The less we know, the better. Take care of yourselves." He escorted his life-mate from the room.

Esán planted a light kiss on Brie's cheek. Their eyes met. She nodded.

Gar groaned. "Will you stop talking in each other's heads? I'm right here." He placed his hands on his hips, then laughed out loud. "I heard you, Brielle AsTar." His spectacles appeared in his hand. Placing them on the bridge of his nose, he rotated, his magnified gaze searching the stone walls. A spot flecked with tiny rainbows of light caught his attention. He took a step closer.

"What are you seeing, Gar?" Esán followed Brie to Garon's side.

He pointed at the wall where a slit of light resembling the one that had brought them to Tao Spirian gradually took shape. A shake of his head preceded a short telepathic message. *"Badness!"* He turned and gripped Brie's hand. The fear flooding his magnified eyes propelled the trio backward. Candle flames flickered and went out. A chilling darkness filled the cavern.

Brie's staff flashed into view. Mittkeer lifted them into its star-spangled embrace and carried them away from the Guardians' Cavern and the planet of Tao Spirian.

A tall, imposing figure stepped free of the ever-night sky. "You did well, Garon Anaru." The next instant, the trio stood in a darkened space, the need for secrecy tangible in the surrounding air.

Esán felt Brie let down her guard as she left his side. A door opened and closed, and then soft footsteps brought her back to their little huddle.

"I know where we are and we're safe. I suggest that a nap might be in order. The less we move or think or communicate, the better."

She edged him toward forward and stopped at the bottom of a ladder. "Bunks. Take the top." She squeezed his hand before placing it on a wooden rung. "Gar can sleep next to me on the floor."

The rustle of fabric told him Gar nestled in blankets. The lower bunk sagged. He climbed up, found a pillow, and curled up on his side. Afraid to sleep, he lay listening; fighting to stay awake. *Where are we, Brielle AsTar?* A vague memory stirred. Oh. *I remember.* A yawn left him smiling in his sleep.

~ Soputto ~

Brie woke sometime later to a chorus of soft snores from her companions. A gentle mental probe informed her that all was quiet beyond the concealed room in which they slept. She pushed herself to sitting and swiveled to rest her feet on the stone floor. *"I wonder how long we've been here?"*

"My question exactly." The telepathic message caused her to smile. Soft rustling preceded the creak of the ladder from the top bunk. Soft footsteps and her mattress sagging announced Esán's arrival beside her. *"Now what, Miss VarTerel?"*

Brie squinted through the darkness. Her acute night vision picked out a lantern from the clutter of supplies on the shelves on the opposite wall. *"Stay here."* Tiptoeing across the room, she lifted it down, carried it to a batter wooden table, and pressed a switch. A flame flickered, sputtered higher, and at her command steadied. She pulled up a rickety three-legged stool and smiled as Esán straddled the one opposite her.

Gar stifled a yawn and rubbed sleep-filled eyes as he shoved a crate over to sit between them. "Do you think w*e're somewhere safe?"*

Brie brushed a curl off her forehead and rested her elbows on the table.

"Vygel and his ship must cross our entire solar system, searching every planet as they go to find our hiding place. We are safe right now, but I recommend we use whatever time we have to our advantage."

Esán looked at her over the lantern's glowing glass chimney. "Are we where I think we are?"

"We're on Soputto at the lakeside cottage owed by Coranna and Barlet, Penee's proxy parents. If we are careful and we keep up the appearance that no one is staying here, we should be safe enough."

Gar's stomach rumbled. "Do you suppose there's any food here?" He grinned. "I'll feel a lot better when my tummy's full."

Brie stifled an Ari-like guffaw and suppressed the desire to tease him. "Penee told me Coranna always keeps the pantry stocked. Promise to be as silent as a tiny mouse, and we'll go up to the kitchen to see what we can discover."

He jumped up and crossed his heart. "I promise!"

Esán picked up the lantern. "Lead the way, Brie. My stomach's grumbling, too."

They crept into the passage and climbed up steep wooden steps. At the top, Brie showed them the lock release on the secret entrance to Barlet's Trophy room. A finger to her lips, she listened for an intense moment before pressing the hidden lever. An opening appeared. Sunlight filtering through a series of small windows painted rectangles on the carpeted floor. Mentally searching for anything odd, Brie took a cautious step forward. Nothing triggered her instinct for danger. Walking a few steps further, she beckoned Esán and Gar to join her.

Esán closed the door, walked around a well-used desk, and moved to the room's center. A slow turn provided an excellent view of the trophies hanging on the walls and filling the shelves. "This is amazing. What does Barlet do to win so many prizes?"

Brie clasped his hand. "He's an expert with the antique longbow and a variety of other weapons. Penee told me he loves working to perfect his skills, but he prefers not to kill unless it is necessary."

Gar, his glasses in place, examined a shelf filled with ribbons in a variety of colors, then wandered along the hallway to the front of the cottage. His head tipped to listen, he studied the floor to ceiling windows with their view of the deck, the water, and the mountains surrounding the lake.

Brie watched her reflection grow sharper as she walked to stand next to him. Memories of her mother's painting of her with Penee reflected on this same window took shape and morphed into the image of a hot air-balloon hovering over the lake. With a thoughtful expression, she smoothed her hair. *So much has happened since I trapped Vygel and Thorlu in a time loop in that balloon.*

Anger sparking deep inside her brought her thoughts racing back to the present. She snuffed it out with a single, sharp command. *The last thing we need is for The MasTer to surface.*

Esán, walking up behind her, helped her to stabilize further. His arm around her pulled her close. "I scanned the house and the shore. We appear to be alone on this side of the lake, so I propose we explore the pantry."

Gar's spectacles vanished as he grabbed her hand and smiled up at her. "Let's eat."

She chuckled and made her way to the kitchen with two hungry comrades in her wake.

Two turnings slipped by with nothing disturbing the serenity of the cottage at their lakeside hideaway. Brie set Barlet's map of the Clenaba Rolas System on the settee beside her, scanned the sky, then turned to smile at Esán, who dozed in a comfortable chair, relaxed, at least for a short while.

Gar plopped down next to her. "You promised if it was quiet to show me the boathouse and beach today, Brielle. Everything feels okay, right, Esán?"

Stormy blue eyes blinked, a yawn stretched his mouth wide, a relaxed smile formed as he surveyed the pair, and the world beyond the windows. "I sense nothing out of the ordinary."

Gar jumped up. "Yippee! We haven't been outside since we got here."

She laughed at his eagerness, rose, and smiled at Esán. "You coming?"

"Nope. I'll keep watch from here. Stay alert." He settled more comfortably in his chair. "Take good care of her, Garon."

Gar crossed his heart. "Promise." He scurried to the door, stepped out onto the wooden deck, and inhaled a deep breath of fresh Soputton air. Late day sun made his dark skin glow and accented the twinkle in his eyes. He looked over his shoulder. "Let's go!"

Brie planted a kiss on Esán's cheek. "See you soon."

5

Soputto

Esán rested his long legs on a leather footstool, scanned the late afternoon sky, and gave himself permission to let his guard down. His head nodding woke him from a light sleep. Thoughts of meeting Gar in Central Park in New York City, 1969, introduced a series of remembered moments. The discovery of his true identity was a pivot point for all of them, but especially for Gar. A smile tugged. *You are changing so fast, Garon Anaru.*

An image of Brie formed in his mind's eye. The smile deepened. His attention drifted back to the windows, where pale green light drifted over the distant shore, its movement resembling silky curtains in the wind. The words *"Angel light. Help!"* whispering through his thoughts propelled him to standing. Two strides carried him to the door.

Feet pounded up the stone steps from the boathouse. "Esán! Help!" Gar's panicked voice ripped through Soputto's dusk. He scrambled onto the deck,

Brie's staff in hand and his glasses lopsided on his nose. A trembling finger pointed across the lake.

Esán whipped around and froze. Beyond the deck's wooden railing, undulating angel light enshrouded Brie's struggling form. His heart pounded a frantic message of helplessness as he watched the light change to a roiling column of clouds and the terror etched on her face intensify.

"Hide!" The single word screaming in his mind thawed his paralysis in time to see a tendril of frothing light snake over the railing toward the VarTerel's staff in Gar's hand.

Gar ducked and scrabbled backward. The light followed and wrapped around Brie's staff. With one long stride, Esán reached for the staff, yanked it free, and, grabbing Gar's arm, dodged inside and kicked the door shut behind them.

Gar pressed his nose to the window. Esán stood behind him, swore under his breath, and gripped Brie's staff tighter.

High overhead, the disc-shaped ship emerged from the billowing clouds and hovered. A shaft of white gold lifted Brie, now limp as a rag doll, upward through a round opening on the ship's underside.

Immobilized, Brie watched Esán rescue her staff and pull Gar out of the tendril's reach. Engulfed in a darkening amber glow, she heard the closing swish of a ship's panel, separating her from Soputto and those she loved.

The Star of Truth's warning seared through her. Shaking long, red curls away from her face, she surveyed her surroundings from beneath half-closed lids. Vapor sprayed from high ceiling vents. Sudden heaviness weighted her body and dropped her to her knees. Consciousness fled.

Esán clutched Gar's shoulder. Horrified, they stared after the saucer-shaped vessel skimming through the air like the Frisbees in Sheep Meadow in New York City. Thunder rumbled as the disc seated into the top of the cylindrical tower of clouds billowing down to receive it. Lightning streaked the frothing column with brilliant zigzags. Undulating vapors forming the anvil-shaped top of the thunderhead boiled higher. Cloud flashers flickered; another clap of thunder resounded over the land; and then the massive cumulonimbus cloud and the vessel within it vanished—sucked from the planet's atmosphere as though by a giant vacuum hose. A faint trail of fading mist followed in its wake, taking the angel cloud with it.

Gar's spectacles emphasized the frustration and fear glistening in his eyes. "Why didn't we save her? Why are we hiding when she needs us?"

Esán clasped the Remembering Stone's velvet pouch on the blue ribbon around his neck. "We are no good to Brie if they capture us, too. Vygel would use us to make Brie do as he wishes." He urged Gar along the hall and down the hidden staircase to the secret room.

Gar jerked around to face him, obstinance tightening his facial muscles. "You let them take her. You—"

Relevart materialized, staff in one hand and his other gripping Gar's shoulder. He acknowledged the boy and then Esán. "You did well, both of you. No good would have come of an attempt to save Brie. We must leave." Mittkeer embraced them. Esán pressed a hand to his churning stomach. When it settled, he focused on Gar and the Universal VarTerel, a deluge of questions almost drowning him.

Relevart regarded Brie's young guard, catching his breath beside him. "We will find her Gar." His gaze traveled the expansiveness of Mittkeer, then came to rest on Esán. "I received word that Vygel knew of your whereabouts, but not in time to prevent him from kidnapping Brielle."

Esán repressed his fear-engendered foreboding. "How did Vygel learn where we were going when I didn't know?"

Relevart frowned. "We are still unclear who our spy is. Henri is laying a trap as we speak." He strolled through star-studded night with Gar at his side. "I made no mention to anyone on *El Aperdisa* what my destination was. Our enemies will assume we will try to rescue Brielle. I expect they will do their best to obscure her whereabouts."

Esán fell in step beside him. "Who provided Vygel with a ship? I can't believe Brie's Grandfather Lorsedi would help them."

The VarTerel paused. Worry lines creased his cheeks. "Lorsedi is certain no one on RewFaar has disobeyed his orders to arrest Thorlu and Vygel and their cohorts on sight." A thoughtful expression took the place of the hardness deepening his facial lines with the mention of their enemies. "Since RewFaar is the only planet in this solar system with technology advanced enough to create something that complex, we must look beyond the DéCussate." He frowned at his companions. "You must both stay hidden. In fact, you must disappear altogether."

Gar came to an abrupt standstill, fisted hands on his hips and lips pressed into a hard, thin line.

Esán folded his arms across his chest and prepared for battle.

Relevart's silver-white brows arched.

Esán realized the recalcitrance prickling up his spine and the stubbornness in Gar's stance would not get them answers. With a disgruntled sigh, he lowered his arms and moved next to Gar.

Glaring from him to Relevart, Gar shook himself and dropped relaxed hands to his sides.

Relevart's amber eyes remained focused in the distance as he continued walking. "We need to go somewhere Vygel and Thorlu will not expect, somewhere no one will disturb us. I have something important to share. Since we haven't discovered who our traitor is, I did not make a plan other than reaching you at the lakeside cottage." He stopped and planted the staff between them. A hand rested once again on Gar's shoulder. "Take us somewhere, Esán, but don't tell us where we're going. Just take us there."

Esán squinted into the distance. He nodded to himself.

The VarTerel's rowan wood staff tingled as Esán's hand gripped it. He inhaled, let a picture form in his mind, and exhaled. Mittkeer vanished, replaced by a forest clearing backed by sun-soaked mountains. He grinned at Relevart. "I doubt Vygel or Thorlu will think to return here."

Gar moved closer to Esán. "Where are we?"

Relevart breathed in the fresh air. "The Isle of Neul. A perfect choice! I gather we are in the Forest of Deora?"

"We are." Esán squeezed Gar's arm. "We're safe, at least for the moment." He looked toward the bay where the incirrata lived, then led the way to the enormous cavern beneath the San Crúil Mountains. "Abarax and La, the island's guardians, are aware of our presence. They'll warn us of trouble." Determination, accented by his tense jaw, lit his eyes. "How long do we let them keep Brie before we try to find her, Relevart?"

A snap of his fingers and the Universal VarTerel's staff vanished. "You and Gar, Esán Efre, will be with her soon."

"You know where she is?"

"No, but Henri gave you a crystal that connects you to Brielle. Correct?"

Esán slid his hand in his pocket, felt the cool smoothness of the crystal, and held it out for Relevart to see. "How will this tell me where she is?"

"It won't, but you will soon be able to follow the tether tying you to her." He settled on a large rock, his expression thoughtful. "Dual Seeds of Carsilem are so rare we know very little about them. You have the powers of a VarTerel, but Chealim hinted your potential is far greater. The only additional information Chealim shared is that to find and save Brielle, you must open yourself to the fullness of the Seeds and accept all that you are."

The Universal VarTerel's eyes glazed over. He came to his feet, staff in hand. Froetise, the crystal topping it, sent rays of light in all directions. With the snap of his fingers, the rays coalesced into one. Bright and white, it swept toward Esán, struck him in the chest, and shattered into tiny firefly sparks that rained down around him.

Gasping in surprise, he pressed quivering hands to his heart and worked to slow his breathing. Waves of heat rippled outward from the ray's point of contact. Weightlessness left him lightheaded. A tingling sensation began at the top of his head, traveled through his body's meridians, and spread from the tip of his spine through the soles of his feet into the ground. He held out a hand and studied the translucent glow emanating from it. A glance down at his body, focused his attention on the glow cocooning him. He saw the astonishment in Gar's expression and sought the Universal VarTerel. Wondrous clarity left him gaping.

Relevart's eyes gleamed dark honey amber. Radiant energy pulsed around him. His smile grew to a grin. "I believe Froetise stimulated the Seeds, Esán. How do you feel?"

"Lighter. Clearer in my head. What does this mean?"

"Chealim can't interfere, but he hinted you might have the potential to walk in parallel dimensions."

Esán wrinkled his brow. "Parallel dimensions? How will that help Brie?"

Relevart sank onto the rock, waved a hand, and vanished.

Gar yelped in surprise. "Where'd he go?" His spectacles appeared. He held them to his eyes and peered through the lenses.

"Esán, Gar, can you hear me?" Relevart's voice reverberated through the cavern.

"We can hear you, but we can't see you."

The VarTerel reappeared. "I sent you to a parallel dimension."

"Wait." Esán bit his bottom lip. "We didn't move. You did."

"No, my boy, I remained where I am." He patted the rock. "You and Gar vanished."

Gar, his specs now perched on his nose, tilted his held. "I didn't move."

Esán narrowed his eyes. "We stood right here. You vanished."

Relevart grinned. "Thus, we have the paradox of the multiverse theory."

"But, Relevart..." Esán frowned. "... VarTerels always travel through Time and Dimension. How is the multiverse different?"

He shook his head. "That is for you to discover. One hint I can give you from my study of Rayn's journals is to explore the possibility of folds in the space-time continuum." He turned his attention to Gar. "What did you see through your lenses before you reappeared?"

The boy pursed his lips and looked from Relevart to Esán. "The light got wavy, then still again."

A smile lit amber eyes. "Pay attention to what your spectacles show you. Remember, they never lie." He grew still, then gripped his staff. "I must go. Esán, you have full use of Mittkeer. Keep your wits about you and keep Gar with you. I will do what I can to distract our enemies." Seriousness cloaked him. "Stay hidden. If they find either of you, Brielle will suffer more than she is already."

The Universal VarTerel embraced Mittkeer and vanished.

Gar's spectacles disappeared.

Esán sank onto a large rock, his mind in a whirl.

~ Surgentin ~

Thorlu Tangorra was sitting at the conference table with his cohorts, Karlsut Sorda and Skultar Rados, listening to them argue when a crewman delivered a message from *Surgentin's* commander. Vygel Vintrusie had boarded the spacecraft with a prisoner named Brielle AsTar, who was now in the ship's infirmary.

A jolt of frustration at being left out of the plan changed to realization as he noted the surprise registering on Skultar's face. Vygel and Karlsut had excluded them both.

Skultar rounded on his half-brother. "You and Vygel planned this and didn't inform either Thorlu or me? I suggest you explain." His narrow nostrils flared above thin, tight lips.

Karlsut's self-satisfaction turned haughty. "I do not have to explain anything. My money bought this ship—"

A fist hit the tabletop. "Your money!" Skultar fired a withering glare at his younger half-brother. "The funds for this venture belong to us, not to you alone. Thorlu also contributed to its purchase and to the hiring of the crew."

Thorlu regarded the men with a growing sense of doom. "You two better discover a way to work together, or our plans will fail before they've begun." He regarded each one. "I'm going to find Vygel and check on Brie. Do not make any other plans without consulting me."

He stepped through the hatch and paused, tempted to eavesdrop. Instead, he hurried down the passageway to Vygel's quarters. The hatch panel slid aside as he approached. Vygel peered out, saw him, and sneered. "Important things are awaiting my attention. Get out of my way, Tangorra."

Thorlu maintained his position in front of the hatch. "You have some explaining to do. Unless you want to share with whomever passes by, I suggest you allow me to join you inside."

Vygel bared his yellowing teeth.

Thorlu remained unmoving.

A series of muttered profanities escorted him into his fellow Mocendi's quarters. The hatch panel slid shut. He took a seat and waited.

Vygel lowered his arthritic crippled body onto the edge of his sleeping couch. A grimaced of pain turned into a gasp. Saliva trickled from the side of his mouth. He wiped it away with his sleeve. "What do you want to know?"

"Everything you chose not to share. I understand Brielle AsTar is on board. Begin there..."

Vygel scowled and started with a stilted description of what took place on ReTaw au Qa and finished with a pride-lathered version of Brie's capture on Soputto. Thorlu swallowed the desire to smack the braggart's pride from his face and, rising, gazed down at him.

"I suggest we check on Brie; and then, Vygel, as we *all* discussed, I am going to find my son. During my absence, I trust you will behave yourself. Do nothing with Brie or the Star of Truth without consulting me first. Do I make myself clear?"

Vygel pressed his thin, colorless lips together and folded his arms across his chest. "I don't answer to you. I am The MasTer's personal Mocendi." Pride tilted his chin.

Thorlu forced his hands to remain unfisted, hid his disgust, and touched the sensor panel. "Are you coming?"

⁘ ⁘

Vygel Vintrusie glared at the infirmary through the two-way mirror. A faint reflection mirrored the sneer of loathing marring his already ugly features. Before he left, Thorlu pointed out the journey to Soputto was only semi-successful.

Vygel glimpsed Brie and allowed himself a moment of self-satisfaction. She was the most important part of his plan. Drugged and strapped inside an isolation pod in the ship's infirmary, she would soon provide all that he desired. His brows bridged his long, narrow nose. "Too bad Esán and the boy escaped. Their presence would have insured her cooperation." He scowled. "Someday, I will find and pay you back, Relevart."

He examined the girl's pale face outlined in the pod's oval window. "You, Brielle AsTar, will soon cease to exist." A ripple of excitement made him chuckle. "The MasTer will reemerge to claim his rightful life." Rubbing his palms together, he leaned closer. "Best of all, I, Vygel Vintrusie, will have a son to carry The MasTer's gene into the next generation."

He straightened with a sense of deep satisfaction. The geno-tech would soon fertilize eggs harvested from Brie with his sperm and then transplant the strongest embryo into the womb of a female crew member. He preferred Brie to host the child, but the geno-tech explained that bringing The MasTer forth would abort the pregnancy. His nostrils flared. *I have no intention of waiting nine moon cycles to see The MasTer freed.*

Satisfied the geno-tech would carefully monitor Brie, he left the observation room and made his way down the pristine corridor to his quarters. After settling his aching body on the sleeping couch, he contemplated the happenings of the past moon cycle.

The Galactic Tribunal, a brutal experience, stripped away his DiMensioner's power, leaving him weaker and more feeble than he could ever remember. The Guardians sentenced Karlsut to solitary confinement for the rest of his life and warned Roween, now under house guard on RewFaar, she would face execution if she tried to escape. They also confiscated her fortune and would have done the same to Karlsut had he not transferred everything to Skultar before leaving for New York City, 1969.

Pain forced him to shift his position to ease his aching body. Sharp twinges in his knees left him searching for a way to distract his attention. His fidgeting fingers played with the folds of his cape. The purple lining gleamed. *At least the Tribunal allowed me to keep my cape.* A moment of gratitude turned to hatred. He hugged the soft, black fabric to his chest. *You are mine. I'd never allow them or anyone else to take you from me.*

Another wave of pain distracted him. His thoughts wandered to the unexpected rescue from TaSneach. As much as he appreciated being freed, Thorlu topped his list of persons to be reckoned with. Vygel scowled. *I doubt Elf will celebrate your arrival, Thorlu Tangorra. However, if by some twist of fate you can bring him around to our cause, we can use all the talented DiMensioners we can find.*

He rubbed a painful knee, stared at the arthritic-swollen knuckles on his emaciated hands, and dodged the nagging sense of death looming closer than usual. In the secret drawer in the wall of his quarters, he studied the last remaining ampules of The MasTer's Reach, the ash from The Master's burned flesh, ash that contained His energy and essence. Beside them, Vygel counted five smaller vials, each containing an elixir, to extend his life by ten sun cycles. He held one up to the light. *I have every intention of walking at The MasTer's side until my son is old enough to take my place.* He replaced the vial and closed the drawer.

Jaw clenched against the pain in every joint in his body, he stretched out on the sleeping couch. Saliva leaked from the side of his mouth. He blinked tears of frustration from his eyes and squeezed them tighter. Sleep, an elusive memory, had been absent for far too long.

He tugged a lightweight blanket under his chin. *Perhaps I can sleep now that Brielle is mine.*

6

Surgentin

Vygel tossed and turned until he threw back the covers, sat up, and wiped the saliva from his face. Frustration magnified his lack of sleep left him pacing from one side of his quarters to the other. Disjointed thoughts made the repetitive journey with him. One idea continued to surface, one idea that brought him to a stop, a gleeful smile on his face.

"Thorlu Tangorra, you are not my boss." He chuckled under his breath. "You may have rescued me from TaSneach and a life sentence in a penal colony, but that doesn't mean you get to tell me what to do."

He ducked into his personal needs space, grinned at his reflection in the mirror and, smoothing the wrinkles from his jacket, draped his cape around his shoulders and left his quarters. At the infirmary, he demanded an audience with the Head Healer. A med-tech listened to his orders, suggested he take a seat, and left to deliver the message.

A short time later, a petite, dark-haired woman entered the infirmary. Her air of authority made his nostrils flare with distaste. Healer De Dilliére's list of questions when Brie arrived in the infirmary infuriated him. *Who is she to question my right to order the removal of the twin's eggs without her permission?*

"Mocendi Vintrusie, shall we talk in my cubicle? It will be more private."

Vygel bit back a nasty retort and stood. "Please. Lead the way."

When they had settled on either side of her desk, she set her data-screen to record and smiled. "What can I do for you?"

"Turn off the screen." He fought the desire to smack the smile from her face. "What I have to say is private."

She studied him in silence, picked up a stylus, and tapped the edge of the desk. "I am happy to keep our conversation between us if it is about your personal issues. If it is about someone else, regulations require me to record it." Replacing the stylus beside the data-screen, her direct gaze fastened on his.

He folded his arms. "Do what you must do. I am here to make certain you understand Brielle AsTar is my sole responsibility. No one else may give you orders regarding her care. Am I understood?"

Healer De Dilliére's expression remained pleasant. "I understand. Is there anything else you wish to discuss?"

He reached over and pressed the off sensor on the recorder. "What I have to share is private. If you ignore my request, I will have the Commander remove you from the ship at our next port of call."

Although he felt her dislike, the woman's demeanor did not change. "As you wish, Mocendi Vintrusie."

~ DerTah - Atkis ~

Thorlu Tangorra touched the sensor pad and entered the Mocendi's Transit Bay. He left Brielle AsTar dozing in the infirmary in an isolation pod. Vygel had promised to go back to his quarters and rest. "I must find my son while I still have time."

At his command, a portal swirled into being. He leapt into its center and four planetary stops later stepped free as the sun stained the DerTanan village of Atkis with a salmon glow. Memories of his last visit produced a frown. *I disliked it then and feel certain I will like it even less now.* Striding between buildings, he scanned the opposite shore. *Tonight, I plan to stay in the village. Tomorrow, I propose to find you, Troms el Shiv.*

A sardonic smile formed and faded. *You thought I didn't know, Vygel*

Vintrusie, that Rayn and I have a son. He laughed. *Protariflee not only gifted Relevart with progeny.*

For a moment, he continued to stare at the sky. He hoped rescuing his boyhood friend and Karlsut would not have negative consequences. Vygel, often blind to the world around him, could stir up trouble with no effort. *"Let it go, Tangorra. You have important things to accomplish."*

He ambled along the dusk-quiet street bordering the harbor and entered the almost empty lobby of the village's only inn.

A pudgy man, busy behind the reception desk, looked up to meet his inquiring gaze.

Tangorra glanced around. He flashed the purple lining of his Mocendi's cape, then let it fall to hide once more in the black folds.

Surprise sparked in the man's eyes. He hurried to greet him halfway and bowed. "My name is Raffe Rundy. I am the inn's keeper. How may I help you, sir?"

"I need your best accommodation, Mr. Rundy. Once I'm settled, I desire a decent meal served as soon as possible."

"I have the perfect room." The Innkeeper scurried ahead of him, fetched a key from a hook behind the desk, and turned the guest register for him to sign.

Thorlu ignored it, focusing his attention on the man's face. "I prefer to remain incognito. I'm sure you understand."

Rundy bobbed his head. "Indeed, I do, sir. Your luggage..."

"None." A note of impatient leaked into his voice.

Without another word, the innkeeper led him up a narrow staircase and along a dingy hall. At the far end, he unlocked a plain wooden door, ushered Thorlu into a large, airy chamber, and handed him the key. "Your supper will arrive shortly. Our Von Baar Peninsula burgundy is excellent."

Thorlu smiled. "Ah. I am familiar with it. Please include a bottle with my meal."

Raffe Rundy bowed himself from the room.

Thorlu regarded his surroundings with a touch of surprise. He had expected it to be as dingy as the hall. Instead, he stood in lodgings furnished for a wealthy patron. A sitting area and dining table arranged in front of windows offered a view of the harbor. Behind a carved wooden screen, he found a double bed draped with brocade curtains.

He left his cape on the bed and moved to the windows. *I hope you are staying out of trouble, Vygel Vintrusie.*

The rescue of Vygel and Karlsut had been his idea. After much discussion, Skultar Rados, who preferred to leave his older half-brother to rot on TaSneach, agreed. Karlsut had stolen their grandfather's fortune and left him to scrape out a living. A con artist at heart, Karlsut made contacts and accrued sources of funding neither he nor Thorlu could match.

Thorlu's self-satisfied smile faded into a scowl. *Vygel gained The MasTer's trust. Something I never did. For that reason, he has an important role to play in what's coming, even though the Council stripped him of his DiMensioner's power.*

A brisk knock at the door announced the arrival of his meal. He turned away from the window. "Come in."

A woman preceded a gawky teenage boy carrying a food-laden tray into the room. She curtsied. "May we set your table, sir?"

"Please."

They left him with a glass of wine in hand and an elegant supper laid out on the table near the window. A quick peek beneath silver covers provided a view of a medley of fish, shrimp, and crab; a fresh green salad; and oven crisp potatoes. The succulent smells made him realize how hungry he was.

He regarded the rich red of his apéritif. *Who is your wealthy patron, Rundy? Ah!* Raising the glass, he proposed a toast. "To TheLise, Dreela of Trinuge and Seyes Nomed, High DiMensioner od DerTah."

Savoring a sip of wine, he sat at the table, placed a linen napkin on his lap, and took his first bite of the best fish he had ever tasted.

~ Surgentin ~

The pinch of probes attached to her scalp warned Brie to keep her mind blank. Straps on her wrists and ankles kept her body stationary. A faint throbbing pulsed around her. The feeling she had lost something vital brought her to full wakefulness. She groaned and fought to focus on the oval window.

A female med-tech peered down at her. "Would you like something for the pain?"

The words vibrated a thin membrane next to Brie's ear. She moistened her lips with the tip of her tongue. "Why am I—" She grimaced and squirmed

The woman's eyes held a warning. "You need to ask the healer's assistant. He'll be stopping by later." She held up a slender silver cylinder. "This should help."

A strange smell permeated the air. Within seconds, drowsiness sent Brie slipping into dreamtime. When she surfaced, the room beyond the small window was dark, except for a panel of lights on the wall blinking on and off. An attempt at a mental scan failed. A surge of panic smothered the breath from her lungs. Shields surrounded the pod, shields that kept her confined. Nothing she attempted budged them. *What if I'm trapped here? What if...* She forced herself to stop the repeated litany. *No what ifs, Brielle AsTar. You will escape.*

A vague memory nudged—Vygel Vintrusie's face in peering down at her, delight making him child-like. She ignored the need to sleep and concentrated on recalling his brief visit. His words reformed:

"Hello, Brielle. Welcome to the *Surgentin*. I wouldn't waste energy on trying to escape if I were you. It won't happen, my dear." His winkles creased deeper. "Besides, soon you and I will be parents. Once we are certain the embryo is thriving in his host mother, you will help me bring forth The MasTer. Then, my dear, you can rest. In fact, you won't have to worry about anything ever again."

Brie shuddered. The MasTer's gene—I will fight it until I breathe my last breath.

A sickening sweetness wafted through the pod's interior. Her breathing grew shallow; her pulse rate slowed. A sense of falling carried her to a place where nothing stirred, except the distance presence of The MasTer waiting.

~ Soputto ~

On Neul Island, Esán contemplated his options. Withdrawing the crystal Henri had given him, he stared into the shimmering depths. When nothing happened, he put it back, slid off the rock he was sitting on, and, offering a hand to Gar, released his sense of defeat with a long exhale. "I'm taking us to a special place. Remember when Penee showed you her incirrata tattoo?"

Gar's eyes rounded. "We're on the incirrata's island, right? Are we going to see her?"

"We are. Hold on." He placed the image of the clearing at the end of the Bolcán Murloch where Penee and Brie had camped in Gar's mind.

A soft squeeze of his hand told him his young companion was ready.

They arrived by the tide pool and stood in the mid-turning sun, gazing over the aqua-blue water at Rina Island, where the Stannag Incirrata lived. The island had not been visible during Esán's previous visit. For almost a century, clouds formed from the tears of Aahana, the Sun Queen's daughter, obscured Neul Isle from view. The return of Aahana's stolen heart had broken the spell and brought sunshine and blue skies back to the sacred island.

The Stannag Guardian of Neul Isle sent ripples dancing over the water as she surfaced and hoisted herself into the tide pool. A jeweled tentacle wrapped around his ankle and tugged. He knelt, drawing Gar down beside him. A second red tentacle caressed his cheek, then Gar's. As they returned to standing, the TreBlayan Astican, Abarax, and La, the Luna Moth, the incirrata's partners in the island's guardianship, materialized beside them.

Abarax straightened to his towering height and scanned the terrain. Celestial blue eyes studied Esán. A taloned finger tapped his dimpled chin. "You have changed since you were here last, Esán Efre." Understanding flooded his cherubic features. "You have discovered more of your power. Congratulations." His interest switched to Gar. "Please introduce your friend."

Esán smiled. "This is Garon Anaru, my distant cousin and my partner in protecting Brielle AsTar."

La fluttered to his shoulder. "Brie in trouble."

Refusing to be daunted by his sense of powerlessness, Esán said, "I know she's in trouble; I'm just not sure how to help."

Gar gazed from the tallness of the Astican to the shimmering pale green wings of the Luna Moth to the scarlet beauty of Rina, the incirrata. A shiver tingled up his neck. *Am I dreaming?*

Gold light flaring above the island made him gulp an astonished breath and gaze in wonder as an elegant staircase materialized. Four graceful women made a stately descent.

He clutched Esán's hand. "Who are they?"

"The two women in front are the Sun Queen and her daughter, Aahana. The two behind them are their attendants."

Transfixed, Gar watched Abarax drop to a knee and La alight on the Astican's shoulder. From her tide pool, the incirrata purred a welcome.

The Sun Queen, her ebony skin glowing, her fire opal eyes gleaming, gazed down at them. Beside her, Aahana, whose eyes matched the beauty of her mother's, smiled at Esán. The attendants, their attention scanning the area and snapping back to their charges, remained several steps behind them. The regal monarch's magnificent smile warmed the group before her focus centered on Esán.

"Esán Efre, I come bearing gifts. I have a great fondness for Brielle and would like to assist in her rescue." She held up a glowing gold key. "This is Tumu Nnoci, the key to the space-time continuum. Your Dual Seeds of Carsilem make you one of the few in this solar system who can access its secrets. Take it. Use it. Return the key to the Stannag Incirrata when Brielle is safe." The Sun Queen pressed the key into his hand. "When you do not require its power, it will shrink. Always keep it with you. When the necessity arises, it will unlock the multiverse."

Her fire opal eyes lowered to rest on Gar. "Garon Anaru, VarTerel Henrietta informed me you have sworn to protect Brielle. She also shared that you possess a special pair of spectacles which she gave to you. May I hold them?"

Gar fought to keep his voice steady, cupped his hands, and whispered, "Repapa." The spectacles appeared, their dark frames glinting in the sunlight. He held them up to the Sun Queen.

She unfolded the temples and peered at him through the lenses. Spectacular fire opal irises filled his senses. Warmth skated over his skin. His heartbeat quickened. His lungs emptied with a quiet whoosh, while the veins in his body pulsed a gentle rhythm.

Her smile embraced him. Holding the spectacles up to the heavens, her magnificence blazed even brighter.

> *"Sunfire emboss these lenses and frames*
> *With embers to decipher truth from games.*
> *Enhance the power of Henrietta's gift;*
> *Allow the wearer to see Time shift."*

She handed them back. "Please, Garon, put them on."

He placed them on his nose, settled the temples over his ears, and looked up at the Sun Queen and her daughter.

Aahana smiled and pressed her palms together in a silent clap. "We are now brother and sister, Garon. I am honored."

Abarax moved to gaze down at him. La squeaked and circled above him.

Esán touched his heart, his attention fixed on the boy's face.

Gar squirmed. "What are you all staring at?"

The Sun Queen pointed at the crystal-clear water. "Your reflection will show what we are seeing."

He knelt at the edge of Bolcán Murloch. As he leaned forward, his reflection left him stunned. Behind the lenses, fire opal eyes blazed, eyes that matched the queen's. He rocked back on his heels, astonishment shaping his youthful features. Climbing to his feet, he faced her, a hand on his heart. "Thank you, Sun Queen."

She acknowledged him with a regal bow of the head. Their eyes met. "You represent me, Garon Anaru, in the search for and rescue of Brielle AsTar."

The staircase began to recede, slowly fading into a haze of soft golden light.

Esán held the key to his heart, his head bowed. Gar removed the spectacles, whispered "Nehidd", and followed his example, but snuck a peek at the disappearing queen from beneath his dark lashes. A quick look at his reflection showed him his chestnut brown eyes. With the removal of his specs, the fire opal blaze cooled. He sighed.

The brilliant blue dome overhead reformed, and sunlight glowed on the Isle of Neul. La's soft squeak in chorus with the incirrata's purring hum accompanied Esán and Gar as Mittkeer wrapped them in stars and carried them skyward. Their last view of Neul Isle—Abarax and La merging with the incirrata and bubbling water flowing over her glistening red body—gave them both a momentary sense of peace.

A hush as tangible as a soft breeze prickled the back of Esán's neck. His overwhelming need for a safe place to study the key's mysteries triggered a change in Mittkeer's star-studded vastness. Bilar, a constellation he knew well, sparkled overhead. The large key grew cool in his hand and shrunk to the size of his thumb. He slipped it into his pocket, clasped Gar's hand, closed his eyes, and pictured his haven.

The Land of All Time and No Time left them standing on a hillside overlooking the village of SumnerTymn, nestled at the foot of the Central Mountains on Thera. Esán's Aunt Merrilea had raised him here until his disease became unmanageable.

He let out a relieved sigh. "Come on, Gar. I'm going to show you where I grew up."

Jogging down the track, he led the way to the cottage on the outskirts of the village. The door opened and his mother's blood-bonded sister motioned them inside. She hugged him, then examined him with serious, gray-blue eyes.

"You were a sickly boy the last time we were together, Esán Efre." She beamed. "Look at you now! You're glowing with health and so grown up." She hugged him again. "Someone is here to speak with you, but first introduce your friend."

Esán drew Gar forward. "Aunt Merrilea, this is Garon Anaru. Gar, this is my aunt, the woman who raised me, cared for me, and loved me from the time I was born."

"I am very glad to meet you." Gar's shy smile made a brief appearance.

Merrilea took his hand. "I understand you are Torgin's cousin, as well as being distantly related to Esán. Please call me Aunt Merrilea."

The shyness vanished. "Thank you, Aunt Merrilea."

She caught Esán's eye and smiled before her attention returned to Gar. "We have a guest who is waiting to meet with both of you. Relevart shared your story with him, Gar, so he is aware of you and all you have done to help Brie." She guided them through her tidy cottage to the living room.

A tall, handsome man in a PPP uniform turned from the window. "It's good to see you, Esán and Garon."

Esán gripped his outstretched hand. "Colonel Jordett. I didn't expect to see you here."

"I received a message from Relevart to escort Merrilea home from the city." He moved to her side. "The VarTerel feels her presence here will provide a distraction while you and your young friend do the work you need to do."

Merrilea moved into the circle of Jordett's arm. "We have something to tell you." She smiled up at the Colonel.

He grinned. "Your aunt and I are Joined and expecting our first child."

The happiness in his Aunt Merrilea's smile lifted Esán's spirits like nothing had for some time. "I am so excited for you both. When do I become a..." He raised a quizzical brow. "How *am* I related to your child?"

Merrilea's eyes sparkled. "I think Uncle Esán would be wonderful. What about you, Jordy?"

Jordett grinned. "Uncle Esán is perfect." He kissed the top of Merrilea's head. "I must return to Idronatti. Why don't you walk me to the RiaTrain while Esán and Gar get to work?"

Esán watched them stroll hand in hand down the path. A touch of longing thrummed. *I wish you were here, Brielle AsTar.*

He turned to find Gar watching him with sadness weighting his shoulders. "My family is your family, Gar, and my home is your home. Let me show you around."

After a brief tour, they walked down the hall to his room. He paused in the doorway to embrace the memories assaulting him from every corner. Childhood escorted him into the room. He caressed the satiny wood of his desk, ran a finger over the spines of his favorite books in the matching bookcase, and smiled at his most treasured toys lined up on a shelf above the bed. Nothing had changed. His aunt had left it ready for him.

He grinned at Gar. "It's just as I remember it. Let's get to work."

Setting recollections aside, he sank onto his boyhood bed and withdrew the key from his pocket.

7

Surgentin

Brie woke from a dream filled with pain. She lay in a drug-induced fog, trying to understand the tremendous sense of loss engulfing her. What was different? Opening her eyes brought the realization she rested on a narrow bed, not in an isolation pod. An attempt to turn her head sent a sharp, shooting pain down her neck. Tears dripped from her chin. *What have they done to me?*

A tiny seed of anger buried at her core fought to gain control. The Star of Truth's lack of activity left her panicked. Her searching fingers found a bandage covering the place on the nape of her neck where the star-shaped birthmark should have been. Dread rose like bile in her throat. *What did they do to it? How will I fight The MasTer without it?*

A door swished open. Vygel peered down at her, glee radiating from him like a child's delight in a new toy. "How do you feel, Brielle AsTar?"

She turned her head, flinched at the stab of pain, and closed her eyes.

He laughed. "I had The Star of Truth removed." His giddiness increased. "Ah, my dear, don't fret. Soon, *He* will rise, and you will never need to worry again." He limped from the room, chuckling to himself.

Brie stared up at the ceiling. "What if I can't fend off The MasTer without The Star? What if…" She bit her lip. "I am not the Star. I am not The MasTer. I am Brielle Ralyn AsTar, daughter of SparrowLyn and Allynae Nadrugia, sister of Arienh Lynae. I will fight for my right to exist. Rayna stirred. The MasTer's essence flared hotter.

Brie summoned her remaining strength to squelch his fire. Exhaustion plummeted her into a bottomless pit of fatigue.

~ DerTah - Atkis ~

From his room at the inn in Atkis, Thorlu Tangorra surveyed Harbor Lane, the village's only street wider than a track, bathed in rosy morning light. His sources had informed him Elf was no longer in Myrrh. They tracked him to this village where Rasiana, Rayn's protector and friend, had hidden him as a young boy after he refused to become a Mocendi.

Thorlu paced to the next window. *If I had known you were my son, Troms El Shiv, I would never have allowed them to cut your vocal cords and erase your memories.*

A flock of white seabirds, mimicking his tumultuous thoughts, rose *en masse* from the surface of the bay, skimmed over the water, and landed in unison on the pebble-strewn shoreline. Raucous squawks and whiney wails accompanied the birds as they launched into the air in unison and flew first one direction and then the other. A series of clipped chirps chorused around them as they glided onto a dock lined with boats and grew quiet.

The twins healed your voice and your memories. His eyes narrowed. *Now you remember your past and your training in DiMensionery.* He turned from the window. "I hear, Troms, that you are talented, more talented than most Mocendi I know." Anticipation made him smile. "It's time we got to know each other."

At the reception desk, Thorlu asked Raffe Rundy to have the horse he had rented earlier brought to the front of the hotel. While a scruffy youngster ran to fetch it, the innkeeper provided directions to the Senndi family home, inquired whether he planned to stay at the inn for another night, and fussed until Thorlu's patience expired. Excusing himself, he strolled outside into the tide-scented air and crunch of horses' hooves and wagon wheels on the hard-packed dirt in front of the inn.

Mocendi shields in place, he remained unnoticed until the stable boy approached the inn, leading his horse. A wave brought him to Thorlu's side. The youngster shot him a shy smile, handed over the reins, and patted the horse's black and gray flank. "His name be Jasper, sir."

A generous tip produced a sizable grin on the boy's face and a happy 'thank ya' to his lips. Thorlu surprised himself by returning the smile before he mounted and rode sedately along Harbor Lane to the forest bordering Atkis.

Once out of sight of the village, he spurred the frisky stallion into a gallop. As the sun hit mid-turning, he slowed the horse to an ambling walk and gave himself permission to enjoy the spectacular view.

In the distance, tall snow-capped mountains formed a backdrop for the rich forest lands bordering a small bay on his left. To the right, trees gave way to fields of tall grass that swept from between the rolling hills. The peace and the beauty lured him in ways he did not expect.

Taken by surprise, he shook himself and focused on the job at hand. Previous experience with Senndi and his sister made him doubtful as to his welcome. He had, therefore, chosen to find Elf and spirit him away. The key problem would be the boy's disdain for him and the world he represented.

Jasper tossed his head and came to a nervous standstill, his muscles twitching. Up ahead, the brown-gold thatched roof of a cottage topped the swell of a hill. Guiding the stallion up the sloping terrain into a thicket of berry bushes, he dismounted, looped the reins over a branch, and searched for a suitable vantage point from which to observe the comings and goings at the Senndi home.

The quaint cottage sat on a rise with a view of sea and beyond. A vegetable garden laid out on the side closest to him bordered a field of tall grass next to the forested hills where he hid. Downhill in the bay, *SeaBella*, Senndi's two-masted sailboat, bobbed at anchor in the sea breeze. He returned his attention to the cottage and its residents.

Thorlu considered Marji Senndi an enigma. Her mystic's power flowed stronger than those of most Mocendi DiMensioners. Although her gifts were similar, fundamental differences set her apart from what he knew and understood. He pursed his lips. *Prior to making a move, I need more information regarding Marji and her brothers.*

A woman exiting the cottage cancelled his decision to retrieve his horse. Protective wards shot up around him. He watched her lower a basket of laundry to the ground and begin hanging a man's clothing on the line. Nothing appeared to belong to a boy of Elf's size. A subtle mental probe found nothing but the simple mind of a peasant focused on her task.

His horse startled and set the berry bushes in motion. Thorlu froze behind his tree. The woman seemed not to notice, finished hanging the last pair of workman's britches, and picked up her basket. When she reached the house, Thorlu shifted to a gull and soared over the cove. A circle of the sailboat provided nothing of value. He found no sign of Elf or the Senndi brothers. From the masthead, he examined the deck and then touched down on the mizzen mast's furled sail. He cocked his head and made a mental search. *SeaBella* rocked on the incoming tide, her wheelhouse and cabin deserted but for a mouse hiding in the galley.

Gull's wings carried him to a cluster of rocks near the uphill path to the cottage. He fluttered to a low bush and pecked at his breast feathers. A change in the lighting brought a squawk of dismay. Frustration lifted him into the air. The garden and cottage shimmered into nothing. He streaked back toward the boat. Legs extended, he dropped lower. His webbed feet brushed the wooden deck a moment before the boat disappeared, leaving him in human form floundering in the sea.

~ Thera ~

Gar walked to the room's center. "Never had a room of my own. Can I touch your stuff?"

"Of course. Touch whatever you like."

Gar turned, absorbing every detail. *I wonder what it's like growing up in a house with a family.* He pushed the longing away. *I had Spyglass and Gin and his guitar.*

During his stroll around the room, he touched the soft fur of a toy rabbit, fingered seashells in a woven basket, and ended at the bookcase. A leather-bound book almost hidden from view tickled his curiosity. He moved aside several books and perused one with a boat on the cover before he pulled it out. Leather binding warmed his fingers. Enthralled and even more curious, he faced Esán. "Will you teach me to read?"

Esán lowered the golden key to his lap. "When Brie is safe, I promise to teach you to read and to write." The fine lines between his brows deepened. "Where did you find that?"

"On the middle shelf of the bookcase."

"I don't recognize it. May I look?"

Gar passed it to him and sat down beside him. "Isn't this yours?"

Esán studied the jumble of letters scattered over the cover. "I've never seen this before."

"What are all the letters? They don't make words, do they?"

"No. Did the cover feel warm to you, Gar? It does to me."

"Yep. Hey, maybe my spectacles can help." A whispered word and they materialized in his hand. He put them on and gulped a breath. Fire blazed around each letter, turning the cover a dark, burnt orange. One blink later, the fire faded, the cover returned to its warm brown, the letters formed six words above a blazing sun. "I can see the words, but I can't read them." He removed his spectacles and held them out. "Do you think these might help you?"

Esán raised them up to the light. "When I looked through Henrietta's, everything became clear. I'll try it."

Gar held his breath as Esán settled the spectacles on the bridge of his nose and studied the leather-bond book. "Well? Can you make out anything?"

Interest lit Esán's face. "The title of the book is *Secrets of the Space-Time Continuum.*" He opened the cover and read:

> *"Time is an illusion, something but not.*
> *Read and Remember."*

Gar shook his head in wonder. "Where do you suppose it came from?"

"Judging by the sun on the cover and the fact that your spectacles allow us to read it, I'd say that Henrietta and the Sun Queen are doing their best to help." Esán angled it to give Gar a clear view and turned to the first chapter. "Let's find out what it contains."

~ *El Aperdisa* - Thera ~

On the living ship *El Aperdisa*, Ari pushed the buzzer next to Henrietta's quarters. *Please still be here, Aunt Henri.* The panel sliding open produced a rush of relief so intense she fought to catch her breath.

Concern glinting, her aunt greeted her. "Are you alright, Arienh?"

Ari replied as calmly as she could. "I need to talk to you and Relevart about something important."

Her aunt stepped aside. "Relevart isn't here, but I'll do my best to help."

Ari stepped through the hatch, clenched and unclenched her fists, and forced herself to speak in a steady voice. "Brie seems to have disappeared. We can always sense each other." She gulped a shaky breath. "The last time I could feel her, she was in horrible pain. Something is very wrong, Aunt Henri. We can't leave for El Stroma until we find Brie."

Henrietta drew her down on the built-in couch beside her. "Try to calm down, Arienh."

Ari grappled with her panicked emotions, swallowed her fear, and focused on her great aunt. "The most important person in my life is in grave danger. Please help me find her."

Henri frowned. "The Galactic Council is sending Relevart and me on an assignment which entails leaving later tonight. Oh, deary me. What a conundrum."

Her spectacles appeared in her hand. Amethyst encircled frames gleamed around her violet eyes. She blinked, removed them, and tucked them away. "I see. Oh my, oh my." Her VarTerel's staff flashed into her hand. "Hold on."

Ari grasped the satiny rowan wood and exhaled as Mittkeer's stars surrounded them. Her aunt whispered a series of quiet words. The star-scape shimmered and blurred into the constellation Bilar glinting overhead.

Her aunt put an arm around her. "I wish I could stay with you, but I cannot. I've brought you to the people who can help find your sister." She planted a kiss on her cheek. "I must go, Arienh. Take care of yourself and find Brielle." Mittkeer vanished.

Ari blinked back tears of relief. "Esán! Gar! Thank goodness."

Gar jumped up from the bed and threw his arms around her. After a delight-filled hug, he gazed up at her. "You came from Mittkeer, right?"

Finally, seeing a ray of hope, she nodded. "Aunt Henri brought me." She looked up to find Esán's magnified eyes staring at her from behind round, black-rimmed spectacles.

His serious expression morphed into one of total surprise as he stood, threw his arms around her, and then looked her in the eye. "How'd Aunt Henri find us?"

"She used her spectacles to discover your whereabouts." A panicked breath left her gripping her knees. Gulping in air, she straightened. "Brie's in real trouble, Esán. If we don't find her soon, we might not find her at all."

"How do you know she's in trouble?" Gar pulled her over to sit on the bed.

After a quick explanation, she looked at Esán. "Aunt Henri believes you can help me discover where she is and what's happened to her."

Esán sat down and handed her the book. "We found this here. I believe it's the key to finding her. First, though, we'll share what has happened since we saw you last."

A quick summary later, Gar handed her his spectacles. "Better look at the book."

"Oh my." She grimaced. "This looks complicated, and Brie doesn't have much time."

Gar squirmed closer and tapped the page. "We'd better get busy."

~ El Aperdisa ~

Henri arrived back in her quarters to find Relevart pacing the cramped space like a caged cat, his expression one of harried concern

Without saying a word, he hugged her to him, planted a kiss on her curls, and tipped her chin to gaze into her eyes. "I was worried something had happened to you, Henrietta. Where have you been?"

She gave a small shake of her head. Darkness surrounded them. A soft snap of her fingers ignited the wick in a lantern. They stood in the hidden room beneath the throne in Rayn's chambers in Soasi. "I didn't mean to worry you. Ari came to me terrified because she has lost her connection to Brie. Until we find her twin, she will not go to El Stroma. I agreed with her and delivered her where she can help the most." A hesitant step took her away from his side. She lifted her spectacles and gazed up at him through the clear lenses.

He frowned. "You know our spy, correct?"

"I do, Rethdun. You will not like what I'm about to share." She lowered her spectacles and ran a finger over the amethyst gemstones encircling the frames. "One reason I removed Arienh from *El Aperdisa* is our spy's deceit puts her at risk more than any of us. Those who manipulate him want her under their thumb so they can use her to bend Brie to their will." She kept her voice calm. "Rethson is our spy. Karlsut and Vygel control him by threatening to hurt Roween Rattori if he doesn't do what they ask."

Relevart lowered onto the bunk. "You're certain it's him?"

She sat beside him and slipped a hand into his. "I played a mind game. While he struggled to prove to himself I was wrong, and he was not betraying his friends, I watched him through my specs. They blocked his awareness while I read his mind."

"My son is working against us. What brought him to your attention?"

"Women's intuition led me to the realization he has been in on all the conversations from which information has gone astray. Also, he has grown more distant with the twins, and has avoided us for the past several turnings."

Pain filled her life-mate's amber eyes. "How did I not see this?" White brows drew together. "I trusted him because he is my flesh and blood."

She took his hand in hers. "Roween and Vygel used and abused Rethson all his life. We can't expect him to behave other than the way they have taught him. I believe he will come to his senses in time. Fear for his foster mother and anger at you for not finding and claiming him sooner confuse his ability to see the truth *or* the damage caused by spying."

Relevart rested his elbows on his knees and covered his face with his hands. Cloaked in emotion-soaked silence, he remained unmoving.

Henri wanted to touch him, but folded her hands in her lap, knowing time was key.

A hand on her knee woke her from a light doze. Relevart brushed a curl from her forehead and kissed the spot where it had rested. "Thank you for your patience, Henri. I needed to remove my emotions from the situation."

Smiling her love for him, she said, "What's your plan?"

"I believe we can use Rethson's connection to our enemies to keep them off balance without making them suspicious. If we appear to trust him, we can also protect him if they decide to harm him. He has a good heart. Time and his destiny will bring him home to himself."

She reached up to touch his cheek. "I'm so lucky I found you."

He kissed her hand and put an arm around her. "I'm the lucky one, Henrietta."

Leaning her head on his shoulder, she stared into the lantern's steady flame, enjoying a quiet moment with the man she adored.

8
DerTah

Near the village of Atkis, Thorlu Tangorra experienced an unexpected shift to Human the moment his webbed feet hit the water's surface. Salty water spewed from his mouth as he broke the surface, fighting the drag of his cape. Anger at himself for not paying attention launched him into sea bird form and into flight. A long glide ended in the trees near his horse. Another shift left him shivering in the coolness of late afternoon.

Curses in several languages accompanied his use of DiMensionery to dry his clothing. With his dry cape draped over his shoulders, he led Jasper to the edge of the Senndis' acreage. *Who teleported the cottage away from Atkis—Marji or Elf?* A search of the lot provided him no hint as to their whereabouts.

Eyes narrowed, he recalled two men talking outside the inn. RayFins, one of the tastiest fish in the Sea of Trinuge, were in season. *Are you out fishing, Gregos Senndi? I'm betting you aren't with Elf and Marji.*

Sunset's transition to night escorted Thorlu on his ride back to the inn. After the stable boy took his horse, Thorlu went in search of the innkeeper.

Raffe Rundy greeted him with wide and effusive smile. "How are we today, Mocendi Tangorra? Did you have a pleasant ride?"

Thorlu shrugged. "At least I enjoyed some beautiful scenery." He smiled his most charming smile. "I'm looking for a friend of a friend whom I seem to have missed. He's a fisherman. How do I discover if he's out fishing and what boat he's on if he is?"

Rundy scribbled a name on a piece of paper. "Tomorrow morning, go to the Harbor Master's Office. Ask for this man. He tracks the fleet and will answer your questions. Is there anything else I can do for you this evening?"

Thorlu tucked the paper into his jacket pocket. "I would appreciate a bottle of your exceptional wine and another of your excellent meals as soon as possible. Thank you for your help."

Annoyed at himself for time wasted, Thorlu sank onto the plush camelback sofa in his room, leaned back, and closed his eyes. *Troms El Shiv, I will have you at my side soon.*

Food and his favorite beverage delivered by a servant, who poured him a glass of burgundy and set the table, focused his attention on the emptiness of his stomach and the need to relax. Once the servant had bowed himself from the room, Thorlu sipped his ruby-red wine and nibbled tasty hors d'oeuvres. Dinner proved as delicious as it was restorative.

Revitalized energy refueled his hope as he crossed the rather seedy reception area and stepped into moonlight and the chaos of last-minute arrivals at the inn. Ambling down to the water's edge, he absorbed the beauty of Fasfro's warm moonlight dancing on the calm surface. For the second time since his arrival, he recognized a longing for a quieter existence. He sighed. *I doubt it will occur in this lifetime.*

A flickered movement pulled his attentions to the gaunt face of Vygel Vintrusie reflected on the water.

A voice whispered in his mind. *"Soon, The MasTer will arise."*

The wake of a passing boat erased the reflection and left Thorlu even more determined to find his son and leave DerTah. The Star of Truth awaited his attention.

In his room, he prepared for bed. A mind frenzied by recent events kept him from sleep. Restlessness darkened his mood and left him sitting on the edge of the bed wide awake. The bottle of wine, still almost full, sat on the table. Pouring himself a glass, he walked to the window to watch DerTah's second moon, Calegri, pursue Fasfro's disappearing saffron light to the horizon. By the time he finished his wine, a series of yawns sent him back to bed. His now groggy brain let him drift into a liquor-induced sleep.

He woke late the next morning, glowered at his weary visage in the mirror in his private bath, and dressed for the turning. Annoyed at himself for oversleeping, he hurried along Harbor Lane to the dirt track leading to the docks. He found the Harbor Master's Office manned by a scruffy, middle-aged fisherman who introduced himself as Zane.

Zane looked him up and down. "You the Mocendi everyone's talkin' 'bout?"

Thorlu answered with a raised brow and a hard look. "I'm looking for Jenvo Narp. Is he here?"

"I'll find him for ya." Zane strode out the door.

A short time later, a stocky, bearded man preceded him into the room, eyed Thorlu with interest, and invited him into his cubbyhole of an office. "What can I do for you, sir?"

Tangorra sat opposite him. "I am looking for a friend of a friend. His name is Gregos Senndi. Can you tell me what boat he's on and its scheduled return to port?"

Narp picked up a clipboard, flipped through several pages, and looked confused. "I was sure Senndi was on the list, but..." He shrugged. "Can't help you."

Tangorra controlled his building frustration and stood. "If you hear anything about his whereabouts, I am at the inn. Thank you." Turning on his heels, he strode from the building. A quick dodge brought him into a shaded passage between the Harbor Master's office and a warehouse. Shifting to a fly, he flew through an open window and landed on the wall as Narp rejoined his colleague in the front office.

Zane scratched at the stubble on his chin. "What did the Mocendi want?"

Jenvo Narp lifted a fly swat from a hook on the wall and tapped the edge of the desk. "He's lookin' for Senndi. Any idea where he is, Zane?"

The fly swatter slapped the wall. The fly buzzed louder and shot up to the ceiling.

Zane shuffled a stack of papers. "He might on the *Blue Sea*, but I can't be certain."

The fly zipped past Narp's nose and out the door. A safe distance from the dockyard, it landed in an empty alley. Tangorra materialized, a scowl of distaste twisting his lips. He muttered a profusion of profanities under his breath, wiped the sweat from his brow, and made his way via a circuitous route to the inn.

A little-used side entrance allowed him to slip unnoticed up the stairs. He stepped inside his room and froze. A silhouetted figure stood in front of the windows.

The figure turned. "Hello, Father."

Thorlu held himself in check. The expression on his son's face suggested he was not excited to see him.

Elf glared at his birth-father. His heart throbbed with hatred. Severed vocal cords and a mind wiped clean of the first twelve years of his life had burned deep scars in his soul, scars that had made him leave Ari for fear of hurting her. He had returned to the people who would protect him from himself. Marji welcomed him, but warned that destiny might not allow him to stay.

Two days ago, a messenger arrived from the village. Thorlu was asking questions about him at the Inn. He now faced the man whose blood ran through his veins.

Thorlu started forward.

Elf scowled. "Don't come any closer, Thorlu Tangorra. Listen carefully. I never want to see you again. Leave Atkis. Do not attempt to find me or to track down Marji and her brothers. If you do, I will make your life miserable." He grimaced with distaste. "Thanks to my gene pool, I am more talented than you can even imagine. Leave, Tangorra, before I do something both of us will regret."

Thorlu regarded him with an expression layered with emotion. "If I had known you were my son, I would never have allowed Vygel to cut your vocal cords or erase your memory. I can't make it up to you, but I can offer you power beyond your wildest imagination. Come with me, Troms el Shiv. We will meet our destinies together as father and son. We will destroy those who seek to reach El Stroma before us and will claim the planet for ourselves and our progeny."

Elf wanted to laugh in his face. Instead, he raised a hand. "Leave and do not come back."

Thorlu's face contorted. He fell to his knees, then pitched forward on his hands. Collapsing on his side, he curled into a ball of searing pain.

Elf glared down at him, loathing painted in every facial feature. "Never forget, Thorlu Tangorra, that I hate you and everything you stand for. Do not come near me again. If you do, I will leave you wounded beyond recognition."

Once more, Elf raised his hand. The inn ceased to be. Marji turned from the sink in the cottage to meet his hate-filled gaze. Was that sadness in her eyes? Power rolling through him doubled him over. He gripped his knees, fighting to regain control.

A gentle hand rested on his shoulder. The power dissipated. He raised his eyes to meet the love shining in Marji's expression. She stepped away. "We must go, Elf. As soon as Thorlu recovers, he will try to track you. Gregos awaits us on *SeaBella*." She held out her hand. He clasped it. The world around them blurred. When it refocused, he stood beside her on the deck of a two-masted sailing vessel. A blast of wintery wind left him shivering.

Marji hurried below deck, leaving him to scan the high, ice encrusted cliffs of TheDa Fiorde. Wind howling up the narrow strait pelted him with snowflakes that stung his cheeks and left him blind. He shivered. The fiord *saved my friends and me two sun cycles ago; it will save Marji and Gregos now.* He blinked tears from his eyes. *And I can't hurt anyone anymore.*

Marji appeared in the hatchway. "Come down and get warm."

He smiled through sadness so pervasive it brought more tears to his eyes. "Promise to stay hidden until Thorlu gives up his hunt. If I'm near, he will find you." He moved to the railing. "I love you, Marji. Thank you for caring about me." Blowing a kiss, he dove into the frigid sea, shifted to a DerTahan, cold water, fang toothed sculpin, and swam into the darkness of forgetting.

E sán laid the Sun Queen's book aside and withdrew the thumb-sized brass key from his pocket. As they watched, it increased in size until it spanned his hand from his wrist to the tip of his middle finger. "This is Tumu Nnoci, Ari." He handed it to her.

She studied it from all angles. "Where did you get it?"

"Aahana's mother loaned it to me to help rescue Brie. Although I'm still confused about how it works, the book has helped to clarify the latest science regarding space and time."

Ari examined the shaft. "What are the symbols engraved here?"

"They're glyphs used by the gods to denote the Sun Queen. It is her key to the space-time continuum."

Handing it back, Ari caressed Efillaeh's jeweled hilt. "We've got the tools to rescue her. Now, we just need to find her."

E sán stared at the key. He could almost feel the wheels in his mind spinning like the miniature spur gears in Tumu Nnoci's bow. Inspired to share Keersé with Ari, he took it from his pocket. "Your Aunt Henri gave this to me. It's a herkimer diamond she programed to find Brie. She told me herkimers are the most powerful of the quartz crystals." He placed it on her palm. "It's called Keersé. I believe it's meant for you. You share a deeper connection to Brie than anyone, so maybe the crystal will amplify it. Try it. Gar and I are ready to help if you need us."

Ari gazed at Keersé, noted its double terminations and its transparency, and curled her fingers around it. Eyes closed, she concentrated on her twin. When nothing happened and frustration tensed her jaw, she opened her eyes.

Esán moved next to her and held Tumu Nnoci above her hand. The stars in the key's bow swirled, forming a meteor-like tail that shot from the bow to engulf her hand in stars.

Coolness spreading up her arm brought her to her feet. She saw Esán's eyes widen as indigo light shimmered around him and spread to surround her and Gar. The room dissolved into the distance as an infirmary cubicle took shape. A panel of lights flickered. Vygel Vintrusie stood at the side of a narrow bed, his shadow obscuring the identity of the person laying there. He tensed and pivoted, searching the pristine space. After a glance around and an uneasy frown, he limped through a hatchway that whispered shut behind him.

Brie's eyes fluttered open. Her hand touched a bandage on her neck. A soft moan mingled with Esán's sharp inhale as the ship's infirmary faded and his childhood bedroom came into focus.

Unsteady legs lowered Ari to the bed. The firmness of the mattress supporting her thighs and the hardness of the floor beneath her leather soled shoes assured her addled brain that reality encased her. She stared at Keersé and then at Esán, who stood with Tumu Nnoci growing smaller as they watched.

Gar looked from the tiny key to Ari. "I just saw Brie. Did you?"

Ari felt the bed sag as Esán sat beside her. "I believe we all saw her, right Arienh?"

Ari juggled emotions ranging from worry to panic. "At least, we know she's alive."

A fter slipping the key into his pocket, Esán fingered the blue pouch under his shirt. "We also know she's in an infirmary similar to the one on *El Aperdisa*. Relevart told me Thorlu and gang purchased a ship from Metchalian rebels." He ran a hand over his hair. "I have so many questions." He counted them off on his fingers. "Where is the ship? Can we locate it again?" Concern made him pause before continuing. "Brie looked awful. What did they do to her? Will she be able to help us when the time comes?"

Ari stared at the small herkimer she still held. Her eyes closed and then flew open. All the color drained from her fair complex. "They removed the Star of Truth, Esán. They intend to bring forth The MasTer. We need to rescue her—the sooner, the better. I researched how the Star connects to the gene. Without the Star, she has no way to control Him. She'll end up like Rayn." She pressed a hand to her stomach. "Do you think she still has the Remembering Stone? The MasTer won't remember who he is without it."

Esán held up the blue pouch. "Brie gave *me* the Stone for safekeeping." The hope in his expression vanished as he tucked it away. "How are we going to rescue her?" He brightened. "Chealim allowed Torgin to keep the time whistle, right?"

Ari gripped Efillaeh's handle. "If you're thinking of traveling back in time, we need two of them, and Chealim kept the second one."

"Going back could cause more problems than it's worth. What if we created a fold in time with Tumu Nnoci? Then we could find Brie, move her to a parallel dimension, and allow the time-fold to help us get away undetected."

Gar licked his lips. "But we don't know how to make a time-fold."

Esán grinned. "Sure we do. We have the Sun Queen's book."

Ari gazed at the small crystal. "Torgin is our science expert. We're going to need his talents, and for sure he'll want to help rescue Brie. Let's go to Idronatti."

"Great minds…" Esán joined her. "Hang on to Keersé. We may need you to use it again. Come on, Gar. I've already let Torgin know we are on the way." He shared a mental image. "That's where he is. On three—ready?"

"Wait." Ari put the herkimer in her pocket. "We don't want to leave an energy trail. Can you still access Mittkeer?"

"You're learning, Arienh." He touched her arm.

The next instant, the trio stood in endless night. While their equilibrium reestablished itself, they gazed at the vastness of All Time and No Time. Esán inhaled. "We ready?"

She nodded. "On three…"

They arrived in a room filled with music stands and chairs, heard voices outside the door, and saw Torgin framed in the square window. His companion hurried away. Torgin entered the practice room, sat down at the anopi, and beckoned them closer.

He played a series of arpeggios. "Relevart warned me I am being watched." His long fingers traveled the keyboard. "I'll be on the roof in ten minutes." He shot a worried look over his shoulder. "Better go."

Mittkeer closed around them. Ari frowned. "How will he make it to the roof unseen?"

Esán drew an oval Time Window. The city she and Brie had grown up in took shape.

Her brow wrinkled. "Bet it's hard for residents of Idronatti to go from total control of every move they made to even a little freedom. Sure am glad Mother taught us to be independent."

The roof of a building in the Arts District of Domlenah Uptown Blue filled the window. Torgin stepped from the stairwell, shaped an eagle, and soared upward.

The door to the rooftop flew open. A young man wearing a Mocendi's cape lined in pale blue darted through. A shout of frustration bounced from building to building and faded into the emptiness of the late afternoon sky.

9
Der Tah

Thorlu drifted from unconsciousness to the awareness of a hand on his arm and a distant voice calling his name. A pain-infused groan shook him. He opened his eyes to find Raffe Rundy bending over him.

"Mocendi Tangorra, are you alright? What can I get for you?"

Thorlu forced his reluctant body to sitting. Pain ripped his head in two, shot through his torso, and left him gasping for air. "Help me to the sofa."

Rundy moved aside. A man's brawny hands gripped Thorlu's armpits, hoisted him to his feet, and half carried him to the sofa. The Innkeeper pressed a glass of water into his shaky hands. Slow sips of the cool liquid assuaged his headache and cleared his thinking. The man who had helped him spoke with Rundy, nodded, glanced over at him, and departed.

The Innkeeper joined him. "I have sworn my man to secrecy. No one will hear of your weakened state."

Thorlu swallowed the last of the water, set the glass on the end table, and came slowly to standing. A slow circuit of the room assured him he had regained his equilibrium. He met Rundy's worried gaze with a gracious smile. "I will be leaving Atkis." He pulled three gold coins from his pocket. "This should cover my bill and provide a reward for you and your man. I'd appreciate it if you did not speak of this to anyone."

Rundy accepted the coins with profuse thanks and hurried from the room.

Thorlu frowned at the closed door. "You have not seen the last of me, Troms el Shiv."

A wave of his hand called forth a spinning portal. He leapt into it, glad for the recovery time provided by the four planetary stops prior to Roahymn. When he arrived at the Mocendi's Transit Bay on *Surgentin*, he went in search of Vygel Vintrusie and found him eating a lavish dinner in his personal quarters.

The gaunt Mocendi, drumstick in hand and grease running down his chin, met his arrival with an inquiring look. "No Elf?"

Thorlu noted the bottle of champagne on the table. "Celebrating?"

Vygel picked at a piece of chicken caught between his teeth and grinned. "The genetic team has harvested Brie's eggs and fertilized them with my sperm." He picked up a glass. "To my son to be!" He drank a gulp of the sparkling wine and held the glass high. "And to the rise of The MasTer!"

Suspicion gripped Thorlu. "What have you done, Vygel Vintrusie? Nothing stupid, I hope?"

Yellowed teeth flashed. "I ordered The Star of Truth removed. Brielle AsTar will soon—"

Thorlu's hand hit the glass from his hand. "Tell me you used the Stone of Remembering and the Star to change the gene from feminine to masculine."

Vygel's anger turned to shocked uncertainty. "I had the Star removed. Isn't that what you said had to happen for The MasTer to rise?"

"I told you to wait until I returned to do anything regarding Brie and The MasTer's gene." He shook his head. "How can I be associated with such a fool?" His hands resting on the table, he leaned eye to eye with his partner. "Tell me the Remembering Stone is in your possession."

Already bulging eyes bulged further. "I don't know if sh—"

Thorlu straightened, turned on his heels, and marched from the room. At the infirmary, he cooled his anger and collect his wits. "Maybe not all is lost."

He entered the sterile environment and approached the med-tech's station.

A sturdy, uniformed male glanced up.

Thorlu schooled his tone to polite and his expression to pleasant. "I need to speak with the person in charge of Brie AsTar."

"I am Med-Tech Bardin. The patient is in my care. How may I help you?"

"I need a list of her personal effects."

Bardin clicked a button on his data-tab and offered it to him.

The contents of the list produced a frown. "Did you find a stone in a blue velvet pouch?"

"I prepared her for surgery. She had clothing and boots. That was it."

Thorlu returned the pad and glanced around. Karlsut's assurance that the Metchalians were as technically astute as the RewFaarans had proven to be true, even here in the infirmary.

Bardin cleared his throat. "Is there anything else I can do for you?"

Frustration leaked into his voice. "I need to see the healer who did the surgery to remove her birthmark."

A small, energetic woman with short, russet brown hair entered as he finished. "I am Healer De Dilliére. Why don't we talk in my cubicle?"

Without waiting for a reply, she led the way down a narrow, pristine passage to a tidy cubic space. From a seat behind the desk, she concentrated on her data-screen, found what she was looking for, and raised intelligent, brown eyes to his. "Please sit. I will answer your questions after you tell me who you are." She folded her hands and waited.

Thorlu felt the tingle of curiosity. Unable to put his finger on the reason, he sat on the edge of a chair. "I am The MasTer's Mocendi Thorlu Tangorra."

She checked her panel and nodded. "Thank you. We have a strict protocol to follow regarding this patient. Mocendi Vintrusie has forbidden me to share anything about Brielle AsTar with anyone but him. Prior to his latest orders, you were on the list of approved visitors. I'm confused as to whom I may discuss her care with."

Thorlu's brows raised. "I can understand the confusion. Vygel has his own motives for wishing to oversee Brie's care. It is my intent to make sure his singular focus does not create a harmful situation for your patient. May I suggest we keep our conversations regarding her between us?"

Her studied expression deepened. "Mocendi Vintrusie has threatened to have my rank and status removed and to have me thrown off the ship if I do not follow his dictates."

"Healer De Dilliére, I assure you Vygel Vintrusie does not have that authority. I promise to keep our conversations private and to protect you from his vindictiveness if the need arises."

She touched a sensor square next to her data-screen. "I just erased our conversation. My patient is my primary concern. How may I help you?"

"You removed a birthmark from her neck, am I correct?"

She relaxed back in her chair. "You are correct."

"Do you know why she had the surgery?" He watched her hesitate.

"I was told she requested it."

He noted the disquiet in her words. "Are you certain you removed all of it?"

"The birthmark in question was vascular rather than pigmented. Although we did our best to remove all the connecting vessels, they ran deeper and were more extensively connected than any I've encountered. It is doubtful we removed them all."

Thorlu pursed his lips while he considered his next question. "Will it grow back?"

She studied her data-screen. "There is no way to guarantee it will not grow back. Is that a problem?"

He shrugged, then took a breath. "I understand Vygel had eggs removed from Brie to be fertilized with his sperm. Would it still be possible to replicate the process with my sperm?"

Her expression grew thoughtful. "I'll check and let you know."

"I'd appreciated it." He rose. "I'd like to see the patient."

"She's heavily sedated. I suggest you speak with the med-tech and visit her before her next scheduled medication."

"Thank you for your time, Healer De Dilliére." He regarded her for a long moment. "Would you be willing to share your first name?"

A quizzical smile curved her pretty mouth. "My parents named me Dianna Divia De Dilliére. My friends call me Dee."

"Thank you, Dee." He stepped through the hatch, his mind in a whirl for more reasons than one.

The eagle Kupar landed in a field of stars, folded his massive wings, and tipped his head. One summer-green eye peered up at Esán. A cackled squawk echoed through the endless night.

Esán's laughter chased the eagle's squawk through the star-studded heavens. "Yes, Torgin Whalend, you can fly in Mittkeer." A delighted chuckle preceded the shift to his favorite kestrel.

His eyes gleaming, Gar shaped his raven.

Ari hesitated, then changed to a red-tailed hawk, ruffled her feathers, and strutted to Torgin's side. *"Lead on."*

Torgin unfurled brown-black wings and lifted into flight. Hawk, raven, and kestrel joined him in a wide circle, soared upward, and then swooped to a landing on a runway of stars.

Their shift to Human happened simultaneously. Ari threw her head back and laughed. Gar stared up at Torgin, his grin stretching from ear to ear.

Torgin hugged his young cousin. "I believe you're getting taller, Garon Anaru."

Gar preened like his raven. "I am taller."

Esán shook himself as though still encased in feathers and grinned. "I haven't laughed like that in ages. Thanks, Torg!"

Ari threw her arms around their friend. "I needed a moment of fun, Torg. Did you ever imagine taking flight in Mittkeer? What a magnificent way to feel free!"

Torgin grinned at her. "I didn't think you wanted to shape shift anything but Ira Raast."

She moved from his embrace and shrugged. "Relevart helped me understand shifting's uses and importance."

His brows rose. "We have lots to catch up on." He grew serious. "Relevart told me someone kidnapped Brie. He also informed me a Vasro was watching my every move."

Gar nudged him. "Was that the guy in the cape?"

Torgin nodded. "Yes. Relevart explained the Vasro are wearing capes lined in pale blue to denote their importance." He looked at Esán. "Do you think he watched me vanishing into Mittkeer?"

Esán shook his head. "If he's aware you can shape an eagle, which is doubtful, you were there and then you weren't. I waited to pull you into Mittkeer until he looked the opposite direction. Did you bring the time whistle, or shall we to go to your apartment?"

Torgin patted his chest. "It's here, along with the compass. I keep them close, just in case."

Esán walked beside him through the ever-night. "How long can you stay?"

"I arranged for a colleague to run the music program while I'm gone. I told him I wasn't sure when I'd be back." He glanced at his friends. "I've regretted my choice to stay in Idronatti ever since I made it."

Ari and Gar joined them. "Why do you regret it? You're creating your own music program for the City's teens, you're playing in the City Symphony, and you've recorded some of the old classics with a group of talented musicians. Aren't you excited?"

"We can talk more at Aunt Merrilea's." Esán urged them into a brisk walk. "Let's put some starlight between us and Idronatti."

Torgin linked arms with Ari and motioned Gar to his other side. "How far before we leave Mittkeer?"

"Keep your eyes peeled for the constellation Bilar." He scanned the heavenly dome. "I love observing things we can't see down there." A shake of the head tossed shoulder-length blond hair in a momentary halo around his once bald head. "There isn't a 'down there' or an 'up here' or even—" He shrugged.

Torgin grinned. "Down and up mean nothing here. In fact, all distances and directions are an illusion in Mittkeer, right?"

"Right. No Time and All Time are happening simultaneously." Esán stopped and rounded on him.

"Torg, you got it. We can rescue Brie by remembering time is an illusion. We have lots to share and to learn." He pointed up ahead.

Two distant spots of light swirled around each other.

"Hold on!" He grabbed Gar's free hand. Ari touched his arm.

His bedroom came into focus as Merrilea poked her head in the door and looked from Torgin to Ari. "I won't ask how you got here—" She handed an envelope to Esán. "Or how this arrived on my dining room table." Her gaze traveled from one to the other. "Will you be staying for dinner?"

"Thanks, Aunt Merrilea. We would love dinner and to spend the night if that's alright."

"Of course you can stay. I'll let you know when it's time to eat." She withdrew.

Torgin peered over Esán's shoulder. "So, what's the message?"

Ari and Gar huddled closer.

Esán pulled a single sheet of yellowing parchment from the envelope and read,

> *"Time is illusion—something but not.*
> *It holds things together. I untie the knot.*
> *Delude those not trusted, a trick of the sight.*
> *This spell holds unbroken til I make it right."*

Ari held out her hand. "May I?" Taking it, she examined curve and flow of the script. "This is Aunt Mira's handwriting. I remember her telling me about hiding her cottage from Lorsedi's soldiers. Relevart must have delivered it." She handed it back. "How does this relate to rescuing Brie?"

Pulling out Esán's desk chair, Torgin took a seat. "First, let's catch up on what's happened since I last saw you and where you believe they've taken Brie."

Gar plopped to the floor while Ari and Esán sat on the bed.

Esán described the trip to Neul Isle and their conversation with the Sun Queen and her daughter, then handed him a key. "See what you think of this."

Torgin fixed his attention on the brass key. He gasped as it grew to the size of his hand and the stars swirled in the bow. The time whistle vibrating against his chest made him glance up to find Esán and Ari watching him. "The key has something to do with time."

"How do you know?" Esán asked.

⁂

"Because the time whistle responded the instant the key touched my hand." Realization flooded his mind. "If we want to rescue Brie, we must discover how to manipulate time. That's why the Sun Queen gave you the key; that's why Relevart wanted me to join you with the time whistle; and that's why Mira sent us the spell."

Vygel's desire to know what Thorlu and Skultar Rados plotted kept him in his seat at the conference table. His concentration drifted from the conversation to the sharp throbbing in his knee. A soft hiss of pain escaped before he could clamp his jaw around it.

Thorlu's piercing gaze flicked from Skultar to him. "What is wrong with you, Vintrusie? You're wiggling around like an impatient child."

Vygel flared his nostrils in distaste. "I have an arthritic knee, Thorlu. So sorry to disturb you. Perhaps I should leave." He forced a pout from his lips by pressing them together.

Skultar, who had been sorting through a stack of papers, paused. "Go to the infirmary, Vintrusie. They'll give you something for the pain. When you return, I'll have found what I'm looking for and we can continue."

With a groan, Vygel placed trembling hands on the arms of the chair and leveraged his aching body to standing. "Don't wait for me. Make whatever plans are appropriate, then fill me in. I'll be back when I can."

The door sliding shut covered a moan of pain. He leaned against the wall. *When did I take my last dose of elixir?* He bit his lip and limped to the drop car. At the level of his personal quarters, he hobbled along the passageway to his compartment and, once inside, pressed the sensor for his couch to change to a bed. Lowering onto it, he forced himself to relax.

Gradually, his heart rate normalized. Relieved, he opened the hidden drawer and counted *five vials of elixir. If I don't stop taking one every time I hurt, I won't make it until my son is born.* A stabbing pain shot from his low back down his thigh to his knee. He rubbed his bald scalp, bit down on another stab of pain, and picked up a vial. The elixir's bitterness slathered his tongue and slid down his throat. The vial fell from limp fingers. His eyes glazed over. Heat flowed from the top of his head to the tip of his spine. The sharp pain in his knee decreased to a gentle throb. He lifted a hand. The consistent tremor had stilled; his sight grew sharper. Stretching out on his sleeping couch, he allowed himself to relax and let the elixir finish its job.

He woke later to find the secret drawer still open. Four vials of elixir remained. His attention riveted to the two ampules of The MasTer's Reach.

Thoughts cycloned around his brain. *What if... What if... What... I'll do it! What's the worst that can happen?*

He slipped an ampule in his jacket pocket and secured the drawer. Pain's absence made him giddy. Intent on carrying out his plan, he hurried from his compartment to the infirmary. After informing the med-tech of his intention to visit Brie, he asked for privacy and pulled a chair to the side of her bed.

When the med-tech focused his attention elsewhere, Vygel gazed at the young woman. "Too bad we need to sacrifice you and your talent for The MasTer to live." He held up the ampule. "Ah, well." With steady hands, he broke it in two. A cloud of black smoke formed, obscuring the girl from view. He held his breath. *Will it work?*

10

Surgentin

The smell of smoke tickling her nose penetrated Brie's drug induced sleep. Her struggle to surface delivered her into a foul-smelling black cloud. A gagging cough wracked her body. Tear dampened tracks crisscrossed her cheeks. The MasTer's gene burned a response that intensified with each breath she took. She fought to hold to the form of Brielle. The effects of the smoke and the drugs in her system worked against her. Her alternate persona fought her way into being. Conscious awareness gave way to drugged confusion.

Rayna awoke in a bed wreathed in smoke to anger prodding her and metal bands trapping her wrists. A frustrated inhale brought smoke slithering up her nose. Her gagged response triggered a fit of coughing. Acid tears burning her eyes prompted a gush of irritation. She flexed the muscles of her arms. The wristbands snapped. Throwing off the covers, she bolted upright into a smoke-formed cocoon surrounding her. Vague images of flesh burning, of ash and smoke being trapped in ampules formed and faded. Rayna fought harder to hold The MasTer at bay, to cancel his anger and thirst for power. The black cloud grew thicker. She gagged. The room spun, leaving her prone on the bed, disoriented and half conscious.

The rattling sound of heavy breathing penetrated her daze. She forced herself to concentrate and searched the compact cubicle.

Vygel Vintrusie gaped down at her, then ran a pale blue tongue over yellowing teeth. "Where is The MasTer?"

Thorlu marched into the infirmary, sniffed the air, and fastened his attention on Rayna. "What have you done, Vygel?"

Vintrusie stared at the ampule's pieces in his hand. "I thought..."

Thorlu glowered. "You thought The Reach would bring forth The MasTer, so you wasted an ampule. Now we have to deal with Rayna Deejara."

Rayna stood and shook herself like a wet canine. The smoky cocoon misted into nothing. She scrubbed a hand through her short, black hair. Glared at the two Mocendi, reached for Brie's essence, and shifted.

Brielle stared at her captors. Vygel gave a howl filled with disappointment. Thorlu shook his head, called the med-tech, and gave him instructions to take care of her. With a firm hand on Vygel's arm, he guided the aging Mocendi from the infirmary.

Brie considered trying to escape, but fatigue forced her onto the narrow bed, where drug induced sleep dragged her into dreamlessness.

She awoke to the awareness of devastating loss. The bandage no longer covered the spot where the rounded, star-shaped birthmark had been. Her stomach heaved. Tears blurred her vision. The realization The Star of Truth was more than a birthmark left her sobbing.

The Star saved me so many times. What will I do without my silent guardian? Will I be able to tell the difference between truth and lies? How will I control The MasTer?

A swirl of questions, mixed emotions, and trepidation churned. Deep in the place where The MasTer's gene resided, a seed of joy pushed up through the rich soil of her despair. A tremor of delight rippled upward. Rayna's feminine power fought to suppress it and failed. Brie's head came up. She acknowledged Ari, her stubbornness and readiness to fight. Esán's battle with illness flashed through her thoughts. Karrew and Almiralyn fighting to return to Human after too long in a shifted form.

"You will never control me, Fisaco." Willpower forced The MasTer's gene back into obscurity. "I will *never* give up. I will fight." She glanced around her cubicle. *And I will escape.*

~ Thera ~

Ari woke up standing at the center of a strange room, coughing, with Keersé clutched in her hand. The smell of smoked drenched the space. Her lungs burned. Her eyes teared. Panic gripped her. *What the heck!* A fit of coughing clawed at her throat. She opened the window and gulped in deep, cleansing breaths of night-fresh mountain air. When her lungs no longer burned, she turned to examine the moonlit room. Memory erased her confused thoughts.

We are at Esán's aunt's. We had a splendid dinner with the Major and Merrilea—a whiff of acid smoke triggered a flashback that left her shaking. She stood on the deck of the sailboat *Melback,* surrounded by the black cloud called The MasTer's Reach. Fear for her twin escalated.

With Merrilea's robe draped around her shoulders, she sprinted to Esán's bedroom door. A quiet knock and she pushed it ajar. "Esán, Torgin, Gar, I'm coming in."

Gar sat up in his midst of his blankets, dark eyes bleary with sleep.

Torgin greeted her with a groggy yawn. "What's up?"

She shook Esán awake. "Something is happening to Brielle."

Ten minutes later, dressed and gathered in Esán's room, the group improvised a quick plan. Ari clutched the herkimer. Torgin balanced the compass on one hand; the time whistle hung on the cord around his neck. Gar, his spectacles in place, tucked the Sun Queen's book under his arm. Tumu Nnoci, full-sized and gleaming, glowed in Esán's outstretched hand. "Concentrate on Brie. Ari, hold out the herkimer. Torgin, when we need you, I'll tell you. Gar, stay alert. Tell me if you see anything strange."

In the bow at the top of the key, a meteor-tail of shimmering light and stars formed and shot around them.

Brie's smoke-filled room came into focus.

Ari, her eyes burning and her lungs tight in her chest, took a step forward and came to an abrupt standstill. Esán and Torgin flanked her. Gar peered from behind them. All eyes were fixed on Brie, lying in a drugged stupor in a ship's infirmary.

Esán whispered. "We're in a parallel dimension."

A ri clutched the herkimer diamond to her chest. *"Wake up, Brielle AsTar."*

Esán held Tumu Nnoci, his eyes riveted to Brie. One question screamed through his brain. *How do we bring you to us?*

Beside him, Ari strained forward. He squeezed her hand. "Steady. Any thoughts on ways to bring her to us?

Torgin held the Compass of Ostradio out to Ari. "Take this and use it with Keersé to focus on her location. Try to establish a connection. Esán, the key unlocks the multiverse. If I can suspend us in this moment with the whistle, I'm betting you can create a fold in time to hide her from Thorlu and Vygel until we discover how to bring her to us. Gar, give Esán your spectacles and the book so he can find the chapters that talk about time-folds."

Esán, his magnified eyes darting over the pages, flipped through the book. "Got it." He handed Gar his spectacles. "Keep your eyes open and hold on to the book."

His quick summary of what he'd read came to an abrupt halt. Arguing voices in the spaceship's corridor spurred the trio into motion.

Esán gripped the key and nodded at Ari. "Go."

Ari, the compass in her left hand and Keersé glowing in her right, held them out in front of her. As she focused all her energy on Brie, the compass needle spun into motion.

Torgin lifted the time whistle to his lips and played one long, sustained note.

The compass needle stopped, showing Brie's position. A single ray of light shot from Keersé's double terminations. Brie's eyes glazed over. The angry conversation outside the infirmary ceased. Another long note held everything steady.

Tumu Nnoci glowed brighter; the dimensional barrier rippled. Esán pointed the key at the wall. The universe within the bow of the key swirled and released a comet of light and stars that engulfed Keersé, the compass, and the book in Gar's hand. It then sped along the single beam, penetrated the wavering barrier, and curved into a glistening indigo mantle enveloping Brie.

Esán recited Almiralyn's charm:

> *"Time is illusion—something but not.*
> *It holds things together. I untie the knot.*
> *Delude those not trusted, a trick of the sight.*
> *This spell holds unbroken 'til I make it right."*

Torgin played a note in a higher musical key and lowered the whistle.

The infirmary hatch flew open. Brie and her light-created cocoon receded, growing smaller and smaller until she vanished. Howls of frustration accompanied Thorlu and Vygel into her empty cubicle.

Ari gaped. Torgin grinned. The room faded.

Esán lowered the key and blinked. He and his friends clustered in the middle of his room in SumnerTymn.

Gar lowered the book and peered up at the companions. "What just happened?"

Beside him, Ari stared from Keersé to the Compass of Ostradio. "Where's my sister?" Her voice shook.

Torgin helped her to the bed and removed the compass from her curled fingers. "Brie's in a time-fold."

Ari clutched the herkimer to her heart. "You know how to find her, right?"

Torgin's knowing smile flashed. "Brie hasn't moved anywhere. She's simply in a different dimension."

Gar plopped down on the floor. "Are you telling us she's still on the ship?" He removed his spectacles and stared up at his cousin, his confusion broadcasting.

"She's there, but..."

Ari's brown eyes glimmered with hope. "I read in Rayn's journal about her grandfather, who taught her to create a time-fold. By using her shameena's powers, she could enter another dimension and watch what was occurring in a parallel one. For her, it was a matter of focused concentration, but it took all four of us. Why?"

Torgin shrugged. "We had to find Brie and isolate her from her captors before we could use Almiralyn's charm to make her disappear into the time-fold."

Esán grinned. "What's our next move, Torg?"

From a skewed perspective, Brie noted the startled gaze of her captors, who stared at the spot where she stood.

Vygel moaned. "Where did she go?"

Thorlu yanked him around. Nose to nose, he growled, "We'd better not have lost her, Vintrusie. Tell me she's still on the ship."

The aged Mocendi licked his lips. "I am no longer a Mocendi." He pulled his arm away. "You are. Can you sense her on board?"

Thorlu scowled and stepped into the ship's pristine passageway. "No, I cannot sense her on board." He marched away, muttering under his breath about Vygel's stupidity.

Vintrusie's bulging eyes scrutinized the infirmary cubicle and paused on the indent created by Brie's body on the cot. "I know you're here somewhere, Brielle AsTar. I will find you." Turning on his heels, he left.

Brie released a held breath. "What just happened? Why can't they see me when I can see them?" She furrowed her brow, crossed to the corridor, and looked up and down. An attendant walked toward her, passed by without a glance, and continued on his way. A few minutes later, she observed a nursing tech enter the room with the silver syringe-tube for administering medication in hand and stop short. Confusion escorted her back through the hatch.

A tired smile crept over Brie's face. "I'm invisible." She yawned and stretched out on the cot. She had read about time-folds and discussed them with her friends. "I can't think of another way to be here, but not visible. I don't know how you did it, Esán, but I'm sure glad you did." Sleep overtook her, sleep so deep and restful that when she woke sometime later, she felt better than she had since her kidnapping.

She'd been awake for a brief time when an attendant entered the cubicle and placed her clothes on a chair and her boots underneath. Brie rolled onto her side. "*If* I'm in a parallel universe, what happens if I move something in the space?" A soft laugh, a sound so expected it made her laugh louder, followed the realization she was no longer in their world, but beside it. A sense of freedom nudged her from the bed to explore her cubicle. In her dimension, she discovered her clothes in a locker next to the cot. After using the cleansing stall, she dressed.

Thorlu entered the parallel infirmary with a geno-tech in tow. The Mocendi glanced at Brie's clothes on the chair, then focused on his companion. "I understand the fertilization of Miss AsTar's eggs with Mocendi Vintrusie's sperm has succeeded, and we have a healthy embryo. When will you transfer it to the surrogate mother?"

The geno-tech checked his comp-pad. "We have scheduled the implantation for this afternoon in Surgery B. Can I help you with anything else?"

"Yes. If the young woman who belongs in this cubicle returns, please inform me immediately. Thank you for your time." He exited, leaving the geno-tech staring after him.

Brie's nostrils flared in distaste. Vygel's fathering her child made her queasy. *I could try to stop it.* She almost laughed. "Really, Brielle, that's exactly what Thorlu wants you to do." Smoothing her hair back into a low ponytail, she sighed. "What I need is food. I wonder if this dimension has a ship's galley?" A look through the hatch showed her an empty corridor. She smiled and began her search.

G ar held his spectacles and whispered the word to send them away. *Nehidd.* He looked at his empty palms and shook his head in amazement. *I'm sure not in New York City anymore.* A glance at Torgin's puckered brow made him smile. "You worried about taking the lead, Torg?"

His cousin shot Esán an inquiring look. "Aren't you in charge? You have the Seeds, I just have—" He tapped his temple and shrugged.

Ari pulled Esán down next to her on the bed. "Torgin, grab a chair. I don't care which of you takes the lead. We need to bring Brie here."

Torgin straddled a straight-back chair, folded his arms across the top and gazed from one friend to the next. "The four of us created the fold. It will take all of us to pinpoint her position and bring her to us." He chewed his bottom lip and raised a brow at Ari. "We could send you or Esán to help her. The removal of the Star of Truth has left her in a weakened state, and I'm betting she could use support."

Ari touched the herkimer diamond she still held in her hand and rolled it one way and then the other. "If one of us joins her, we risk being used against her." She almost smiled. "If *they* unravel her mysterious disappearance, that is."

Esán rubbed his chin. "If we remained aboard the ship, there's a risk, but removing her to a safe place where you can use Efillaeh on the Star of Truth before we disappear is another story."

Torgin hugged the chair back and narrowed his eyes. "Does it feel as though our mentors have been rather silent?"

"I expect they're busy." Esán moved to the window, his shoulders slumped, then squared as he turned to face them. "They also trust us to do what we must do."

Gar cleared his throat. "I know what we need! We need a break and food."

Pulling the chair from under his tall frame, Torgin set it by the desk. "Gar's right. We need a break, and we need something to eat. I suggest a quick snack and a walk."

Much to their delight, they entered the kitchen to find that Merrilea had anticipated their need. After thanking her, they washed down thick chicken sandwiches and fruit with tangy, cool lemonade. As soon as they finished, she shooed them from the kitchen. "You all need some fresh air. I'll clean up."

A hike through the woods at the edge of SumnerTymn lightened everyone's mood. Torgin leaned against a tall, leafy tree, his expression distant. Gar joined Esán and Ari in a game of kick the pinecone.

Gar darted after a rolling cone, gave it a sidewards kick, and giggled as it hit Torgin's knee. "Hey, Torg, come play."

His cousin smiled, picked up the cone, held it in the light, and drop-kicked it, but remained by the tree. "Gar, come here and don your spectacles."

With a glance at the cone hitting the ground, Gar shrugged. Summoning his specs, he perched them on his nose and walked over.

Torgin pointed at the sky. "Tell me what you see."

Gar tipped his head back. Overhead, the sky glowed with the coming of dusk. "The planet of..." His brow creased in concentration. Surprise washed over him. "ReTaw au Qu, Thera's Evening Star, is twinkling over there." He pointed and turned to Torgin. "How'd I know that? Oh. My specs, right?"

Torgin, revelation filling his smile, nodded. "Yep. When I looked through your spectacles, I knew they'd come in handy. Let's go."

He strode to where Ari and Esán stood enjoying the quiet of the woods. "We need to resume our discussion. Let's head back to Merrilea's. I have an idea."

Gar removed his specs, looked at them with a sense of wonder, and sent them into hiding. With a last glance around, he jogged after his friends. *Wonder what Torgin discovered?*

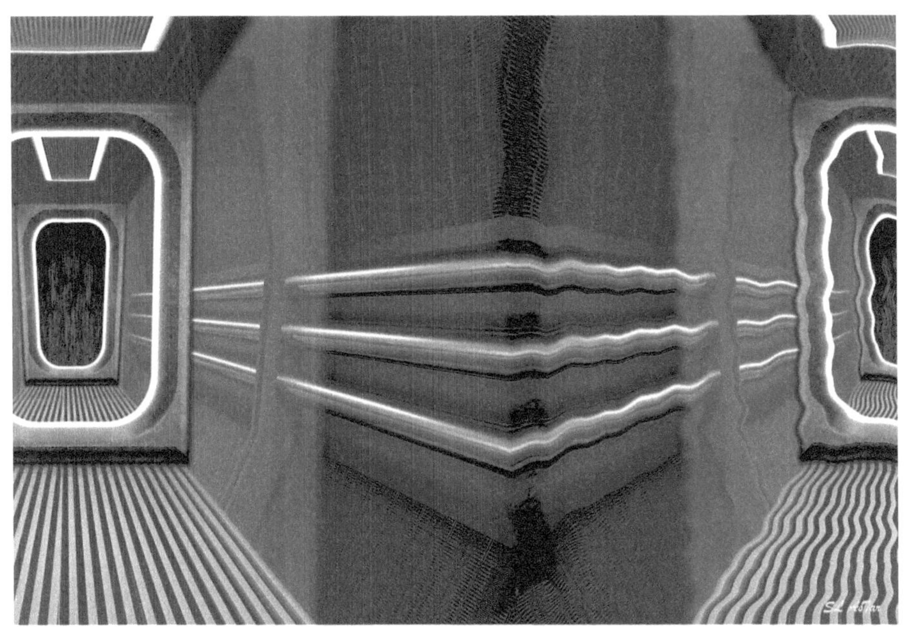

11

Surgentin

Brie wandered along passageways until she found the crew's dining hall. From her perspective above the parallel reality, she observed a man use the food dispenser. When he settled at a table, Brie followed his example and soon carried a food-laden tray to a corner as far from him as possible. The unnecessary precaution made her smile as she prepared to enjoy a proper meal.

Mouth watering and stomach growling, she shoveled in a spoonful of well-seasoned eggs. Munching a crisp piece of breakfast meat, she let her thoughts wander. *If I can find Thorlu and his colleagues, I might learn what they're planning.*

A female in a med-tech uniform stopped in the hatchway and peered around the crew's dining hall. The crewman looked up and smiled. "Skylyn, join me." He pulled out a chair and gave her a quick kiss on the cheek when she sat down. "Glad you could get away." His expression questioned. "How do you feel about being chosen as the host mother for the Mocendi's baby? It's quite an honor."

The woman ran a hand through her chestnut curls. "I'm not sure how I feel. The geno-team didn't consult the female patient. Without her permission, they kept her drugged and harvested her eggs." She shivered. "I wish I felt better about this."

"Careful." The crewman's murmured warning received a slight nod. He smiled. "When's the procedure take place?"

She sighed. "Later today, so no food or drink until after." A glance at the ship's chrono-clock by the food dispenser prompted another sigh. "Gotta go. Thanks for letting me know you would be here. I needed a last chance to be normal. I expect I'll have no time to myself after they transplant the embryo." She pushed her chair back. "I'm glad we're alone here. Please remember not to say anything to anyone else." Head high, she left.

Brie followed her along the passageway. The host-mother-to-be paused outside a hatch close to the main infirmary. A long breath later, she pressed the hatch release and stepped inside.

A med-tech met her with a brisk nod. "Right on time, Lt. Uranne. Thanks. Let's get you prepped and resting." She led her to a cubicle, handed her a medical gown, and pulled a curtain across the end. Settling at her data-screen, she pulled up Skylyn's file and began inputting information.

Brie peered over the med-tech's shoulder and studied a picture of the host mother, then read the information pertaining to why they chose her to host Brie and Vygel's child.

Lieutenant Skylyn Halo Uranne was twenty-eight and grew up on the planet of KcernFensia. Not only did her blood-type match Brie's, but her distant relatives were related to Gerolyn, SparrowLyn's mother, and thus to Brie.

The hatch slid open. Thorlu entered and looked down at the med-Tech. "I requested a security detail to be present at this afternoon's event." He glanced around before continuing. "Thank you for alerting me to the success of the second fertilization. Two fertilized embryos improve the potential of producing a healthy child. Please remember this is our secret. No one else, not even Vygel Vintrusie, is to know. Understood?"

The female med-tech looked up. "I have given my word and so has the surgeon. Your secret is safe with us, Mocendi Tangorra."

Thorlu's charming smile flashed. "Thank you." With a last glance at the curtained cubicle, he left.

Skylyn pulled the curtain aside. Her changing expressions read like a book. The med-tech gave a slight shake of her head and continued to make notes on the data-screen.

From the time-fold, Brie observed the two women. Her emotions, already conflicted by the situation, grew more disturbed. Questions piled up in her mind: *Whose child? Male or female? Why keep it a secret? What happens to the child when it's born?*

Vygel Vintrusie fidgeted in a seat at the table in his quarters while the crew searched the ship. He massaged a swollen knuckle and tried to wade through confused thoughts. *Brielle AsTar has escaped, taking The MasTer with her. Is she still on board, or did her friends steal her away?* Pain pierced his knee like a knife. He wiped a drizzle of saliva from his chin with a trembling, arthritic hand. *They don't know where she is. How could they help her?*

The hatch opened, and Thorlu entered. Narrowed, gray-blue eyes drilled into him. "I hope you have done as I asked." He pulled out the second chair. "No sign of the VarTerel. Any idea how she left the ship?"

A nasty retort shot to the tip of Vygel's tongue. Biting it off with a gurgle of dislike, he glowered. "I don't know." He shot Thorlu an accusatory glare. "You're still a Mocendi DiMensioner. Do you?"

The curse of his existence laughed, a laugh frothing with dislike. "Work with me, Vygel Vintrusie. We can't accomplish anything if we continue to hate each other. Skultar and Karlsut are not stupid. If they discover they can play us against each other, they will." He moved to the hatch. "We have important things happening this afternoon. After they are complete, I suggest we figure out how to find Brielle AsTar."

Vygel slumped on the chair for some time after Thorlu's departure. He licked pale lips and mutter to himself. "I think you're still on board, Brielle AsTar. Not even your friends are smart enough to find you." He shuffled to the couch bed and lowered his pain-ridden body onto it. A peek in the secret drawer produced a groan as he counted the remaining vials. *Only four...* The drawer clicked shut.

The chronometer chimed the hour. "It's almost time. Soon, Mistress VarTerel, I will be the father of our child."

Brie considered going in search of Thorlu and Vygel but chose instead to remain near the infirmary. *I'm sure my adversaries will come to me. Besides, I would rather be close to Lieutenant Uranne.*

After what seemed like forever, the med-tech began preparations for Skylyn's upcoming procedure. Collecting the slender, silver cylinder, she ducked into the Lieutenant's cubicle. The murmur of voices drew Brie closer. She focused on Skylyn.

"No one told me I'd be carrying two babies." The Lieutenant seemed to listen. "I know I have to obey orders, but..." Skylyn's voice, pitched low, held a note of anger. "It's my body and my life." Again, she listened. "Can you at least tell me if it's a boy or a girl?" The med-tech answered under her breath. "So, you can't tell me—or you won't? Just drug me and let's get this thing done."

The chrono-clock chimed as the hatch to the corridor opened. Healer De Dilliére, followed by Thorlu Tangorra, entered. While the Mocendi kept his distance, the healer pulled the curtain aside; moved for the med-tech to exit; and took her place on the chair at the Lieutenant's bedside. After taking Skylyn's pulse and running a body-scan, she smiled. "This is a big day. We've given you something to help you relax. When it has taken effect, a med-tech will take you to the surgery. This is a simple procedure, so it won't take long. The most important thing is that you rest afterward. Do you have questions?"

Brown eyes darted to Thorlu and back to the healer. "No." She squeezed her eyes closed and then directed a steady gaze at the Mocendi. "Promise me that once the child is born, I will get my life back."

Thorlu moved closer. "You have my word."

The Lieutenant looked at Healer De Dilliére. "You are my witness."

The healer nodded. "You relax and soon this turning will be behind you." After one last check, she left the cubical and preceded Thorlu into the hall.

Brie followed.

Healer De Dilliére faced the Mocendi. "If anything happens to that young woman, I will hold you responsible."

Thorlu regarded her for a long, tense moment. "Unlike many in my profession, Dee, if I give my word, I keep it. Shall we view the implantation together?"

The healer studied his face, then turned. "Please follow me."

Brie, torn between staying with Skylyn to make certain she made it to surgery and back and the desire to keep tabs on Thorlu and Vygel, made a snap decision to stick close to the Mocendi.

Thorlu sat in an observation booth to the side of the surgery bay. He considered going to find Vygel. A glance at the ship's Head Healer changed his mind. *I'd rather spend time with the first intriguing woman I've met in sun cycles. Vygel knows what time the surgery is. He'll either show up or not.*

He turned his attention to a med-tech preparing the bay to receive a patient. A geno-tech double checked his station, made some adjustments, and checked again. Two gowned figures entered the compact operating theatre and hurried to their stations. Dee explained that the med-tech's station monitored the patient; the geno-tech's monitored the embryos. Not long after, a surgical stretcher bearing the Lieutenant arrived, floated into the operating theatre, and seated into place on its pedestal.

Thorlu, surprised to find himself fascinated by what he saw, turned to Healer De Dilliére. "Please explain what we will be—"

"Why didn't you come for me?" A flustered Vygel burst into the observation area. "Have I missed anything?"

Healer De Dilliére shifted on the bench. "Please sit with us. I was just about to explain what you'll be seeing."

Vygel shuffled to the bench, gave a hiss of pain as he lowered onto it, and clasped quivering hands in his lap.

Thorlu ignored him and listened to the Head Healer.

When she finished, she smiled. "It's a simple procedure, one we have perfected to protect the mother and the embryo. For the process of Protariflee, the genetic specialists even developed an anesthetic to leave the mother unaffected, in order to give the embryo the best chance at survival. The med-tech assisting the surgeon will use 4-D imaging to monitor what's happening."

She looked from Vygel to Thorlu. The younger Mocendi gave a small shake of the head. Keeping her eyes on his face, she continued. "The screen on the wall will show the insertion tube and where it places the embryo."

Thorlu's mind raced. *How do I keep Vygel from knowing there are two?* He gave the man beside him a sideways glance before smiling at the healer. "How long before we'll know if the embryo is healthy?"

"It will take one to three days before tests show it has implanted in the uterine wall and is stable."

Lights dimmed in the observation booth. The wall screen below glowed. Thorlu forced his attention away from a squirming Vygel.

👁 👁

The surgeon placed two embryos created from her eggs and the sperm of Vygel and a mystery donor in the womb of a stranger. A part of her hated what was happening, yet she found herself fascinated.

As Brie watched, a plan to protect the babies took shape. The challenges were many. Its success would depend on her ingenuity and that of Esán. She frowned. *I'll need Torgin's help... and Ari's.* A tiny smile flickered. *We'll make it work.*

When the medical team had finished the procedure, she followed Skylyn to the recovery cubicle and sat on the cot in her reality, formulating different ways to execute the plan until her head ached and fatigue caught up with her. When guards took their places outside the infirmary and Skylyn finally slept, Brie curled up and let herself slip into a deep sleep.

Angry voices penetrating her dreams propelled her to sitting. Below her, Vygel Vintrusie faced off with Thorlu Tangorra. Confusion turned to realization. *The time-fold carried me to the Mocendi's quarters.*

Vygel's bloodshot, bulging eyes glared at the younger man. "How dare you order a second egg fertilized without telling me? Do you honestly believe I would want *my* child to gestate in the same womb as yours? I want the pregnancy aborted and a new host mother to carry my child, the child who will carry The MasTer's gene into the next generation. I want—" He grabbed his chest and staggered. "C-c-can't b-breath—" Collapsing to the floor, he lay still.

Thorlu knelt beside him. "Vintrusie, can you hear me?"

When the older man remained unresponsive, Thorlu rose and pressed the intercom button. "I need medical help, and I need it fast." A quick explanation later, and he returned to Vygel's side.

Brielle's thoughts raced. *Thorlu Tangorra's sperm fertilized the second egg.* Her nostrils flared in distaste. The hatch opening below returned her attention to Vygel's prone body.

A med-tech hurried to the Mocendi's side. A body scan later, the tech called for help and turned to face an impatient Thorlu, who snapped, "Are you going to tell me what's wrong or leave me guessing?"

"I can't tell you for certain, but it seems likely he's had a cardiac event." The med-tech's calm reply did little to stem Thorlu's obvious concern. Before the Mocendi could reply, a second technician maneuvered an air-stretcher into the space.

As Thorlu stepped into the corridor after the stretcher and the hatch slid shut, Brie refocused her attention on the woman who carried her future children.

12

Thera

Esán led the way down the tree-covered mountainside to his aunt's cottage. The smell of roasting meat met them as they entered through the front door.

Merrilea, followed by Jordett, exited the kitchen and greeted them with a cheerful smile. "Look who's joining us for a turning or two."

The Major grinned. "I couldn't seem to stay away." He drew Merrilea closer and nodded at Esán. "You have important things to do. I suggest we catch up over dinner so you can get to work."

Serious conversation, held at bay by good food and unexpected company, hung in the air around the table. Esán swallowed his last bite, folded his napkin, and pushed his chair back. He stood and kissed his aunt's cheek. "Thanks, Aunt Merrilea. We needed a good meal before we tackle our next challenge. Now, we must excuse ourselves."

Merrilea caught his hand. "Please be careful." She glanced at the Major. "Before you go, Jordy has some news."

Jordett nodded. "A group of Vasro have descended on Idronatti, looking for you, Esán. They appear to be a rebel band and are younger than we expect. Rumor has it they are under the direction of Karlsut Sorda."

"Thanks, Major. We appreciate your help." He squeezed his aunt's hand. "I doubt we'll be here in the morning, Aunt Merrilea. Thank you for everything." He smiled at her and then Jordett. "Take care of each other."

After saying their goodbyes, Ari, Torgin, and Gar followed him to his childhood sanctuary. He sank onto the bed; Ari sat cross-legged next to Gar on the floor; and Torgin straddled his favorite chair.

Esán didn't waste time. "You said you have an idea, Torg. Care to share?"

Torgin gripped the sides of the chair back. "What if we removed Brie from the time-fold on the ship into Mittkeer? Neither Vygel nor Thorlu can enter the Land of Time. Since we're dealing with moving through time and dimension, it will be a quicker way to rescue Brie and get us away, too."

Ari tilted her head and gave him a teasing grin. "Were you reading my mind, Torgin Whalend? I thought of Mittkeer, too." She narrowed her eyes. "It makes sense. We know the compass and Keersé will help us pinpoint her location. We need to discover how to move her from the time-fold to Mittkeer."

Gar held up the Sun Queen's book on the space-time continuum. "I bet this will help."

Torgin took it and flipped through the pages. "I can't read this. It's nothing but a bunch of letters scattered on a bunch of pages." He reached out to put it aside, then hesitated. "Wait. You said you've read several chapters, right, Esán? How did you get words to form?"

Black-rimmed glasses appeared in Gar's cupped hands. "He used these."

Torgin rested the book on the chair back and settled the spectacles on the bridge of his nose. His mouth rounded a surprised. "I can read it." He skimmed several pages. "I even understand what's written here. Give me a chron circle, and I bet I'll have figured out how to remove Brie from the time fold to Mittkeer."

Esán nodded his approval. "Gar needs to stay with you. If you run into trouble, he sees with the eyes of Sun Queen when he is wearing the spectacles. Ari and I will rest."

The red-haired twin's stubbornness appeared in the set of her jaw. "I'm staying right here."

Torgin's long legs straightened. He returned the chair to its place at the desk and faced Ari. "You and Esán need to rest, so you're ready to help rescue Brie. Gar and I will work in Merrilea's study."

Anger colored her cheeks almost as red as her curls. Muttering under her breath, she crossed to the windows, gripped the sill, and sighed. She marched back to her friends. "I'll try to rest. Please find a way, Torg. Brie doesn't have much time."

"We'll work as fast as we can." He ushered Gar from the room.

Springs sighed as Ari plopped down on the bed and dropped her face in her hands.

Esán watched her, but said nothing.

She lifted her head. Worry glistened in eyes so like Brie's, Esán felt his throat tighten.

"As soon as we have her, Esán, you both need to disappear—I mean— really disappear somewhere neither Torgin nor I nor Gar knows about. Vygel won't stop searching for you as long as he lives. The MasTer gene is too important to him."

Tucking his hair behind his ears, Esán frowned. "Thorlu and Vygel aren't the only ones searching for Brie and the people she loves. All of us are targets, too. Our power will enhance theirs; our presence will keep Brie in line."

Ari stretched out on the bed. "I'm just her twin, Esán. My power won't add much, but yours will."

Esán looked down at her. "Why do you refuse to acknowledge your gifts, Arienh AsTar? You are every bit as talented as your sister. Your gifts are unique to you. Accept, Arienh, that you are a target worth capturing. Now, get some rest."

In Merrilea's study, Torgin bent over the yellowing pages of *Secrets of the Space-Time Continuum*, grateful for his love of math and science and his ability to decipher and assimilate unfamiliar material. Each chapter of the book provided new insights. A solution to removing Brie from the time fold to Mittkeer hovered at the edge of his senses. Then, without warning, the pages refused to unscramble.

He groaned, stretched, and fixed his attention on Gar. "How well do you read?"

"Not so good, but the glasses help. Why?"

He held up his hand, his thumb and index finger forming a small space between them. "I'm this close to understanding, but the letters on the pages of the next chapter are scrambled." He took off the spectacles. "Put these on. Let's see if they will form words for you."

Gar donned his specs and pulled a chair up to the desk beside Torgin. He looked up at his cousin.

With a startled gasp, Torgin bent to look him in the eye. "You have fire opal eyes. The last time you put on the glasses, they didn't change color. What's going on?"

"They turn to fire opal when I need the Sun Queen's help." Gar gazed at the book, wrinkled his brow, and adjusted the spectacles. A slow smile grew until he gave a soft laugh. "I see the words. Can't read many of them. What do we do?"

Torgin studied the boy next to him, his mind racing. "We can both use telepathy. You put a picture of the page in my mind. I'll squeeze your shoulder when I'm finished reading, then you can do the next page. How's that sound?"

Gar's gaze darted from his face to the open page. "I can try. You ready?"

"Sure am." He put his hand on his young cousin's shoulder. A long moment passed. Insecurity radiated around him.

Torgin communicated telepathically. *"The Sun Queen gave you everything you need, Garon. Breathe, see the page, and put an image in my mind."*

The boy's shoulders sagged. He blew out a long breath and scooched forward on the chair and fixed his gaze on the page.

Torgin laughed softly. "I'm reading the page."

For the next two chapters, Gar's images materialized, slipping one into the other with the ease of a seasoned professional. Torgin caught his breath and reread the latest page. "I've got it, Gar. You can relax."

Gar blew out a relieved breath. "I did it! Whew. Wasn't sure I could. What did you discover?"

"Don't want to waste any more time. Bring the book and let's go wake up the others." Torgin hurried along the hall to Esán's room.

Gar, book in hand and spectacles still in place, traipsed after him. He came to a stop. "Something's wrong. Where'd they go?"

Before Torgin could respond, a grinning Ari appeared with Esán beside her. "We've been practicing. I helped create a time fold. What did you discover?"

Torgin put an arm around Gar's shoulders. "We worked together. Mittkeer is the key. It is over-arching. No matter what dimension or time we are in, it remains constant. It is All Time and No Time for the entirety of All."

Ari looked confused. "So how does that help us rescue Brie, Torg?"

"If we go into Mittkeer in a group, we will arrive together in Time. Make sense?"

"Sort of. You're saying that Mittkeer is never-changing and is present everywhere?"

Gar wiggled beside him. His fire opal eyes darted from one to the other. "Something is trying to track us. Gotta go soon."

Esán frowned. "Just one more question. How do we alert Brie?"

Torgin beckoned everyone closer. "Gar's spectacles are the key to helping us bring Brie to us."

He glanced out the window. Two men, the pale blue lining of their black capes flashing as they walked, hurried down the hill toward the cottage. "We've got company."

The room vanished. Mittkeer's star-studded vastness enclosed them. Silence embraced them as their senses adjusted and their nausea passed.

~ Surgentin ~

Thorlu sat beside Vygel's critical care pod and studied the older man's face. Heart surgery had almost killed him. Even now, Dee had explained, the chances of Vygel recovering were slim. *You've been in my life longer than anyone I know. As angry as you make me, I don't want you to die. I remember you as a boy eager to serve, half in love with Rayn, and filled with dreams for a future on El Stroma, without Pheet Adolan vermin. We planned how to end the RomPeer's rule and free all the Eleo Predan prisoners he'd taken. Oh, Vygel, we were such idealists. What turned us to greedy, angry men?*

Bulging eyes popped open. Large nostrils flared. Lights on the wall monitors blinked and a high-pitched buzzer sounded. Two med-techs entered and began checking the monitor and the CC Pod. One ushered Thorlu to the hatch. "You need to go."

The med-tech hurried back to his monitoring station. Thorlu stood by the hatch, unable to make himself leave. His attention remained riveted to his friend's face in the pod's oval window.

Dee arrived, nodded his direction, and consulted with the med-techs. A second buzzer set everyone in motion. Dee pressed an indentation on the pod's sensor pad. Paddles maneuvered to press against Vygel's chest. The med-techs stepped back. The pod hummed as the electrical current stimulated the old man's heart. Oxygen flowed into the pod. Monitors showed improved vitals. The heart reestablished a strong rhythm.

Dee pressed a second indentation. The pod's interior glowed a soft green. She nodded and spoke with the med-techs. "Watch him and call me if he shows signs of waking or if his condition deteriorates. Good work."

Beckoning to Thorlu, she led the way to her office cubicle and sat behind her desk. "Please sit down, Thorlu. I'm sure you have questions regarding Mocendi Vintrusie."

He sat opposite her and sighed. "Vygel and I were boyhood friends."

Her calm demeanor took the edge off his distress. She smiled. "You and Vygel are of Eleo Predan decent, correct?"

His brow raised. "Why?"

She held his suspicious gaze. Hers stayed open and honest. "Eleo Predans have a longer life span than almost any race of Human's in the Inner Universe. You and Vygel were born on El Stroma. He has aged in ways you have not. Do you know why?"

"He spent some time in a Pheet Adolan prison camp. Although he has shared little, I know from others he suffered both from torture and from long periods of isolation."

"Are you the same age?"

Thorlu almost laughed. "I'm over a decade younger."

She stared at her data-screen. "Why is it so important to Vygel the Brielle AsTar's eggs were harvested and fertilized with his sperm?"

Thorlu scrutinized the face opposite him. Dee's brown eyes show no malice, only concern. She regarded him with quiet interest and respect. He made a decision he hoped he would never regret. "I will share his reasons, but first you must promise what I share will remain privileged information. You may tell no one. If that feels wrong to you, let's change the subject."

Dee's expression told him nothing. Her gaze never wavered. A small nod prefaced what was to come.

A buzzer stopped her response. She hit a red square beside her data-screen. "Vygel is in trouble. I'll find you when I can." She hurried from the cubicle.

Thorlu swallowed the sudden bitterness in his mouth. "Vygel Vintrusie, we have too much to do for you to die now." He left the cubicle and went in search of Skultar and Karlsut.

● ●

From her parallel reality, Brie sat on her cot, watching Vygel Vintrusie fight for his life. A med-tech flipped a switch on the side of the Critical Care Pod. The top split down the center and slid open, allowing Healer De Dilliére and her team to work hands on. Complete concentration cloaked everyone.

A specter-like figure of a young Vygel Vintrusie floated free of his physical body and drifted upward. It hovered near the ceiling, attention fixed on the activity below. Glowing figures materialized on either side of the translucent Vygel, their attention fixed on his struggling, aged body.

Brie rose slowly. *What's happening?* Understanding left her breathless. *I'm seeing through Vygel's eyes and feeling his response, like it's my own. Pain and fear ripped through her.* Vygel's essence recoiled as the body on the table went rigid. Brie clutched at her chest. Gray haze filled her consciousness. White light glowed in the distance.

On the table, Vintrusie's eyes rolled back in his head, breaking the connection to Brie. Staring down at the once Mocendi, she gasped and dropped to sitting, her heart a pounding drum beat in her chest.

Defibrillator paddles placed on his chest arched his physical body. It slammed back onto the table. His hovering essence reacted. This time more curious than alarmed, his attention remained fixed on those fighting to save him. A drug administered into the heart muscle sent shock waves throughout the body. It shuddered and lay still.

Near the ceiling, pearlescent figures gathered around Vygel's essence. One pointed at something invisible. Another seemed to instruct. Vygel's ghostly presence stared hard at the unmoving body below. He looked from one figure to the next and nodded. They faded. The ghost-like Vygel floated lower, hovered, and vanished, sucked into his physical form through the top of his head.

The aging body convulsed. Bulging eyes flew open. The wrinkled face contorted in pain. Healer De Dilliére administered a drug with the slender silver cylinder. Vygel Vintrusie slept the deep sleep of a fighter, who, at the last moment, won the battle against death.

Everyone in the Critical Care Unit breathed a sigh. Healer De Dilliére outlined instructions for the patient's care, thanked everyone for their diligence, and left them with instructions to call her if there were changes.

Brie pondered what she had undergone with the man whose dream of walking beside The MasTer had brought her to this place. She had read about near-death experience in the Galactic Library. None of her sources mentioned the possibility of anyone other than the person experiencing it being aware it happened.

What does it mean? She rolled onto her side and stared down at Vygel's pod. *I learned near-death leaves the person changed. Will Vygel be different when he awakens?*

Vygel Vintrusie's dreams filled his world and faded, leaving nothing but vague impressions. He awoke to find his wrists and ankles strapped down. A struggle to unravel why brought beads of sweat to his brow. Drugs administered by a strange man dropped him into sleep, where dreams of his childhood on El Stroma reminded him of a time when innocence left him vulnerable. The horror of the prison camp brought him face to face with the man he had become. Dreams of Thorlu Tangorra and Rayn Palmira sent him tumbling into memories of destroying El Stroma, of releasing chemicals to end all life on the planet he loved. His journey to TreBlaya and the eventual emergence of The MasTer pursued him through hallways bathed in the deaths he had helped to cause.

He woke with a start, wishing never to sleep again. He tried to call out, opened his mouth to shout, and snapped it shut. His thoughts flew to Elf that turning on Treblaya when his vocal cords were severed and his memories wiped clean. Another attempt to speak ended in failure. More memories rose and fell. The desire to forget brought his thoughts back to Elf. A lump formed in his throat. *The MasTer ordered me to have it done. I watched the process with self-righteous glee, knowing Thorlu's sperm had been used to fertilize Rayn's egg. I knew Elf was his son.*

A sedative misted the air inside the pod. He fought to stay awake until his eyelids grew so heavy he feared they might close forever. Sleep carried him like a small boat on a vast sea into the land of dreaming.

The sound of voices murmuring around him penetrated his drug-heavy sleep. He blinked. His eyes bulged. Confusion flooded his mind. Coherent thoughts refused to form.

A figure bent over him. "How are you feeling, Mocendi Vintrusie?"

His head jerked from side to side. The slurry of words spoken by the figure made no sense. He did not recognize anyone or anything. The one thing he grasped terrified him. *I don't know who I am.*

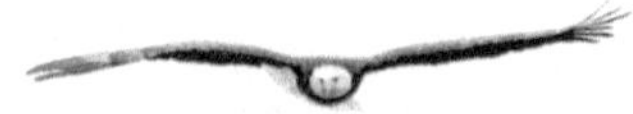

13
Mittkeer

The nausea and dizziness caused by entering Mittkeer did nothing to improve Ari's mood. Brie's capture scared her more than she liked to admit. Thorlu and Vygel, scoundrels in the extreme, would go to any lengths to release The MasTer, even if it meant destroying Brielle. *At least, she's safe in the time-fold.*

Torgin's summer-green eyes held a hint of pity. "Are you alright, Arienh?"

"No. I'm not." She rounded on Esán. "Why didn't you warn us you were bringing us here?"

Esán's serious expression added to her fear. "We couldn't afford to get caught, Ari." He eyed his best friend. "Who was out there, Torgin?"

"There were two young Vasro headed toward the cottage. The pale blue lining in their capes suggests they are Karlsut Sorda's recruits. Thanks for getting us away so fast, Esán."

An impatient Gar wiggled beside him. "Those Vasro guys had a tracker. I could hear it getting louder the closer they got. Do you suppose they felt us leave?"

"I doubt it." Torgin shrugged. "But it's a good thing we left when we did. What's our next step, Esán?"

Tumu Nnoci in hand, Esán scanned the star-lit vista. "We know the *Surgentin* was near ReTaw au Qa. I suggest we begin there. Gar, see if you can spot the constellation Drazil's Tail." He drew a line in the air that curved up at the end. "It has six stars in a line and two additional to make the curve. The fourth star from the left has a golden corona around it."

Ari tugged at a red curl. "We're wasting time. Why can't we repeat what we did before?"

Torgin cleared his throat. "May I explain?"

Esán looked relieved. "I wish you would."

In a business-like tone, Torgin began. "We knew when we started our original search, we wanted to create a time-fold to hide Brie until we could figure out how to rescue her. Our goal now is to remove her from the fold to Mittkeer. The closer we get to the *Surgentin's* position, the easier it will be. I doubt it is near ReTaw au Qu, but it's the best place to start."

"Thanks." Esán gazed at the endless night sky. "We can decide our next move when we get to our destination. Ari, hold Keersé and concentrate on Brie. With luck, you'll have a better sense of her as we move closer."

"Hey, I think I see the tail thing." Gar pointed into the distance. "It's way out there."

Esán grinned and gripped his shoulder. "Good work, Garon. Please hold on to Ari. Torgin, I need you to touch my shoulder. Gar and I are taking us to Drazil's Tail. Everybody ready?"

Ari held onto Gar and concentrated on her sister. The leap through the star-studded heavens left her gasping. Above her, in the dome of unending stars, a constellation gleamed brighter than those surrounding it. She pointed. "Up there! See it." She hugged Gar and smiled at Esán. "You two make a great team!"

Torgin cleared his throat. "What's next?"

Ari pressed Keersé to her heart. "Brie's not anywhere near here." A nagging thought produced a memory of their time in New York City, 1969. "Oh! Esán, when you worked for Karlsut Sorda in New York, didn't you discover he and Skultar grew up on Roahymn?"

His eyes gleamed. "Yes. Dwight, or rather Rethson, told me."

Torgin stared at the starry dome. "Roahymn is close to the Outer Rim *and* a magnetic bridge that connects it to El Stroma's solar system. I'm betting the ship is near there."

Expectation made Ari giddy. "Do you know what constellation is the marker for Roahymn, Esán?"

He grinned. "No, but I'm pretty sure the VarTerel of the Inner Universe does."

She groaned. "Great. Wolloh's on the other side of the solar system."

"Maybe not." Torgin turned her to face the opposite direction, where a white-haired figure limped toward them. The hazel eye on the unscarred side of his face glowed in the starlight. Scars on the opposite cheek glinted with the luster of moonstone. His distorted smile reached out to them.

At the top of his staff, the crystal Vinredi sent a shaft of light to pool around them. Drazil's Tail vanished. Wolloh Espyro, now standing with them, pointed ahead. "The constellation Vêrco, the marker for my home planet, comprises sixteen stars that create the outline of a male deer."

He scrutinized them, one by one. "Relevart shared some of your adventures. Garon Anaru, I have looked forward to meeting you. I see you are making good use of the spectacles Henrietta gave you. Arienh, your aunt will be glad to know you and Keersé have connected. Torgin, your research and your theories regarding Mittkeer and its role in Brie's rescue are exceptional. Good work. Esán, it seems the unknowns associated with the power of Dual Seeds of Carsilem are coming to the fore in you." Seriousness cloaked him. "We will need all our gifts to rescue Brielle and escape from the *Surgentin*." He limped toward Vêrco.

Ari ran to his side. "How did you find us, Wolloh?"

He stopped. His pleasant expression underwent a change. Anger glinted like the sharp edge of a dagger in his hazel eye. "Since Relevart and Henri are on a special mission, they asked me to assist you. Brie is one of my best students. I do not want her to fall prey to the Mocendi, especially Vygel and Thorlu. Secondary to that are Karlsut Sorda and Skultar Rados and their band of young, untested Vasro. They care not for the return of El Stroma, but for their fame and their bank accounts." He scowled. "They believe bringing The MasTer forth will help their cause." Scars pulsed on his injured cheek. His feathered left brow quivered. "They do not realize the devastation they are about to unleash on the Universe."

He drew Ari with him over the carpet of stars. His good eye seemed to assess her strengths.

She squirmed. "What do you want of me, Wolloh?"

"I need you to do two things: give me Efillaeh and Keersé."

An angry 'no' choked her.

"We don't have time to argue, Ari." He held out his hand.

She unbuckled the scabbard, considered walking away, and then handed it to him along with the small herkimer diamond.

"You do not yet understand your true power, Arienh AsTar." He raised his staff. Vinredi's center blazed blood red. "Think of Brielle. Good. Never doubt yourself, Arienh, or your ability to overcome."

Stars spun into a blur of white light. Mittkeer vanished. Ari gasped and gripped her head with both hands. Garbled voices nearby drew closer. She blinked, trying to bring her environment into focus.

A voice she recognized called her by a name she knew well. "Who do we have here? We have missed you, Brielle AsTar."

Her blurred vision regained its focus. Thorlu Tangorra's sardonic smile made her sicker than her exit from Mittkeer.

Esán grabbed Wolloh's arm. "What have you done? Where's Ari?"

The VarTerel of the Inner Universe angled his injured side to him. The scarred cheek pulsed. His blind eye glinted with the fire of white topaz. The feathered brow raised.

Esán, reminded of meeting Wolloh for the first time, removed his hand.

Wolloh turned and brought his good eye in line with his. "Thank you, Esán. I have sent her where she will do the most good." The eye narrowed as he passed him the crystal. "The sooner we rescue Brielle, the sooner we can bring Ari back to Mittkeer."

Anger, dismay, and fear intermingling made Esán's head ache. His fingers curled around Keersé. "Did you even warn her?" He glared at Efillaeh. "Or did you just send her unarmed into battle?"

Gar, fear in his magnified eyes, gazed from him to the VarTerel of the Inner Universe and moved closer to his cousin.

"Esán, perhaps we should let Wolloh explain." Torgin's calm voice penetrated his rush of emotions.

A breath soaked with fear wafted through Mittkeer. "You sent her to the *Surgentin*, didn't you? She's not in the time-fold with Brie, is she? What happens when Vygel and Thorlu discover who she is?" Esán nearly choked on the words.

A sustained note on the time whistle followed by an unexpected quiet pulled him up short.

He stood on the bridge of a ship where two crew members tracked readings on several monitors. Neither man seemed aware of his presence. One screen, he realized, charted the ship's course and position. A repeating bleep showed the *Surgentin* maintained a stationary position behind Roahymn's moon. The need to concentrate erased all emotion. *I'm in a time fold, or they would notice me.* His attention jumped from one screen to the next, his eidetic memory recording everything he saw.

The ship's bridge blurred. Stars focused. Torgin's relieved laugh infiltrated Esán's dazed reentry into Mittkeer.

Gar clapped. "You did it, Torgin!"

Wolloh's hazel eye gleamed. "When you've stabilized, Esán, I will scan your memories. As soon as I have the ship's location, we'll travel in that direction."

Esán gripped his knees, worked to lower his blood pressure and calm a heart muscle that ricocheted off his breastbone. When he could breathe again, he looked his friend in the eye. "You helped him. Thank you, Torg." A half turn brought him face to face with Wolloh. "I'm fine. Please see what you discover in my memories."

~ Surgentin ~

From her position in the time-fold, Brie gripped the edge of the cot and gasped in dismay. "Ari! What are you doing here? I mean there?"

Thorlu entered the infirmary, his eyes blazing. He stopped in front of Ari. Focused anger bored into her. "You didn't think I'd realize you were here?" He beckoned to the med-tech who had followed him into the infirmary. "Give her the medication and go."

Brie sensed Ari's desire to pull away and felt her force herself to hold still.

The med-tech produced the slender syringe cylinder and touched it to her twin's arm. Ari swayed, then shook herself.

The med-tech departed. Thorlu folded his arms and glared.

Brie's pulse rate accelerated. *Calm down, Brielle. You can't help if you pass out.* Her brow wrinkled. Her thoughts raced. She spoke aloud. "Arienh, you told me Rayn's grandparents had spoken to her from a time fold. I wonder if you can receive a telepathic message?" She crossed her fingers. *"Twin secret."*

Below, Thorlu's gaze hardened. "Where have you been hiding, Miss AsTar?"

"It's a twin secret."

Ari's voice, a great imitation of her own, almost made Brie smile. That Ari heard the telepathic message made her want to jump for joy.

Thorlu shoved her sister toward a cubicle and pushed her down on the cot. "Don't play games with me. Where were you hiding?"

She hugged herself and groaned. "I don't feel so good."

He stooped to look her in the eye. "I'll be here when you wake up."

Another groan, her only reply, earned her an irritated scowl. She laid down and closed her eyes.

From her reality, Brie watched him go. As soon as the hatch closed, she got to work. Neutralizing the drug in Ari's system would take them working together. *"Ari, do not react. Listen closely. You are being monitored. Just do what I say. If you understand, yawn."*

A yawn informed Brie that she received the message. *"Don't communicate with me. Thorlu will know. Continue to act drugged. If you remember how Penee neutralized the drug Karlsut's men gave her in New York City, move your right hand."*

The hand moved.

"Good. I'll help from here. Signal me when you're finished by turning on your side."

Several minutes passed. Brie thought Ari had fallen asleep and was deciding how to wake her when the med-tech entered, checked the monitor next to her cubicle, and left again.

Ari turned onto her side and heaved a sigh.

Brie smiled. *"You sensed he was coming, right?"*

A hand twitched.

"Whenever they drug you, the sooner you neutralize it, the better. Always act a little dazed. One more thing, I have a small scar on my neck where the Star used to be." She swallowed. *"I'll put an image in your mind so you can create it on your neck."* Closing her eyes, she pictured the small incision and projected it to Ari.

Moments later, the hatch opened. Thorlu marched to Ari's side. He pushed her hair from her neck and muttered to himself. "Something about you bothers me. Sleep while you can." He took his leave.

Brie exhaled a relieved breath. She could see the scar on Ari's neck. "You're good, Arienh."

A soft snore covered what Brie knew was a snort.

~ Mittkeer ~

Esán sighed as Wolloh's mind probe withdrew. "Did you find what you needed?"

"I did. With your permission, Torgin will perform a mind scan to calibrate the compass of Ostradio for Vêrco."

Esán noted the surprise on his friend's face. "It's good, Torg. You can do it. I'm ready when you are."

Torgin, looking dazed, turned to Wolloh. "Can't he just tell me the coordinates? You can remember them, right Esán?"

"I can, Torg, but it'll be quicker if you just do it."

Wolloh touched Torgin's arm. "You hold Ostradio in your left hand, and I'll hold your right and guide you through the process. Let's not waste any more time."

Torgin withdrew the compass and, with a doubtful look, clasped Wolloh's smooth hand. The VarTerel of the Inner Universe gave him a reassuring smile.

"Esán will stand right there and open his mind to you. Close your eyes. Good. Next, relax. A mind scan is a matter of simple concentration. Give yourself permission to connect to Esán and allow his thoughts to become your own. That's good. Now, seek the memories of his time on the *Surgentin*. Gently. Don't panic and don't rush. There you go. Open your eyes and look."

Stars on the back of Ostradio had rearranged to show Roahymn's sky. Torgin flipped the compass. The needle spun in a blur of gold over the red letters and numbers and stopped.

Esán grinned. "I told you it would be quicker."

Wolloh placed his staff in front of them. "Please hold on."

As Esán's fingers touched the smooth shaft, a flash of blue light obscured the night sky. When his vision cleared, he stood beneath the constellation Vêrco. The next instant, it vanished. A feminine gasp of surprise made him turn.

Brielle, eyes wide with wonder, threw her arms around his neck and sobbed. As he kissed her tears away, the nausea of their unexpected reentry into Mittkeer left them clinging to each other. He looked up, noted Torgin's relief, Gar's wide grin, and Wolloh with a crooked smile. Ignoring them, he kissed the woman he loved.

14
Mittkeer

Torgin stood apart from his friends in the quiet of Mittkeer, fighting to keep his racing thoughts in check. *I wonder what other talents I possess.* His lips pressed into a firm line. *Concentrate, Torgin, Ari needs your help.*

With one long stride, he closed the gap between himself and the VarTerel of the Inner Universe. "We can't leave Ari alone with Thorlu and Vygel. They'll figure out she isn't Brie, and then we'll be in worse trouble."

Brie hugged Esán, accepted a quick hug from Gar, and faced Wolloh. "He's right...at least about Thorlu." She quickly explained what had happened to Vygel. "The last time I saw him, he was still in a coma, so he's not a threat to Ari at the moment." More serious than ever, she fastened her unblinking gaze on Wolloh's. "You wouldn't leave Ari on the ship without a plan to rescue her. So, what do you propose?"

"Getting you to safety is my primary goal. To accomplish that, we need to distract Thorlu Tangorra. His is astute, so diversion is key." Wolloh studied her from his seeing eye. "Something else is worrying you. Please share it with me."

Brie slipped a hand into Esán's. "Without my permission, the *Surgentin's* genetic team extracted my eggs. Vygel's sperm fertilized one egg and Thorlu's another. A member of the ship's crew is the host mother for the two babies."

Torgin sensed her fighting back tears and stepped in. "You don't want to leave the host mother behind, right?"

A tear lingered and slipped down her cheek. Sniffing like a small child, she wiped it away. "I don't want my children raised like Elf and Penee or Rethson were, even if they can't be with me."

Gar's hand crept into hers. She flashed him an understanding smile, gave the hand a squeeze, and returned her complete attention to her mentor.

Wolloh's taloned hand stroked his chin. "You've connected with this woman, Brie?"

"Did I speak with Skylyn? No. I was already in the time fold when I discovered she was the host mother."

"Is she aware you are the mother of the babies she is carrying?"

Brie nodded. "She is."

The VarTerel stared up at the crystal topping his staff. His distorted features twitched. "You understand we will have only one chance to remove Ari and Skylyn—one chance and one chance only."

Torgin frowned. "Why only one?"

Wolloh looked up at the star-sprinkled doom. "I'm certain Thorlu knows we are close. Karlsut and Skultar tried to convince him to continue the hunt for Troms el Shiv, but he chose not to leave and lose Brie. Now he has her, or at least an excellent substitute, back on the ship."

"We need to hurry." Esán pulled Brie closer. "I've been monitoring the *Surgentin*, and it is preparing to leave orbit."

Brie blanched. "Please tell us what to do, Wolloh."

The disfigured VarTerel seemed to grow taller. "Brielle and Gar, you focus on Skylyn. Torgin, locate and connect to Ari. Esán, you will assist me with preparing their way from the ship to here. Everyone, tell me when you're ready."

~ *Surgentin* ~

Ari felt Brie's departure like the slicing away of part of herself. The desire to reach out, to discover where her twin disappeared to, almost gave her away. A light flashed on the monitor panel. The hatch opened to admit the med-tech, followed by a woman she assumed to be a healer.

Ari met her puzzled gaze with one of her own. "Do I know you?" She hugged herself. "I feel so strange."

The baffled expression changed to one of professional observation. "We missed you, Miss AsTar. Please tell us where you've been hiding."

Ari flashed a dazed look at the healer. "I remember..." She looked around. "...Thorlu finding me." She pressed her hands against her eyes and lowered them. "Anything before is like someone pulled a featureless curtain in front of it." Her voice trembled. "What's happening to me?"

The woman held a palm-sized round instrument over her head and ran it down the length of her body. Appearing more baffled than ever, she drew the med-tech aside, addressed him in low tones, and, after he left, closed the end of Ari's cubicle. She adjusted the settings on a side monitor and sat on a chair facing her. "We have little time. You're not Brielle AsTar. Although the readings on the body scan are identical to hers, I can find no trace of the vascular roots of the birthmark I removed. Thorlu told me Brie is a monozygotic twin. You're her sister, correct?"

Ari could not detect animosity, only concern. "Who are you?"

"I'm Healer De Dilliére. And you are..."

Following her instinctive response to the healer, Ari answered. "Arienh. Ari for short."

"Ari, Thorlu will discover you're not Brie. When he does, I can't guarantee your safety. You need to go wherever your sister went."

"Why are you helping me? Thorlu can be vicious if he's crossed."

A light on the monitor flashed. Healer De Dilliére adjust a sensor and switched her attention to Ari. "You need to continue your charade. Thorlu is on the way. Let him think you have amnesia and, Ari, escape as soon as you can."

The end of the cubicle slid open. A female med-tech preceded the Mocendi into the small space. Healer De Dilliére moved to one side. Ari covered her face with shaking hands.

Thorlu marched to the bedside and glared down at her. "Are you ready to tell me where you've been hiding, Brielle?"

Confusion dulling her expression, Ari lowered her hands and raised her stunned gaze to Thorlu's face. "I don't remember. All I can remember is you finding me." She looked at the healer. "Did the drug you gave me steal my…" She touched the scar on her neck. Her eyes widened. "You removed the Star of Truth. I don't remember anything else." She lay down on the cot and curled into a ball, her mind empty as a blank slate.

Thorlu joined Healer De Dilliére at a monitor station. "Could the drugs you prescribed give her amnesia?"

The woman held up a hand. "Give me a second, Thorlu, I'm checking."

The Mocendi paced the width of the infirmary. A quick about face and three long strides brought him to Ari's side. She sensed confusion, anger, and another emotion she could not put her finger on.

His absence from her side left her hugging herself tighter. She peeked from beneath an eyelid. He hovered over the healer, impatience wafting from his person in a perfume-like mist. His astonished gaze shot to her face and back to the healer.

Healer De Dilliére appeared to be busy entering data. His hand on her shoulder stopped her. She glanced up, saw his expression, and lowered her eyes.

When he spoke, Thorlu's gentle tone surprised Ari. "I know what you have discovered, Dee, but I'd rather hear it from you."

The woman hesitated, then stood. She crossed to the cubicle and gazed down at Ari. She mouthed the words 'I'm sorry', then turned to the Mocendi. "This isn't Brielle AsTar, Thorlu."

The full range of emotions rushing through him left Thorlu Tangorra staring first at Dee and then at Ari. He wondered in a distant part of his brain why surprise was absent from the list. A quick march to the ship's intercom helped him to diffuse his prominent emotion. Anger dissipated as he spoke to the duty officer.

The commander's face appeared on the view screen. "How may I help you, Mocendi Tangorra?"

"It is imperative the ship leaves Roahymn's airspace as soon as possible."

The man's calm demeanor remained intact. "We have already begun preparations and will be underway within the next half chron circle."

Thorlu controlled a gasp of surprise and forced a sense of calm he did not feel into his voice. "Who ordered you to leave orbit?"

"Karlsut Sorda gave the order. Is there anything else I can help you with?"

"Nothing else. Thank you." The screen went dark.

He faced the healer. "How long will she be out?"

The twin sat up and pushed her red curls back from her face. "I'm awake, Thorlu."

He glared down at her. "You heard everything?"

She nodded. "I'm Arienh. Brie is no longer on the *Surgentin*."

The ship's emergency alert sounded. Lights flashed above the hatch.

Ari jumped to her feet. The infirmary wavered, refocused, and wavered again.

Thorlu shouted, "Nooo!"

~ Mittkeer ~

The urgency vibrating through Mittkeer fixated Esán on summoning his power. Deep inside, the Seeds of Carsilem responded with a surge of energy that almost knocked him over.

A hand on his shoulder calmed his momentary panic. Wolloh stepped into view. "Breathe. Allow your power to flow naturally. Good. When I open the path from the ship to Mittkeer, your connection to Brie will direct you to her twin and then to the *Surgentin*." He gripped his staff.

Esán matched Wolloh's power with his own. Energy thrummed through his raised palms and hummed in his ears, opening a path to the ship.

The VarTerel nodded. "Good work, Esán. Brie and I found Sky. Torgin, do you have Ari?"

Torgin frowned. "One minute I've got her and the next she's gone. Hold on."

"Keep your focus on Ari and use the time whistle to hold the path to the ship steady. Tell me when you are linked to her."

Esán listened with half an ear as he fought to hold the ship to its place behind the Roahymnian moon. He fell to his knees, and, forcing himself to remain conscious, gathered the reins of the Seeds and held firm.

Torgin shouted, "I've got Ari! Help me, Wolloh."

Wolloh responded. "On my three, bring the girls here."

Torgin yelped and doubled over.

A flash of brilliant white light flared across the star-scape.

Brie let out a cry. "I lost Sky. I lost—" Sobs echoed through Mittkeer.

Esán fought harder to hold the *Surgentin* to its orbit. His connection to the ship snapped, leaving him fighting to breathe. Acute anguish left him facing Brie. "I'm so sorry, Brielle. We'll find Sky and the babies. I promise."

A silhouetted figure dashed from the fading light. Ari ran straight to Brie. A second figure hugged his mid-section and groaned.

Vinredi blazed royal blue before it faded. Wolloh leaned on the staff, his breath coming in gasps.

Brie, her heart pounding with gratitude, accepted hugs all around. She fastened her pleading gaze on Wolloh's face and, moving closer to Esán, gathered all the courage she could muster.

Her teacher and mentor's seeing eye blinked. His feathered brow trembled. "I feel your agitation, Brielle. Explain your need."

She drew Esán with her a step closer. "Send me back to the ship, Wolloh. My children-to-be and their host mother are there and unprotected. Even with Vygel ill, they are not safe. Karlsut Sorda is determined to use my children to get his way and doesn't care whom he hurts. Please send me back to help protect them."

Ari moved next to her twin. "If Brie goes back, so do I."

"Me, too." Gar chimed. "I'm her protector."

Torgin gaze over Brie's shoulder. "I think we have a problem." Everyone turned. Brie stared, examining her emotions. Dismay was not among them.

Thorlu, fighting his disorientation and nausea, sought a way to make sense of his sudden arrival in a place he had never expected to visit.

The last things he remembered were the ship's alert sounding; a flare of light obscuring his surroundings; and nausea doubling him over. Sobs penetrating his discomfort brought him upright to the sight of unending night. His startled gaze darted to the VarTerel of the Inner Universe.

Wolloh's unscarred cheek and hazel eye gleamed. "Welcome to Mittkeer, Thorlu Tangorra. I suggest you join us."

Thorlu examined the group gathered a short distance ahead. Red-haired twins stood next to the VarTerel, one on either side of Esán Efre. Torgin Whalend tucked something beneath his shirt and pulled a young black boy behind him.

Thorlu maintained his distance. "Why did you bring me here, Wolloh Espyro?"

The VarTerel of the Inner Universe smiled. "I didn't, but circumstance most surely did."

"Send me back."

A feathered brow rose above an unseeing white eye. "If I could do so, I would, however, *Surgentin* left orbit and approaches the Décussate. I have no jurisdiction in the Outer Universe, and, even if I did, returning a human to a moving object is almost impossible."

Thorlu's mind raced. One thought jumped to the top of the list. *How will I get back to Dee?*

Esán considered teleporting Brie through the Land of Time away from The MasTer's Mocendi and the threat he presented.

Wolloh's hazel eye glinted in the starlight. "I suggest we return to Shu Chenaro and decide what our next move should be." The turn of his head brought his gaze to rest on the Mocendi. "You may discover, Tangorra, we have similar goals." He placed his staff ready for travel. Vinredi glowed.

Torgin, with Gar at his side, rested a hand on Wolloh's arm. Ari moved to stand beside her twin.

Esán glanced at Brie, felt her acceptance of Thorlu's presence, and abandoned his plans to escape with her alone. Ignoring his dislike of the man, he focused his attention on the VarTerel.

Wolloh regarded the hesitant Mocendi with a touch of impatience. "Unless you wish to remain in Mittkeer, please join us."

Thorlu walked over stars and night, scanned the companions, then touched Ari's shoulder.

A corona of rainbow light surrounded the group as the constellation Uruao, the Scorpion's Tail, appeared overhead. A breath later, they arrived in the sitting room at Shu Chenaro, where Stebben Stol waited, expression watchful and stance that of a warrior.

Before anyone could speak, the magnificent figure of Chealim materialized at the room's center, his cherub blue eyes fixed on Thorlu.

Surprise coupled with astonishment flashed across the Mocendi's face, then transitioned from uncertainty to acceptance.

Chealim scanned the group. "Stebben, you may relax. Everyone else, please take a few minutes while Thorlu and I conference in the library. When I return, we have things to discuss." He stepped to Thorlu's side. They vanished, leaving everyone talking at once.

"Excuse me." Wolloh cleared his throat. "I have a couple of things I'd like to say. Please take a seat."

Esán and Brie moved to the sofa, while Torgin and Ari each settled into the leather wingbacks. Gar gripped the back of Torgin's chair and stood, taking in his surroundings with a look of surprised wonder. Stebben, the alert protector, remained close to his mentor.

Wolloh regarded them from his seeing eye. "First, my compliments to you for Brielle's rescue." He handed Stebben the leather scabbard containing Efillaeh. "Please return this to Arienh." A smile followed her nod of thanks. "I hope you realize your talents are developing much faster, Ari, than any of us expected. If I thought you wished to be a DiMensioner, I would offer to train you. Since I know this is not your desire, I honor your choice with the caveat that should you ever change your mind, I am at your service."

Ari stood and belted on the scabbard. "Thank you, VarTerel Espyro, for understanding my temperament is not conducive to the discipline required for such a role." She kissed his cheek, grinned at his surprise, and sat down.

His distorted smile melted into a studied gaze that switched to Torgin. "Torgin, you, too, are in the process of discovery. Do you have questions regarding your talents and their development?"

Chealim's reappearance left everyone silent. The MasTer's Mocendi was nowhere to be seen.

The Galactic Guardian nodded to their hosts. "Wolloh and Stebben, thank for your help. I suggest you get some rest. I will be in touch when we need you again."

His attention fastened on the young people. Shu Chenaro's sitting room faded.

15

Surgentin

On board the *Surgentin*, Skultar Rados and Karlsut Sorda, Penee's cousins, glared at the young officer cowering in front of them in the conference room.

Karlsut snarled under his breath and lunged to his feet. "Did I hear you correctly? Thorlu Tangorra and Brielle AsTar are no longer on the ship?"

Skultar Rados pursed thin lips, his unshakable gaze on the young man. "Did you say the ship has left its orbit around Roahymn?"

The officer swallowed and snuck a look at Karlsut Sorda. "As ordered, the ship is on its way to the magnetic bridge on the far side of the Décussate." A nervous tick jerked his head. "Healer De Dilliére just informed the captain that Mocendi Tangorra and the young woman vanished."

Karlsut glared. "Vanished? What do you mean by vanished?"

Skultar cleared his throat. "Please ask Healer De Dilliére to join us. We'd like to hear her story."

Relief prompted a dignified dip of the head. "Yes, sir." Without waiting for dismissal, he hurried from the conference room.

Karlsut rounded on his brother, narrow nostrils flaring. "Why didn't you let the man explain, Skultar? We need answers."

Although Skultar's outrage demanded release, he spoke in a controlled voice tempered with steel. "We are partners, and yet you ordered the ship to leave orbit without discussing it with me first." His tone hardened further. "Explain."

His younger brother squirmed, stammered a start, and snapped his mouth shut.

Skultar did not come to his rescue, but maintained a chilling silence.

Clasping and unclasping his hands, Karlsut glared at the tabletop. "We had Brielle. Vygel had his baby implanted. Thorlu has been overseeing the girls' care." He looked up and shrugged. "I decided it was time to leave for El Stroma."

Skultar glowered. "Correct me if I am wrong. We—you, me, and Thorlu —are equals in this enterprise. We, the three of us, decided to wait until the Vasro had taken control of *El Aperdisa*. Then, as I recall, we were going to travel to our home in the living ship, which will, unless you have been an idiot and destroyed it, be the basis for our financial success."

"*El Aperdisa* is fine." Karlsut floundered, then licked his lips. "I meant to tell you, then Vygel had heart surgery and Thorlu and the girl vanished, and —" A grin spread from ear to ear. "Think, Skultar." He tapped the edge of the table. "With Vintrusie and Tangorra out of the way, we can pursue our own plans. Best of all, if we need them to do our bidding, we have Vygel's baby to use as bait." Sly laughter shook his stooped shoulders. "Do you think for a moment, the girls, including Penee, won't come running if we threaten Brie's baby?"

"By the RomPeer's gods, I've always known you were devious..." Skultar shook his head.

"I am not. You're the conniving one, Skultar Rados."

Skultar spoke through bared teeth. "When Grandfather died, who ran off with the family fortune?" He controlled the hatred leaking into his voice. "While you lived a life of luxury, I protected our future in the form of Penee by working on a winter moon in a Penal Colony." He squeezed the bridge of his nose, then lowered his hand. Squinting brown eyes, rested on his half-brother. "Fortunately, you had the forethought to transfer your personal funds to me before leaving for the past. My question now, Karlsut Sorda, is whether we can work together? I'm not willing to sacrifice everything to have you steal whatever attention, prestige, and money we may earn."

Karlsut sat back and steepled his fingers.

Skultar observed him from a frigid silence. Transitory memories formed. They were half-brothers, birthed from two of the RomPeer's consorts. Although they were both tall and thin, with the narrow faces and long noses from their grandfather's genetic heritage, their resemblance ended there. As the younger brother, Karlsut had to fight harder to be recognized. Skultar realized he had hated his older brother, whom he thought always claimed the limelight. When the chance presented itself to disappear with the family fortune, it didn't enter Karlsut's mind not to cut and run.

Intertwining his fingers, Skultar pressed his palms together. "We are going back to the planet where our grandfather ruled. From what we've been told by the Metchalians, opportunities abound there. El Stroma is coming back to life. Once we take over *El Aperdisa* and have her resources at our disposal, we'll be on the road to extreme wealth. If we work together, it will make it harder to keep us from ruling as Grandfather ruled before us."

"So, Skultar Rados, are you promising to share equally?"

Skultar met Karlsut's loaded question with a prolonged silence. Negative emotions kept him seated. He gripped the table's smooth edge.

Impatience brought his brother face to face with him. Karlsut offered his hand. "Equal partners."

Skultar stared at the hand, looked him in the eye, and folded his arms. "I will shake when we have said the Pheet Adolan Pledge of Honor."

In order to hide his distaste, Karlsut lowered his head and struggled to school his expression to pleasant.

Skultar realized his brother hoped he had forgotten The Pledge, which bonded those who embraced it to a shared destiny. If one party broke the pledge, disaster befell both.

The stubborn set of Karlsut's jaw warned him of a battle to come. Rather than wait for the attack, he cleared his throat. "Do I trust you enough to tie my life to yours, Karlsut Sorda? No. But unless we recite The Pledge, I will walk and take Thorlu and the *Surgentin* with me."

Opposite him, his younger brother observed him without expression.

Heavy-lidded eyes riveted to his flashed a flint-like gleam. He summoned a smile. "If we are to make a success of future ventures on El Stroma, The Pledge will insure our loyalty to each other and to our mutual cause." He stood and extended a manicured hand. "I challenge you to join with me to establish Pheet Adolan rule on El SyrTundi *and* El QuilTran."

Karlsut shuddered, clasped the hand and, with him, repeated,

> *"With this pledge, we're bound forever*
> *To support and share, forsaking never.*
> *Our destinies, lives, and successes are one.*
> *If this promise is broken, both are undone."*

A charged silence cloaked the compartment. Neither man moved, their attention focused on each other.

Thorlu Tangorra arrived in his quarters on the *Surgentin* and shook his head in amazement. Chealim had sent him back to the ship through Mittkeer. A 'time tweak' allowed him to arrive a short time after his disappearance from the infirmary. Hurrying down the passageway, he found Healer De Dilliére behind the desk in her cubicle.

She looked up and raised a brow. "Thorlu Tangorra, *where* have you been? You and the twin vanished half a chron circle ago. I'm on my way to share with your partners what happened." She cleared her data-screen. "Care to come along?"

Moving to the hatch, she scanned the corridor. "Is the twin back as well?"

He joined her. "I'll explain later. Let's go see Karlsut and Skultar. They are, I'm sure, anxious about my disappearance." A touch of sarcasm leaked into the words.

Dee shook her head and hurried along the pristine passageway. At the conference room, she pressed the sensor. The hatch slid open. She entered and moved aside.

Thorlu ducked in and acknowledged the startled disappointment on his partner's faces. "Hello, gentlemen. You look surprised."

Karlsut sank into his seat. Skultar remained standing and smiled at Dee.

"We haven't met. I'm Skultar Rados. You know my brother, Karlsut Sorda. Please sit down." He flashed an acerbic smile at the Mocendi. "I'm sure Thorlu will share what happened."

Thorlu sat opposite the two men. "It's really quite simple. I realized Brielle was about to be removed from the ship and lunged forward to grab her. Someone teleported her elsewhere." He rubbed his shoulder. "They dumped me in a storage unit and left me there unconscious. When I came to, I went in search of Healer De Dilliére, knowing she would report what happened to you."

Karlsut snorted. "Do you expect us to believe that you, a great Mocendi DiMensioner, couldn't hang onto a drugged girl?"

"Take or leave it, Karl." Thorlu shrugged. "My head aches, so I'm going to lie down."

Dee stood. "I'd better check you over in case you have a concussion." She led the way from the compartment.

Thorlu took his leave with a quiet statement. "I will share more when my headache is better." He left the brothers staring at the closing hatch.

Back in Dee's cubicle, she pulled out a chair. "How are you, other than your headache? Any nausea or dizziness?"

He stopped her with a hand on her arm. "I don't have a concussion."

Dee slipped behind her desk and studied him with an intense, professional look. "In the event they check, I suggest we fill out a report." She sat back and tapped her chin. "You didn't hit your head or lose consciousness, correct?"

A wave of longing held him quiet. Then he once again made a decision he hoped he would not regret. "I am not at liberty to tell you everything, but I can share that those who combined their knowledge and power to rescue Brie and then Ari removed me from the ship. After being challenged to reconsider my course in life, they sent me back, so I can protect Skylyn and the babies she is carrying."

Dee's attention never wavered. "Why did Vygel have Brie's eggs harvested without her permission? What is so special about her and the babies?"

Thorlu took a deep breath and shared The MasTer's story.

A slight arch in her right eyebrow was Dee's only visible reaction.

When he finished disclosing how he discovered that the Star of Truth controlled The MasTer's gene, he paused, lowered his eyes, and stared at his folded hands resting on the gray desktop.

The healer tapped her stylus on the edge of the desk. "I believe you have something more to share?"

A swallow cleared the tightness in Thorlu's throat. He looked up. "I have played the villain throughout this little adventure, Dee. As a young man, I held myself to high ideals and fought to save my people, the Eleo Preda. One turning not long after leaving El Stroma, I realized I harbored more anger than I could control. Recently, someone whom I value and trust informed me The MasTer planted the seed of anger. He recognized my talent and my fervor for a cause and made use of it. I can't undo the past. I can, however, move forward as the man I hoped to be. My intention is to protect the children and their future."

With studied attention, Dee fingered the length of her stylus, then placed it on the desk. "How do you intend to do that? Neither of your partners appeared to be happy to see you."

"Before I answer that, how did you come to be on the *Surgentin*?"

"A friend accepted the position as the Infirmary Head but backed out. Prior to informing the ship's captain, he asked if I was interested. He warned me that the men who were financing this enterprise were unscrupulous, and he wasn't certain what their game was." She smiled. "The temptation to help revitalize a planet, to travel beyond the Décussate..." The smiled vanished. "For the sake of the twins and Skylyn, I'm glad I said yes."

Honesty rang true throughout her explanation. Thorlu inhaled a relief-filled breath. "In order to protect her and the babies, I need a partner. Are you interested?"

Her steady gaze did not waver. "If you swear to set aside your nefarious role and assume that of the defender of good over evil, I will stand by you and do everything I can to help."

Thorlu felt a surge of surprise, followed by gratitude. "You realize I must continue to play the role of the villain. Karlsut and Sorda cannot know that I have more honest interests than bringing forth The MasTer and filling my pockets. Vintrusie wants to walk at The MasTer's side and to see his son become his personal Mocendi. We must, therefore, find Brie and return her to the ship. *Surgentin* is no longer in orbit around Roahymn. Once it crosses the Décussate into the Outer Universe—" He shook his head.

A buzzer buzzed. Dee held a person intercom to her ear. "I'll be right there. Keep him calm." She pocketed the intercom and stood up. "I have just learned two things: Skylyn has disappeared. No one knows where she's gone, and Vygel is awake. If you'll search for Skylyn, I'll see to Vygel. Thank you for trusting me."

She left him sitting in her cubicle, his thoughts careening several directions. He stood. "I must bring Karlsut and Sorda around to Brie's importance for our joint ventures."

16
Mittkeer

B rie's heart gave a sickening twisted as she regarded the Galactic Guardian surrounded by a backdrop of stars. "Thorlu is back on the ship?"

Chealim did not reply, but affirmation radiated from his intense presence.

The desire to be heard almost choking her, she moved into his line of vision. "I need to be on that ship, Chealim. Skylyn carries *my* babies. Please let me help to protect them and her. Please, Chealim." Her plea was calm; her demeanor, respectful. Fighting an impulse to touch his hand to enhance the power of her request, she stepped back.

Esán's arm encircled her. Gar's hand crept into hers.

The radiant being's gaze traveled from the star-studded night to those present. "Your destinies are as ever-changing as the choices you make. I cannot reveal what is to come or the part you will each play. What I can do is help you find your way." His intense focus swept over the companions to

Esán. "Your illness keeps you from achieving your highest potential. For that reason, you must pursue its cure. Ari and Brie, you must help Penee find Troms el Shiv. Not only has the council promised Thorlu an opportunity to know his son, but Elf's presence is vital to the success of El Stroma's return."

Gar cleared his throat and peered through his spectacles. "What about me? Who do I go with?"

Chealim's finger lifted the boy's chin until their eyes met. "You may choose what is right for you, Garon." He straightened.

Brie tried not to sound frantic. "What about Skylyn and my babies?"

"Thorlu will see to their safety until you can remove her from the ship." Again, his all-encompassing gaze took in the group. "Follow your instincts. Work together. Your destinies call. *El Aperdisa* is your staging ground. I suggest you go there now."

Pale blue-white light scintillated around him as he faded, leaving only the memory of his presence.

Suppressed frustration held the group silent. Brie sagged against Esán, her battle with fatigue stealing her vitality.

Ari bit her lip. "How do we know Thorlu is truly on our side? Why charge us with finding his son? If the Guardians want Elf found, why don't they just use their power? I'm not sure I want to find him. He made it clear he didn't want to be around me."

Brie found the strength to put an arm around her twin. "Stop worrying about Elf. Once we've found him, he may surprise you."

Gar's gaze, free of his spectacles, darted from them to Torgin. "We're going to *El Aperdisa*." He grinned. "How long will it take? Henrietta promised Spyglass would be there. Do you think he is? Penee is there too, right?"

Torgin laughed. "Your questions will be answered when we're aboard the ship." He withdrew the Compass of Ostradio and turned to Esán. "I'm ready when you are."

Esán surveyed the group. "Chealim would not have interfered if it were not important to the CoaleScent Cycle. All of us have personal goals. For now, let's put them aside. *El Aperdisa* won't stay put forever. Besides, I miss Penee and Spyglass."

Gar grinned. "Lead the way, Captain Esán."

Brie linked elbows with Ari and moved to Esán's side.

Esán fixed his attention on the compass. "Ask it the way to TreBlaya, Torgin."

The needle spun and stopped. A chart of Mittkeer formed and floated above it. Highlighted was the star-defined shape of a firefly. Its central star glowed the brightest and the tiny incandescent stars forming the wings glimmered in the darkness. Written beneath it: Constellation of Riffley.

Brie felt a stir of anticipation.

~ El Aperdisa ~

Penee sat in her quarters on *El Aperdisa* with the last of Rayn's journals open in her lap. She ran a finger over her full name, Penesert Tamahine el Stroma. *I am pure-blood Pheet Adole. My father-donor was a cousin of the Pheet Adolan RomPeer and my mother-donor was from one of El SyrTundi's wealthiest families.* A sigh whispered. *Sometimes I wish I were Eleo Predan like everyone else.* She placed a hand, fingers splayed, on the cream-colored pages. *We are not that different. Only our thoughts and perception of our history sets us apart from one another. Ari is Eleo Predan, and we are comrades in arms. Our nationalities don't negate that or our friendship.*

A shiver prickled the hair on the back of her neck. *"Where are you, Ari? Brie? Esán? Are you safe? Why haven't we heard anything?"*

Terrier claws striking the floor brought her head up. Spyglass scampered into her quarters, jumped up beside her, and curled into a ball of white and black fur next to her thigh.

Suppressing the growing fear for her friends, she stroked the terrier's back. His ribcage expanding and contracting acted like a catalyst of hope. Her fear receded. "I bet you miss Gar as much as I miss the twins and Esán and Torgin." She ran a finger down the inner joint of the book's spine and continued in a conversational tone. "Rayn's journals have gotten me thinking."

Spyglass' pointy ears perked.

Penee touched her name. "I'm just realizing, Spy, I'm full-blooded Pheet Adole, and our friends are Eleo Predan. If we had all been born on El Stroma before Vygel and his Vasro destroyed it, we'd have been raised to hate each other."

As if he understood, the small dog jumped up and licked her cheek.

She put her arm around him. "Kind of like Gar in New York City, right? Because his skin is black, he learned to be careful around certain people. Why are people afraid of those who differ from themselves, Spyglass?" Penee closed the journal. "It seems to be a human characteristic. I've seen it wherever I've been." Restless fingers stoked the dog's back. "Mostly, we're taught what to embrace and what to fear, based on the history of our people and the perceptions of our parents and teachers." She lifted his chin. "In order to feel safe, people surround themselves with those who see the world as they do."

Penee scratched Spyglass's ears. "I wonder if we can change things on El Stroma?" A thought tugged her lips into a frown. "Guess it depends on what we find when we get there."

She scrubbed her hand over her short hair and cocked her head. "How many people do you suppose survived the chemical rains? I wonder if they reestablished tribes?" She opened the journal, reread an entry, and set it aside. "You know, Spy—"

The hatch bell chimed. A grinning Ari stepped over the threshold, followed by an excited Gar. Spyglass yipped a clipped welcome. Before Penee could say anything, Gar threw his arms around her. "We missed ya, Pen." He plopped down beside her and hauled Spyglass into his lap.

Penee hugged Ari. "I'm so glad to see you. Are you alright? You look worn out."

Ari's deep voice filled the compartment. "I'm fine." She lowered on to the seat next to Penee. "We have lots to share. Chealim and the Council assigned us a couple of important jobs that we must accomplish before we leave for El Stroma. Brie is here, too, and she's checking in with Mom and Dad."

"You're sure you're fine, Ari?" Penee examined her more closely.

"I promise I am."

Penee pressed further. "And Brie... how is she?"

Ari lowered her eyes, but only for a moment. "She's had a difficult time, but she's recovering. I'll let her share her own story."

"What about Esán? Are they together? I haven't seen them since they disappeared from Myrrh."

Gar squirmed to see her better. "Torgin's here, too. He's gonna go with us to El Stroma."

"That's great news." Penee gave him a quick hug, then folded her hands in her lap. "Tell me why you're here, Arienh, and how I can help."

Tumultuous feelings left Ari tugging a red curl, her thoughts reeling. *The past few turnings have been crazy.* Emotional pain flicked its snake-like tongue. *Elf's defection still hurts. Chealim's request that we find him has stirred up a bunch of feelings.*

She gave the curl a final tug, took a breath, and gave her friend a crooked smile. "Sorry, Pen. Too many emotions…" An inhaled breath left her calmer. "The Galactic Council is asking you, me, and Brie to find Elf and bring him back. Thorlu is committed to helping us, especially if we can reintroduce Elf into his life. Also, Elf's presence on El Stroma is vital to the outcome of the CoaleScent Cycle. The Guardians believe when he learns he is going to have a little sister, he will come willingly." She grimaced. "Even though the father is Thorlu. They're hoping father and son can mend the rift between them."

"Elf has a sibling?" Penee's brow knit. "If Thorlu is the father, who's the mother?"

Ari took a breath. "Vygel had Brie's eggs harvested and fertilized with his sperm. When Thorlu found out, he provided sperm samples, too. The *Surgentin's* genetic team implanted both embryos in a host mother named Skylyn."

"What's the *Surgentin*?" Penee looked from one to the other.

"It is the ship Karlsut, Skultar, and Thorlu purchased to take them to El Stroma."

Penee frowned. "Is it as well-equipped as *El Aperdisa*?"

Ari tapped her chin. "*Surgentin* is smaller and faster and every bit as advanced as *El Aperdisa*."

"Do you know where Elf's hiding?" Penee swiveled to face Ari.

Ari kept her response emotionless. "Nope. That's what we must find out. Chealim suggests we begin by finding Marji Senndi. She raised Elf after The MasTer ordered his memories erased and vocal cords cut. She lives with her brothers on DerTah's Von Baar Peninsula near the small town of Atkis. Brie and I have been there. As soon as she's had time to rest, we'll begin our search."

Penee breathed a discouraged sigh. "At least we have a place to start." She brightened. "You realize going on a search for Elf is a perfect way to hide Brie from our enemies?"

Ari bit her lip, then smiled. "Thank you, Pen. That makes the hunt for Elf less personal."

A return smile glinted before Penee grew serious again. "What about Torgin and Esán? If they're not coming with us, what will they be doing?"

"The Council believes that finding a cure for Esán is vital if he is to reach his full potential. Torgin received word when we arrived on board *El Aperdisa* that the Pentharian Medical Clan has new knowledge to share, so they're off to ReTaw au Qa. Once Torgin and Esán have collected the information, they're making the journey to Tao Spirian to deliver it to the research team working on it there."

Curiosity made Ari bring her eyes level with Gar's. "Chealim said you can choose whether to help find Elf or to go with Esán and Torg. Have you decided what's right for you?"

His gaze darted to Penee and back. "Will you be okay if I go with the guys?"

Penee's lips pursed. A thoughtful nod later, her mouth relaxed. "We'll miss you, but it feels right for you to go with Torgin and Esán. Any objections, Ari?"

"None. I suggest we let them know your decision, Gar. Brie and I left them in the Plantitarium. She said she'd meet us back there."

Ari preceded Penee into the passageway and glanced back to make certain Gar and Spyglass followed. Concern for his safety made her edgy.

A soft whisper brushed her cheek. "They'll keep him safe. Stop worrying, Ari."

Rather than nullifying her discomfort, Penee's words magnified the current of unease pulsing through her.

Torgin and Esán, both lost in thought, sat in silence after the girls left *El Aperdisa's* plantitarium. Torgin stared straight ahead. Chealim's instructions seemed incomplete, but they often did. *The Guardians always leave room for choices.* He grimaced. *And mistakes.*

Esán spoke behind him. "I remember visiting *El Aperdisa* for the first time and realizing she's a living ship. The originals of these plants and insects came from El Stroma, Torgin, and we're taking them back there."

Surprise spun Torgin around. "I thought you and Brie weren't coming with us."

"Even though Thorlu committed to protecting Skylyn and the babies, we need to rescue her from the *Surgentin*. You and I are going to Tao Spirian to discover what we can about Sisohprommate, the bacteria which causes my disease. Chealim hinted that the Pentharian medicine clan may have discovered a way for me to go to El Stroma and not succumb to it before or after we get there."

The hatch slid open. Gar darted through. Spyglass ran straight to Torgin, dropped to his haunches, and barked. His young cousin halted beside him, his fists on his hips. "Chealim said I could choose whether to go with the girls or the guys."

"And..." Torgin and Esán proclaimed as one.

"I'm going with you to see Yaro, and to visit Tao Spirian." His succinct nod of the head messaged 'so there.'

Ari peered in the hatchway. "May we join you?"

The black and white terrier barked and wagged his tail.

A deep guffaw shook her shoulders. "We accept your invitation, Spyglass." She ushered Penee ahead of her. "Look who I found."

Torgin put an arm around Penee's shoulders. "Sure am glad to see you, Pen. Has Ari brought you up to date?"

"She has." Penee accepted a quick hug from Esán and looked around. "If Brielle, Den, and Rethson were here, we'd all be together again."

· · ·

Brie hurried into the Plantitarium, fatigue deepening the faint lines around her eyes and worry tightening her jaw.

"Relevart's youngest son has disappeared. Rethson isn't on the ship. Den has gone in search of him and will meet us back onboard when he can. Commander Odnamo has orders to leave for El Stroma in half a moon cycle, so everyone needs to be back by then." She drooped onto a bench and covered her face with her hands.

Esán put an arm around her. "I'm here, Brielle. All of us are. Tell us what you need."

She reached for his hand and produced a shaky smile. "I'm just so tired. Since I expect we will all go our separate ways in the morning, let's catch up. An early dinner is being set up in the officers' dining hall, so we can converse in private. I suggest we head that way."

Ari, with Gar and Spyglass at her side, led the way. Esán and Brielle followed, talking in low voices.

Torgin touched Penee's arm. "Let's hold back so we can talk. Any idea where Rethson might have gone?"

She slowed her pace, her beautiful eyes thoughtful. "If I were to guess, I'd say he has gone to find Roween Rattori. A group of Karlsut's Vasro trainees have been threatening to hurt her if he doesn't spy for Karlsut and Skultar." She glanced at Brie and Esán. "I sure wish Relevart and Henri were here. As it stands, Den spoke with the Commander yesterday and left last night."

"So is Den headed for RewFaar, Pen?"

"He is. Cross your fingers, he gets there ahead of Rethson." Linking her arm through his, she met his gaze. "I'm glad you're coming with us. It seemed odd not to have you around." Absorbed in their own thoughts, they entered the dining hall, where Brie and Esán sat at a long table, food trays untouched. Penee joined Ari in the buffet line.

Gar scurried to Torgin's side. "Can I sit by you?"

"You bet. Let's go fill our trays."

His young cousin ran ahead. Torgin followed more slowly. "*You are such a gift, Garon. It's almost like having a younger brother.*"

The next morning, Brie sat, brushing her tangled curls. Dinner had been an informative meal. After dessert, they hugged each other goodbye; the boys headed to their quarters and the girls to theirs. Acute loss made her shaky. Esán, her anchor, had departed earlier with Torgin and Gar for ReTaw au Qa. She, Penee, and Ari would soon begin their search for Elf.

Nimble fingers worked a tough snarl free. Her brush glided through her long hair and smoothed red curls into a low ponytail. Pulling on her drango tunic, the one given to her by the Atrilaasu, she ran a hand over the tanned skin. It looked like she received it yesterday. She smiled. *I love that it changes to match its environment like the chameleon drango of its origin.*

After pulling on matching boots, she called her VarTerel's staff into being and wrapped her fingers around it. Her hands tingled as it made contact. She smiled. "I'm so glad Esán saved you from Vygel."

The hatch's buzzer escorted Ari and Penee into the compartment. Her twin hugged her. "Are you sure you're ready for this?"

Brie cast a look at the rainbow light glistening in the tourmaline crystal at the top of her staff. "I'm fine, Ari. You and Penee will help me, and Musette will guide us."

As Penee gazed up at the glowing tourmaline, her head jerked toward the hatch. "We need to go. The Commander sent us word trouble heads this way." She reached for the rowan wood staff.

Brie snapped to attention and forced her fatigue into the background. "You can fill me in when we reach Atkis."

Ari's hand on her shoulder sent a jolt of energy through her.

"Thanks, sis. Hang on. Here we go."

Mittkeer's cool, starry darkness enveloped them. The ensuing nausea passed and a chorus of exhales floated through the ever-night. Brie glanced around. "We're looking for the Constellation Uruao, gateway to DerTah, but first, tell me what the captain relayed to you."

Penee's direct glance received a nod from Ari. "A rebel battleship from across the Décussate heads toward *El Aperdisa*. The information Commander Odnamo received suggests its manned by Vasro and a Mocendi sent by Karlsut Sorda to find us. One of Grandfather's personal militia infiltrated the crew and, when opportunity permits, smuggles information to him. That's as much as he's shared so far."

Brie bit her bottom lip. "Sounds as though we'd better find Elf fast. Hold on to my staff, and I'll take us to Uruao."

She closed her eyes, perceived the power of her friends supporting her, and whispered the songline she had created for the constellation. "Scorpion's Tail up in the sky. Next to Irgov, virgin on high."

A flare of golden light left them standing beneath the gateway marker for DerTah. Without waiting to discuss their next move, Brie took them to the forested hills near the site of the Senndi cottage.

17

Surgentin

On the ship *Surgentin*, Vygel Vintrusie felt the viperous darkness sucking the life from him. Straps binding his wrists and ankles held him prisoner. The ever-present blackness grew colder and colder. A shiver quaked through his body. *I will not die. I must not die. I will not die. I must not die.* The mantra repeated over and over seemed to steady him. A slow warmth crept beneath his skin.

His eyes blinked open. Blinding brightness squeezed them shut. A constant hum and a faint rhythmic click blended with his heavy breathing. The sound of his own swallowing fascinated him. His tongue ran over his teeth, licked his lips, and withdrew as though it had a mind of its own.

Like a rogue wave, confusion rushed over him. Nothing within his defined view seemed familiar. Though he fought to remember, his identity remained shrouded in some dark place he could not access.

Trapped hands fisted and relaxed. Fatigue fought to drag him back into dark nothingness. He struggled to stay awake. An anguished moan filled the confined space. His eyes flew open.

Above him, framed by the oval window, a woman peered down at him. "Vygel, how are you feeling?"

He froze as though hit. *Vygel? Who?* His head whipped from side to side. He held it rigid and stared at the face. The awareness of pain burning in every joint, of blurring memories... His jaw tensed. *I will not die. I must not die.*

Blackness wrapped its arms around him.

☙ ☙

Anxious to see Vygel, Thorlu gave Dee time to reach the infirmary, then prepared to follow. Her face on the data-screen stopped him. Her expression held a warning. She mouthed one word. "Help."

He strode into the anteroom of the infirmary and stared through the observation window. Dee completed her instructions for Vygel's care and joined him, her expression blank.

She pointed at him, then at herself, and beckoned. Without further explanation, she stepped into the corridor and walked away from the infirmary and past her office. When she reached a companionway that led to a lower deck, she took it. At the bottom, she guided him along a narrow corridor and ducked through an unmarked hatchway, waited for the panel to slide shut, and faced him. "Vygel regained consciousness with no memory of who or where he is. The heart attack has left him weak. He needs rest. I have sedated him. We will perform a more detailed examination when he awakens."

Thorlu looked around. "Why did you bring me here?"

Dee's expression held a hint of anger. "Karlsut Sorda has ordered me not to discuss Vygel's condition with you or anyone else. He has also warned me to stay away from you. If I don't, he will confine to my quarters." She took a breath. "What is going on, Thorlu? Who's in charge and why are you being ostracized?"

"You need to be careful, Dee. There are mini lenses hidden all over the ship. Skultar and Karlsut are the most suspicious men I know. They distrust everyone, and in particular, each other. I'm a threat because I have talents which they do not possess or control. Return to the infirmary and remain there until I let you know it's safe. If asked, I stopped by. You shared only that Vygel is stable. If anyone asks where you have been, tell them you needed to check the details of Vygel's latest tests and wanted privacy to do it."

"And you, Thorlu? How are you going to find Skylyn?"

"It's better that you don't know. Go. I'll be in touch when I can."

When he was certain she was in the infirmary, he teleported to his quarters. He had redirected the mini-lens installed by Skultar to show them empty. Satisfied things were as he left it, he withdrew a mini screen from its hiding place and prepared to discover what his cohorts were up to.

Skultar Rados stared at a report on his data-tab. "Would you care to explain, Karlsut?"

His half-brother scowled at his mini screen. "That report's meant for me, not for you. My name is in the header. Did it ever occur to you it might be private?"

"We swore allegiance to each other. You and I do *not* have secrets, understood?" He scanned the report, reread a section, and frowned. "So, dear brother, you have gathered a group of young Mocendi wannabes to find Brie. What happens then? We are about to cross the DéCussate. Do we turn around and go back?"

Karlsut's tongue flicked over his lips. "I've already spoken to the Captain. He's returning the *Surgentin* to Roahymn."

Skultar's chair crashed to the floor. "You did this without consulting me? When did you plan to tell me?"

An angry flush reddened Karlsut's narrow face. He clamped his mouth shut and scowled.

"I suggest you remember the pledge, Karlsut." Skultar yanked his chair upright. "If you chose not to be honest with me and I make a mistake based on your lack of communication, we both will suffer." Ice-cold eyes shot daggers at his brother. "Now, why don't you fill me in?" He sat down, his penetrating gaze razor sharp.

Nostrils flaring a hostile message, Karlsut lowered onto a chair. "I have gathered a group of twenty-odd Vasro. Most of them are young and in the training to become Mocendi." Pride crept into his tone. "Two men who trained under Vygel and Thorlu lead them. Their names are Raiherr Yencara and Zori Sedrin." He sneered. "Rethson continues to spy for us. He has taken two Vasro trainees to find Brie on DerTah. Rethson is certain that's where they will begin a search for Elf."

Skultar reread a section of the report. "It says here Sedrin is the captain of the fast attack ship headed to the ship *El Aperdisa*."

Karlsut's shoulder jerked; the corner of his mouth twitched. "Their orders are to destroy the Eleo Predan ship."

"What the…" Skultar slapped the table and fought for control. "You plan to destroy our means of making a fortune? Care to explain?"

His brother paced the small conference space. "I thought it would keep the VarTerels from following us."

"You idiot! VarTerels don't need a ship. They have Mittkeer."

A snide look stretched Karlsut's expression into a sneer. "I've heard that Mittkeer stops at the Décussate, so how do you expect them to reach El Stroma without a ship?"

Skultar covered his face with his hands and sighed.

Thorlu listened to the conversation between Karlsut and Skultar with a growing sense of revulsion. After they grew silent with the bitter taste of betrayal on their tongues, he considered how to stoke the distrust between them and how to commandeer control.

Even though Skultar spent time on the winter moon, TaSneach, while his half-brother ran around spending their inheritance, he was the smarter and better informed of the two. From his reaction to Karlsut's idiotic statement that Mittkeer stopped at the Décussate, he assumed Skultar realized the truth. Mittkeer transitioned to Mittidee, a fluid, flowing land of time, extending to the furthest reaches of the Universe.

A decision to take matters into his own hands propelled him from his quarters. He walked into the small conference room without buzzing, his stance broadcasting his mood.

Karlsut squirmed and looked away.

Skultar met his obvious displeasure with a shrug. "How's your headache?"

Thorlu used his DiMensioner's skill to project himself bigger than life and towered over the two men. "I suggest you bring me up to date on what's been happening. Do not lie to me. If you do, I will take immediate action."

Both men struggled to hide their duplicity behind stoic faces. Karlsut, the least successful, shot a nervous glance at his older brother. Skultar kept his face blank and did his best to hide his thoughts. Neither man spoke.

"Just to remind you both of my position here. I am the only remaining MasTer's Mocendi who is functional. My powers can leave you senseless and, if I choose, can end your lives. Oh, yes." His eyes narrowed. "I will use a mental probe to learn what you have been up to, or you can save yourselves extreme agony by telling me why we purchased a fast attack ship, why Rethson is no longer on *El Aperdisa*, why you warned others on the ship not to have anything to do with me, including the ship's Commander—Shall I continue?"

If the situation had been different, the agitated, guilty behavior of his two adversaries would have made him laugh outright. Instead, he made a choice. With a wave of his hand, he left Karlsut slumped, unmoving, in his chair, and scrutinized Skultar.

"Explain your pledge of allegiance and what your plans are—other than removing me from the equation—or I will imprison you in the ship's brig. When we reach our orbit around Roahymn—"

Skultar smothered a choked gasp and turn sheet white. "How did you…"

Thorlu raised a brow. "As I was saying, Skultar Rados, once the ship returns to its orbit, I will send you to a place from which you will never escape."

A trembling hand smoothed Skultar's goatee. "Please sit. I will tell you everything."

Thorlu threw his head back. His laugh ended with a cold, emotionless stare. "Don't playact with me, Skultar Rados. I don't care if you live or die. Do we understand each other?"

The once Governor of the Soputton Penal Colony on TaSneach shifted in his seat. Thorlu watched his fear and dislike dissolve into acceptance.

Beady dark eyes stared up at him. "Please sit, and I will bring you up to date. I have one condition *you* must meet."

Thorlu controlled the desire to wipe the complacent smile off the man's face. "Your condition?"

Skultar turned a sour look toward his brother. "I want Karlsut to be a part of this discussion. As noted, we made a pledge. If we don't include him and he does something stupid, he and I will suffer the same fate, and you will inherit our mess."

Thorlu released the illusion of massive size and lowered onto a chair. "Your younger brother is prone to making poor decisions. I suggest you figure out how to control him before I wake him up."

18
Der Tah

Ari's arm supported her twin as they surveyed the acreage stretching from the forest to the shore of a small bay. "You got us here, Brie. Do you need to rest?"

Brie's staff vanished as she allowed her sister to bolster her fatigued-drained body and emotions. "I could use a short breather. Penee, let's sit on that log. I'll share what happened on *Surgentin*, so you can understand why I am so tired and what we're facing."

When they were situated, she provided a recap of the past few turnings. Penee's attention never wavered.

Ari listened with her anger building. Brie's detailed narration made Ari dream of wringing Vygel Vintrusie's neck. Penee's narrowed eyes and tight jaw broadcast similar feelings.

Brie finished, sighed, and stared at her hands clutched together in her lap.

Outrage launched Ari into an angry marched along the forest's border and back. "If I ever see Thorlu or Vygel again…" She clamped her mouth shut around the desire to shout her fury.

Penee offered Brie a hand and helped her to stand. "The sooner we find Elf and return to *El Aperdisa,* the better. Which way to the Senndi's place?"

Brie scanned the forest and hills. "This way." She led them down a narrow tail ending at the empty land where she had last seen the cottage.

Ari walked into the open. "What now? Marji and her brothers are our only lead, and they're not here."

The atmosphere across from them wavered. Shimmering light flickered and expelled a rosy-cheeked woman whom Ari recognized. Marji Senndi put a finger to her lips and beckoned them to her side just as a stocky, white-haired man broke from the cover of the trees and sprinted toward them.

Gregos Senndi reached his sister's side, nodded at the girls, and glanced behind them. "Just received word a pair of Vasro arrived in Atkis last night. They asked a bunch of questions, searched the village, and now head this direction. Better get yourselves gone. Tamosh is waiting on *SeaBella.* I'll run interference at this end."

Horses' hooves pounding the dirt road increased in volume.

Marji caught Brie's eye. "Now."

Ari gasped and gripped her sister's arm. A burst of light blinded her. When her sight cleared, they stood on the deck of *SeaBella.* The icy fiord surrounding them triggered recollections of her first visit to the Fiorde of TheDah with The MasTer's reach in pursuit. She shivered and moved closer to Penee, whose panted breath clouded the frigid air.

Marji preceded them down the ladder to the cabin. Tamosh Senndi handed them warm sweaters, then set steaming mugs of tea on the table. With a pleasant smile, Marji introduced herself and Tamosh to Penee. "We have looked forward to meeting you, Penesert. Gregos, Tamosh, and I have known of you since the Guardian's placed Elf in our care. He, of course, did not remember you until the twins gave him back his memories and his voice." Sadness wreathed her. A shake of her head sent it into hiding. "Please sit, and I will share what we know of Elf."

Tamosh shrugged on a heavy wool coat, mittens, and a watch cap. "We're glad you're here, girls. Marji'll help you decide what we must do to bring Elf home. I'll stand the watch. We don't know how powerful your pursuers are, and I don't want anyone sneaking up on us."

Marji moved with him to the hatch, where they shared a short, soft-voiced conversation.

Ari used the time to reacquaint herself with *SeaBella*, a forty-two-foot, two-masted sailing vessel. The main cabin, divided into two levels, slept six. In addition, the V-berth accommodated the captain and first mate. To the port side of the upper level, where they gathered, a table surrounded by bench seating became a berth. A bench on the boat's starboard side provided an additional place for sitting and sleeping. Two steps descended to the second level, where a larger table to starboard made into a double berth opposite the galley. The head, a boat-sized personal needs space, was between the galley and the door to the V-berth. She experienced a wave of longing. *I forgot how much I love this boat.*

Ari waited for Marji to claim a mug of tea and sit on the starboard bench opposite her. "How did you know we needed you?"

"Chealim sent word to be on the lookout. As Tamosh said, we are glad you're here. Shall we discuss our options?"

Ari gripped her mug. "First, please tell us where Elf is."

Marji cleared a throat tight with emotion and described the last time she saw him. "He blew me a kiss, jumped overboard, shaped a DerTahan fang tooth sculpin, and disappeared beneath the water."

As Elf's foster mother talked, Ari peered through the steam rising from her mug. Marji Senndi intrigued and disturbed her. A glance at Brie and Penee suggested they sensed nothing out of the ordinary. She took another sip. *What about you bothers me?*

Eyes the color of the ocean when storm clouds churned overhead swept her direction. "Arienh AsTar, you hold Elf's love in your heart as he holds yours in his. You also possess Efillaeh, the sacred blade. You must be the one to call Elf forth. Penee will stand at your side. Beware, girls. He's lived in depths of the fiord's glacial water for far too long. It may be harder than any of us expect to return him to his human form."

Ari's hand rested on the handle of the healing blade. Suspicion surged. "What do you know about Efillaeh's power? Who are you, really?"

Brie's startled expression stopped her from continuing, but not from glaring at the woman across the table.

Penee's expression flashed surprise.

Marji's lips twitched. "Chealim told me to expect the unexpected from you, Arienh. You and I have much in common. Like you, my gifts showed up later than my twin's. But that story is for another time. The tide is almost out. Before it turns, we must call Elf forth. Once he is aware of your presence and Penee's, we could lose him forever."

She distributed jackets and scarves to Penee and Ari. "Brielle, I suggest you rest and conserve your strength to help Elf return to human and you and your companions to return to *El Aperdisa*. If we need you, you'll know. Ari, please be ready with the sacred knife. Penee, open your heart to your birth-mate. Let's climb on deck."

Cold slapped Ari's cheeks and stung her eyes as she stepped into the glacial cold. Penee moved ahead of her, hugging herself to keep warm and to protect herself from the wind.

Tamosh stood at the helm. "All clear for now. Best get to it."

Marji guided the girls to the bow of the boat where the anchor rode stretched down into the water. Around them, the tide-exposed shoreline lay spotted with glassy patches of ice. The few bare trees visible on the shore wore ice droplets like diamond jewelry. The wind's whistling whine traveled the fiord, bringing with it gusts of frigid air and stinging flakes.

Marji squinted through the haze. "Efillaeh, now."

Ari gripped Efillaeh's handle, lifted it high, and called out, "Troms El Shiv, come forth." She pointed the silvery tip of the scared blade at the water and watched the emerald etchings glow brighter.

Beside her, Penee sang love-filled words that filled the cold, cloud-heavy sky.

> *"Efillaeh, please bring Elf hither!*
> *Do not allow his soul to wither.*
> *Shape a path for his memories;*
> *And end the curse of his enemies.*
>
> *Return him whole and filled with life,*
> *Leaving behind his present strife.*
> *Efillaeh, please bring him here,*
> *To those who love and hold him dear."*

As she finished the last verse, the wind ceased. Above *SeaBella,* her iceincrusted words sparkled in the late afternoon light. The amethysts in Efillaeh's handle shot rays of purple into their midst, captured them in a glowing bubble of protective light, and lowered it to the water's mirror-smooth surface. Total quiet engulfed the fiord. A group of lily-white laridae gulls circled the bubble. A dolphin leapt free of the sea, caught the encapsulated song in its mouth, arched its body, and plunged below the surface.

Ari's hand pulsed. She raised the knife to the heavens, then lowered it. Penee gripped her shoulder and pointed.

Silver-gray water near the glacier-blue shoreline churned into frothing white foam. Green spikes lining an arched spine preceded the back of a huge seaweed draped head. The spine straightening carried the creature to standing. A shake of the head tossed water droplets in all directions.

Ari held her breath as it made a slow pivot to face *SeaBella*. Penee gasped and clutched her arm.

The fang-lined mouth opened in a roar of despair. Gills on either side of the slimy neck flapped a frantic rhythm. The seaweed-draped head whipped from side to side, sending drops of water to form a sparkling halo around it. Scaly arms twice the length of a man's stretched high. A second roar filled the lagoon. *SeaBella* rocked on the ensuing wake caused by the creature as it waded into deeper water and swam to the boat's side.

Webbed fingers curled over the low railing. Kelp green eyes larger than fisted hands bulged with bemusement. Clear membranes slipped over them. Orange-gold irises contracted in the late afternoon light. A sigh smelling of low tide and winter sea blowing across the deck tossed Ari's red curls out behind her.

She returned Efillaeh to its scabbard and, with her emotions threatening to choke her, stared in awe at the sea creature.

Penee's frigid hand clasping hers tightened. Their eyes met, then returned to the extraordinary creature.

Marji moved to the railing and laid a hand on a scale-covered cheek. Webbed-fingers covered it.

SeaBella tipped. Ari pulled Penee to safety as they slid over the wet deck. The boat righted, with the creature standing across from them. It curled a dragon-like tail around its webbed feet, lifted its head, and howled until the fiord quaked and water rolled over *SeaBella's* bow. Then, in a silence teeming with misery, the creature shrunk to the size of a man, sank onto the deck, covered its face, and sobbed.

B rie, her attention fixed solely on the sea creature now prone in front of Ari and Penee, climbed on deck and walked to Marji's side. No one else stirred. Only the occasional squawk of a laridae mingled with the creature's sorrowful moans.

Tamosh gave a soft whistle. "We've got company heading up the fiord. What's the plan?"

Brie swiveled her head as a sloop-rigged sailboat rounded the curve of the shoreline. Three men stood on the deck. She touched the back of her neck and sighed. *I miss you, Star of Truth.*

Ari looked over her shoulder at Tamosh. "Do you know them?"

A bitter-cold gust pushed *SeaBella* to port. "No. Marji, whatcha sensing? Friend or foe?"

Tamosh frowned. "Whoever's on that boat is playing with us."

Marji's eyes narrowed. "Two Vasro and someone with power to equal a Mocendi's. Any thoughts on how to get beyond them, Brielle?"

Fatigue smacked Brie, leaving her as limp as the slack lines of moments ago. Ari's arm around her waist helped, but a foggy mind left her reeling.

Her twin examined her with a high level of concern. "What just happened, Brielle? You were fine, and now you're not?"

"I almost recognized the third person in the boat. He put up shields and cut off my mental probe." Her shoulders sagged. "I don't think I'm going to be of much use to you."

Marji scrutinized the boat, narrowing the distance between them. *Unless we use DiMensionery, they've blocked our only escape route.* She knelt beside the sea creature whose moans had muted into stillness and whispered, "Troms el Shiv, come to our aid."

The body trembled. A webbed hand fisted and flattened on the deck. The creature pushed itself high enough to peer down the fiord. A threatening growl escaped the fanged mouth as it slithered to the opposite side of *SeaBella* and slipped over the railing into the sea, its rippling wake barely rocking the boat. No sign of its seaweed covered body marred the surface of the glacial water.

Brie couldn't stop shivering. Penee and Ari snuggled closer, one on either side of her.

"You don't have to stay on deck, Brielle." Ari's words misted the air. "Go rest. If we need you, you'll know."

"Will I?" Defeat left her shoulders drooping. "I seem to have lost more than the Star." She shrugged off Ari's attempt to hug her and shuffled to the hatch.

Ari's heart ached for her twin. "I never remember Brielle feeling sorry for herself." She turned to Marji. "How can I help her?"

"Let her rest. Our enemies are closing in. We need to get busy." She pointed. "Elf!"

At the stern of the enemy sailboat, a massive puddle of seaweed surfaced. A webbed hand ripped away the rudder and sent it skimming over the fiord. The boat swung to port. Seaweed and moss rose from the ocean. Bulbous eyes and long fangs glinted as massive scale-covered arms lifted the boat free of the water. One man skidded across the deck and tumbled overboard. A second clung to the crazily swinging boom. With a howl, the man's grip failed. He flew through the air and hit the water near the shore with a resounding splash that echoed off the icy cliffs. The creature lifted the boat higher and flung it. Rocks and debris exploded where the hull slammed into the frozen shore. The third occupant of the boat, balanced unharmed on the tilting deck, lifted a hand and flung a spear of fire across the space between him and the creature.

A webbed hand snatched it from the air and shoved it, sizzling and crackling, into the sea. Three huge strides carried the creature to the wrecked boat. It glared down at the astonished man, picked him up, and lifted him to eye level. Startled gazes locked. The man's eyes rounded. He went rigid.

Fanged mouth gapping wide, the creature howled, a sound so gut-wrenching Ari's heart ached. She saw tears in Penee's eyes and reached for her hand. They watched the creature make its way along the shore, the man clinging to its mossy forearm. Opposite *SeaBella*, the creature waded deeper and, hugging the man close, side-stroked to the boat and dumped him onto the deck where he landed in a water-soaked heap.

A long hollow, melancholy cry echoed through the fiord. The creature dove from sight, his wake rocking *SeaBella* as though she joined in its cry of despair.

Ari ran to the railing. "Elf, come back. We love you. Elf…" Her knee's hit the wooden deck; she reached for the water with both arms. When the surface remained unbroken, she collapsed over the railing, tears raining down her face into the frigid fiord.

Brie's hand on her shoulder brought her head up. Sympathy and sadness registered on her twin's tired face. "Ari, look behind you. He brought us a gift."

Marji knelt beside the shivering man, who lifted his head to peer up at her. His shoulders sagged. Long legs rotated him to face the twins and Penee.

Ari's jaw clenched. Penee gasped.

Devoid of emotion, Ari climbed to her feet and glared. "You are why Elf returned to the sea, so you'd better have an exceptional reason for sitting on this deck in his place, Rethson Jacy Vilandree."

Marji stepped in front of Rethson. "We have problems to solve, so put your anger on hold, Arienh. Rethson, let's get you some dry clothes and then we require some answers."

Ari saw the hard set of his jaw and the fear in his eyes when he edged by her to follow Marji into *SeaBella's* cabin. "Did you see his face, Brie? He won't tell us anything."

Penee cleared her throat. "He's afraid for his mother's life, Ari."

"She's not his mother, Rayn was. Besides, Roween Rattori used him and lied to him. Why would he even care?"

"You and Brie have always known your mother. Rethson, Elf, and I didn't enjoy that privilege. Stand-ins raised us." A half-smile appeared on Penee's face. "Elf and I were lucky. Good people stepped in and loved us. Rethson only knows one mother…Roween. She may have used him, but she also took care of him from the time he was a baby. Give him a chance, Ari. He's only realized recently who she is, *and* who he is."

At the helm, Tamosh nodded his agreement. "Well said, Penee." He glanced the length of the fiord. "The weather is gonna get nasty. We need to take shelter in Natlaki Bay." He opened the hatch. "Marji, a storm's moving in this direction. We're getting underway."

She appeared at the foot of the ladder. "Tamosh, the TheDah beach patrol will pick up the men on the beach."

His full lips pursed. "Will they keep them busy long enough for us to get away?"

"They will. Do you need me up there?"

"The girls can help. You secure everything below." A glance at the sky brought a frown, he waved Ari to his side and started the auxiliary engine. As it hummed to life, he checked his gauges, then stepped aside. "Ari, man the wheel. Penee and I will check to make sure everything's secure while the engine warms up." He shot her a curious glance. "You remember how to do that, right?"

She almost smiled. "I do, Tamosh. You taught me well."

"Good girl. Penee, come with me."

While Ari remained at the helm, Penee followed him to the bow. Pieces of their conversation drifted back to Ari. Tamosh gave explicit instructions. Penee executed them. Triumph beamed as she made her way back to the helm. "There's so much to learn."

Tamosh nodded at Ari. "I'll take it from here. As he and Ari changed places, his gaze hesitated on Penee. "You're shaking like a leaf, Penesert. Get yourselves below and warm up. As soon as Marji gives the word, we'll pull the anchor. I'll shout if I need help up here."

Penee, teeth chattering, hurried to the hatch and descended the ladder.

Ari moved to the railing. Her heart ached. *We're leaving, Elf. Will I ever see you again?* Stubbornness raised its head. Resolve not to leave him behind held her motionless. With a furtive glance over her shoulder, she unbuckled Efillaeh's scabbard and lowered it to the deck. *"If you won't come back to us, Troms el Shiv, I'll come to you."* She shed her winter jacket.

"Arienh! Stop! Don't do—"

Bitter cold closing over her head cut his warning short. Shock waves rolled through her. Reflexes leapt into action. She gulped icy salt water that stung her nostrils and fought to enter her lungs. Struggling not to breathe in, she sought the surface. Water-heavy clothing and frigid cold dragged her downward. Flagging energy produced a feeble kick, and then another. She broke the surface, spewing water, coughing, and fighting for air. Voices calling her name scattered her already confused thoughts. She grasped for threads of reason. *"Troms el Shiv, I need you. Come and hold me one last time."*

No response left her foundering and despondent. Cold invading every cell in her body triggered uncontrolled shivers and left her confused and disoriented. Numbness stole her senses one at a time. Vision, the last to go, blurred. Her mind blanked.

*M*an overboard! Man overboard!" Tamosh's shout propelled Brie up the ladder from the cabin and across the deck to the railing as Ari's head broke the surface. Panic made Brie dizzy. Penee and Rethson, joining her, calmed her. She lifted a hand. Her staff snapped into view. "I need your help, both of you. Focus your intent on Arienh, and together, we'll use Musette's power to bring her to us."

Marji called from the hatch. "Bring her into the cabin. I'll prepare the bed. Hurry!"

Brie pointed the staff's tourmaline crystal at her twin.

> *"Musette, weave your web of light*
> *Around my twin; hold her tight.*
> *Lift her from the rising tide;*
> *Place her on the bed inside."*

A rainbow cocoon formed around Ari's sinking body. Brie called over her shoulder. "Help me lift her."

A sucking sound echoing off the tall cliffs accompanied Ari's exit from the glacial sea. Concentration intensified. As though made of air, she floated above the water to *SeaBella* and through the open hatch, where Marji settled her on the port side bench.

Brie vanquished her staff, climbed down the ladder, and hurried to her twin's side. Penee followed, the scabbard in hand. At Tamosh's bidding, Rethson remained on deck.

Marji bent over Ari, frowned, and placed hands on her chest. "She's not breathing. We need to resuscitate."

Brie reined in her growing panic and watched Marji apply pressure in a repeated rhythm. *Please come back to us, Arienh. Please.* After what seemed like forever, a gagged cough brought water spewing from Ari's mouth. Brie helped Marji to roll her onto her side. More water dribbled down her chin. Kneeling, Brie brushed wet hair back from her cheek. A soft exhale produced a rush of relief. "She's breathing."

Marji straightened. "She is. Turn her onto her back. Let's get her wet clothes off."

Penee waited with Efillaeh drawn while Brie and Marji stripped off Ari's soaked clothing and wrapped her in blankets. Accepting Efillaeh from Penee, Brie placed the sacred blade on her chest, sank to the floor, and let the tears flow.

Heat trickling into her extremities edged Ari closer to consciousness. Warmth seeping into her chest muscles relieved the ache in her heart and lungs. Sluggish thought nudging her to remember produced an anguished moan.

A face moved into her line of vision. She blinked and looked away. The distress in her twin's expression chilled her more than the water had.

Soft whispering penetrated her semi-conscious state. Warm lips kissed her forehead. "I love you, Arienh AsTar. Sleep. I'll be here when you wake up." The familiar voice melted away.

Unable to move beyond the chilled fatigue weighting her body, she slept.

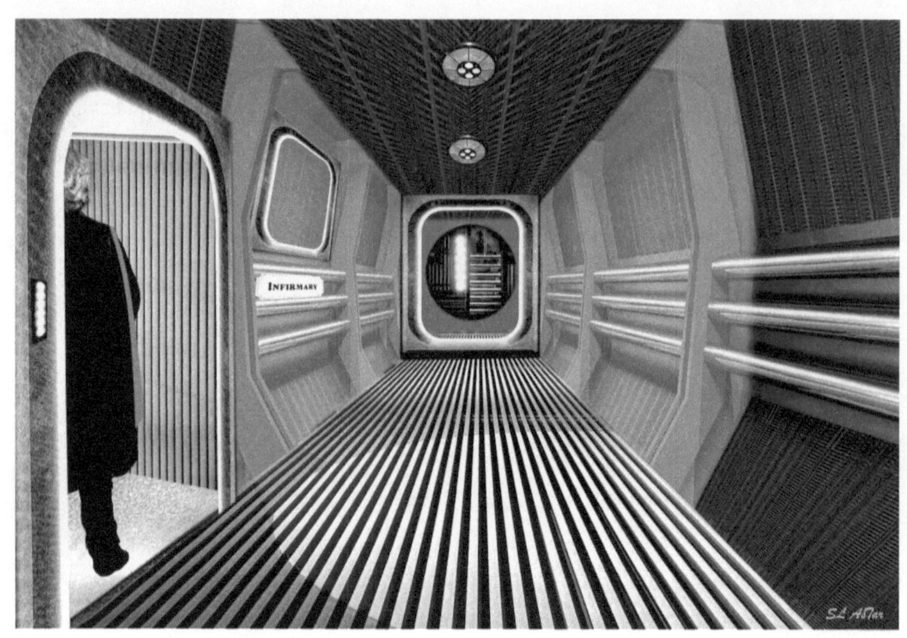

19

Surgentin

Thorlu's instincts fought waking Karlsut, and yet, Skultar was right. If they left his brother out of their discussion, they might face a catastrophe created by his ignorance and lack of judgment. He focused his hard-edged gaze on Skultar.

"How do you intend to keep him under control? He is unpredictable and deceitful. I don't have time to keep track of him. Do you?"

Skultar frowned. "What job can we give him that will keep him interested and out—"

The hatch buzzer sounded. Skultar swiveled his chair. Thorlu motioned him to stay seated and stepped to the hatch. The panel slid open, and a med-tech passed him a note.

Thorlu nodded and returned to his seat as the panel shut with a soft click. He read the note, whispered a quiet word, and watched it disintegrate into nothing.

Skultar folded his arms and glowered. "What was in the note?"

A tense moment passed. Thorlu lifted his hand.

Karlsut Sorda pressed his palms to his temples and groaned. Anger turned his paleness a deep rosy red. "What did you do to me? How dare you—" Pain twisted his features.

Thorlu moved to stand over him. "What have you done with Vygel's Mocendi cape?"

The man squirmed like a child caught breaking the rules. His chin jutted forward. "I didn't steal his—" He cringed and hit the table with a fist. A frantic gaze darted to his brother.

Skultar shook his head. "Tell him what you did with it."

Karlsut dropped his chin to his chest, muttered a smattering of nonsense, and pushed up from his chair. "I don't have to tell you anything." He glared first at his older brother and then at Thorlu, who raised a brow.

Thorlu waited, the desire to remove him from the room growing by the second. "Unless you wish to spend time in the brig, sit down and tell us where the cape is."

A violent shudder dumped Karlsut into his chair. Shaking hands skated over his sparse hair and dropped to the table. "Rethson informed me Esán, Torgin, and Gar travel to Tao Spirian after a brief stop on ReTaw au Qa. I gave the cape to Yencara. He has hired a jumper craft and has taken a SorTech and three Vasro to find Esán Efre and his two friends."

Thorlu lowered into his seat. "Skultar, I suggest you go for a walk while Karlsut and I take care of some business."

Skultar's features hardened into a stubborn mask. "I'm not leaving. We all stick together. There's too much to lose if one of us makes a mistake. What's so important about Vygel's cape?"

Thorlu studied the half-brothers through narrowed eyes. "I will share its importance, but only after you both swear to keep the information to yourselves."

Skultar stood, walked around behind his brother, and rested manicured hands on his shoulders. "We swear to keep what you tell us to ourselves, right Karlsut?"

An exaggerate shrug tried to displace the hands keeping him in his chair. Karlsut jerked himself free of Skultar and scowled at Thorlu. "I don't answer to you. My money paid for this ship and its crew. I call the shots. The only power you have here, Thorlu Tangorra, is the power I allow you. Get out of my sight."

Skultar shook his head in disgust and looked at Thorlu. "Now what?"

"I suggest you help your younger brother understand the importance of working together." He touched the sensor panel by the door and strode down the passageway.

S kultar sat down across from his half-brother. A variety of solutions to the problem of Karlsut Sorda came and went, leaving him staring at his folded hands.

A malicious laugh from the other side of the table brought his gaze to his brother's crazed features.

Karlsut glared. "Why are you siding with that no good Mocendi? We're partner's—you and me. Tangorra is expendable. We don't need him." His face blanched. "He knocked me out. You two made plans behind my back. How dare you!"

Skultar, keeping his growing animosity from leaking into his voice, spoke in a calm and controlled manner. "Tangorra and I had a discussion. It seemed best to include him in our plans. We need the power he wields to be part of our arsenal. You missed nothing you don't already know. If you want to remain a player in this game, help me keep the last MasTer's Mocendi on our side."

"We still have Vygel to do our bidding. We don't need Thorlu." Karlsut frowned. "Vygel is still with us?"

"Vygel has awakened from his coma, but he remembers nothing—not even who he is. And Karlsut, because of your disastrous visit to New York City, 1969, he no longer has the powers of a Mocendi DiMensioner."

A disgusted sneer twisted the narrow face. "So, is Tangorra taking over, or are we in control?"

"I would suggest that we use him until we don't need him any longer. Right now, we need his power on our side. Agreed?"

Karlsut rocked nervously, muttered, and after an obvious battle with himself, nodded. "Agreed."

"Good, then I suggest we do our best not to anger him, at least for the time being."

I n his quarters, Thorlu watched the brothers' maneuvering on his mini-screen. "What a pair." He stroked his close-cut beard. The note, delivered to him in the conference room, contained a two-part message: the missing cape and the second part, which he kept to himself. A satisfied smile lifted his mustache. Lorsedi Telisnoe's men had boarded Karlsut's fast attack ship. Captain and crew would spend the rest of their lives in a work-camp on RewFaar. *El Aperdisa*, her cargo, passengers, and crew were safe.

His thoughts turned to Vygel. Few knew the power of a Mocendi's cape. Most thought it was simply for show. He ran a hand over the soft fabric of his where it lay beside him on his bunk. VarTerels had their staff to augment their power. Mocendi had their capes. That Karlsut had given it to a man with little training, whom Thorlu remembered as arrogant and deceitful, made him edgy.

His hatch buzzer alerted him to a visitor. A harassed-looking med-tech gazed up at him as the panel slid open. "Healer De Dilliére says come fast. Karlsut Sorda is ordering Mocendi Vintrusie to be moved."

Thorlu touched the man's shoulder. He flashed a look of surprise as they arrived in the infirmary where the *Surgentin's* head healer faced off with Karlsut.

Dee shot Thorlu a warning-filled glance. "In answer to your order to move the Mocendi, Karlsut, Vygel is much too ill to leave the infirmary. If you insist on doing so, you will be responsible for his death."

Skultar ducked through the hatch in time to hear her last words. His displeasure written in every aspect of his presence, he glowered at his brother. "What do you think you are doing, Karlsut Sorda? I told you to leave Vygel in the infirmary. Now, I discover you have given orders to move him. Care to share your reasoning?"

Child-like fidgeting edged Karlsut toward the hatch.

Thorlu blocked his exit. "I suggest we allow Healer De Dilliére to do her job." He caught Skultar's eye, touched Karlsut's arm, and, the moment Skultar touched the other, he teleported them to their conference room.

After helping a resistant Karlsut into his seat, Thorlu sat on the table's edge, his acerbic gaze steady. "If you try to interfere with Vygel's care again, I will be true to my former threat and put you in a hidden section of the brig. A reminder, Karlsut Sorda, I paid my share of the cost of this ship, as did Skultar. We are equal partners in this venture. Do not tempt me again to end your participation. In front of your brother, swear to keep us both informed."

Karlsut squirmed beneath his scrutiny, tried to come to his feet, and dropped back into the chair. "How dare you—"

Skultar's fist hit the table. "Stop behaving like a moron. If you are unwilling to put your brain to work helping us achieve our goals, I will have Thorlu put you in that cell."

Thorlu felt a tug of surprise. He stood. "I'm leaving you in your brother's care. Please don't continue to create more problems than you're worth, Karlsut Sorda."

20
ReTaw au Qa

Esán, Torgin, and Gar, with Spyglass at their heals, stepped free of Mittkeer onto the planet of ReTaw au Qa. High overhead, the sun glowed behind semi-opaque wisteria-tinted clouds. Giant root-skirted trees encircled the marshland. A breeze moved iridescent leaves one way and then the other, showcasing different shades of magenta and honey amber. Close by, a sluggish, algae-covered river meandered its way through mounds of swampy, raisin colored soil.

Gar wrinkled his nose. "I forgot about that smell."

Torgin sniffed the moisture-laden air. "Damp moss and standing water, if I'm not mistaken."

Gar knelt and hugged Spyglass. "Stay close, Spy. Wouldn't want to lose you."

Esán led the way to the riverbank between burgundy puddles and grassy mounds. He stopped and pointed. "Here come the Pentharian." His hand rested on Gar's shoulder.

An Auqan vulture spread massive brown and cream wings and, using the tip feathers, turned in a circle, its orange-gold eyes scanning the world below it. Wing-wind whipped the pale orchid grass and tossed Esán's hair back from his face. Dark brown talons dug into the burgundy river mud. The vulture hissed, shook its feathers, and shifted form.

From its towering height, a Pentharian gazed down at them. Brown braids highlighted with gold cascaded to the waist of a human-like torso covered in tattoos. Golden scales shimmered on reptilian legs and a long, slender tail. Earrings lined human ears; a gold ring pierced the nose. Lizard eyes in a humanesque face gleamed a warm yellow-gold.

Gar grinned a welcome. Spyglass sniffed, but stayed close to his master.

The Pentharian waded through the shallows, gazed down at Torgin, and offered his lizard like hand, palm up. "Welcome, Torgin Wilith Whalend, brother of my heart."

Torgin touched the upturned palm. "It is good to see you, Yaro, my heart-sworn brother."

Spyglass dart forward, barked, and rested his front paws on Yaro's scaled lower leg.

The Pentharian's generous mouth curved. He bent down and offered his hand.

Spyglass sniffed, then licked it.

"Do you have a name, little dog?"

Gar stepped closer. "Name's Spyglass. He likes you, Yaro."

A golden hand stroked the black and white back. "I, too, like this dog." He straightened.

Torgin put an arm around Gar's shoulder. "My cousin tells me the three of us are heart-brothers."

Yaro's smiled widened as he offered his palm to Gar. "It is good to see you once again, Garon."

Gar touched it and then touch his heart.

The golden Pentharian acknowledged Esán with a bow of his head. "Esán Efre, the Seeds of Carsilem have matured. You are a powerful presence. Let's move to safer ground so we may converse with more ease." He eyed Torgin. "I sense many changes in you, too, my brother. Is it possible you have learned to shift shape?"

A wide smile flashed. "I can shift. Are we flying to our destination?"

Yaro bent down to look Gar in the eye. "Do you think your Spyglass would like to ride on my vulture back? Will he know to be still?"

"If I ride with him, he'll be good, right Spy?" Excitement made Gar's eyes shine. Spyglass wagged his tail and yipped.

Yaro nodded his approval. "It is good. We fly. Follow me and stay close. Your enemies continue to monitor ReTaw au Qa."

He shifted to a vulture. Torgin helped Gar onto the feathered back and placed Spyglass in front of him. Vulture eyes observed his change to eagle before taking flight.

Esán shifted to his rusty-brown and pale blue kestrel and followed, his senses alert for danger.

T he thrill of flying beside his heart-brother tempted Torgin toward giddiness. Gar and Spyglass perched on Yaro's vulture back kept his head clear and his attention focused.

The vulture swooped lower, skimming treetops and gliding over ponds of still water reflecting the wisteria-colored clouds. A break in the trees loomed ahead. Torgin experience a thrill of surprise as they swept through the opening into a fertile valley tented beneath ancient vine-covered branches. A sharp bank to the left brought him down beside Yaro's vulture form. Gar's delighted laughter stimulated his shift to human form.

The boy's excitement reminded him of his first ride on a Pentharian's back during his first visit to Myrrh. He grinned and lifted Spyglass to the ground. Gar slid down a brown and cream wing and landed beside him, grinning from ear to ear. "That was a blast!"

Yaro materialized. "I'm glad you enjoyed the ride, young Garon." His lizard gaze rested on Torgin. "You have chosen your shifted shape well, my brother." He scanned the canopy of vines. "Where is Esán?"

A kestrel swooped through a gap overhead, alighted on the ground, and shifted. "We have company."

Yaro's tail twitched. "Come with me. I have things to share before you leave ReTaw au Qa."

He led the way to an enormous Ficus Fig, ducked between the curtain roots, and descended a steep trail leading underground to a cathedral-like space.

Torgin gazed at the far end of the room. Memories of attending Yaro's initiation to Venerat of his clan flooded his thoughts. Seyes Nomed and the Dreelas TheLise had accompanied him to ReTaw au Qu, where, as an adopted member of the Snake Clan, he took part in the ceremony. The entire experience remained one of the most treasured of his life.

Gar pulled on his hand. "Hey, you okay? You seem pretty far away."

Torgin forced himself to be present. "I was thinking about the last time I visited my heart-brother." He studied the boy in front of him, then searched their surroundings. "Speaking of Yaro—where is he?"

"I'm here." The golden Pentharian walked from a door near the altar. Voer, his blue scales shining, followed him. Both Pentharian stopped to greet Spyglass, who pranced around them and yipped a welcome.

Voer's vibrant gaze traveled from Torgin to Gar to Spyglass and settled on Esán. "You carry great power, Esán Efre. We welcome you to our homeland."

Esán touched Voer's offered palm and bowed his head.

Voer's gaze moved to Torgin. "It is good to see you, Torgin Whalend, heart-brother of Yaro." He smiled down at Gar. "Ah, young Garon, welcome back to ReTaw au Qa." He offered his palm.

Gar wiped his on his pants and touched it to the Pentharian's blue one.

Voer touched his chest with a fisted hand and bowed his head. Long bluish braids fell over his shoulder. He straightened. "Come. We have information to share."

Yaro placed several carved wooden stools in a circle. "Stee and Yuin stand guard. They send their regards."

"How is Jeet?" Esán observed the Pentharian. "Has he recovered from his battle with the Brotico?"

Voer touched a braid and sighed. "Our brother, Jeet, remains in a death-like sleep from which he may not awaken." He breathed a deep inhale and released it. "Please, let us move on. Yaro, explain what you have learned."

Yaro's nostrils opened wider, then narrowed. "I oversee the comings and goings of foreigners on ReTaw au Qa. A short time ago, one of my sentinels reported a military air ship that landed near his clan's ancestral land on the other side of the planet. Humans disembarked and set up a camp where men train to be killers.

"Uneasiness made him shift to a scavenger hawk and eavesdrop. The more he learned, the more his worry increased. The men call themselves Vasro. They are mercenaries who work for a man named Karlsut Sorda. My informant learned they plan to find the girl with the Matriarch's Eyes and your friends, Brie and Ari, and use them as bait to capture and kill every VarTerel in the Universe. They are also determined to destroy all the Eleo Predans they can find.

Yaro shook his head. "We Pentharian hire out as mercenaries, but only undertake jobs of honor. We cannot condone murder for the sake of destroying an entire people."

Voer's beak clicked open and closed. "Yaro has something to tell you."

Yaro touched the snake tattoo on his chin. "We have saved the most important sharing for last." He lowered his hand. "Our medicine clan's researchers have learned, Esán Efre, that Sisohprommate, the bacteria causing your disease, is endemic to the swamps of ReTaw au Qa." He held up a clay vial. "Here is a sample. It is our hope the contents of this vial will help your Tao Spirian healers to find a cure."

As he passed it to Esán, an emerald-green Pentharian strode into the space and stopped beside Voer.

The Pentharian clan leader acknowledged him with a nod. "What is it, Stee?"

"Vasro travel this way. Yuin has gone to warn the clans to seek obscurity in the swamps."

Vulture eyes gleaming, Voer stood. "You must go, my friends. Do not venture above ground. It is safe to open the way to Mittkeer within these sacred walls, but nowhere else." He touched his heart. "May honor be yours always."

The Pentharian shifted and flew from their place of worship.

Yaro knelt in front of Gar and glanced up at Torgin. "I would like to seal the three of us formally."

Torgin knelt beside Yaro, his serious gaze on the boy's face. "Are you ready to be sealed to Yaro *and* me? If we do this ceremony, the three of us will be heart-brothers forever."

Gar pressed a hand to his heart and looked into Yaro's lizard-gold eyes. "I am honored to be sealed to you both." He blew out a breath. "What do we have to do?"

The Pentharian stood and offer his hands to him and to Torgin. "Let us circle. Repeat after me," Yaro directed.

> *"Comrades of Heart, as brothers we join.*
> *A trio that's sealed and none can purloin*
> *Arg doo me teekay. Dio ordek od pier."*

The Pentharian touched his forehead to Gar's and then Torgin's.

Gar exhaled and grinned. "Can I hug you both?"

Yaro opened his arms, his golden eyes gleaming.

Gar pulled Torgin with him into a group hug. Spyglass barked.

Torgin caught Esán's eye where delight sparkled. He rested a hand on Gar's shoulder. "Thank you, Yaro. We will return when time permits." He picked up Spyglass.

Esán withdrew the VarTerel's stone from his pocket and clasped Gar's hand. The Venerat's Sanctuary melted into a globe of stars.

Gar swallowed and gazed from Torgin to Esán. "I have a brother on another planet." Awe made his eyes glow brighter than usual. He knelt beside Spyglass. "Spy, you and me have family *and* we have friends!" He hugged his dog, stood, and hugged Esán, then Torgin. "Thank you for letting me come to the future with you."

Torgin brushed a sneaky tear from his cheek, noticed Esán doing the same thing, and put an arm around Gar. "We're just glad we found you. Are you ready for another adventure?"

Gar's head bobbed against his side. "Yes. What constellation are we looking for?"

Torgin withdrew the compass. "I'm ready."

Esán surveyed the heavens. "We're looking for Cesspi, the Tao Spirian sailfish."

"What's it look like?" Gar tipped his head back and stared.

"It has nine stars resembling a fish with a large, sail-like fin. The brightest star is the eye of the fish." He looked over Torgin's shoulder at the compass face. The needle spun and slowed. A chart of the heavens materialized above it.

Torgin pointed. "There you go!"

Esán held out the VarTerel's Stone. The star carved around a fox glowed. "Hold on."

Torgin put the compass away and picked up Spyglass. Gar moved next to Esán. Stars blurred and refocused. Cesspi shone overhead. Before he could speak, Mittkeer withdrew, leaving them on a coral pink beach.

Esán waited by his father's boat slip in the harbor, remembering his last visit to Tao Spirian. Chealim and Relevart had summoned him, Torgin, and Brie to discuss the theft of three Corps Stones, and thus their journey back in time to New York City, 1969, began. *What an amazing adventure that was!*

Torgin waving from the bottom of the ramp and Gar's shout of delight as he chased Spyglass down the dock heightened the memories. His gaze wandered the curve of the island and picked out the white sail of his father's sloop, *Capee Iwa. Soon, we'll be together even if only for a short time.*

Gar arrived at his side, fastening the float coat Torgin had purchased for him. "I love it here. The ocean is beautiful. And all the boats—wow! Is your father close?"

Esán pointed. "See the sailboat turning at the end of the dock? That's *Capee Iwa,* my father's boat."

"Torgin says he's cool. I can't wait to meet him." He scurried to the end of the finger and ran back. "Do you think he'll like me?"

"Yes, Gar, I do. He'll be pulling in soon. Go get Spyglass and Torgin."

Somay waved, then guided the boat into the slip. *Capee Iwa* bobbed gently as he made his way forward and tossed the bow line to Esán. "Secure her." He jumped on the finger and hurried to the stern.

With the boat secured, Somay hugged Esán and grinned. "I am always so amazed when I realize you are my son!"

A sharp bark and the dull patter of paws on the wooden dock heralded Spyglass and Gar. Somay knelt to greet the terrier with a scratch behind the ears before offering his hand. "Welcome to the Island of Tautian, Garon. My name is Somay."

Gar touched his palm to Esán's father's. "My friends call me Gar." He patted his dog on the head. "This is Spyglass. We're from the Island of Manhattan."

Esán saw the twinkle in Torgin's eye and cleared his throat to smother a chuckle.

Somay didn't hide his delight. "You ever been on a boat, Gar?"

"No, sir." Eagerness infused the two words.

A sea shuttle putted to the end of the dock. Somay waved at the captain. "Esán, you and Torgin take the sea shuttle. Gar and I will meet you at the clinic."

Gar's whole person wiggled with excitement. "I get to ride in a sailboat. What about Spy? Can he come, too?"

Somay smiled. "Yes, he can stay in the cabin while we sail *Capee Iwa*."

Gar gave Torgin a big hug and grinned up at Esán. "See ya later." He looked at Somay. "What do we do first?"

Esán and Torgin watched Somay help Gar on board and hand him Spyglass. He couldn't help wishing he had known his father when he was Gar's age.

Torgin gripped his arm. "Look. On board the sea shuttle."

The figure of a man stepped into the sun's light, the purple lining of his knee-length cape announcing him as a MasTer's Mocendi. He pointed at Esán and pulled open the door. Two men detached from interior shadows and jumped to the dock.

With Torgin at his heels, Esán raced for *Capee Iwa*. Somay shouted an exclamation that got lost in their pounding footsteps. He fought to slow the boat's momentum out of the slip by reversing the small inboard engine and catching a cleat with a gaff hook. Esán leapt aboard and reached for Torgin.

A man grabbed his friend by the shoulders and hauled him backward. The second man ran down the finger as *Capee Iwa* backed beyond reach. With a shrug, he turned and hurried to help subdue their struggling captive. Each gripping an arm, the men escorted him along the main dock toward the sea shuttle.

Esán locked his gaze on Torgin. Messages flashed between them. As they reached an empty slip, the men cringed, their faces contorted in pain, and stumbled. Torgin yanked free, sprinted down the finger, dove into the water, and with long, powerful strokes, swam toward the sailboat.

Spyglass barked excited encouragement. Gar clung to the top of the cabin. "Come on, Torgin!"

One man regained his footing, dashed down the finger, and jumped. He splashed to the surface, shouting in pain. The second man stared after the escapee but chose not to follow. Esán couldn't resist one last mental shot. Knees buckling, the man hugged himself and groaned in agony.

Torgin reached the boat. With the engine in neutral, Somay helped him up the ladder. Moments later, they cruised behind an incoming barge. He spoke over his shoulder. "Can't stay here."

An imaged flashed into Esán's mind. "Got it."

The tree-lined shores of an estuary surrounded them. Somay edged the boat up to a rickety wooden dock. Esán jumped off, tied the bowline to a rusty cleat, then took the stern line from his father and secured the boat.

Torgin hugged Gar to his soaking wet chest. Esán caught his eye. "You did great. I wasn't certain you could swim."

"Every kid in Idronatti learns to swim when they turn eleven."

Gar peered over the side. "You mean you learned when you were my age?"

"I sure did."

Gar pursed his lips. "Guess I'd better learn soon, huh?"

Somay joined them. "Who was the man on the shuttle?" He rummaged in a side compartment and tossed Torgin a towel.

Esán jumped aboard. "I don't know him, but he's wearing the cape of a MasTer's Mocendi."

21

Der Tah

Penee studied Ari's pale face. *What a crazy thing to do, Arienh AsTar.* She glanced at Brie in the bunk on the opposite side of the cabin. Almost as pale as her sister, she, too, slept. In the galley, Marji prepared a meal to serve once *SeaBella* was safely anchored in Natlaki Bay.

After straightening Ari's blankets, Penee pulled on her jacket and woolen hat and climbed up on deck. The wind yanked at her clothes and pressed her against the closed hatch. One hand clinging to the boom, she peered between Tamosh and Rethson at the storm-agitated sea.

The wind raging through the fiord added power to the engine carrying *SeaBella* toward safety. Tamosh finessed the boat over the rolling waves with the skill of his many sun cycles at the ship's wheel. Rethson clung to the boom, ready to spring into action should Tamosh need his help.

SeaBella swung to port, shuddered in the wind, and steadied. A howl of despair beat against the hull. Penee caught her breath. The sea creature's massive head rose above the waves as it swam toward the boat. Webbed hands clung to the railing. The head jerked higher. A powerful kick sent the seaweed-covered upper body onto the deck. *SeaBella* listed to port, her deck almost even with the water.

Tamosh shouted. "Don't capsize her, Elf."

The creature shrunk to human size. Rethson skidded to a stop beside it and grasped an arm. Penee slid over the deck as the boat returned to level, gripped its hand, and helped it to climb aboard. Tamosh steered the boat into the wind and headed for shelter between an island and the shoreline.

Marji climbed on deck and fell to her knees by her son. "Elf, come forth."

Brie peered from the hatch, disappeared, and returned with Efillaeh.

Marji accepted the sacred knife with a nod of gratitude. She touched the seaweed-covered head. Shudders shook the body. Scaled arms lifted. Trembling human hands materialized and lowered, palms pressed against the soaked wooden deck. Repeated tremors continued. Howls of dismay echoed off the ice-covered cliffs and stilled. Fingers curled, then pressed splayed against the wood as the creature pushed up to sitting. Bulging eyes and the gaping fang-toothed mouth morphed into a human face. A final quake left a flaccid-skinned, pale Troms El Shiv sitting dazed and expressionless on the deck.

Penee's heart leapt, then settled into despair for the bedraggled and confused young man in front of her. Marji held the knife to her heart and tapped his temple. His eyes cleared. Creases furrowed his brow and smoothed. He lifted a hand and stared at the palm. Then, gently touching her cheek, he curled up on his side and slept.

Marji passed the knife to Brie. "Go check on Ari. We'll be down soon." She retrieved Tamosh's jacket and covered her son.

Penee reached out.

"Let the boy be, Penee." Tamosh spoke in a hushed voice. "Marji, take Penee below. I need a sleeping bag and pillow for Elf." When they hesitated, his brows raised. "Rethson and I won't let anything happen to him or allow him to leave until he's spoken with you. But I need my coat back, so get me that sleeping bag." Levity laced the words.

Marji kissed his cheek and ushered Penee ahead of her into the cabin. A quick rummage ended with the required sleeping bag and dry winter clothing in hand. "I'll take them up and help Tamosh anchor the boat. You both rest. There's nothing you can do until he wakes."

Brie's knees buckled. Penee caught her arm and helped her down the steps to the table in the galley. Sinking onto the bench, Brie lowered her head to rest on her arms. Fatigue's tears squeezed from her closed lids to pool on the tabletop.

Penee checked on Ari and stretched out on the bed opposite. *What brought you back, Troms el Shiv? I saw your confusion.* She sighed. *And your fear.*

On deck, Marji covered Elf with the sleeping bag and took the wheel while Tamosh guided Rethson through the process of anchoring *SeaBella*. Wind tossing her hair inspired a sense of exhilaration that reminded her how much she loved her life afloat.

The purr of the engine mixed with the wind demanded her attention. A chart depicting the chain of islands at the mouth of the fiord formed in her mind. She turned the wheel to navigate around submerged rocks and eased the boat through a narrow opening into an unpretentious anchorage sheltered behind the central island in the chain. The best place to spend the night lay a short distance ahead. Tamosh and Rethson were ready at the bow. At her signal, they dropped anchor. Tamosh hurried back to the helm, checked his gauges, and secured the engine. Calm winds and quiet water held *SeaBella* steady.

Rethson joined them, a smile lighting his eyes. "Thanks for letting me help, Tamosh." His gaze dropped. Restless fingers played with the hem of his jacket. He looked up at Marji. "I have to go. My mother is in danger."

Marji kept her tone amenable. "We can help Roween, but we have to know what she's up against. Share what you know, so we can make plans. I suggest we get Elf into dry clothes and you get a good night's rest. In the morning, we'll sit down and figure out the best way to help your mother."

Once again, he looked away. A sigh creating a foggy cloud relaxed taunt features. "I will trust you to keep your word. How can I help with Elf?"

She moved aside. "Why don't you go below and get warm? We'll take care of Elf and join you."

He hesitated before sliding open the hatch and disappearing into the cabin.

Tamosh put an arm around her shoulders. "You are a diplomat, for sure. Let's see to the boy, shall we?"

Unable to move, Elf did little to help Tamosh strip off the wet, tattered clothes he had worn when he shifted to a fang tooth. Loving hands dressed him in winter pants, a shirt, and a warm wool sweater. A moan of gratitude accompanied the wool socks slipped onto his freezing human feet. Two pairs of hands worked together to slide his limp body into a down sleeping bag. His eyes fluttered open.

Marji bent over him, eased a wool watch cap onto his head, and kissed his cheek. "Sleep, Elf. You are safe." Her footsteps retreated.

Tamosh created a makeshift tent and slipped into a second sleeping bag beside him. Strong arms pulled him closer. His warmth and Marji's proximity dispersed the hysteria gathering in Elf's throat. Lethargy weighted his body. Heavy lids closed as sleep's healing cradled him.

Cognizance made a slow return. Memory of the moment he shifted to a fang tooth cold water sculpin brought with it the reason he had left his humanness behind. At the last possible moment, Efillaeh's magic helped him to overcome the desire to end his life. One minute longer and he, Troms El Shiv, would have ceased to exist. Mixed emotions left him shaking and awake.

A strong, loving hand on his shoulder eased the turmoil. Exhaustion overtook him, allowing slumber to cloak his turbulent thoughts.

He woke a second time to total darkness. Tamosh's warmth inspired images of his boyhood after Rasiana had stolen him away from The Master. A rush of gratitude for the Senndi's, the only family he had ever known, left him snuggling deeper into the sleeping bag.

To Tamosh's soft snores, he stared from under the tented tarp at a cloudless night. Stars flickered their welcome. DerTah's golden moon, Fasfro, cresting the high cliffs, felt like a celebration of his homecoming. *Calegri will follow soon.* Profound longing swelled in his heart. *I missed seeing the moon and stars and feeling the coldness of the wind on my face.* Doubt nagged. *Should I even be here? Will I hurt someone? How can I face Arienh?*

Tamosh raised up on his elbow. "Easy, Elf. Everyone on the boat loves you. When you have rested, we'll help you reclaim yourself. Let's you and me sleep while we can." He nestled closer, his snores floating over the bow and out to the Sea of Minus.

Elf closed his eyes and let the gentle rocking of the sailboat and the unconditional love cocooning him send him into dreaming.

The sun rose over Natlaki Bay, bringing with it blue skies and a scattering of rose-tinted clouds. Penee pulled her woolen cap lower and tipped her head back. A sigh of contentment misted the crisp air, as she lowered her gaze to the make-shift tent where Elf slept. Tamosh had gone below and didn't want him to awaken alone. She had seemed the logical choice.

The rustle of fabric and an audible yawn suggested her birth-mate stirred. Situating herself to peek under the edge of the tent, she met his emotion-filled gaze. The depth of his sadness and something else she could not define made her want to crawl in beside him, to hold him close. Instead, she hugged knees to her chest, rested her cheek on her kneecaps and she and her birth-mate studied each other in silence.

He adjusted the sleeping bag around him, squirmed to sitting, and touched the deck. "Please come closer."

She repositioned herself to sit beside him. "I'm glad you're back, Troms el Shiv."

A paled hand traced the curve of his head as he brought his gaze level with hers. "I think I'm glad, too." The hand fell to his lap. He bit his bottom lip. "What if I hurt someone? My anger builds so huge sometimes I can't contain it. What if I hurt you or Ari..." A tremor shook the hands covering his face. He held them out and examined them for a long moment before he moved closer to her. "Penee, you are my sister and my friend—" His loud exhale clouded the air. "What about, Ari, Pen? I am terrified I'll hurt her."

Penee sandwiched his hand between hers. "We will all help you with the anger. What is important is that you're here to help us save El Stroma."

"But, Penee, I'm not as important as you or Brielle or Esán."

She kissed his cheek. "We all have our parts to play. It's like putting a puzzle together. If one piece is missing, the whole is incomplete. One step at a time, Elf. Are you up to hearing what's happened since you disappeared?"

"I'm good—just tired. Once I sleep some more, I'll feel better." He leaned his head on her shoulder. "I'm listening."

By the time she finished telling him about Brie's kidnapping and rescue, he had moved to see her better.

"Is Brie alright?"

"She, like you, is fighting emotional as well as physical fatigue. Losing the Star of Truth has left her scrambling to remake herself." Penee shook her head. "I've never seen her like this—depressed, lacking confidence, and defeated. Ari jumping overboard compounded the problem."

A horrified gaze fastened on her face. "Now I remember! I couldn't get to her, Penee." Shame shook him. "I was too deep and too entangled in my grief and remorse. By the time I realized she had jumped overboard and called to me, you all had rescued her."

Distress and hopelessness filled his gaze. "How do I undo the hurt I've inflicted on the woman I love more than life itself?"

Penee put a hand on his shoulder. "You begin by letting her know, Elf. Tell her you love her. Tell her why you left."

His jaw went rigid. He threw his head back, hugged himself, and rocked back and forth. The howl of dismay he struggled to disarm exploded into a shuddering sob. He choked it down and wiped his nose with the back of his hand. "What if—"

The hatch sliding open prompted a look of total dismay. He put a finger to his lips. "Tell 'em I'm still sleeping."

She reached for the tarp.

He grabbed her arm. "Don't leave me alone."

"It's alright, Elf. One of us will always be close, I promise. When you calm down, we can decide what's next." A quick kiss on the cheek and she crawled into the brightness of the morning.

22
Der Tah

The sounds of Tamosh checking the engine compartment, the wind rustling the tarp overhead, and the gentle lapping of water against *SeaBella*'s hull lulled Elf's raging emotions into abeyance. Blustery wind slapping the lines against the masts reminded him how much he loved the ocean and life on a sailboat. *Maybe someday, either here or on El Stroma, Ari and I can live on a boat.* A tiny smile quivered into being. *Am I accepting that I am back?*

Beneath a squawking trio of laridae, *SeaBella* danced on her anchor rode. Close by, a fish jumping free of the water and its reentry splash made his smile bigger.

Tamosh knelt and looked under the tarp. "How are ya, boy? Need anything?"

Elf wiggled to sitting. "I need some time to prepare for seeing everyone, especially Arienh. Please stay close, Tamosh. I'm afraid to be alone."

"I'll be at the helm. Marji's on deck preparing the boat to get underway with Rethson and Penee. Ari's just waking up, so Brie is sticking close to her. Call me when you're ready to face the music." He grinned. "Or in this case, the ladies."

The boat's captain moved away, humming to himself.

Elf stared beyond the tarp. Penee gripped handholds, made her way toward him, and smiled down at him. "You're looking better, Troms el Shive. May I join you?"

A smile twitched. He touched the corner of his mouth. "I'm Human."

She crawled in beside him. "You are. I'm so glad!"

He lifted a hand and stared at it. "What I don't understand is how I became the creature. When I shaped a fang tooth, I knew I wouldn't last long. I didn't realize until Efillaeh called to me I was something else." Confusion bubbled over. *Focus, Elf. What's important right now?* He gripped Penee's hand. "Is Ari awake yet?"

"She is. Shall we go below?"

Shame squeezed a long, misty hiss from his lungs. "No. I need more time. You go. I'll come when I'm ready."

Understanding flashed between them. She crawled from under the tarp, and moments later, the hatch opened and closed.

❦   ❦

Ari woke to the morning sun streaming through the portholes. Fuzzy thoughts and an aching body stirred up memories of icy water and the fight to catch her breath. *I remember calling for Elf. He didn't come.* The realization left her dispirited and lonelier than she could ever remember. *What do I do now?*

Heavyhearted, she curled onto her side. The soft sounds of lapping water lulled her into a half doze. Her semi-conscious dreams unfurled like *SeaBella's* mainsail. Images of the sheet billowing in the wind and the memory of skimming through the water felt strangely real.

On the starboard side of the boat, Brie watched her from sad, bleary eyes. When she didn't move, Ari tried to say her name but couldn't form the word, cleared her throat, and failed again.

Brie traveled a long way back from wherever her thoughts had taken her. Her eyes cleared, and she pushed herself up from the bench. "Arienh?"

Ari labored to leverage her weakened, sleep-drugged body upright. "Brie—please—sit with me."

Her twin studied her for a long moment. "Are you sure you don't want to lie down and rest?"

Untangling a hand from the blankets, Ari pulled Brie down beside her and strove to croak words from her sore throat. "Sorry I scared you. I wanted Elf, and I couldn't get beyond that." She glanced around. "How did I get here?" Fighting to control the urge to cry, she pressed her trembling lips together.

Brie put an arm around her. "We all worked together, Penee, Rethson, and I." She lowered her gaze. "You were on the brink of death, Ari. Marji brought you back." She looked her straight in the eye. "Never scare me like that again." Tears streamed down her face.

Ari's emotional dam broke. She put her arms around her twin, and they held each other and sobbed.

Gradually calm reestablished itself, tear ducts ran dry, and depleted emotions drained away.

Brie sniffed, pulled two paper hankies from her pocket, and offered one to her twin. As though the stage manager called their cue, they blew their noses in chorus. Brie choked and giggled.

Ari snorted.

Their fit of laughter ended in a hug as Penee climbed the two steps from the galley and handed them each a cup of tea. She looked at Ari. "I knew I cared about you, Arienh, but when we almost lost you—" She lowered onto the starboard side bench. "I love you two like sisters. Please take care of yourselves!"

Ari repeated her apology, then savored the warm, minty tea, soothing her sore throat and warming a body that had suffered the shock of hypothermia. Her foggy mind seized a memory from just after she awoke. "Is *SeaBella* underway?"

Penee bobbed her head. "We're in Triple Moon Strait, headed north toward the Province of Geran. Marji got word from Gregos that TheDah's soldiers spotted more Vasro racing in our direction."

Ari cradled her mug. She swallowed a lump in her throat. "Are we leaving Elf behind, then?"

Penee glanced at the hatch, fixed a questioning gaze on Brie, and arched her bow.

Brie clasped her hands in her lap. "Tell her."

"He's on the boat, Arienh."

"He's what?" Ari set her mug on the bench. Trembling hands covered her mouth. Her mind numbed, then buzzed with joy, then fear, then hope. "Is he alright? Is he Human? What brought him back? Does he want to see me?" Weariness overwhelmed her. Glad for Brie's arm around her, she sagged against her. "Tell me—"

"Elf is Human. He is much better now than last night." Penee looked puzzled. "He's pretty confused about how he became the sea creature. All he remembers is hitting the water as a fang tooth and swimming as deep as he could go. When Efillaeh called him forth, he learned of his strange form for the first time." Pale fingers plucked at a loose thread in the cuff of her shirt. A bewildered gaze moved from Ari to her twin. "Any ideas, Brielle?"

Brie's eyes closed. When they opened, she looked somewhat dazed. "There's something at work here I don't understand. Something or someone inspired the change." She sipped her tea and stared at the porthole between her friends.

Ari wiggled to look at her. "What are you sensing, Brie? Is it good or evil?"

Brie's auburn brows lifted; her head tilted; and her lips rounded. "Oh." Her attention returned to *SeaBella's* cabin. "I think I might understand."

Ari swallowed her impatience. *Brie will share when she's certain.*

Brie's findings around Elf's new form didn't surprise her. *What took me so long to figure it out?* She pinched the bridge of her nose and sighed. *Maybe the residue from the drugs has clouded my mind.* A glance at Ari brought another sigh. *I'm just too tired to think.*

The hatch slid opened. Cold air accompanied Marji down the narrow ladder. Wood slid over wood, cutting its chilling flow. She stood on the sole and turned to study each girl.

"Please, Penee, fetch me a mug of tea."

Ari shot her a wide-eyed look and pulled her blankets tighter around her.

To the sounds of Penee moving around the galley, Marji sat down at the table opposite. The kettle whistle shrilled. A spoon clinked against the thick sides of a mug. Penee climbed the two steps to the first level, handed their hostess her steaming tea, and slid onto the bench next to her.

Brie clasped Ari's hand. "I believe you have things to share. We promise to hold whatever you tell us as a sacred trust."

Marji set her mug on the table, but continued to cup her hands around it. "My life will be at risk, as yours are, if what I share becomes public knowledge." She bowed her head. When she raised it, her cloudy gray eyes had changed to celestial blue and her brown hair lightened to a buttery blonde.

Ari's mouth rounded in a silent 'O'. Penee gulped a breath. Brielle simply waited.

Marji sipped her tea and replaced the mug on the teak tabletop. "In my home world, had I remained, I would be a Galactic Council member, which did not appeal to me. After much soul-searching, I approached my brother, Chealim. He arranged for me to meet with the leadership circle. My desire to help the Guardians maintain Trilemma throughout the Universe by living among a human population met with resistance from some and enthusiasm from others. After much deliberation, they gave me permission to join Gregos and Tamosh, who are both working with the Guardians. The Council made one stipulation: no one could know my true nature. Now, because of the magnitude of what is occurring, they asked me to share my secret with you. Any more questions before we move on to Elf's story?"

Brie leaned her elbows on the table. "Is anyone else we know aware of your secret?"

"Relevart and Wolloh as the Universal VarTerels and Henrietta know. Esán's dual seeds informed him, and now the three of you have joined the circle. Anything else?"

When no one put forth a question, her eyes and hair returned to the color of her DerTahan persona. She sat back and looked from Ari to Penee. "Rasiana placed Elf in our care at the request of the Guardians. His destiny dictated he not remain in the Mocendi hands. The eventual discovery of his talents would have led to you, Penee." She paused, her gaze resting on Elf's birth-mate. "You have a question?"

"Why didn't you stop him from jumping into the ocean?" Her tone accused. Blood rushed to her cheeks. "I didn't mean to be disrespectful, but..." She shrugged.

"Your question, Penesert, is fair. Getting him away from Thorlu distracted me. I didn't realize his intent until he flipped his fang tooth tail and disappeared."

"Would you have stopped him if you had known?" Ari's voice trembled, but her gazed remained steady.

Marji pursed her lip. "Could I have kept him from jumping? He had decided that you and Penee wouldn't be safe if he continued to live." Sadness etched the lines in her face deeper and dimmed the brightness in her eyes. "His terror of the anger he carries and the power he wields played a large part in his decision. I knew his goal was to let a larger predator feed on his flesh. Interfering is never my goal, but Elf is the son of my heart, and I could not let him die. I gradually shifted his aquatic form to that of the creature you saw rise from the sea. When I did it, I knew he might feel betrayed." She lowered head.

A blast of cold air filled the cabin. Elf climbed down the ladder and regarded the women.

No one moved. Slow, weighted steps carried Troms El Shiv from the hatchway to stand looking down at Marji. "I heard you telling them about changing my shape." He kissed her upraised face. "Thank you, my heart-mother. I love you."

A tear leaked from his eye. He flicked it away and looked at Penee. "I love you, Penesert." His gaze dropped to the cabin's wooden deck, then moved to Ari. "I love you, Arienh AsTar. You filled my heart the first time I saw you." He knelt in front of her. "Can you ever forgive me?"

SeaBella pitching to port, sent everyone tumbling. Rethson's angry shout sent them scrambling for the ladder. Brie climbed up first. Tamosh struggled to steer the boat into the wind. The lines on the mainsail slapped. *SeaBella* heaved over a high wave and dropped into the trough.

Marji brushed past her and hurried to the helm. Wind shoved her the last few steps. Only Tamosh, grabbing her and pulling her to his chest, kept her from pitching overboard. She scanned the sky. Her eyes narrowed. "This is not nature at work." She turned aft as a large motor vessel appeared from behind a small island. "There's a SorTech on board that boat."

Brie sent a mental probe flashing through the space between their sailboat and the one racing to close the gap.

The captain of the boat and three of Karlsut's Vasro manned the craft.

The fifth occupant reacted to her probe by setting wards around their boat. Brie responded by shielding the sailboat and her crew.

A blast of wind shook *SeaBella*. A line on the mainsail snapped.

Marji hurried to her side. "We need to go where they can't follow."

Penee climbed on deck. "What can I do?"

SeaBella mounted the side of a wave and shot toward the trough.

Brie slid into Penee's arms. "We need to vanish." She stuck her head through the hatch. "Ari, stay there. Keep Elf with you."

She lifted her hand. The solid wood of her staff gleamed between her fingers. Penee gripped her arm. "Where to?"

"Blank your minds." Marji's hand clasped the rowan wood.

Tamosh gave a shout of frustration as *SeaBella* bucked.

Brie focused and breathed.

The wind ceased. *SeaBella* glided with effortless grace through a rippling ocean of stars.

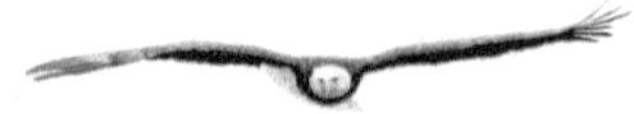

23
Tao Spirian

Esán and Somay had left Torgin, Gar, and Spyglass concealed in a grove of casaurina trees and sailed the boat to a nearby village where Tianna, his mother, waited in a small hut near the beach with her trusted friend, a member of the Tecôlta tribe.

Tianna greeted him with a quick embrace and made introductions. "Esán, this is my friend Annjoa. She is an Arrenduca healer from the Island of Sicreetô and wishes to share important information with you."

In the way of Tao Spirian, Esán, head bowed, pressed his palms together and rested his thumbs on his heart. He looked up to find Annjoa returning the ritual welcome.

Her smile warmed him. "Let us sit together while your parents take the bottle given to you on ReTaw au Qa to the Research Center."

He passed the clay bottle to his father. "Yaro told us the contents may help better define my disease and help with the cure."

Somay handed it to his life-mate. "Since our pursuers know me but not you, Tianna, please take this and keep it safe. I'll teleport you to the Center but remain hidden. We can rendezvous on the boat when your business is complete."

Tianna slipped the bottle into a hidden pocket in her long, full skirt and turned to Esán. "The sooner you can leave Tao Spirian, the better. Annjoa told me about Karlsut Sorda and Skultar Rados. I think you will find what she has to share very informative." She hugged him, clasped Somay's hand, and together they flashed from view.

Esán took a seat next to the Arrenduca and waited for her to begin.

Annjoa studied him with focused concentration. Her gaze softened and her expression relaxed into a smile. "My only experience with Dual Seeds of Carsilem is you. I can tell you, however, they have matured in ways none of the Arrenduca community expected." She caught his flicker of surprise. "Yes, Esán, you have been the subject of much discussion among those of us who oversee the spiritual needs of Tao Spirian."

Esán's skin tingled with a warning. He tensed.

Her attention darted to the window and back. "Listen closely. You must return to the VarTerel, Brielle AsTar. She is in grave danger. Since Karlsut Sorda's Vasro commander and his accomplices arrived on Tautian, their greed and hatred alerted the Tecôlta women, whom, as you know, are sensitive to the harmful wishes of others. The commander wears a Mocendi's cape. His name is Raiherr Yencara. He felt certain you would come here in search of a cure for your illness. His small jumper craft arrived two Tao Spirian day-cycles ago. Since that time, I tuned in to his thoughts. Not only was the Star of Truth removed from Brie, but Karlsut ordered a med-tech to inject her with a series of pellets that dissolve at differing rates. These seed-sized pellets release toxins that cause fatigue and listlessness. They also induce a sense of worthlessness in the victim."

From the pouch at her waist, she withdrew two seed pods that spanned her palm. "These are Wrené Tree pods. When the seeds are placed in hot liquid and ingested, they destroy the pellets and revitalize the victim. The sooner you reach Brielle, the better her results will be." She tucked the seeds in a small pouch and handed them over.

"I gave you two so that you may also ingest their restorative goodness. Use yours only, Esán Efre, when you feel your symptoms manifesting. They will help to keep your illness at bay for a time at least. Do you—" She frowned. "Yencara and his men have almost reached this end of the island. It won't be long before they discover the Research Center. Unless you have questions, Esán, you'd better go."

Esán stuffed the pouch in his pocket as he rose. "I'll contact you through my father if I need more information. Thank, Annjoa, for your help. Go in safety." He once again bowed his head and pressed his palms together.

The last thing he saw was the Arrenduca offering the ritual farewell as she vanished and his feet touched a wooden deck.

Tianna Efre waited in the Research Center, hashing over her last conversation with Somay. Yencara and his men searched for their son. Although Sorda knew little about her, he knew Esán's mother lived on the planet of Tao Spirian. Her life as a traveling birther and etheric healer obscured her whereabouts and fine-tuned her instinct for approaching danger. Trouble headed her way.

A man's arrival in the Center screamed beware. She wiped memories of her from the mind of the young woman behind the desk and, adjusting her appearance, turned to the window. A man in a Mocendi's cape strode into the reception area. While he interrogated the receptionist, Tianna observed a second man pacing back and forth at the front entrance. The Mocendi finished his discussion, glanced Tianna's direction, and marched from the room.

As he exited the building, she resumed her natural appearance, returned the receptionist's memories of her presence, and stood to greet a young technician who requested she follow him. At the end of a long corridor, they entered a laboratory where an older gentleman waited.

"Tianna Efre, I have discovered several things of interest in the specimens you brought to me earlier. We are most grateful to your son for providing such excellent samples from ReTaw au Qa. I have prepared a packet of dehydrated antibodies for him to take on his journey. These antibodies live in the oceans of Tao Spirian. When he comes home, we treat him with seawater enriched with them. Tell him to pour the contents of the packet into the ocean at his final destination. If there is no ocean, he must combine salt, water, and the minerals in this second packet with the antibodies." He pressed both packets into her hand. "I wish him well." His hand on hers held a warning. "Your stalker is at the reception desk. Go out the back door. I'll do my best to slow him down."

Tianna whispered a sincere thank you and slipped through the service entrance. Somay flashed into view and grabbed her hand. The Center vanished. The deck of *Capee Iwa* solidified under her feet.

E sán paced *Capee Iwa's* deck, eager for his parents to return. When at last they flashed into view, he glanced around. "Where are Torgin and Gar?"

"I alerted them to trouble. They are on the way." Somay gripped the tiller. "We can't stay put much longer. In fact, the further from Tao Spirian we can get, the better. Let's cast off in case we need to leave quickly."

Esán jumped onto the dock, released the stern line, and tossed it to Somay. The sounds of a motor vessel growing louder shot a jolt of adrenaline through him. He caught his father's eye, untied the bow line, scrambled aboard, and pushed off.

A screaming sound careening over the water increased his need to act. Relief boiled over when Torgin, with Spyglass in his arms and Gar at his side, his spectacles in place, materialized on *Capee Iwa's* bow. "Get back here, you two. Gar grab Spy."

Relevart's stone burned Esán's palm as his friends flashed to his side. An explosion sent waves rolling through the estuary. *Capee Iwa* bucked, sending her occupants to the deck. Water roiled around the pitching sailboat. A blast of air reeking of explosives flapped the sails and slapped the lines.

A blaze of white light transitioned to cool dimness. Gar scrambled to his feet, holding his spectacles in place. "Where are the stars? This isn't Mittkeer. Where are we?"

"Someplace safe. Stay alert." Esán stood up and helped Tianna to her feet. "Are you alright, Mother?"

She tugged at her long skirt. "I'm fine."

He turned to Somay. "Thanks for your help. How long do you think we'll be safe here?"

Somay gazed at the dark rock enclosing them. "That depends on how sensitive Yencara's equipment is. I suggest you leave without delaying."

The VarTerel's stone vibrating against Esán's curled fingers made his Seeds of Carsilem hum. His father nodded. Mittkeer's stars rushed toward them, hit a barrier, and vanished. A long, low, malicious laugh echoed around them.

Somay's expression flashed a warning. No one spoke. Not even Spyglass made a sound. Esán summoned his resources, motioned his companions closer, and held Tumu Nnoci close to his heart. The key to the space-time continuum grew to its full size. Dark rock walls vanished into sunlight and fresh air. The warmth of a sea breeze caught *Capee Iwa's* sail and sent her skimming over the calm, blue sea. Torgin grinned. Tianna let out a sigh. Somay put an arm around Gar and smiled at his son.

Gar made a squinted survey of the landscape. "This isn't Mittkeer either. So..." The question hung in the air.

Torgin knelt to put Spyglass on the deck. "We are in a time fold, Gar. Our enemies cannot follow us here." He stood. "What stopped our transition into Mittkeer?"

Esán replaced the key in his pocket. "It appears Karlsut's SorTechs have been busy. They can't enter the Land of Time, but they have discovered a way to make it harder for us to do so." He looked at his parents. "You need to come with us. When it's safe, I'll bring you back. Right now, thwarting our enemy's attempts to catch us and finding Brie are my priorities."

Eyes shaded, he gazed over the open sea. Nothing alarmed him. "It's time to go." Before anyone could respond. The ever-night sky formed a glittering globe around them.

Gar's wide grin brightened his features. "Hey, we're sailing on an ocean of stars."

Esán took a moment to catch his breath. "Torg. Get out the compass and find Uruao, the Scorpion's Tail. It is the gateway to DerTah."

Ostradio gleamed in the starlight as Torgin held it in front of him and made a slow rotation. The needle spun into a blur of gold and slowed. *Capee Iwa* sailed on a beam of shimmering light and glided to a stop. Through the shields still surrounding them, her crew stared beyond the bow.

~ Mittkeer ~

Capee Iwa bobbed gently on a sea of never ending-night, tiny ripples traveling out from her sides. Mittkeer's all-consuming silence swaddled the boat and its crew until Spyglass' sharp yip broke their trance-like state.

Torgin knelt in the cockpit to stroke the terrier's back, then stood to study the compass. "I wonder if we can sail to Uruao?"

A whispered breeze caressed the length of the hull. Somay grinned. "Let's try it. Esán and Gar, help me raise the mainsail."

The large triangular canvas rode the rigging lines to the top of the mast, billowed in the increasing breeze, and eased *Capee Iwa* forward through stars and deep blue night. Esán grinned. Gar clapped his hands in delight.

Somay sat, tiller in hand, his gaze darting from the compass to the sea of stars. "Why aren't we moving?" He chuckled at Torgin's all-knowing grin. "All Time and No Time, right?"

Torgin nodded. "Time is illusion, something but not." He smiled. "I'm quoting Almiralyn."

Esán's head cocked to one side; his brow wrinkled. "Did you hear that?"

Tianna peered ahead. "Do you mean laughter? How can that be?"

Gar peered through his lenses and pointed. "I see another boat way out there."

Somay passed Esán an old-fashioned monocular telescope. "See if you can pinpoint what Gar is seeing."

Torgin waited, his impatience growing. "Care to share."

Esán handed him the telescope. "Tell me I'm seeing what I believe I'm seeing."

Torgin raised the brass scope and gazed at a familiar shape floating beneath the Constellation Uruao. "If you saw the sailing vessel *SeaBella,* then we're seeing the same thing, which would suggest that a VarTerel is on board. Do you suppose the girls found Elf with Marji? Shall we move closer?"

Esán frowned. "Call it being overcautious, but I'd like to explore before we all venture toward it. I'll—"

Torgin shook his head. "You stay put. If this is a ploy, they'll need you here. I'll go." He looked at Gar. "Keep me in your sights."

Gar touched the rim of his spectacles. "Will do."

Torgin vanished into the shape of an eagle and soared through the star-studded immenseness. Nothing about the Senndi's ketch caused him alarm. People he recognized gathered on the deck, their focus on one another. He landed, shaped Human, and grinned at the astonished looks on the familiar faces.

"Torgin Whalend!" Brie's tired expression brightened. "Somehow, I didn't expect to find you flying around Mittkeer. Where are Gar and Esán?"

Although he felt nothing that suggested a threat, his scan of those gathered left him unsatisfied. He peered over her shoulder. "Is Ari on board? Did you find Elf?" He caught Rethson's eye. "How did you get here, Rethson? The last I heard, you were in RewFaar."

Marji, whom he knew and admired, moved into his line of vision. "We need to find a safe place to compare notes, Torgin. DerTah is not it, nor if I am not mistaken, is Tao Spirian." She moved to the stern, a hand raised. *SeaBella* eased along the port side of *Capee Iwa*. She smiled at Somay. "Raft her up, Captain, and bring your crew aboard. A quick conference is in order."

A short time later, Torgin sat atop the cabin, observing his friends. Elf helped Ari to climb on deck and sat next to her, his back resting on the bulwark. The only one who appeared to be missing from the impromptu reunion was Den. Esán drew Brie to one side and pressed a seed pod into her hand. After speaking quietly, Brie, pale and shaking, disappeared into the cabin.

Marji assumed the role of leader. "We must leave Mittkeer. Although we are safe at the moment, we cannot assume our enemies won't gain access to the Land of Time. Suggestions for a safe place to confer and make plans?"

Esán gazed at the group. "Where will Karlsut and Skultar not expect us to go? Not Myrrh, DerTah, or Tao Spirian. ReTaw au Qa is unsafe." He chewed on his bottom lip. "What about Thera's Sea of Mystéer? I doubt they'd guess we'd go there."

Torgin shuddered. "No one goes there and for good reason. What makes you think we'd be safer than anyone else?"

Attention fixed on Esán, everyone waited.

Torgin glimpsed a moment of surprise on Marji's face, a nod from Somay, and a look of careful curiosity in Tamosh's expression.

Brie hurried on deck, vitality humming around her. "What did I miss?"

Esán clasped her hand. "I suggested we go to the Sea of Mystéer on Thera. Share what you know of it, Brielle."

Torgin smiled to himself as he observed a hint of color in her cheeks and the return of aware intelligence in her eyes. He saw a knowing smile on Tianna's face as she watched her daughter-to-be.

Brie pursed her lips. "In school in Idronatti, they taught us the Sea of Mystéer is an enigma. They said little, except the military allowed no one to go there. Since we couldn't leave the city—" She shrugged. "Mother grew up in Singtil in the Central Mountains. Her stepfather told her it was a place where secrets flourished, and he shared stories of people escaping in boats that simply vanished. Marji, what do you think?"

Eyes narrowed, Marji stared into the starry vastness. "I think it's time we got underway. The Sea of Mystéer will provide a place to regroup. I doubt we will be there long." She turned to where Tamosh and Somay stood to one side, conversing in low voices. "Gentlemen, you have both been to Thera's ocean. Thoughts?"

Tamosh frowned. "It is no worse than other places that come to mind. What's good—Esán is correct—no one will think we'd go there." His gaze darted over the heavens. "We've been in Mittkeer too long." He glanced at Somay, who nodded. "We'll put a picture of Mystéer in the minds of our VarTerel and bearer of the Dual Seeds."

Torgin held up the compass. "I'm ready."

Brie and Esán stepped forward.

"Wait!" Rethson stood red-faced and shaking. "What about my mother?"

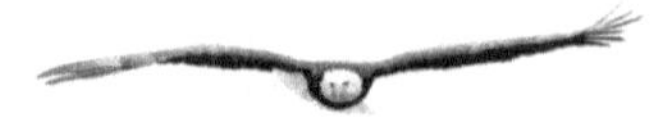

24
Thera

Brie turned as Rethson's face contorted in pain. He clawed at the side of his neck and crumpled to the deck. Marji hurried to his side. Nimble fingers felt for a pulse, then touched a small white scar on his neck. A nod brought her to standing, an urgent warning broadcasting from her dark eyes.

"We need to take a moment. Tamosh, stay with Rethson. She beckoned Tianna, Penee, and Brie to follow as she descended into the cabin.

Brie climbed down and slid the hatch closed.

Marji frowned. "Rethson has a tracker disc implanted in his neck. Penee, you've had one removed. Is there anything you can tell Tianna to help her before she attempts to remove it?"

Penee touched the small scar on her neck. "She will need Brie to assist with her VarTerel's skills."

Brie nodded. "I'll help. You understand that once Karlsut realizes he can no longer track Rethson, Roween will be in grave danger?"

Marji stepped further into the cabin and bowed her head. When she looked up, she looked less worried. "I have done a scan of RewFaar. Roween is well-hidden and well-protected. Lorsedi Telisnoe is more than a match for Karlsut and his Vasro. They have no way of knowing her whereabouts. Lorsedi has offered a bounty to anyone who brings him a Vasro member. He has also sent Den to oversee Roween's protection until he is certain the Vasro have left RewFaar." She glanced up at the hatch. "First, we'll take care of Rethson. Then, putting distance between us and our last known entrance into Mittkeer is vital."

Tianna led the way on deck, spoke to Somay, and moved to Rethson's side. Marji motioned everyone else to gather around her as Somay climbed onto Capee Iwa and returned with a leather bag, which he placed next to Tianna. Brie called forth her VarTerel's staff and joined the Tao Spirian healer. "How long do you think he will remain unconscious?"

"I'm uncertain." With careful precision, Tianna cleaned the area around the white scar. "I understand you named your crystal Musette. Please use it to detect any traps that might hurt Rethson."

Brie touched the facetted tourmaline to the scar and shook her head. "We need Efillaeh. It is the only knife that can remove the disc without harming him."

Hurrying to her twin, she explained her need and returned with the sacred healing blade. Tianna took it; Brie placed Musette next to the scar. The sharp point of the knife made a small, shallow slit. The crystal glowed. A sliver of silver glinted. Efillaeh's amethysts shimmered. Emerald engravings on the blade spilled healing green light into the tiny incision. Tianna lifted the disc free and handed it to Brie. Efillaeh's light faded, leaving smooth, unblemished skin on Rethson's neck.

Dark amber eyes fluttered open. Rethson looked from Brie to Tianna. "What did you do?"

Brie held up the disc. "You are no longer tied to Karlsut."

Fright widened his eyes. "You should have asked me. He will have the Vasro kill Mother. We have to find her first."

Marji's reassuring calm quieted him. "Karlsut and Skultar do not know where Roween is hidden. They have been using your love for her to keep you under control. Once we are further from our enemies, I will share more." She touched Rethson's temple and stood. Pressing the disc between her palms, she whispered,

"All Time, No Time, this disc prepare
To vanish soon into thin air,
Keep it active till we depart
Then work your special magic art."

Holding it high, she tossed it in to the foreverness of the Land of Time.

Brie felt Rethson's fear dissipate as she helped him to his feet. He rubbed his neck. "I'm grateful to you both." He mustered a smile. "Esán, your mother is amazing."

Esán kissed Tianna's cheek. "She is, isn't she?" He slipped a hand into Brie's. "We need our VarTerel."

With everyone on SeaBella's deck surrounding them, Brie and Esán prepared to transport two boats, twelve people, and one frisky terrier.

Torgin held the compass where they could see it. "Take us to the Trio of Noori, gateway to the Theran sea."

The needle spun. Two sailboats seemed to glide through the immensity of Mittkeer, stars blurring into streaks of white in their wake. Beneath three bright stars forming a line across the heavens, the needle stopped. Night withdrew its cool darkness, depositing them in the cloud-dimmed brightness of mid-turning. A clammy breeze smelling of decay rustled the water's dirty gray surface.

Brie's staff vanished. Esán slipped the VarTerel's Stone in his pocket. Torgin studied the back of the compass as the stars and constellations transformed into the Theran night sky. Silence thick with uncertainty pressed the friends closer. Brie peered beyond the stern at the glare of the sun burning its way through the clouds.

Gar's youthful voice broke the alert silence. "Where are we? Can't see anything but water and clouds."

Tamosh moved to Torgin's side. "The boy's right. We need to know where we are. Ostradio will give charts of the area, correct? We don't want to run aground."

Somay joined them to watch a chart float above the compass face and grow bigger.

👁 👁

Somay looked up, met Torgin's questioning gaze, and pointed to a small island on the chart. "Can Ostradio zoom in on this spot?"

Without a word from Torgin, the Island of DeWin filled the floating chart. Somay and Tamosh studied it.

Tamosh nodded. "Hydd Cove looks to be a perfect spot and from what I remember about Mystéer, the island is uninhabited."

Somay pinpointed their present location in the Bay of Silvering and traced the course to the island with an index finger. He glanced at the clouds obscuring all but the incandescent glare of the sun and frowned. "We need to use what light is available to get us there. The wind has stilled, so it looks like engine power is our best bet. Let's get under way. I suggest we divide into two groups, but stay close together."

Tamosh studied the chart a moment longer. "Each boat needs a captain and either Esán or Brie. The goal is to find the anchorage and raft up for the night."

Somay nodded his agreement. "If the cove is safe, staying for a couple of turnings isn't a bad idea, either. Do you want to lead in *SeaBella*?"

"Nope. You have the smaller boat. Let me follow you. Pick your crew."

Somay looked over at the group. "Why don't I take those who arrived with me in Mittkeer. That will give me Esán in case we need to disappear, Torgin with the compass, Gar as my first mate, Tianna, and Spyglass."

Tamosh conferred with Marji. "Sounds good. Let's communicate telepathically as we go."

Heads bent over the compass-created chart, they studied the narrow entrance, widening into a deep, rounded basin. The chart showed the way there was through a narrow, abyss-like channel between undersea rock formations. A warning next to the channel flashed: Beware kelp forests; best navigated at slack tide. The date and time glowed beneath it.

Somay pursed his lips. "Slack tide is in about half a chron-circle. We'd better get moving." He regarded the group. "Keep your wits about you and your eyes open."

After calibrating *SeaBella's* compass to Ostradio, Somay climbed on *Capee Iwa* and assisted Tianna aboard. Torgin followed, put Spyglass on the deck, and helped Gar. Esán handed Tianna her healers' kit, kissed Brie, and jumped aboard.

Somay assigned his crew their tasks and waited for Tamosh to give the command to cast off.

Tamosh gazed at the expectant faces peering up at him. "Ari and Brie go below and rest while you can. Elf, I need you at the helm. Rethson, stand at the bow. Look for debris or obstacles that might damage the boats. Penee, you and Marji watch for anything strange or out of place." As the crew dispersed, he moved to the helm and started the engine.

On *Capee Iwa*, Somay followed suit. When both engines were humming, Tamosh gave the order to cast off and Somay motored ahead of *SeaBella*. Torgin, with Ostradio in hand, stood nearby. Esán coiled the lines and took his place at the bow. Tianna and Gar stationed themselves as lookouts on either side of the cabin.

Somay, at the tiller, gazed over a sea that appeared featureless beneath the sun's cloud-muzzled glare. The oppressive silence intensified. Clouds billowed and roiled, obscuring the sun like a theater curtain closing at the end of a performance. Moisture sodden grayness pressed closer.

"Tamosh, all stop."

SeaBella slowed. When her forward motion ceased, Somay eased *Capee Iwa* to a stop. *"Can't see a thing. You?"*

Tamosh responded. *"Elf has an idea. Hold on."* A tension-filled pause suggested they spoke. *"I'm sending him to you."*

Elf materialized on the deck of *Capee Iwa*. "I'm going to change and swim ahead. If it's safe, I'll lead you into the cove. Try to maintain this position."

The next instant, a two-legged, scale-covered sea creature slipped over the side and disappeared beneath the water's surface.

❧   ❧

E lf savored the feel of water caressing his scaled body. Webbed hands and feet propelled him forward. He marveled at the sense of freedom returning to the sea gave him. The sailboat bobbing beside him focused his attention on his task. Diving deeper, he explored the channel-like abyss. As the island drew closer, he stopped, his sculpin eyes searching. *Something watches. What?*

He analyzed the sensation and his response. *I'm not afraid.* Treading water, he touched down on a flat-topped crystalline formation. The water in front of him wavered. Two glowing green orbs floated upward. A toothless mouth followed. A sea snake wiggled a zigzagged path through partially submerged kelp and stopped in front of him. Empathy flowed between them. Shared thoughts took shape. Elf sensed only the snake's curiosity and willingness to help. His mind adapted to the creature's way of communicating.

"Where you go?" Green, unblinking eyes stared.

"Hydd Cove." Elf waited.

"Boats go too?"

"They're my companions."

The snake's paddle-shaped tail flicked right then left. *"Must hurry. Tell boats to follow. I lead."*

Elf swam to the surface and focused his thoughts on Tamosh and Somay. *"Follow me. We must hurry."*

He submerged but remained visible to Somay. The creature navigated the abyss, leading Elf and his companions closer to their destination. A surge of movement at the mouth of the cove brought the sea snake to a halt. The message, *"Stop boats,"* ran through Elf's mind.

A quick relay of the message caused the boat captains to slow and reverse engines. Rushing bubbles exploded on the water's surface. Expectant faces peered ahead. Elf swam after the sea snake, anticipation building as he went.

The approach to the cove brought them close to a bright orange bolt of electrical current that shot from one side of the entrance to the other. Swimming a wide semi-circle, Elf followed the sea snake to a coral reef. Wedged between two rocks, a cylinder glowed iridescent green. On the other side of the entrance, a second cylinder glinted orange. A lightning-like bolt shot upward from each cylinder, met to form an arch over the water and dissipated.

The sea snake quivered beside him. *"See next."*

Elf counted in his mind. The next flashed occurred a minute-and-a-half later, followed immediately by a second bolt of light. Quiet settled over the cove for another several minutes. The sequence repeated. Within the stillness between, Elf dove down to the green cylinder, studied it and swam back to *Capee Iwa.*

Treading water at her side, he shared what he had discovered. A telepathic conversation ensued. Elf listened to Somay explain that the PPP had set up traps throughout Thera's oceans. He did not know if the traps were still being monitored. He, Tamosh, and Marji discussed options. It was decided that Esán would shape a fish and join him. Once they made certain the cove itself was safe, Esán would set up shields around the cylinders during the longest pause, the boats would enter the cove, and he would release the shields. With luck, if the short interruption was detected, it would be interpreted as a brief malfunction.

Esán in the shape of a yellow-tailed sea bass joined him and they swam back to the waiting sea snake and the flashing currents of light.

At the next long interval between bolts of current, Esán and Elf swam beyond the entrance to Hydd Cove, leaving the sea snake hidden in a kelp forest to keep watch. Sunlight penetrating the water pulled them upward. Esán's sea bass surfaced. Fisheyes fought the brightness. Here in the cove scattered puffy clouds replaced the heavy gray fog. Filtered sunlight formed a patchwork of light and dark pools on the water's surface and illuminated the dark green foliage lining the shore and the golden hue of a small sandy beach not far ahead.

Elf's creature walked onto shore, his scales, fins, and long kelp hair glistening with water and sunlight.

Esán materialized as Human at his side and scanned the modest-sized expanse. "I'll shape a bird and fly over the area while you make sure the cove itself is safe. Let's meet back here as soon as we're satisfied."

"Good plan." The creature waded into the water until it reached his hips, and dove.

Esán shaped a kestrel and flew an exploratory circuit of the shoreline, his keen raptor sight searching for anything out of the ordinary. After completing the loop, he swooped low over the water and arrived back at the beach to find Elf, in human form, waiting.

Elf flicked fluid droplets from his cheek. "I found nothing underwater to cause alarm. You?"

"Everything seems fine. Nothing bothered me." He glanced at the sun gliding gently toward the horizon. "We need to get the boats anchored before the sun sets. I'll place the shields around the cylinders. You fetch the boats."

Elf nodded. "Be careful down there."

Esán grinned. "You, too." He strode into the water and shifted. Flipping his yellow tail, he swam to the cove entrance where the sea snake waited. The snake's telepathic *"go ahead"* sent him in a circle of the first cylinder. Assured that it was safe, he set up the shield and glided across the channel. Orange light glowed along the upper side of the second cylinder. A bolt of light shot directly at Esán. Quick reflexes carried him out of range. A tight flip brought him behind it. He set a shield and signaled Elf to bring the boats.

25

Thera

Onboard *SeaBella*, Penee stood at the railing scanning Thera's Mystéer Ocean. Cool, damp air brushing her cheeks made her shiver and look up at the thick, gray haze overhead. Memories of Neul Isle, where the cloud cover engendered warm sadness, flickered. Here, 'festering anger seethed within the dark pewter clouds. Another shiver raised the hair on her neck.

Penee's gaze skimmed over the gray-brown water toward Hydd Cove. *Where are you, Elf?* The fear his shift to his sea creature might tempt him to break for freedom chilled her as much as the ocean breeze. His kelp-covered head surfaced on the port side of *SeaBella*. His bulging eyes fixed on her made her dizzy with relief.

Somay moved to her side, his attention on Elf. A short telepathic exchange later, Elf swam ahead of *Capee Iwa*, leading the way through the narrow channel. Penee marveled at his athletic stroke and powerful kick as he glided through the water. *I wonder what it's like to be you right now, Troms el Shiv?*

A guttural laugh filled her head. *"It's wonderful, Pen! Someday—"*

His teasing cut short left her mind empty and her heart pounding. *"Elf? What happened? Where—"*

Marji touched her shoulder. "He's fine, Penee. He'll explain when he can." She turned to the hatch as the twins climbed on deck. "Perfect timing, girls. Brie, please go forward and help Rethson. You remember how to work the winch and how we set the anchor, correct?"

Brie's smile. "I do. If we need help, we'll yell." Gripping the grab rail along the top of the cabin, she side-stepped her way to the bow.

Penee followed her progress with a sense of relief. The seed pod Esán had given her friend appeared to be working.

On *Capee Iwa,* Torgin, compass in hand and his eyes flitting between it and the cove entrance, provided Somay with information as needed. Tianna and Gar prepared the lines to toss to the crew on *SeaBella* once the bigger boat was anchored.

Somay cast his experienced eye ahead. "Looks like we made a good choice. The cove is well-protected from the wind and, therefore, a calm place to anchor. We'll move to the port side of the cove as we enter, which will give Tamosh room to maneuver SeaBella." He looked up at Torgin. "You've shared the best anchorages with him?"

"I have. He will choose from the two best places once he's inside. Esán and Elf are also keeping him informed."

"Good." Somay shaded his eyes. "Looks sunny." He gripped the tiller. "Here we go."

Torgin marveled at the skill with which Esán's father steered the sailboat through the narrow passage. Once *Capee Iwa* was safely to the port side of the cove, Torgin provided Tamosh telepathic instructions from Ostradio's chart and watched SeaBella glide into the cove's center.

Tamosh's voice drifted over the water as he shouted directions to his crew. "Brielle, drop anchor. Ari, hold her steady."

"Anchor's down." Rethson yelled.

"Prepare to set the anchor." Somay took over the tiller. The boat's engine revved in reverse and the anchor rode when taut.

"She's set!" Rethson's grin made Torgin smile and remember his first time helping to anchor *SeaBella* on DerTah.

At Tamosh's signal, Somay eased *Capee Iwa* next to the larger boat, and Tianna and Gar tossed the lines to Brie and Rethson.

Tamosh and Somay congratulated their crews on a job well done as Elf's sea creature climbed the starboard side ladder, tossed a large black and silver scaled fish onto the deck, and shifted to Human. He caught Marji's eye and smiled. "Thought I'd provide the main course."

She chuckled. "So you're hungry, right?"

He hugged her. "I'm glad you brought me back." His smile at everyone. "Thank you all."

Esán's head appeared above the railing. "Did I hear something about dinner?" He climbed aboard to the light-hearted laughter of his companions.

Tamosh tossed him a towel. "What about the shields? Did you lower them?"

"I did. I thought it would be better in case they're being monitored."

Tamosh, his expression pleased, picked up the fish and carried it to the cleaning station at the stern. A quick slice exposed the fish's innards, which he removed and threw over the side. Slipping a finger under the gills, he held the prize high. "I'd say it's time to relax and have a sumptuous meal. Thanks, Elf." He turned to Marji. "Can I help with dinner?"

She took the fish. "You've done your share of the work today. Torgin and Gar will help me in the galley, right, boys?"

Torgin housed the compass in its pouch, opened the hatch, and took the fish from her. "After you, Chef Marji."

Gar giggled and urged Spyglass down the two steps ahead of him.

Accompanied by the sounds of chatter on deck and Spyglass's excited bark in the cabin, Torgin climbed below to cook his first meal in the galley of a sailboat.

A sense of safety allowed everyone to enjoy a delicious, laughter-filled meal. When they had eaten their fill and the galley was spotless, Brie curled on the bench at the stern of *SeaBella* next to Esán, her head on his shoulder. Ari and Elf sat cross-legged on the deck, fingers intertwined. Penee, with Gar sitting beside her, gazed up at the coming of night.

Torgin, followed by Rethson, climbed on deck with a guitar in hand. "Look what I found, Gar." He grinned. "How about a song?"

Gar jumped to his feet, took the guitar, plucked the strings one by one, and nodded his approval. "I'll play if Ari and Pen will sing."

Tianna and Marji joined them from below and sat on the seat at the helm. "We'd love to hear you sing, girls."

Somay smiled. "I have a wooden flute on *Capee Iwa*, so, Torgin, you can join the performance, too. I'll get it."

Soon, Torgin found himself surrounded by Gar, Ari, and Penee. Gar strummed the guitar. "What do ya wanna play?"

Torgin blew a few experimental notes. "I suggest something from 1969."

Ari beamed. "You know *This Land is Your Land,* right? We didn't get to perform it in New York City, so this would give us a chance."

Gar did a little dance. "I know it. Torg?"

"I can follow along." Torgin played a few notes of the song.

A quiet practice moment later, they gathered by the closed hatch. Gar played a series of chords and nodded at the girls. Their voices rang out across the cove. Torgin played the melody with Gar and watched the delight on the faces of their audience.

The concert ended with everyone joining in and then a round of applause. Tianna hugged Gar. "I understand you play classical music. Maybe someday you can play for me." She yawned. "It's bedtime. We have a lot to decide tomorrow."

Murmurs of agreement filled the night. The boats rocked as she, Somay, and the boys climbed aboard *Capee Iwa*.

Torgin stood for a long moment before joining the group below deck. Moonlight glowed behind the clouds overhead. Rays of cool light slipped through intermittent openings, turning the water's surface to diamond sparkles. Peace filled him, peace he knew would not last. *But for now, I will treasure every moment I can get.*

Brie woke from dreams filled with the *Surgentin* in pursuit and danger stalking Skylyn, the host mother for the embryos of her babies.

She slipped from her bunk and peered through the porthole at the moon's lingering light glowing along the horizon. Soft voices on deck penetrated her sleepy daze. Sliding the hatch cover back, she stuck her head out.

A variety of stimuli, the cool dawn breeze; the pungent odor of low tide; the unusual sound passing overhead kept her silent but stole her sleepiness, leaving her skittish and alert. Esán, appearing in front of her, made her jump. She read the warning in his stance and bit back a yelp of surprise.

He motioned her below, climbed down, and slid the hatch closed, its sound muffled by a whispered charm. "We have company in the bay. Something mechanical flies a patterned flight, suggesting a search. Marji called the clouds to cover the boats. Don't make any noise."

The boat rocked. He peered out the porthole, then silently slid the hatch open.

Torgin climbed down. Voice, as soft as a bird's wing in flight, he explained. "A robotic drone is searching the area. We need an invisibility charm to keep us from detection. Tianna and Marji suggested I check with you, Brie. Since you were born in Idronatti, your energy carries more of the essence of Thera than either of them."

Brie let her dream fade and reviewed Almiralyn's charm; she stepped out on deck where Marji waited. The older woman nodded and mouthed the word, *'now'*.

Focusing her intent on both boats, Brie whispered:

> *"Time is illusion—something but not.*
> *It holds things together. I untie the knot.*
> *Delude those who seek us, a trick of the sight.*
> *This spell holds unbroken 'til I make it right."*

The drone's soft whine overhead inhibited discourse of any kind. Brie clutched Esán's hand. Torgin's gaze searched the clouds. Gar, his spectacles in place, peeked over the gunnel on *Capee Iwa*, his eyes huge, and arms encircling a mute Spyglass.

SeaBella rocked gently as bodies below deck responded to the unfamiliar but threatening sound. Ari, sleep dulling her expression, poked her head out of the open hatch with Penee staring wide-eyed over her shoulder.

On *Capee Iwa*, faces peered through portholes. Nothing moved.

The drone passed overhead for the third time, hovered, and flew on. The gradual fading of its continuous hum acted like a tonic to those suspended in the timelessness of dread.

Marji, her gaze intent and her stance rigid, finally lowered onto the seat at the helm. "For the moment, it's gone. We need to decide our next move. I don't believe Mittkeer is the answer, at least not yet. Any other ideas?"

Elf climbed onto SeaBella. "A better understanding of the cove might help us."

"I agree." Torgin cradled the Compass of Ostradio in his hands. "Show us a chart of Hydd Cove."

Everyone gathered around as the chart floated above the compass face and enlarged.

Somay pointed at a large dark spot and read, "Chideho Cavern. Will Ostradio share more?"

A detailed map of the cavern filled a corner of the chart.

To the soft sounds of breathing, they all studied the chart.

Tamosh traced the outer limits of the cavern with a finger. "It goes deep under the mountains, and on the south side there is an exit."

Marji nodded her agreement. "I suggest that Elf and Esán—" She whipped around, her gaze darting over the shoreline.

Everyone froze.

Brie moved to her side. "I thought I heard a slow rumble."

Marji's eyes narrowed to thin slits. "We have to move now. No time to explore. My mental probe of the cavern picked up nothing suggesting danger." Her head tipped back. She grabbed Brie's arm. "Esán, Somay, quickly. Help us."

A picture filled Brie's mind. Esán grabbed her hand. She gasped and dropped to her knees.

Rethson joined the group, along with Penee.

Gar scanned the cove, his spectacles' black rims gleaming red. He gasped and pointed. "By the cove entrance!"

Lightning arced over the cove. A high-pitched shrieking sound whistled through the air.

Spyglass growled.

Marji's voice rang out. "Now!"

Gar sat up, straightened his lopsided spectacles, and searched the darkness for his companions. Beside him, Spyglass lay as though sleeping. One by one, he picked out his friends prone on the deck, unmoving and silent. Even so, he was not afraid. Asking his spectacles to show him where they were, he climbed to his feet, his back against the hatch.

The world around him took shape. *Capee Iwa* and *SeaBella*, still rafted, floated together in an underground lagoon. No light penetrated the space. Sound limited to the soft breathing of his friends was all he could hear.

Spyglass twitched into wakefulness and scrambled to his feet, then dropped to his haunches beside him, his tongue hanging out the side of his mouth. A small whimper sounded like thunder in the enclosed silence.

Gar turned his attention to the bow of the boat, where a soft glow of light enlarged into an adult male. Forcing himself to remain still, Gar waited.

The figure floated over the deck and stopped in front of him. A translucent hand touched Gar's temple. Coolness flowed through his body. Something settled over his heart. A deep voice filled his head.

"I, Heyo, the ghost of an ancient shaman, transported you and your friends into the land of the Cannesti. In you, I sense the ancestral dream and have given you the knowledge to access your gifts when the time is right." The voice stilled, then resumed. "We must save you and your companions. Awaken the most powerful among them. I will help you move undetected into the Land of Time. Speak not of me until all are away from the planet of Thera." He faded. "Trust who you are."

Gar blinked away the sense that he remained trapped in a dream and knelt beside Brie. "Brielle, wake up." When her eyes opened, he moved onto Esán and then to Marji. Soon they gathered around him. "We have to leave this cavern. I..." He pressed his lips together. "We have no time to waste."

Marji studied his face, her expression solemn. "I sense a change in you. Tell us what we must do."

He touched the slight pressure resting over his heart. Heyo's deep voice spoke in his mind. He repeated his directions. "Take us to Mittkeer. Our enemies cannot detect us."

Brie's staff flashed into her hand. Esán withdrew the obsidian stone, where the star glowed golden around the carved fox. Marji shed her alternate persona. Blue eyes glinted as she allowed her power to encircle the two boats.

Gar called Spyglass to heel.

Stars blurred into being. Capee Iwa vanished. SeaBella faded from view.

Gar scanned the group. Somay and Tianna vanished as he watched. Marji and Tamosh followed suit. Images filled his mind. Both boats and their occupants, one on DerTah and the other on Tao Spirian, were safe.

Brie scanned the Land of Time. She caught her breath. "We need to separate." She pointed at the constellation Riffley. "Penee, Elf, and Rethson, must take Spyglass to *El Aperdisa*. Relevart and Henri will join you soon." Before they could respond, they faded into the star-sprinkled night.

Gar frowned. "Why did you send Spyglass away?"

Brie looked him in the eyes. "I knew you would want him safe, and we have a dangerous job to accomplish."

He heard the truth in her words and nodded.

She straightened and placed her staff in the center of those remaining in Mittkeer. Tension filled the surrounding air. No one spoke.

26

Jumper Ship

B rie fought to control the drag and pull of an unexpected force. Stars focused, then vanished, replaced by total darkness. Her staff thrummed against her palm.

Esán pressed closer. "Let your staff go."

She released it, as he, Ari, Torgin, and Gar huddle around her.

Pernicious laughter held them silent. A dim glow illuminated the metal bars of a cell window. "You figured you'd get away," an unknown male voice sneered. Close-set, eager eyes peered between the bars. "You can't escape. My ship is in motion and will be until we reach our destination." He chortled. "Thanks for getting rid of your friends." More nasty chuckles left him sneering once more. "You are my prize, my ticket to becoming a MasTer's Mocendi." Metal clanked against metal, leaving them in total darkness.

Brie drew her friends closer until they formed a tight circle. After constructing a shield around them, she created a hologram of them sitting on the floor. "We can talk, but only in whispers. Thoughts?"

Esán cleared his throat. "The man at the window was Raiherr Yencara. He wore a Mocendi's cape when he pursued us on Tao Spirian, but, based on his last comment, I believe he is only a Vasro."

"Where did he get the cape?" Torgin whispered question met with silence. "Will it enhance his power like it does for a Mocendi?"

Gar tugged at Esán's shirt. "What's the difference between a Vasro and a Mocendi?"

Torgin bent lower. "Vasro are students of DiMensionery like Brie was before she became a VarTerel. Mocendi's are graduates in the art, who are initiated into the MasTer's service."

"Thanks. That helps."

Brie sighed and touched her neck. "I sure wish—"

Ari gripped her hand. "I have an idea. Do you think Efillaeh can heal the Star of Truth? It would give us an extra layer of protection."

Brie's heart jumped. "Ari, please try. Esán, hold the shields in place. Torgin and Gar work together to maintain the holograms." She lowered her head and lifted her lush red curls off the back of her neck.

Efillaeh slipped soundlessly from its scabbard. The cool metal against her scar, sent a shiver of hope racing. A tingle of sensation started at her shoulder blade and tiptoed upward.

"Company." Gar's urgent whisper cut the process short.

Brie stepped away. Ari put the knife in its scabbard. Esán released the shields. The holograms melted into nothing, as the companions sank silently to the floor and wrapped themselves in the semblance of fear.

Raiherr Yencara and his SorTech, Callum, stood outside the jumper craft's small prison. While Callum set up The Box to monitor the activity inside, Yencara savored the weight of the Mocendi's cape. The longer it remained in his possession, the stronger his DiMensioner's power became.

He and his SorTech had tracked *Capee Iwa* through the ocean of Tao Spirian. After the sailboat vanished into Mittkeer and Callum continued to report Rethson's position, Yencara took full credit for their success.

And then, the unexpected occurred. No signature. Not an echo of Rethson's presence anywhere. Frustration exploding into rage, Yencara had marched down the passage, paused, and strode back to the SorTech. "What happened?"

Unruffled and smiling a knowing smile, Callum had explained he had gathered enough information about Rethson's companions to reprogram and attune The Box to the only VarTerel in the group. Yencara almost laughed out loud as he now faced the cell imprisoning the companions. "Prove yourself, Callum. Show me the VarTerel."

The SorTech adjusted a setting on The Box and gave him a thumbs up.

Raiherr Yencara opened the metal window cover and stared between metal bars at his captives huddled together on the floor. "My SorTech tells me you've been up to something. One of you'd better tell me what, or someone will get hurt."

Esán struggled to his feet. "We are trying to figure out where we are and who brought us here. Wouldn't you do the same thing?"

Yencara whispered something over his shoulder and stepped aside. A second male face appeared in the window. The intrusive gaze scanned the group and paused on the twins before he turned to speak with Yencara.

A lock clicked, and the door opened, casting a path of light across the cell.

Esán, captured in the glow, did not move. "How did you bring us here?"

The SorTech moved to Yencara's side. "I rather doubt we'll be sharing that piece of information." His piercing gaze darted from one twin to the other. Confusion tainted his reed-hollow voice. "Which one of you is the VarTerel?"

When neither twin responded, he strode forward and grabbed Gar. "Stop playing with me, or I will break the kid's arm."

Yencara fingered the purple lining of his cape, his confidence ebbing and flowing with the changing currents of his self-doubt. *I am a Mocendi. You're just a wannabe.* He tugged the cape. *I am a Mocendi.*

The tall, brown-skinned boy nudged the one with the Seeds of Carsilem to one side and stepped into the light. "Let the boy go, or are you afraid to pick on someone your own size?"

His friends huddled behind him.

Yencara straightened the cape. "What makes you think you can stand up to a MasTer's Mocendi?"

The young man's summer-green eyes gleamed. "What makes you think you are a Mocendi? I sense you're a low-level DiMensioner."

Fury blazing, Yencara shoved his SorTech aside. The boy yanked free and dodged into the huddled companions. Without warning, the five prisoners vanished.

Howling his disappointed and fury, Yencara turned on his SorTech. "Where have they gone, imbecile?"

Callum stepped into the hall to check the settings on The Box. "I programed everything correctly to block their entrance into Mittkeer. I don't know what happened."

Yencara stormed down the passage. A stop to wait for the turbo-lift cooled his anger. He held the door for his SorTech and followed him inside. "Do you know where they ended up?"

Callum shook his head. "It's like they vanished into nothing."

G ar studied an open door and moved closer to his cousin. "Where are we, Torg? Is this a time fold?"

Torgin remained unresponsive, frowned, and turned to Esán. "Did we do it? Are we in a time fold?"

Esán stared at the open door. "It doesn't seem right. Stay here." He walked into the shadowy passageway. After looking both ways, he rejoined his friends. "Nothing sets off an alarm, but I'm still unsure that we're safe."

Brie touched Gar's shoulder. "Put on your spectacles. Examine the cell and the passageway and tell us what you see."

In silence, Gar called them forth, settled the temples over his ears, and walked a circle around the cell. Brow furrowed, he strode into the passageway, turned one way, then other. Puzzlement buzzed as he walked back. "It's kinda weird. I don't see the walls or the floor. It's like looking at the blank screen before the show starts in a movie theater. It's just white all around us. The ceiling is round overhead. I'm not sure where we are, but we're not in a cell."

Torgin took his hand. "Lead me to the exit."

Gar reexamined the space, scrunched his features into a confused frown, and shook his head. "I didn't find a way out—just plain white." He took off his spectacles, rubbed his eyes, and put them back on. He whispered encouragement, then gave a soft laugh. "Oh! Sun Queen, come to my aid."

The round, black rims glowed like embers. Fire opal eyes surveyed the space.

Gar grabbed Torgin's hand and led him to a section of wall that was slightly darker than the rest and handed him the spectacles. "Look straight ahead."

Torgin settled the spectacles on the bridge of his nose and looked through the clear lenses. A rectangular section of wall the size of a ship's hatch jumped out at him. He laid a hand against it. When nothing happened, he looked more closely at the wall next to it. A glint of lighter white caught his eye. With a silent wish for luck, he touched it. A panel whispered open. Warm light flooded the area.

A step beyond the hatchway triggered a gasp of surprise. An excited bark brought Gar to his side. Spyglass darted forward as he dropped to his knees. Laughing, he hugged his wiggly terrier.

Penee, Rethson, and Elf laughed at their antics. Penee grinned, pulled Gar to his feet, and enveloped him in a hug.

Ari stepped through the hatch, caught sight of Elf, and ran into a welcoming embrace.

Rethson's wistful expression made Torgin flinch. He moved to his side and opened his arms.

"It is good to see you, Rethson."

Relevart's youngest son grinned and gave him a quick hug. "Glad you all made it."

Esán and Brie joined them. Questions from all sides collided. Laughter erupted and gradually silenced. Brie looked up at Rethson. "We are on *El Aperdisa*, correct?"

Penee put an arm around her. "We are. Rethson came up with a plan to track you. When we realized you were prisoners on a Vasro ship, the three of us put our heads together, reviewed our resources, and waited until the right moment to help you escape."

Elf nodded. "We knew we had to be careful not to attract attention, so we bided our time. To bring you to us, we needed you off the ship. The instant we sensed you preparing to create a time fold, we got ready. You entered the fold, and we brought you here." He grinned. "I'm so happy to be back with all of you."

Torgin indicated the door. "What is that space? I don't remember seeing it before?"

Rethson brushed his hair from his forehead. "It's the Holographic Center. The crew members use it to practice defending the ship or to relax. In the event the Vasro could track you, the Center was the best destination point on El Aperdisa. All they would see was the cell or worst case, the white walls."

Ari tugged at a curl. "How d'you bring us here without the use of Mittkeer?"

Elf joined the conversation. "Since we knew that Yencara and his SorTech had discovered a way to block your entry into Mittkeer, we asked your grandparents, Mairin and Lanli, to help. They are both VarTerels." Elf smiled. "After years of working for the Galactic Guardians, they have developed several ways to pass through Mittkeer unnoticed. They helped us to create a tunnel through All Time and No Time."

Penee, eyes glistening with excitement, jumped in. "It wasn't like the tunnel we used to go back to 1969. Instead, we created a vacuum through No Time. By doing so, we kept Yencara from being able to sense your entrance and exit from Mittkeer."

"So, he doesn't know where we are." Esán draped his arm over Brie's shoulder. "Where are Mairin and Lanli now?"

"They're meeting with the ship's commander to decide if it would be better to leave orbit around TreBlaya now or after we rescue Skylyn, Thorlu, and the babies." Elf shook his head. "I can't believe I'm about to have a little sister."

Ari registered a moment of surprise, then smiled. "Are you accepting Thorlu as your father?"

"I'm accepting that he may be a better person than I thought he was. Time will tell. I suggest we adjourn to the dining hall. Penee felt certain Garon would be famished, so she arranged for a meal to be waiting."

Torgin chuckled. "Gar's not the only one who's hungry. Let's eat and then plan our rescue mission." He shot Brie an understanding smile. "Alright with you, Brielle?"

She smiled back and, linking elbows with Ari, followed Penee and Elf down the passage. Gar and Spyglass trailed after them.

Rethson turned to him and Esán. "Den sent word Roween is safe. Lorsedi's men have imprisoned the crew of Karlsut's attack ship and the three Vasro sent to find her. He'll be returning to *El Aperdisa* once Commander Odnamo decides what the next step is."

Torgin lagged as Rethson and Esán strolled after the others. He reviewed the happenings of the last few turnings. A sense of urgency built. *Thorlu and Skylyn are not safe on Surgentin.*

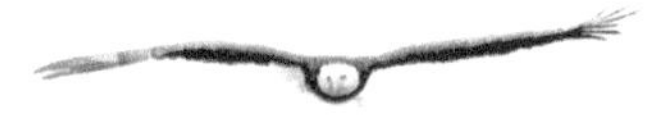

27

Surgentin

Thorlu arrived at the infirmary as two med-techs closed Vygel's isolation pod and reset the life-support system. His emotional response to his friend's potential demise surprised him. Their friendship had always been tumultuous, and yet his sadness was deep and enduring. *We had some amazing adventures, my friend.*

The faint whiff of Dee's favorite scent pulled him from his emotional upheaval. She moved to his side and motioned him to follow her. Once again, she led the way to the hidden space on *Surgentin's* lower deck. As the panel slid into place behind them, she turned.

"I went to check on Skylyn this morning." She frowned. "She's missing. No one has seen her since yesterday. I've looked everywhere I can think of. I even spoke with her boyfriend." She lowered her eyes. "I'm sorry, Thorlu."

With effort, he suppressed a wave of fear-generated anger. "It's not your fault, Dee. Thank you for trying to find her and for telling me." He put his hands on her shoulders.

Eyes the color of sunlit cognac looked up at him. The trust reflected there reminded him of how much he wanted to keep her safe.

"Dee, please be careful. Although Skultar may not be a danger to you, Karlsut Sorda is. Stay out of his way. If you need my help, picture me in your mind. I'll know and come as fast as possible."

"I'll be careful, Thorlu. Do you think Karlsut is behind her disappearance?"

"I'm about to find out. If anyone asks, you haven't seen me. I'll find you when I have some answers." He did a mental scan of the passageway. Satisfied, he pressed the sensor tab by the hatch panel. "I'll leave first. Give me time to reach the top of the companionway before you follow."

Once in his quarters, Thorlu switched on his mini-screen. Determined to maintain his hold over the half-brothers, he prepared to discover their latest antics before confronting them with Skylyn's disappearance.

The conference room focused. Karlsut reclined in his seat, picking his teeth. Skultar, his expression less than pleased, studied his screen. His face pinched in annoyance. "Why didn't you tell me Yencara had made contact?"

Karlsut shrugged. "Yencara doesn't report to you. I hired him."

Skultar opened his mouth, snapped it shut, and continued to read. "You didn't think it was important to tell me Brielle AsTar and her friends escaped. Yesterday, you were bragging about his successful capture of all of them and about his SorTech's latest discovery." He leaned back and tapped his chin with an index finger. "Let me see if I can remember." Tap, tap. "Ah yes, Callum…" He shot his brother a sardonic look. "That is the SorTech's name, correct?"

Karlsut didn't move. His already narrow features seemed to grow narrower.

"I'll take that as a yes." Skultar stood up, walked around the table, and stopped beside him. "If your SorTech is so smart, where are the companions?" He swiveled Skultar's chair to face him and rested his hands on the padded arms. "You—don't—know. We have now lost The MasTer and our leverage with the Universal VarTerel."

"We didn't lose The MasTer's gene. The geno-tech assured me that Vintrusie's son carries it."

Thorlu switched off the screen, donned his Mocendi's cape, and marched down the passageway to the conference room. The panel slid open. The brothers froze as he stepped through the hatch, his power radiating around him, his dissatisfaction broadcasting from every pore.

He glared from one to the other. "Where is Lieutenant Skylyn Halo Uranne? I understand she has been missing since yesterday morning."

Karlsut drew a series of circles on the tabletop with his index finger. "Why should you care? She has nothing to do with you."

Glad he had ordered the healing team who had done the Protariflee process to keep his involvement in strictest confidence, he glared down at Karlsut. "I have known Vygel Vintrusie since we were children together on El Stroma. He is the closest thing I have to a brother. What happens to his child is vitally important to me, especially now that he is so ill. Which one of you is responsible for her disappearance?"

Both men looked surprised. Neither appeared to be bothered by his scrutiny.

Skultar moved out of his brother's line of vision. His gaze fastened on Thorlu's, a warning in its depths.

Thorlu switched his attention to Karlsut. "Since we all seem to be puzzled, let's keep each other informed. I spoke with the boyfriend. He's as lost as we are." He took a seat. "What's the latest news from Yencara?"

Karlsut sneered. "He and his SorTech lost Brie and her companions. They all vanished. He promised he'd find them and bring them back." Disgust erased the sneer. "I rented the jumper craft for nothing. What a waste."

Skultar's mouth worked around a response Thorlu felt certain was caustic. He jumped in. "Since the *Surgentin* is back in orbit around Roahymn, I assume Yencara will return to the ship. When he arrives, I would like a word with him."

Karlsut bristled. "Why? He's working for me, not you."

Thorlu forced a smile. "He possesses something of Vygel's that I know he will want when he awakens."

Pushing himself to standing, Karlsut brushed by him and paused by the hatch. "I've had enough of you two." He wagged a finger. "No secrets. I'll know." Arrogance escorted him from the room.

Although fatigue threatened to drag him ever deeper, Vygel fought against it with the last of his remaining strength. Rewarded by the gradual ascent from his pit of darkness, he fought harder. A distant glow drew him upward. His eyes fluttered open. Confusion pressed them closed again. The sense of falling brought his senses to his aid. A soft hum enlivened his hearing. Numb hands tingled with life. He wrinkled his nose as the smells of the pod's interior assailed him. Light leaked beneath his lids.

He stared up at an oval window. Confusion hit him hard. *Where am I? Who am I? What happened to me?*

Blurry edges of darkness crept closer. *No! Not that nothingness.* He struggled against the bonds holding him still. A moan of pain escaped his chapped lips.

A male face peered in the window and disappeared. Time crawled by. An eternity later, a vaguely familiar face gazed down at him.

"Vygel, it's Thorlu. Look at me. I am your friend, Thorlu Tangorra."

Who is Vygel? Thorlu? Where—A cough shook his body. Spittle coated the window. The face called Thorlu disappeared. A woman took his place.

"Vygel, I am Healer De Dilliére. I am going to remove the top of your pod. Don't be afraid."

Humming accompanied the opening of the top. Cool air brushed his cheeks. A hand touched his wrist. The healer moved aside. A man in white released the bonds on his wrists and ankles. Gentle hands helped him to sit, wiped the spittle from his face, and changed his soiled gown for a clean one.

When he was once more prone in his clean pod, Vygel searched the faces of those who assisted him. He formed a word from recent memory, brought it to his tongue, and pushed it out with a breath between his lips. "Thorlu?"

A man moved to his side. "I'm right here, Vintrusie."

Vygel flinched, his eyes questioning.

The man bent over him. "You are Vygel Vintrusie."

Vygel examined the gray-green eyes, the dark blond beard and mustache. He noted the shoulder-length hair and the handsomeness of the features. "Do I—know—you?" The words emptied his lungs. He gulped in a breath.

The woman stepped into view. "It is time to rest, Vygel. Thorlu will visit again soon."

The man called Thorlu watched as the pod's top lowered into place. A sweet smell permeated the air. Sleep tiptoed over him.

Skultar Rados waited in a small cubicle for Thorlu to return from the infirmary. Impatient and edgy, he paced to the hatch. "Vygel is regaining consciousness." He frowned. "Is that good or bad?" He glared at the hatch. "Leave or stay?"

An answer to his question presented itself as the hatch slid opened and Thorlu Tangorra stepped through, selected one of two chairs attached to the wall, and sat down. "Vygel is awake but still unable to recall anything. Healer De Dilliére will keep us informed."

Skultar took the remaining chair and cleared his throat. "I'm the one who hid Skylyn, Thorlu. I was afraid Karlsut would do something stupid. The rise of The MasTer is vital to the success of our plans. The genetic team can duplicate the gene to place it in another subject." He cleared his throat. "When Vygel's baby is strong enough, I will become The MasTer's carrier." The note of defiance in his statement made him cringe.

Thorlu's expression did not change. "Would you have shared this with me if I hadn't discovered Skylyn was missing?"

Skultar considered the question, one he had ignored answering for himself until this moment. "I am certain I will not share it with Karlsut." His brow smoothed. "But, although I am unsure why, I am trusting you. Don't ask me to explain because I don't understand it myself."

The purple lining of the Mocendi's cape glistened as he sat back, his arms folded and his intense, gray-green eyes unblinking.

Fighting the desire to squirm like a child, Skultar forced stillness and kept his gaze steady. Thorlu, as an enemy, was not on his wish list. He cleared his throat. "I admire you, Thorlu. I would prefer to work with you rather than against you. How do you suggest we continue moving forward?"

"First, we have to figure a way to manage your brother. Karlsut is a comet on the loose. If we can't control him, we must put him under lock and key."

Skultar shook his head. "I couldn't control him when we were kids, and I certainly can't now."

Thorlu sighed. "I suggest we sleep on it. Before I go, where have you hidden Skylyn?"

"She's in a room made up for her in the crewmen's quarters. Three men, hand-picked by the commander, are standing guard.

"Excellent, Skultar. Let's meet tomorrow after breakfast and make plans for our favorite partner."

Skultar watched him go, dropped his face in his hands, and muttered, "What are we going to do with you, Karlsut Sorda?"

Thorlu hurried along the passageway. His goal—find Dee. He had questions that required answers, and she was his best bet.

At the infirmary, he checked on Vygel, was informed that Healer De Dilliére was in her cubicle, and hurried to her door. She opened the hatch with a polite smile that changed to a long, exhaled breath. "I was afraid it might be Karlsut." She stepped aside. "What can I do for you?"

He whispered in her ear. "We need to talk in private, but not in your special place. Will you trust me?"

She didn't hesitate before giving him an affirming nod.

He touched her shoulder. A cell surrounded them; a globe-light glowed above them.

She caught her breath and laughed softly. "That was my first experience of teleportation." Her eyes sparkled in the dimness. "Shall we sit?"

He drew her down beside him on the cell's only bunk. "I will come right to the point. Skultar informed me your team can duplicate The MasTer's gene and put it into another host. Is this true?"

"Yes, it is."

He looked her squarely in the eye. "This is very important. Can the genetic team remove the gene from the original host's DNA?"

Curiosity flashed through her cognac eyes. "Why is this important to you?"

"For two reasons. The most important to me is that my daughter may carry the gene. I don't want her to experience what Rayn and Brielle experienced."

She nodded. "Based upon what you've shared with me, that's understandable. What's your second reason?"

"If they can remove it from Brie, she can live a more normal life, and—" Emotions choked him. He swallowed. "I have a son named Troms el Shiv, whom I hope to get to know. Right now, he'd rather die than be near me. If

The MasTer's gene no longer haunts Brie, he might give me a chance to repair the rift between us."

Dee's beautiful face softened, and her eyes glistened with tears. "We can make this happen, but we need to bring Brielle to the *Surgentin*. The genetic team I work with here is exceptional. Do you think we can get her aboard without Karlsut and Skultar knowing?"

He leaned forward and kissed her forehead. "I'm certain we can. You understand that your joining forces with me puts you at risk?"

She smiled. "Can't think of anyone else I'd prefer to go to battle with. Did you discover where Skylyn is?"

A quick explanation of Skultar's hiding place made her arch a brow. "Can we trust him not to move her now that he has told you?"

"I believe we are safe for the moment. Let me take you back to your cubicle before I check on the mother-to-be."

She clasped his offered hand.

He did a mental scan, and they arrived by her desk. "Be careful."

A moment later, he arrived in his quarters to find Skultar pacing back and forth. At the sight of him, the harried man barked, "Where have you been, Tangorra? We have a problem, and I couldn't find you."

Thorlu noted his escalating frustration. "Sit down, Skultar, and tell me what's happened."

28

El Aperdisa

A frantic search through dark corridors lined with locked doors woke Brielle from a nightmare and left her gasping for breath. *Why am I running and who is calling my name?* Squeezing her eyes shut, she struggled to reconstruct her dream. Fragment by fragment, the puzzle came together. *It's Skylyn! She's in trouble.*

A quick cleanse later, she dressed and hurried to the dining hall, where the girls and Gar sat together at a table near the entrance. Gar waved. She waved back, then honored her unexpected hunger by filling her tray with tantalizing breakfast treats.

By the time she reached the table, Ari had pulled up another chair. "Sit and eat. We have lots to tell you."

Brie corralled her increasing agitation and made herself concentrate on eating. She washed a bite of crisp brown toast down with a long drink of juice and looked up to find her twin studying her.

Ari rested her elbows on the table. "Something's happened. Tell us."

Brie shared her dream. "Where are Esán and Torgin? We need to rescue Skylyn and Thorlu, and it can't wait until *El Aperdisa* leaves orbit."

Penee sipped from a steaming mug. "The boys are consulting with Commander Odnamo to see what his timetable is for leaving TreBlaya." She gazed at the tea in her mug. "Brie, I'm staying here with Rethson and Elf to wait for Den to return while you make the rescue run."

Ari rested a hand on her arm. "I'm staying here, too, Brielle. If anything goes wrong, Keersé will help to pinpoint where you are."

Gar walked around the table and stood beside her. "I'm going with you and the guys and Spyglass is staying with Penee and Ari."

Brie looked around the table at her friends. "You've been busy." She couldn't decide if she felt left out or relieved. The scar where the Star of Truth had been grew warm. "Oh."

Ari leaned closer. "Are you alright?"

Brie smiled. "I'm great. The Star reacted for the first time since the surgery." She hugged her sister. "Thanks for using Efillaeh on it. It may never return to its former power, but at least it seems like it has recovered a little."

A light gleamed in Gar's eyes. She looked up to discover Esán and Torgin smiling at her.

Esán kissed her forehead. "Did I just hear you say the Star is making itself known?"

She laughed. "You did. Good morning to you, and to you, Torgin. What did the Commander have to say?"

Torgin grew serious. "I suggest we find somewhere quiet. We've got lots to talk about."

Chairs scraping and the shuffling of feet ushered them into the passageway. Torgin led them to a conference room big enough for up to eight people. "The Commander had the hatch panel programed with our fingerprints, no one else can use it." He waited for everyone to take a seat. "Esán and I each have information to share."

Penee scanned the group. "Aren't Elf and Rethson joining us?"

"Esán, you're up." Torgin sat down.

"I spent the morning with them." Esán grinned. "We were in the Holographic Center. The Commander has given them permission to learn to fly a small explorer craft, one they will use once we are in orbit around El Stroma. They will remain here to continue their training."

The excitement in his voice and the twinkle in his eye made Brie consider interrupting to suggest he stay and continue the lessons.

He swiveled his chair to face her. "You, Torgin, Gar, and I are going on an important rescue mission, one I wouldn't miss for anything. We will use our gifts to travel through Mittkeer. The Commander informed us before we joined you that the *Surgentin* is once more in orbit around Roahymn. That will be our destination."

Gar wiggled, his excitement buzzing. "When do we leave?"

Torgin took over, his attention on Brie. "You've been through a lot. Since you are primary to the success of this mission—"

Ari's deep chuckle stopped him. "You sound like you're one of the crew."

He looked down his nose at her.

His unsuccessful attempt to control a smile made her shoot him a sheepish grin. "Sorry to interrupt. When do you leave?"

"Since Brie's been through a lot, the Commander suggests we make a preliminary plan, get some rest, and leave in the morning. He reminded me our plans must be flexible enough to change at a moment's notice. Also, *El Aperdisa* with remain in its TreBlayan orbit until we're back."

Brie listened with a half-smile. Although the seeds from the Wrené tree continued to replenish her energy, additional rest was vital. A wave of apprehension produced a shiver. Esán's arm around her steadied her. She leaned her head on his shoulder and sighed.

The rest of the turning crawled by. When Esán stretched out on the bunk in his quarters, he let out a long sigh and reviewed their tactical meeting and the resulting plan. The trickiest part—the exit from Mittkeer onto the *Surgentin* while it was in orbit. The Compass of Ostradio would be key to their success. He sat up and wrapped his arms around his bent knees. The weakest part—they'd arrived on the ship unprotected by a time fold. Once they stabilized, they would create one.

He sighed. "I dislike taking Brie aboard without proper cover, but..."

"You talking to yourself?" Torgin stood in the hatch. "I promise we will have everything in place, Esán. The time fold will happen. Don't worry so much." He plopped down on the end of the bunk. "Have you decided how to bring Thorlu and Skylyn to us in the fold?"

"The time whistle and Tumu Nnoci are central to our success. You will use the time whistle to create a vibrational change in the fold; I'll use the key to open a gate in the space-time continuum. Brie and Gar will teleport Thorlu and Skylyn into the fold, and we'll close the gate. How does that sound?"

"It sounds simple enough." Torgin touched the whistle on the lanyard around his neck. "Why am I not confident it will succeed?"

Esán laughed. "We both know things can go wrong, even when we do the right thing. At least we have the tools and the knowhow to adapt."

Torgin's expression grew distant. "I wish..." He sighed and shook himself. "Better get some rest. See you in the morning."

The desire to hold Brie left Esán sitting on the edge of the bunk.

"Are you awake?" Her telepathic question made him smile.

"I am. Want to meet?"

She flashed into being, took his hands, and pulled him to his feet. A long kiss later, she stepped back and studied his reaction. "I love you, Esán Efre. See you in the morning." As quickly as she had appeared, she vanished.

"I love you, too, Brielle AsTar."

A soft giggle filled his mind. Smiling to himself, he prepared for bed. Sleep overtook him almost before his head settled on the pillow.

~ Surgentin ~

Thorlu Tangorra glared at Skultar, his finger pressed to his lips.

Skultar huffed an exasperated breath and furrowed his brow. "I—"

For the second time, Thorlu patted the built-in sofa unit. "Sit."

"B-b-but—"

Thorlu mouthed the word "quiet" and mimed searching his pockets.

His mouth working, Skultar made a thorough search. Beady eyes snapped to Thorlu as he withdrew a thin, black disc the size of his thumbnail from his back pocket.

Thorlu took it and wrapped it in the corner of his purple lined cape. "We can talk now."

Skultar stared at the hand holding the offending disc. "Karlsut put that in my pocket, didn't he? That means he heard me telling you where Skylyn is hiding. What a rascal. What do we do now?"

"We don't let him know we found out about Skylyn. Tell me how you learned she was missing."

"One of her guards came to tell me. He was pretty rattled." He scratched his goatee. "There was a disturbance in the crewmen's quarters. When things settled down, Skylyn had disappeared. Have you discovered anything?"

Thorlu nodded. "I did a mental probe. Raiherr Yencara and his men are back from Tao Spirian. They arrived while you and I were meeting after Karlsut left."

Realization ignited. Skultar grimaced. "They created the distraction. No one knew they were back." He looked at Thorlu. "Karlsut has always been a conniving, spurious piece of work. Since I am emotionally entangled in this mess, thus unlikely to make the best decision, what do you think we should do?"

"Foremost, we let him give himself away. You stay out of sight for a bit. Let me do some prowling around. I'll report back when I can."

"What about the disc?"

Thorlu held it tighter. "I'm going to give it back. Then you'll tell me you have an awful headache, and I'll leave. Keep the disc with you. When I come to report in, hand it to me. I'll hold it until we're done with business, then give it back. Are you ready to moan about your head?"

Skultar held out his hand. Thorlu placed the disc on his palm and watched him slip it into his pocket.

A short time later, Thorlu observed Yencara climbing up the companionway from the landing bay. Vygel's cape draped around his shoulders rankled him in ways that surprised him. Reminding himself his primary goal was to find Skylyn, he obscured his presence by blending into the passage wall, allowed the arrogant Vasro to walk by him unmolested, and followed him. *You are only a first level DiMensioner. I wonder what Vygel's cape has done for you.*

Yencara slowed, glanced up and down the passageway, and ducked into an open hatch, closing it behind him.

Thorlu tuned his senses to listen. Karlsut, the other occupant of the space, spoke in a controlled voice. "I lost track of Skultar after Thorlu found him in his quarters. I'm sure they discovered Skylyn's missing."

Yencara sneered. "They know nothing. I erased the guards' memories of us. Relax. Thorlu is smart, but not that smart. Besides, why should he care about the woman and Vygel's baby?"

A silence weighted with strain followed. Then Karlsut, authority ringing in his voice, said, "When I am sure I can trust you, I will share his reasons and mine. Until then, keep Skylyn out of sight where I told you to hide her and don't hurt her. Am I clear?"

Thorlu could almost see Yencara bristling with irritation.

"You are clear." Faked respect dripped from each word. "If you will excuse me, I'll go check on her."

"I'll expect a report at the scheduled time." The panel opened. Karlsut Sorda stepped through and stalked down the passageway.

Yencara followed, watched his boss disappear around a corner, and strode the opposite direction.

Thorlu tailed him. At a companionway to the lower deck, the Vasro stopped. A casual lean against the wall allowed him to survey the passageway. Flicking the cape over his shoulders, he descended.

Rather than give himself away, Thorlu remained at the top of the steps, his senses attuned to Yencara. When he felt certain the man continued along the passageway, he followed. The man's energy signature, acting like a signpost, led him straight to the storage area off the cargo bay. Hidden by stacks of boxes and supplies, he discovered a well-disguised hatch.

Merging into his surroundings, he listened to the voices beyond the hatch. Skylyn's, the higher of the two, held his attention.

"Who are you? Why am I here?" Her voice was steady and uncompromising.

Yencara gave a harsh laugh. "You're pretty cheeky for a someone who is a prisoner."

Thorlu heard her move. The next moment, the sound of a fist hitting bone followed by a howl of surprise bounced off the walls. Not waiting for the Yencara's response, Thorlu touched the sensor. His presence filled the open hatch. Two startled faces turned his direction. Skylyn's relief was palpable; Yencara's surprised outrage flashed from the woman to him.

Thorlu motioned Skylyn to his side and whispered, "Go to Dee. Don't let anyone see you."

She nodded and slipped into the storage area.

Yencara, his eye already swelling, lunged. Thorlu caught him with an elbow to his jaw and shoved him deeper into the space. The panel closed, and they faced off in the light of a radiant lantern.

The furious Vasro glued his gaze to Thorlu and did not move. "Well, if it isn't Thorlu Tangorra, the only remaining MasTer's Mocendi, except for..." He flipped his cape over his shoulder to show the purple lining. "... me!"

Thorlu kept his expression devoid of emotion. "Mocendi Yencara has a nice ring to it." He waited for the younger man to preen and then bluster.

"You trained me well, Tangorra." He didn't cover the sneer in his words.

Thorlu looked down at the man, whose overblown pride bristled like porcupine quills. "I am certain you know that to steal another Mocendi's cape brings nothing but disaster to the thief."

Again, the man preened. "I did not steal it, Tangorra. I earned it."

"How? By taking it from a dying man; by trying to kidnap the youngest VarTerel in the Inner Universe; by holding a pregnant woman prisoner? You're a coward, Raiherr Yencara, and always have been. Give me Vygel's cape."

"Never. It's mine. Vygel is as good as dead. Besides, he liked me. Who better to inherit his most cherished possession?"

Thorlu considered his options, came to a quick conclusion, and raised a hand. Yencara doubled over, his features bulging with pain, dropped to his knees, then fell flat on his face. Thorlu touched him with a toe.

They arrived in the conference room to find Skultar waiting. Thorlu put a finger to his lips, pointed at himself, and shook his head. After removing Vygel's cape from the prone figure on the floor, he pointed at the unconscious heap and mouthed, "Be careful." Pivoting, he left.

Once in his quarters, he studied the cape. "Once upon a time, I might have done the same thing. You have so much to learn, Raiherr Yencara."

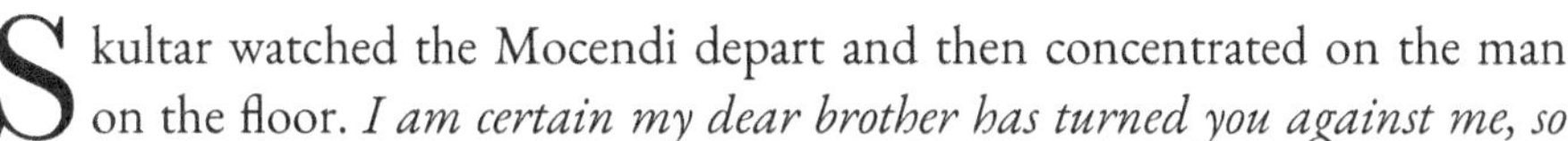

Skultar watched the Mocendi depart and then concentrated on the man on the floor. *I am certain my dear brother has turned you against me, so*

what do I do with you? Did Thorlu find Skylyn? Will I be safe with you once you are fully conscious?

The Vasro groaned, gathered his splayed limbs, and pushed himself to sitting. After touching his puffy eye with a tentative finger, he surveyed his surroundings. His gaze fastened on Skultar. A trembling hand reached for his cape. Hatred flooded his bruised features. "Where is my cape?"

"How would I know?" Skultar shrugged. "One minute I worked alone in the room; the next you appeared."

Yencara tried to stand but dropped back onto the floor, panting. "What did you do to me?"

Skultar laughed. "I did not touch you. Can I get a healer for you?"

The Vasro leaned against the wall, his breath coming in small gasps. "Where's Tangorra?"

"You have so many questions. Let's just wait until my brother gets here and then perhaps we can figure out what happened to you."

The slight swishing sound of the hatch panel escorted Karlsut into the conference space. He stopped short. His stunned gaze darted from Yencara to his brother.

His emotions well-hidden, Skultar, raised a brow. "Look who appeared out of nowhere. I don't suppose it occurred to you, Karlsut, to share that he had returned. I expect he has some things to tell us about his trip."

Again, Yencara attempted to stand. He arrived on his feet with white-knuckled hands gripping the edge of the table. A gasp of pain propelled him to the chair next to him. Collapsing into it, he fought to catch his breath.

With no hint of sympathy, Karlsut glared down at him. "How did you get here?"

The Vasro licked his lips. "I don't know."

Karlsut leaned closer. "I suppose you don't know *who* gave you the black eye either?"

Yencara rubbed his bruised jaw and flinched.

Skultar rose and crossed to the water dispenser. He filled a glass and placed it in front of Yencara. "Let the man have a few minutes to recover. Then I'm sure he will share with us."

As Karlsut reached for the glass, Skultar stopped him with a hand on his wrist. "Leave it there and let the man catch his breath."

An abrupt yank jerked the wrist free. "Don't touch me. And don't tell me what to do. Leave us." His tone suggested that not heeding his word would create more trouble than it was worth.

Folding his arms, Skultar shot his brother an unyielding glare. "You forget yourself. We are partners. I suggest you sit down, and when Yencara is ready to talk, we will both listen."

Artificial acceptance manifested in his brother's demeanor as he struggled to cover his desire to deceive. He sat down, twitchy fingers tugging at his earlobe.

The obvious need to distract his attention made Skultar even more alert and ready to react.

Yencara sniffed and wiped his nose with the back of his hand. "I need to rest. I'll give you a full report after I've slept."

Karlsut jumped to his feet. "Let me help you to your quarters."

"Sit down, Karlsut. No one leaves this room until we have heard Yencara's story. When he has shared what happened to him and where he hid Skylyn, he can go to his quarters and rest."

Like a spoiled child, Karlsut plopped onto his chair. Skultar watched him, calculating the risks associated with ignoring his older brother.

29

Surgentin

Thorlu went in search of Dee and Skylyn. At the infirmary, he checked on Vygel, whose condition remained unchanged. When Dee's cubicle and her quarters were empty, he descended the companionway and walked with ghost-like silence to the space where they had met before.

A mental probe pinpointed the women huddled behind a protective ward. Surprised and intrigued, he put an image of himself in Dee's mind. The panel slid open. A woman's hand pulled him inside. The closing click brought a relieved sigh from the darkness. The light from a small hand torch highlighted two pairs of eyes filled with abating dread.

His slight smile erased whatever remained. "It is good to see you both. Skylyn, you're a brave woman and an adversary to be reckoned with. I'm glad you're on our side. Dee, thank you for bringing her here." Sensing a flood of questions behind the women's relieved expressions, he cut them off with a shake of the head. "I'll tell you everything I've discovered after we find somewhere safer for you to hide. Is there a place unknown to Karlsut and Yencara, their gang of Vasro, and Yencara's SorTech? You know the ship better than I do. Any ideas?"

While the two women compared notes, Thorlu analyzed his unexpected response to Dee. *She intrigues me. I want to be near her.* His brow wrinkled. Surprise smoothed it. *Am I falling for you, Dee De Dilliére?*

Dee finished her conversation with Skylyn and looked up at him. "You look surprised."

He smiled. "I am. What have you two discovered?"

Skylyn spoke up. "The Metchalian rebel who sold the ship to you showed me a cell no one else is aware exists. Not only is it unknown, but the Metchalian stocked it with rations and water. They originally built it for smuggling political prisoners off their home planet."

As he expected, Thorlu heard nothing to suggest she lied. "Have you been there?"

"Yes. He took me to see it and to teach me the entrance codes."

"Good. I want to check it out before I take you there. Can you picture it in your mind?"

She smiled. "I can do better than that."

An image flashed into his thoughts. He swallowed a gasp of surprise and examined the woman who carried his child.

"I am Eleo Predan, Thorlu. When we have more time, I'll tell you my story. Right now, I feel Callum searching for me."

Thorlu nodded. "I'll be right back." He arrived in a cell containing bunk beds and a personal needs cubicle. Lockers lined one wall. The windowless cell door did not have a visible lock or sensor pad. Nothing set red flags flying, so he teleported, arriving in Dee's secret space to the sounds of Callum's voice in the passageway. Without hesitating, he teleported the women to the safe cell.

Skylyn grinned. "I am three generations removed from my Eleo Predan grandparents, so my talents are minor. Thank you for your help."

Dee examined the space, then bit her bottom lip. "Wouldn't we draw less unwanted attention if I continue my role as Head Healer?"

"My concern, Dee, is that Karlsut and Yencara will use you to get their nefarious needs met. Making the choice between saving you or Skylyn versus achieving something vital to all of us is not high on my list.

She appeared surprised.

Skylyn hugged her. "You are important to both of us and to the unborn babies I carry. Please stay here with me where it is safe."

Her uncertainty morphed into an accepting smile. "I'll defer to our group needs, but if Vygel worsens, he'll require my expertise."

"If Vygel needs you, I'll come for you, otherwise, hide here out of harm's way." Thorlu prepared to leave. "While you have time, answer Skylyn's questions. Explain about The MasTer and why the babies are important to our enemies. I'll answer any others after I check on what's happening with our enemies."

Skylyn touched his arm. "The SorTech found Dee's secret space. Your quarters are being watched as well."

"I'll be careful. Take care of each other." He teleported to Dee's office cubicle. Wards shot up around him, shielding him from the seeking energy of The Box. Callum, Yencara's SorTech, waited nearby.

Skultar, his thoughts blank, watched the two men opposite. His brother's deadpan suggested a devious plan in the making. Yencara's pain-contorted face covered his true thoughts.

Karlsut, his voice lathered with concern, sent a pitying gaze in his henchman's direction. "Shall I call the infirmary and request that a med-tech come and fetch you? I'm sure a healer can administer pain medication that will make you more comfortable."

The Vasro produced a feeble grimace that Skultar felt certain was fake. "I'm not sure I can make it on my own." He hunched over and tipped his head up to look at Karlsut. "You could take me, Karl. When I am better, we'll come back, so I can explain my injuries." An even more feeble smile flew Skultar's direction.

Skultar kept his demeanor pleasant. "Why don't you explain how you got the black eye, Yencara, and where you planned to hide Skylyn without informing either of us? I'm certain Karlsut would be interested."

Although Yencara appeared mystified, Karlsut's narrow features underwent a series of fast-forward contortions that stopped abruptly on suspicion. "You planned to move Skylyn without telling me?"

"Your brother is just trying to sew mistrust between us." Yencara whimpered. "You know I am loyal to you, Karlsut Sorda."

"If you are loyal to me, share how you got that eye and the bruise on your jaw."

Yencara squeezed his eyes shut, winced with pain, and moaned.

A pale gold light flared behind him. Thorlu rounded his chair, his imposing presence filling the room. "I suggest you tell them what occurred, Raiherr Yencara, or I will."

The Vasro writhed under his probing stare and whimpered. "I only remember waking up here."

Thorlu perched on the edge of the table. "Ah, Raiherr, you are just like your idol, Vygel. Prove that you are smarter—tell these men what happened." He leaked contempt into his expression. "You know I have little tolerance for liars."

Skultar circled the table to stand where he could observe all the players in the game. As kids, he and Karlsut played a Pheet Adolan board game, much like the Old Earth game of chess. He smiled at the Mocendi's gambit. Karlsut was about to lose, big time.

Yencara could feel the trap closing. He let out a moan as he struggled to sit up straighter. A glint in Thorlu's eye silenced any further attempts to gain sympathy. The Mocendi wouldn't hesitate to insure the pain was real. He glanced at the hatch. No escape there. He hiccuped a breath. Truth appeared to be his only option.

Noting the mocking expression on Skultar's face, Yencara doubted there would be any help from that quarter.

Get it over with, Raiherr. He bit down on his bottom lip, tasted the tang of blood, and swallowed. "I found Skylyn where you hid her, Skultar. She's a good bargaining chip, so I hid her from all of you." He touched the corner of his blackened eye. "She took me by surprise and gave me this. I didn't expect a fight, especially from that woman. Then Tangorra appeared and let her go. When I went for him, he hit me in the jaw with his elbow. I'm guessing he teleported me here. It also seems likely he stole Vygel's cape. I would have told *you* Skylyn's whereabouts, Karlsut." He folded his arms and glared at each member of his audience.

◉ ◉

Karlsut listened. Each admission was like kindling added to a fire. Fury threatened to overtake him. A dagger-filled look carried his animosity straight to his brother. "You hid Skylyn without telling me, Skultar. Now who is the traitor?"

Skultar's disparaging expression snapped Karlsut's mouth shut. Self-preservation kept him silent.

His older brother loomed over him. "This blame game is getting us nowhere, Karlsut. You continually forget our pledge. If I thought it would keep you out of trouble, I'd throw both you and your henchman in the brig." Disgust flared his narrow nostrils. "Go to your quarters and stay there. If you attempt to leave, the crewman assigned to guard you will escort you to the brig. Do I make myself clear?"

An adrenaline rush made Karlsut shake. "You can't lock me up, Skultar Rados. I am your brother and your partner." He rounded on the Vasro. "I trusted you, Yencara, and you betrayed me. I want you and your SorTech off this ship. I want—"

◉ ◉

Yencara sneered. "You are nothing to me but a simpering, whimpering moron." Pain exploded through his body, leaving him shaking and doubling him over. Thorlu touched his arm. Different walls enclosed them.

"Listen closely, Raiherr. Behave yourself or be gone. Your choice. You are in your quarters. If you leave them, I will escort you from the ship using methods I'm certain you will dislike. If you so much as open the hatch to Callum, I will destroy The Box and erase every single memory he possesses. DiMensionery is off limits until I tell you otherwise. It would be too bad if, like Vygel, you lost the use of your power."

Yencara cringed with another wave of pain and curled up on his bunk.

Thorlu vanished.

Skultar looked up as Thorlu reappeared. "I had Karlsut escorted to his quarters. You would think he would learn to discern friend from enemy."

Thorlu sat opposite him. "The pact with your brother has the potential to destroy you both unless you learn to work together."

Skultar scowled and gave an affirming tip of the head. "I thought if Karlsut and I made the pledge, it would help me control him." He sighed. A pensive thought narrowed his eyes. "Callum is as untrustworthy as Yencara or Karlsut. When the search team finds him, the commander has ordered him confined to quarters until they can remove him from the ship." Humor sparked. "Skylyn gave the Vasro that black eye. That must have taken him by surprise. Where is she and is Vygel's baby alright?"

"The baby is fine. You'll have to earn the privilege of more information."

His graying brow arced. "You don't trust me?"

Thorlu laughed, then sobered. "Do you trust me?" He vanished in a flash of golden light.

Skultar pursed his lips. "I'll let you know when I've decided."

Thorlu made a sweep of his quarters, found a mini-cam, and crushed it. Tempted to lie down and relax, he instead took off his cape, laid it on the end of his bunk, and sat down. His hand resting on the folds of the purple lining triggered a memory from his training as a Mocendi. He made himself relax, focused on the sensor panel by the hatch, and let his mind go blank. The memory rose again, this time in greater detail. A long inhale followed by a longer exhale brought it to the forefront of his mind.

He settled his cape on his shoulders and recited an excerpt from the training manual. "The cape of a Mocendi is tuned to the individual's energy signature. Capable of healing and/or easing pain, it can redirect molecules in the body."

Vygel's cape in hand, he strode to the infirmary and asked to visit the ailing Mocendi.

The young healer fixed her fearful gaze on his face and tipped her head toward a drawn curtain. "I'm sorry the patient is unavailable."

Thorlu motioned the young woman out of sight and lifted a hand. The curtain moved aside.

Callum stood looking down at Vygel, his hand resting on The Box next to the open isolation pod. His head turned. A sly smile of recognition gleamed. "Be very careful, Tangorra. I have wired your friend to The Box. If you want him to go on living, I suggest you put his cape on the end of the pod and leave."

Thorlu met the man's gaze. "My friend is dying. Put him out of his misery, and then you and I can decide what happens next. Of course, I doubt your partner, Yencara, will be happy when he hears you killed his mentor."

A minuscule flicker of insecurity vanished as quickly as it appeared. "You don't scare me, Thorlu. I am as powerful as you."

A sardonic laugh turned to a sneer. "You are a SorTech, Callum. I, my friend, am a Mocendi who has attained the rank of High DiMensioner. A contest with you would end almost before it began. Check The Box. It is no longer connected to my friend. It is, however, connected to you. Care to try it?"

Callum jerked around, reached for the sensors on The Box, and snatched his hand away. A gaze teeming with animosity transitioned to curiosity and darted to Thorlu. "How did you do that?"

The hatch to the infirmary opened. Two crewmen entered. The taller man reported to Thorlu. "We understand you require help to remove this man from the infirmary."

"I do. Please confined him to his quarters. Thank you for your quick response." Thorlu stepped aside. "If we meet again, Callum, and if you have matured beyond your need for hurting others, I may teach you a few things."

The SorTech glowered and reached for The Box.

"I wouldn't touch it if I were you."

Callum's hand hovered, then curled into a fist. Pressing it to his side, he allowed the men to escort him into the passageway.

Thorlu shook his head in disgust and then addressed the healer as she stepped from her curtained station. "What is your name?"

"Healer Adina, sir."

"You summoned the crewmen, correct."

She nodded. "The SorTech threatened to kill my patient and me."

Thorlu thanked her and then moved to Vygel's side. "I'm going to spend some time with my friend. Why don't you take a quick break? I promise not to leave his side until you return."

She closed the curtain behind him. He heard the panel open and shut. After disarming The Box and moving it to the floor, he spread Vygel's cape over his still body and sat down beside him.

30
El Aperdisa

Brie stared at her reflection in the small mirror in her quarters and imagined Ari smiling back at her. *I wish you and Penee were coming on the rescue mission.* As she tugged her curls into a ponytail, a warm tingling ran up her neck. Trembling fingers traced the small scar. *Healer De Dilliére thinks The Star might grow back.* Another tingle made her smile. Ari's work with the Efillaeh had begun the process.

The light above her door glowed. A glance at the viewer told her Esán waited outside. A thought opened the hatch panel.

He entered and studied her with an intensity that made her giggle. His growing smile lit his eyes. "How do you feel?"

"I'm much better. The Star is stronger. With luck, it will continue to heal. Are you ready for this?"

"As ready as I can be without knowing what's coming." He turned serious. "Listen, I just spent some time in the ship's science library, reviewing the latest information on the space-time continuum. What do you know about time crystals?"

Brie did a quick mental inventory. "Not much. Does it have anything to do with our rescue mission?"

Esán's brows scrunched together. "I'm uncertain, but it helps to keep quantum particles in consistent motion."

The entrance light glowed, and Torgin stepped through the hatch. "You two look serious."

Brie smiled. "Esán has been telling me about time crystals. Do you know anything about them?"

"I just finished reading an article describing their ability to control the flow of time at an infinitesimal level. I wondered if one might help stabilize the time fold." He held up a small quartz crystal. "So, I worked with one of the research scientists and, with his help, created this crude one by using a laser beam to reset the particles. I thought about trying to change your staff's crystal, Brie, but didn't. Accidentally creating difficulties getting in and out of Mittkeer would be disastrous."

Esán shot him an admiring grin. "You continue to amaze me, Torgin Whalend. Have you seen Gar since breakfast?"

"He's spending time with Penee and Spyglass. He'll meet us in the Holographic Center. Commander Odnamo believes that is the best place for us to enter Mittkeer. We can put up shields to obscure our exit from anyone watching from inside or outside the ship."

Esán put his arm around Brie. "We should be going. Do you have everything you'll need?"

"Yes, but I want you to know I left the Remembering Stone with Ari. Since Vintrusie requires it to bring The MasTer forth in his masculine form, it seemed better not to bring it with us. The only other thing I'll call forth is my VarTerel's staff when we are ready to leave the ship."

"Sounds good. Torgin, do you have everything?"

He touched his chest. "One time whistle, one compass, and one time crystal. How about you, Esán?"

"Tumu Nnoci and the VarTerel's stone are in my pocket." He touched the sensor, stepped into the passageway, and led the way to the Holographic Center.

Penee and Ari rounded a corner and hurried to meet them.

Brie looked from one to the other. "You're excited. What's up?"

Ari rubbed her hands together, her smile widening. "Our grandparents, Mairin and Lanli, came to find us. The Galactic Council asked them to train us in the arts of DiMensionery. They feel we are a danger to ourselves and others until we master our gifts. Elf and Rethson will join us."

Brie hugged her twin. "I am so excited for you." She held her at arm's length. "You sound comfortable learning more about your gifts."

"I'd rather know how to use my talents than risk hurting myself or someone else. Besides, even if I train in the arts of DiMensionery and chose not to become a DiMensioner, I'll have the knowledge to safely use my gifts." Ari planted a kiss on her cheek. "Be careful."

Gar, with Spyglass at his heels, jogged down the passageway. His eyes sparkling, he stopped by his friends. "When we're on the way to El Stroma, I get to train, too." Spectacles appeared in his hands. "I've got my specs, so I'm ready whenever you are."

After hugs all around, Torgin touched the hatch sensor. He and Esán entered the center. Brie waited as Gar nuzzled his terrier and then sat back.

"Take good care of Ari and Penee. See you soon."

Spyglass yipped and moved to Penee's side. Gar nodded and followed Brie. The hatched whispered shut, enclosing them in unblemished white. Shields shot up around them.

Torgin pulled out his compass. Brie's staff flashed into her hand. Gar placed his spectacles on his nose and adjusted the temples. Esán surveyed the group and nodded.

Brie lifted her staff. Musette's rainbow light pooled around them. Mittkeer opened. The Holographic Center changed to a terrene of night sky.

~ Surgentin ~

Thorlu watched Vygel with growing concern. As still as death, his lifelong friend lay in his isolation pod, seeming to grow paler and smaller. A buzzer on the panel sounded. Healer Adina hurried into the infirmary and straight to the wall of monitors. A thorough check brought her to Vygel's side.

"I need to close the pod in order to give your friend oxygen and run some tests. Do you know where Healer De Dilliére is? She should have heard the alarm."

Thorlu stood. "I'll find the healer, but first I require two things. Vygel's cape must remain with him. *No* one else may touch it except you, myself, and the Head Healer." He moved aside to show her The Box. "We need to hide this somewhere that only you and I are aware of."

Adina examined his face as closely as she had examined the monitors. "Healer De Dilliére trusts you, so I am going to follow her lead." She crossed to a monitoring station, moved the seat to one side, and pressed the toe of her shoe against the wall. A cavity appeared. "Put The Box in here. Since I am the only one aware of its existence, I need to show you how to access it."

After they stowed The Box, she pointed out a minuscule indent on the station wall near the floor. Thorlu touched it with his toe and nodded as the cavity vanished.

"Thank you, Healer Adina. Please tell no one that you trust me. It could get you hurt."

"I promise." Her gaze lingered on his face. "My first name is Marsili." She checked Vygel's monitors, pressed a call button, hurried to his side, and tucked his cape around him.

Thorlu paused by the hatch. The isolation pod's cover lowered and the team went to work.

~ Mittkeer ~

Gradually, Torgin's equilibrium stabilized, the nausea faded, and his blurred vision cleared.

Beside him, Gar grimaced. "I love Mittkeer, but getting here is yucky." He twisted to look around. "Something's weird." His spectacles flashed into view. He scanned the stars and frowned. "Anyone else feel anything?"

Brie gripped Esán's hand and pointed into the distance. Torgin's gaze followed. A luna moth detached itself from the night sky and alighted on Brie's shoulder. She listened with fixed attention, then nodded.

"The Sun Queen sent La to warn us someone is tracking us through Mittkeer. She says the tracker-signal began the moment we entered. Gar's spectacles, along with the key, will help to pinpoint its exact position. Until we've found and destroyed it, we're not to leave Mittkeer."

La's antennae brushed Brie's lips, then Esán's before she flew to Torgin and touched his cheek with a moth-soft wing. The frames of Gar's spectacles assumed the Sun Queen's ember glow as the luna moth hovered above his head. Her soft, parting squeak whispered through Mittkeer, and, with her, melted back into the night sky.

Esán withdrew Tumu Nnoci from his pocket. It grew to full size in seconds and emitted a reddish-gold glow.

Torgin, frustrated at his inability to help, shoved a hand in his pocket and wrapped his fingers around the time crystal. "I wonder if this might help?" It gleamed on his outstretched palm.

Musette's rainbow light shot shafts of color from crystal to crystal and then engulfed the key to the space-time continuum. A laser thin beam rocketed from the tip of Tumu Nnoci through Mittkeer.

Bespectacled eyes tracked it. Gar pointed. "Where the beam stopped, there's something the size of my fist." He started forward.

Torgin's hand on his shoulder pulled him up short. "No one goes closer until we have a better understanding of what we're dealing with. Stay here, but focus your spectacles in that direction."

Gar's gasp echoed through the darkness. "Got it. My spectacles are acting like binoculars."

Torgin faced his young cousin. "Your eyes are fire opals. The Sun Queen is helping you. Tell us what you're seeing."

Gar moved a few steps. "I'll put an imagine in your minds."

His irises and the frames of his spectacles blazed red and gold with touches of green. He gulped in air and pressed shaking hands to his heart.

Torgin gasped as an image formed. Brie aimed her Musette's light along the laser-like beam. Esán grew taller. Blue eyes glowing like the ocean after a storm, he flashed to the opposite side of the object. The beam from the key fashioned a light-constructed cage around a shiny black square.

The Compass of Ostradio throbbed against Torgin's chest. He pulled it free and held it next to the time crystal. The arrow spun into a blur and stopped, pointing at the glistening object. A low hum filling Mittkeer sent a second beam streaking from the compass and a third from Musette.

Gar's voice filled the night. "They all met and created a prison for whatever is there." He dropped to his knees. "I don't know how, but we have to remove it from Mittkeer." A quake shook his youthful body from head to foot. He scrambled to his feet, holding his glasses in place. "Esán, the Seeds know."

Torgin moved a step closer to him. "Hold on to me and keep telling us what's happening."

Opal-tinted eyes squinted. "A constellation's forming beneath us." His gaze widened. "It's a fire serpent with a gaping mouth. The Sun Queen sent it." He flinched, doubled over, then straightened. "Put the cage in its mouth and prepare to expel it from the Land of Time." Gar shuddered and clutched Torgin's pant leg.

Without hesitating, Torgin took command. "Everyone, create a mind-link with me." His gaze skimmed the group. "Now."

He felt them each connect. "Esán and I will hold the tracker in the cage steady. Brie, illuminate the fire serpent with Musette. Gar, keep filling our heads with information."

Brie shifted her staff and traced the shape of the serpent's gaping mouth with rainbow light.

Gar's images faded as the mouth, outlined in tiny, multi-colored flames, opened wider.

Torgin handed him the time crystal and pulled out his whistle. One long note suspended the cage directly above the mouth.

Esán's chest glowed ruby red. A tentacle of the ruby light writhed forward, wrapped around the cage, and dropped it into the fiery opening, where it burst into flame as the serpent's mouth closed.

Gar gripped the time crystal. "I know where to send it, Torg." He placed an image in his mind.

Torgin saw the heat of the desert rising over red sands. Prison walls in a box canyon came into focus. Words poured from his mouth into Mittkeer.

> *"Fire serpent, our enemy take*
> *To the desert of fire, where none are at stake.*
> *In a prison of death, let it expire;*
> *Its power undone in the depth of your fire."*

The serpent launched through the starlit space to the constellation of Uruao, the gateway to DerTah. A jagged tear formed in Mittkeer's vastness, releasing the fire serpent and its burden over the Desert of Fera Finnero to the prison in the Toelachoc Mountains. The Land of Time rewove its tattered edges into a seamless expanse of stars. Impenetrable silence gripped the never-ending night. No one moved.

A soft sob whispered. Gar hugged himself, rocking to the quiet pulsing of All Time and No Time. Black-rimmed spectacles disappeared. His trembling hands covered his face.

Brie, her staff in hand, walked over starlight and moonbeams to stand by the man she loved.

Torgin knelt, cradling his young cousin.

Esán, bemused by a sense of wonder, sought each companion. Their enemies had wanted them dead, or at least trapped forever. They had, instead, each discovered new powers and grown. He touched his chest. *The Seeds of Carsilem showed me a glimpse of my potential power.* Awe left him breathless.

He drew Brie into an embrace, holding her to his chest where the ruby light had glowed. She touched his cheek and gripped her staff. "Are you alright?" Her whisper blew a warm breeze over his cooling skin.

"I'm fine, just filled with wonder and curiosity. How about you? You and Musette breathed in the same breath. Your combined light stimulated the Seeds."

She nestled closer. "I know."

Torgin and Gar walked down a star-studded path to join them. For a moment, they all huddled in a group hug. Then Gar wiggled and peered from one to the other. "Did you see what we did together! I never saw you do the stuff you did before. I've never done what I did."

Brie smiled through her tears. "We need time to digest what happened. You were amazing, Garon. Torgin, you created a charm and so much more. Thank you for taking the lead."

Esán understood their amazement. "I wonder if the Sun Queen helped with what just happened to us?"

"Who can say?" Torgin grinned. "But I'll never forget it."

Gar handed him the time crystal turned to Esán. "Who was tracking us?"

He shook his head. "What type of device was it, and how did it get into the Land of Time?" Esán gazed into the distance. "Not just anyone can enter this land."

Torgin followed his gaze. "I wonder if one of us brought it from *El Aperdisa*? Could one of the Vasro spies the commander warned us about have planted it?"

The group stood together in the tranquility of Mittkeer. Esán could almost hear their thoughts seeking the answer.

31

Surgentin

Thorlu hurried along the passageway in search of a secluded spot from which to teleport. He slipped into an empty meeting space and created protective shields around him. A quick scan of the area and his destination satisfied him that no one watched. He teleported to the secret cell.

Dee stepped in front of Skylyn, then smiled as he dropped his shields. "You certainly get around."

He clasped her hand. "Vygel needs you, Dee. I'll bring her back as soon as I can, Skylyn." Shields shimmered and the empty quarters snapped into view. He studied his companion, once again surprised by the effect she had on him. "I'll leave you at the infirmary and hide close by. When you're finished, picture me in your mind and I'll come."

She returned his studied gaze. "You stay here. It's better if we're not seen together." Without waiting for a reply, she stepped into the passageway.

The truth of her words kept him from following. *You continue to amaze me, Dianna Divia De Dilliére.*

Vygel realized the muffled moans thrumming against his eardrums were his own and opened his eyes. Through the oval window of the isolation pod, he saw only the soft lights in the white-blue of the ceiling. He wiggled his fingers, then lifted a hand. *I'm not strapped down.* The folds of his cape sent a wave of gratitude racing through him. A flash of purple as he pulled it under his chin brought with it a surprised breath. *This is my cape. I am a Mocendi!* He sought his name, felt its tug from some deep place in his memory. His eyelids, fluttering shut, wrapped him in darkness like the folds of his cape. A name floated upward. *My name is...* Clarity dodged, dipped, and dropped from sight, leaving behind a groan of frustrated disappointment.

The light dimmed above him. "Vygel, it's Healer De Dilliére. Can you hear me?"

His eyes fluttered open. A blurred face in the window gazed down at him. He licked his sore lips, fought to find words, wondered if he spoke a language and, if so, what it was.

"Vygel, can you see me?" The woman's voice triggered a memory.

Her features took on shape and design. Dark curls framed a pretty, feminine face etched with the fine lines of middle age. The intelligence shining in her brown eyes suggested she would be hard to fool.

His hands clutched the fabric of his cape as he fought to understand where his memories had gone. A word formed. Again, he licked his lips. "Healer." The whisper ricocheted off the pod walls.

She smiled. "Good. Now you must rest."

A sweet scent wafted around him. A sense of peace sent him slipping into a deep and tranquil place.

~ Mittkeer ~

Brie contemplated the expanse of endless night, only half-listening to her friends trying to solve the mystery of the tracker. *Did I bring it with me?* Reviewing her movements left her shaking her head. She considered her companions. "Which of you was close to another person, besides one of us, before we met at the Center?"

Esán frowned. "I was in the library, using the reading screen." His bit his bottom lip, stared into the distance, and nodded. "Then I came here."

Gar cocked his head and furrowed his brow in thought. "I was with Penee and Ari until they left, so I could spend time alone with Spyglass. After that, I met you guys at the center."

Torgin stared at the time crystal on his palm. "I worked with the scientist to create this. When we were finishing up, a technician rounded the corner, bumped into me, excused himself, and hurried away. I'm betting he's our Vasro spy, and that he left something on me somehow, something with a trigger catch programed to release once we entered The Land of Time. I'm sorry I put you at risk."

Esán's mouth twisted with apprehension. "We left from the Holographic Center, so you had no way of knowing." He paced over stars and night sky, then turned. "We can't go any further until we alert Commander Odnamo that his spy is on the research team. It's too dangerous to leave the Vasro loose on the ship. I'll return to *El Aperdisa*, deliver the message, and come back here."

Brie shook her head. "We stick together. I'll send Ari a message."

"They'll be watching your sister, Brielle, but they might not be monitoring Penee." Torgin fiddled with the compass. "No one on board knows Gar's ancestry, so they won't be watching him either." He held up the time crystal. "What if we create a time fold paralleling the ship? We need the practice, right? Then, Esán can use the key to thin the wall so Gar can send Penee a telepathic message, and away we go."

Gar put his hands on his hips. "I think we ought to get it done. We have folks to rescue."

Brie marveled at the efficiency with which they all prepared to play their role as silent consensus propelled them into action. She raised her staff. "Everyone focus on Penee. Torgin, you take the lead."

He raised the time whistle to his lips. A long, steady note pierced the quiet of Mittkeer. Musette's rainbow light formed a shimmering tunnel vibrating with the note's frequency. Ostradio replaced the whistle in Torgin's hand. Tumu Nnoci's bow glittered as it formed shooting stars that skimmed down the tunnel to create the fold. Mittkeer grew faint. They stood in a replica of the Plantitarium. Below them, the girls sat on a bench, sharing a snack and chatting.

Penee looked up, her expression puzzled. Ari turned.

Gar stood beside Esán, ready to send his telepathic message. The key to the space-time continuum touched the fold's barrier. It wavered and thinned.

Torgin placed the image of the technician in Gar's mind; Gar placed it in Penee's with an explanation. When he finished, he opened the conversation to all his companions. *"Have you got it, Pen?"*

"I heard you, Gar, and saw the image. Go before you're discovered. We'll alert the Commander."

Gar blew out a sizable breath and grinned. "We did it."

The time fold vanished, leaving them in the vast stillness of the Mittkeer.

Brie turned to Torgin. "Please have the compass show the way to Vêrco, Roahymn's gateway. Once we're there, we can figure out how to board the *Surgentin*."

Holding Ostradio out in front of him, Torgin stated their need. The chart of Mittkeer took shape above the compass. "We're here beneath the constellation Riffley." A second group of stars on the chart glowed. "That is our destination point."

Brie clasped Esán's hand and waited for Gar and Torgin to move closer. Without seeming to move, they arrived beneath the gateway to Roahymn.

Gar plopped down on the star-spangled carpet. "I gotta catch my breath."

Torgin tucked the compass beneath his shirt and sat next to his cousin. "Since no time passes in Mittkeer, we won't be letting our friends down if we rest. In fact, we'll be doing them and us a favor."

Esán drew Brie down beside him. Her head resting on his shoulder, she allowed her racing mind to slow down and slip into restful quiet.

~ Surgentin ~

The tingle of DiMensionery caught Thorlu in the middle of thoughts of Vygel. His nostrils flared. *Yencara—*

Masking his mind and his movements, he made his way to the Vasro's quarters. The guard sat on the floor, his glassy eyes staring at nothing. A mental probe beyond the hatch panel confirmed his suspicions. *Where are you, Raiherr Yencara?*

Instinct pressed him further down the passageway. Karlsut's guard greeted him with a nod. Thorlu touched the sensor and entered his quarters to discover them empty. Alerting the guard to be on the lookout, he hurried to the conference room. Skultar sat at the table, his face in his hands. Karlsut, as Thorlu expected, was not there.

Skultar lifted his head. "The guard informed me Yencara and my brother are missing. No, I don't know where they are, although I expect they're searching for Skylyn."

Thorlu watched the man opposite him. "You realize your pledge may get you killed?"

"I do." He stood up. "How can I help find them?"

"Stay here. I've asked Karlsut's guard to report to you in half a chron-cycle. If anything disturbs you or if either your brother or Yencara shows up here, I'll know and return. You have not seen me, Skultar."

In the passageway, he created an invisibility cloak and hurried to the storage room off the cargo bay. Though empty, it tingled with their fading energy signatures. Stepping back through the hatch, he stood in silence behind a stack of containers. *Wish I could teleport. Can't. Yencara will sense it the moment I do.*

An image of Dee flickered in his mind and faded.

So did Dee send the image or did the Vasro?

Skylyn's voice whispered through his thoughts, *"Outside the cell."*

Torn but determined, he headed to the brig.

Yencara stood close to the entrance to the hidden cell. He ran a hand over the wall. "You are here, Skylyn. I can feel you."

Thorlu considered his options. *Appear and drag Yencara to a cell? Shield Skylyn—not without a distraction.*

Karlsut strode around the corner. "I'm telling you, she's not here. No one has seen her. I found Healer De Dilliére with Vintrusie. She hasn't seen Skylyn or Thorlu."

Yencara faced him, his expression one of disgust. "We can't trust De Dilliére. So, where did you lock her up?"

After a sputtered attempt to lie, Karlsut shrugged. "I didn't. I figure Thorlu will seek her out sooner or later, and we'll have him."

"How will we know if he does?"

"I have a med-tech on our payroll. He's keeping watch."

While the two men argued, Thorlu constructed a shield around Skylyn and hoped she wouldn't fight it. A telepathic thank you expressed her gratitude.

The angry growl of men's voices ended with Karlsut stalking away. Yencara replaced his hand on the wall and muttered. "Where did you go, Skylyn? I'm certain I felt you close by." A frustrated string of profanities filled the passageway. With more muttering, he marched toward the companionway.

The moment the Vasro had reached his quarters, Thorlu ducked into the cell camouflaging Skylyn's hideaway, entered the code on the invisible sensor pad, and allowed his cloak of invisibility to fade.

She smiled as he stepped through and lowered her protective shield. "I can put up wards, but they aren't as comprehensive as yours. Thank you."

"Tell me how you and the babies are doing."

"We're fine." Her hand patted the round of her belly. "They gave me a therapeutic drug to speed their development during the first trimester, so they are already almost three moon cycles. I should start feeling movement soon. How is your friend?"

"Vygel is struggling. I need to check on him and Dee. Let's see if I can help you strengthen your shield. It should be easy. Picture a curtain of light around you, then—"

A solid shield flickered into place. She grinned. "My gifts grow stronger along with the babies."

Thorlu studied her, then smiled. "We'll explore your gifts later. Use the shield only when you're sure you are in danger. Yencara is more adept than either of us would like to believe. If he comes looking, be careful. Wait until he's distracted if you can."

A snippet of Dee's face flickered through his mind. He frowned. "I need to go."

Careful to remain unseen, he made his way toward the infirmary. Down the passageway from Yencara's quarters, he stepped into visibility. The guard no longer sat on the floor. Thorlu approached and glanced at the hatch. "How's he doing?"

"He's still there, but..." Confusion infused the man's face. "I was monitoring our prisoner via a vid-screen when he started getting edgy. I thought he might try to leave, so I came to remind him he's being watched. The next thing I knew, I woke up on the floor. When I checked, he was in his quarters asleep, but…" The guard shook his head. "Something doesn't feel right."

Thorlu held up a hand for quiet. The man nodded. A mental probe later, he motioned the guard to follow him. At the curve in the passageway, he stopped. "Don't engage with him. If he leaves his quarters, get a message to me as soon as possible. If you can't find me, go to Skultar Rados. I suggest you get back to your vid-screen."

The guard nodded his understanding and left.

Thorlu confirmed Yencara's presence in his quarters, hurried to the infirmary, and peered through the observation window.

Karlsut stood over Dee. "Tell me where he is, Healer De Dilliére, or I will make you wish you had."

"I told you, he doesn't check in with me."

Karlsut's hand flew back.

Thorlu gripped it as he prepared to make his threat a reality. "Hitting a lady is below even you. What is it you need from me that is so important you would threaten the ship's Head Healer?"

Karlsut jerked his hand away and turned, hatred shredding any semblance of cordiality from his features. "Tell me where Skylyn is, or I will see that your lady friend pays the price."

Thorlu regarded the distorted face. "I was coming to ask you the same thing. She has disappeared yet again. Yencara is the most likely suspect. Have you asked him? I couldn't find him?"

Suspicion flared Karlsut's nostrils. "Are you suggesting that damnable Vasro moved her without telling me?" He marched to the door. "I'm going to make him sorry he ever boarded this ship."

Thorlu made certain the hatch panel remained close. "I suggest you cool off first. Go to the conference room, tell Skultar what's happening. After I check on Vygel, I'll join you. The three of us can put our heads together and decide the best way to deal with our rogue Vasro."

Skepticism gleamed in the man's eyes. "How do I know I can trust you? You're as big a liar as Yencara." He hit the sensor. The panel responded. "I'll find that woman and hide her where you'll never find her." He shoved past Healer Adina as she attempted to enter the infirmary. The panel closed on his retreating figure.

The healer acknowledged them with a nod and a whisper. "I'll keep watch."

Thorlu flipped the right side of his cape over his shoulder and faced Dee. "Please tell me how Vygel is doing."

She pulled aside the curtain enclosing her patient's cubicle. "Would you like time alone?"

He moved to the side of the isolation pod. "Stay and fill me in on his condition."

The curtain dropped closed as she moved to his side. She gave him a long, searching look. "The games you play are intriguing and dangerous. You realize you're putting yourself in danger?"

"I do." He gazed at Vygel laying in the shadowy interior of the pod, looking pale and unmoving, and sighed.

Dee spoke in an undertone. "He woke briefly, said "healer", and slipped back into unconsciousness. He is very weak. I seriously doubt if he will make it, Thorlu. You need to go to Skylyn. I'll stay here in case I'm needed."

A pang of anxiety made him grip the edge of his cape. "Yencara and Karlsut realize you and Skylyn are important to me. You aren't safe here."

Healer Adina stuck her head in. "I didn't mean to eavesdrop, but I think you should go. I'll stay with Healer De Dilliére." She held up a thin silver tube. "If either of them shows up, we'll be ready."

Thorlu noted the stubborn set of Dee's jaw and the powerful will shining in Marsili Adina's eyes and capitulated. "I'll be back when I can."

His long stride carried him down the passageway, his goal—the conference room.

32

Surgentin

Esán's hand on Brie's arm woke her from a gentle sleep. She yawned, stretched, and looked from him to Gar and Torgin, who sat studying the Sun Queen's book on the space-time continuum.

Climbing to her feet, she peered over Gar's shoulder. "Where did that come from?"

He held up his spectacles. "It appeared when I called these into being. Torg and I think there's something we're missing."

Esán handed her a nouri bar. "We've all eaten. I suggest you do so while you can."

Her stomach rumbled as she took the first bite. "Thanks, I needed this." An image of her mother in Idronatti flickered. *I hope you are safe.*

Torgin turned the page and continued reading. A soft 'ah-ha' suggested success. He glanced up, repeated something under his breath, and perused the next section. A satisfied nod preceded the book's closing and disappearance.

Gar gasped. "Wait. Where did it go? What if we need it again?"

"If we need it, I bet it will reappear with your spectacles." Torgin grinned. "Right now, I understand what we need to do to exit Mittkeer onto a moving object. Between us, we have everything necessary to make it happen. The time crystal is the key."

Brie swallowed the last of her snack. "Care to explain?"

"Sure. The compass will pinpoint the *Surgentin* and track it for us. Gar, with his spectacles on, will hold the time crystal and focus on our destination. A single note on my whistle will stabilize the crystal's vibration and suspend the ship in time. Tumu Nnoci will open the way. Brie and her staff will take us from Mittkeer through space-time. We just need is to confirm a destination point on *Surgentin*. Once we have that, we're ready to go."

Fascination glimmered in Esán's expression. "What a mind you've got, Torgin Whalend! You take the lead. Any thoughts on where we should end up?"

Torgin looked at Brie. "You explored the ship when you were in the time fold. We need a place that's spacious but also people-free."

She reviewed her search. Instinct focused her attention. She smiled. "Our best bet is the storage room off the cargo bay.

"Good." He gazed around the group. "Are we ready to go adventuring?"

Brie called forth her staff. "I'm ready."

Esán withdrew Tumu Nnoci as Gar settled his spectacles on his nose and accepted the time crystal.

Torgin held out the compass. "*Surgentin* cargo bay." The gold need spun. An aerospace architect's drawing formed with an area circled in blue. "Got it." He played a steady note on the time whistle.

"The crystal's vibrating and getting warm." Gar gulped.

Brie put an image of the cargo bay in his head. "Tell us when it is in focus."

Mittkeer's silence deepened. Gar's breath quickened. He nodded. "Now."

Tumu Nnoci's bow glowed. A shooting star flashed, circled them, and vanished into time.

Musette's light blazed, blinding them with vibrant rainbow colors.

Gar's moan brought them to their senses. The light faded, leaving them crouched at the back of the cargo bay.

A hatch opened and closed. Low, angry words bounced off the wall. "I told you, Karlsut Sorda, I—did—not move Skylyn anywhere."

Another voice murmured. A snarled response changed to a growl of dislike. "Thorlu suggested I hid her? Karlsut, you idiot! Ever heard the phrase divide and conquer?"

Brie peeked around a stack of boxes.

A man's silhouette filled the open hatch. "You coming, idiot?" Yencara moved into the shadows.

Karlsut Sorda followed. The hatch shut.

Esán's soft 'sh' kept the companions silent.

The hatch whispered open.

E sán recognized the voice. Raiherr Yencara crept toward them. *I can't use telepathy or teleport my friends.*

"Time fold." Brie's barely discernible message brought the companions into a close huddle, their skills merging, their knowledge preparing the way.

A time fold forming created a ghostlike shimmer in the dark space. Quiet footsteps made Esán turn his head. The time fold wavered. He forced his attention back to the process at hand. *If we could bring it into being—*

Brie gave a sharp gasp and fumbled for his arm. He felt her yanked backward. Before he could respond, the fold solidified. He and her friends stared down at her, held captive by the would-be Mocendi.

Y encara flashed a hand-beam. Light flooded the area. "Where are your friends?"

Brie jerked free of the hand gripping her arm. "Not here." The Star's warmth almost brought a smile. She covered it up with a carefully worded demand. "I came to see the ship's Head Healer."

A laugh echoed through the storage bay. "What you want is of no interest to me, youngest VarTerel in the Universe. You are now my prisoner. I don't know where your friends went, but I suggest you get them back here." Again, he grabbed her arm. Half dragging her, he maneuvered her to a well-camouflaged door. "I believe you will find this little hideaway to your liking. If your friends don't come back, I will make certain you regret it." He shoved her inside and locked the hatch sensor.

Brie blanked her mind and held herself statue-still. Yencara's mental probe swept through the cell. His failed attempts to invade her thoughts allowed her to gauge his level of talent and training. Although his energy suggested a low level Mocendi DiMensioner, something had elevated his abilities enough to make him more dangerous.

A recent conversation with Esán nudged her memory. *Oh, yes. He told me he had worn a Mocendi's Cape on Tao Spirian.* Focused again on Yencara, she discovered his festering anger over the cape's return to Vygel Vintrusie. Withdrawing from his mind, she scanned the cargo bay. Karlsut Sorda waited in the shadows. A quick probe of his mind gave her a scrambled sense of what had occurred since she left the *Surgentin.*

Armed with the information she required to begin her search for Skylyn, she teleported, leaving Yencara behind, howling in frustration at the empty cell.

E sán felt almost as frustrated as the man below them. *Where have you gone, Brielle?*

"Ship's library."

Torgin turned. "Did I just hear Brie say she's in the ship's library?"

"You did. Now what?"

Gar's magnified eyes peered at the storage bay. "We could wait right here so she knows where to find us."

The Compass of Ostradio gleamed in Torgin's hand. "Or we can explore the ship, starting with the library. We know where the infirmary's located, but not how to get there. What are you thinking, Esán?"

Esán stared at the cargo bay, then nodded. "We learn as much as we can about the ship. And keep our eyes open for Skylyn and Thorlu while we do it."

Torgin directed the compass to show them the library. The plans of the ship materialized with the library highlighted. "I'll guide you. First, we cross the cargo bay and take the companionway to the next level."

Gar, his spectacles still in place, led the way.

Esán followed, absorbing every detail and marveling at how the time fold mimicked the dimension in which Brie now roamed.

⚬ ⚬

Brie waited in the quiet library to make sure that if Yencara could track her, he would end up there. When she felt certain he had lost her, she teleported to a storage cubicle across from the infirmary. A mental scan of the area assured her it was safe to approach the observation window. Healer De Dilliére and a younger female with a healer's insignia on her tunic were the only two in the area. Brie pressed the sensor, observed a light flash at the Head Healer's station, and waited with her impatience roiling upward.

The younger woman checked the view screen beside the hatch and hurried back to Healer De Dilliére, who glanced at Brie's image. Surprise ignited, then vanished as she hurried to open the hatch. Without speaking, she motioned Brie into a curtained cubicle. After quietly instructing her companion to stay alert, she slipped between the curtains.

Urgency filled her quiet undertone. "How did you get here? If Karlsut and his partner find out, you will be in grave danger."

Brie replied in a whisper. "My friends and I came to rescue Skylyn and Thorlu. Yencara snatched me as the time fold we were creating formed. My friends vanished into it. The Vasro locked me in a cell. Fortunately, he didn't stop to think I might have more power than he does."

Healer De Dilliére shook her head. "I doubt if he recognizes anything but his own. You must find your friends and have them remove you to the time fold. I'll let Thorlu know you're close by."

Brie smiled. "I thought you might help." She took a breath. "Please tell me where to find Skylyn?"

The healer shook her head and leaned closer. "Can't talk here. Please get yourself to safety. Thorlu will tell you when he can."

Healer Adina's voice penetrated the curtain. "May I help you, Vasro Yencara?"

"I want to see Vintrusie." The demand was less than polite.

"One moment, while I check to see if you're on his permitted list of visitors." A brief scuffle insured.

"Ouch." Yencara yelped. "What did you do to me?"

Brie peeked between the curtains as he staggered, then dropped to his knee and toppled onto his side, unconscious.

Healer De Dilliére motioned Brie to stay and stepped from the cubicle. "Marsili, keep watch." She hurried to her station. The emergency sensor for intruder flashed green.

When Thorlu arrived in the conference room, Karlsut sat at the table with his forehead resting on folded arms. Skultar glared at his brother with a look of sheer disgust.

At Thorlu's entrance, he straightened and sneered. "I bet you didn't even try to find that traitorous Vasro, did you?" A hard look from Thorlu snapped his mouth into a thin line.

"Karlsut, you have a choice to make. Work with Skultar and me, or we will end your charade."

Karlsut scowled. "You can't touch me. Anything you do to me will impact my brother. Why don't you just leave us to make our own plans. In fact, why don't you leave the ship for good?"

Skultar's dislike for his brother chilled his expression. He turned to Thorlu. "You wouldn't know how to undo the Pheet Adolan Pledge of Honor, would you?"

With a purposeful lift of his arm, Thorlu flashed his cape's purple lining in Karlsut's line of sight. Thorlu narrowed his eyes and regarded one indignant face, and then the other. "As it so happens, I do."

Karlsut jumped to his feet. "Just because you are a Mocendi, you think you are all powerful. You don't know everything, Tangorra. You can't break the pledge. No one can. It says so in the ancient texts, so there."

Thorlu raised a hand. Confusion replaced Karlsut's red-faced anger. The brig materialized. The astonished young crewman standing watch lurched to his feet. "What the—"

Thorlu silenced him with a frown. "I want this man locked in a cell until I tell you to set him free."

The crewman looked doubtful.

Not giving him time to speak, Thorlu said, "If I find him anywhere but in his cell, you will answer to the ship's commander."

Still looking uncertain, the crewman led the way to an empty cell. Thorlu escorted Karlsut to the bunk, where he moaned and buried his head in the pillow.

Outside the locked door, Thorlu faced the younger man. "No one but you, me, and commander may know this man's whereabouts—not his brother, not the Vasro or his SorTech—no one. Understood?"

"Yes, sir. I understand."

Thorlu took a step closer, his stern gaze making it clear he meant what he said. "Swear, on your honor as a member of *Surgentin's* crew."

A swallow bobbed the crewman's Adam's apple up and down. "I give you my word."

Mocendi cape flaring, its purple lining glinting a warning, Thorlu turned on his heels. Once in the companionway, leading down to the brig, he teleported.

Skultar stood as he materialized. "What did you do with Karlsut?"

"He is safe until we can decide the best way to neutralize his lack of judgement. Are you still interested in dismantling the pledge?"

Skultar pinched the bridge of his nose and sat down. "I only made it to keep Karlsut under control. Obviously, it hasn't worked, so, yes, please undo it. How can I help?"

"You swore the Pheet Adolan Pledge of Honor, correct? Repeat it for me."

An exhale later, Skultar recited:

> *"With this pledge, we're bound forever*
> *To support and share, forsaking never.*
> *Our destinies, lives, and successes are one.*
> *If this promise is broken, both are undone."*

Thorlu listened with a touch of misgiving. "This may be painful as it unwinds from your essence. Are you prepared to undo the pledge for yourself and for Karlsut?"

Skultar did not hesitate. "I am. By being bound to him, I'm putting all of us on the ship in danger. I must be free to do what's best rather than wasting time fixing the problems he creates."

"Alright. You will say the pledge and then repeat after me. Are you ready?"

A slight pause, an inhaled breath, and Skultar repeated of the pledge. When he finished, he paused, his gaze uncertain.

Thorlu settled his cape more comfortably on his shoulders. "I'm uncertain what will happen, Skultar. I suggest you sit down."

Narrow features twitching, he took his seat.

Thorlu's grey-green eyes held his gaze. "If you are ready, nod."

A nodded response came without hesitation.

"Repeat after me. I, Skultar Rados, am aware of the consequences of breaking this pledge. I do so for the good of all concerned." Thorlu paused before continuing.

> *"Unbind that I may support and care,*
> *A task Karlsut has chosen not to share.*
> *Our destines must be our own.*
> *The promise broken, leaves us alone."*

As the last word faded, pain ripped across Skultar's face. He pushed away from the table, hugged himself, and groaned. Terror filled his gaze as he sought Thorlu. Shaking hands gripped the table's rounded edge. Knuckles whitening, he pulled himself to standing, threw his head back, and howled. A tortured sob sent a tremor throughout his body.

The room grew still. As suddenly as the pain had begun, it ceased. Skultar stared at his steady hands, then wiped the tears of agony from his face. "Will Karlsut have felt this?"

"No. He will not know we have rescinded the pledge unless you or I tell him. I suggest we keep it to ourselves. It may temper his actions a little."

The sensor light above the door flashed. Thorlu, sheltering Skultar from view, opened it. A med-tech gave him a short, urgent message and hurried away.

"I have to go, Skultar. You get some rest and I'll contact you later." He stepped into the passageway, created an invisibility cloak around himself, and made his way to the infirmary.

Torgin, Esán, and Gar explored the ship and now stood in the time fold replicating the infirmary, their attention glued to the man sprawled on the floor. They discovered Brie hiding in the curtained cubicle next to him. Esán's need to act felt like fists pounding at Torgin's side. He pulled his gaze from Yencara.

"Esán Efre, calm down or they will sense us three dimensions in all directions. Let the Healer deal with Yencara's removal, then we will bring Brielle to us."

"I thought the Healer summoned help." He clenched and unclenched his fists, his stormy gaze darting from the hatch to the man.

Gar, his spectacled eyes fixed on Yencara, frowned. "I think the Vasro guy is coming around."

The younger healer slipped behind the prone Vasro, a slender, silver syringe in her hand. She caught the Head Healer's eye and received an affirmative nod.

Yencara groaned and pushed up to sitting. She stepped closer. His hand shot out to grab her tunic. As he pulled her to her knees, she pressed the syringe to his neck and scrambled out of reach. Profanities filled the space. He tried to stand and fell back to his knees.

The panel slid open, and two guards stepped through. The leader spoke to Healer De Dilliére, then turned around as Yencara crumpled to the floor.

Together the guards half carried, half dragged the Vasro from the infirmary.

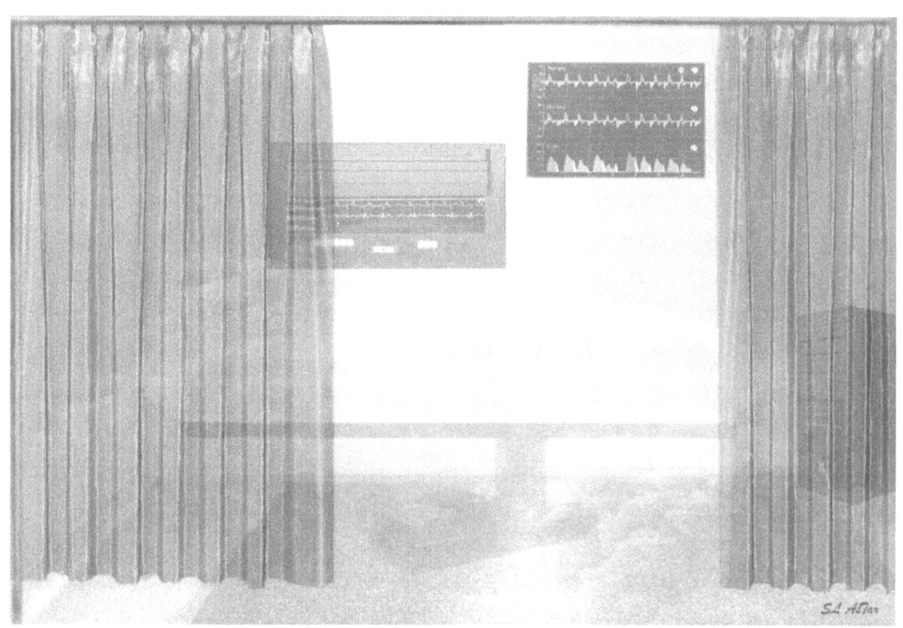

33

Surgentin

Thorlu arrived in time to watch Yencara's removal. He spoke to the crewman in charge. "Please lock him in the brig and inform the commander we spoke and where the prisoner is. Tell no one else."

"Yes, sir."

He waited for the crewmen and their prisoner to round the slight curve in the passageway before entering the infirmary. Surprise and then relief made him smile at the red-haired twin who stood in a cubicle half hidden by the partially open curtain.

Without acknowledging her presence, he addressed the Head Healer. "How is Vygel doing?"

Healer De Dilliére motioned him into Vintrusie's cubicle. "Periodic returns to consciousness and steady vitals suggest he is doing better. We're keeping him under close observation to make sure he continues to progress. His cape seems to help him, although I am uncertain how much."

She touched the instrument panel and spoke in an undertone. "I have alerted my genetic team to standby. Her friends..." She indicated the next cubicle. "... are close. You should talk with her, so she can inform them if her decision is to move forward."

Thorlu flashed her a gratitude-filled smile. "Please stay here." His murmur shifted to a normal tone. "Thank you for the update, Healer De Dilliére. I'll check in later in the turning to see how Mocendi Vintrusie is doing." He left the infirmary, wrapped himself in a cloak of invisibility, and returned. Slipping into Brie's hiding place, he touched her arm.

The next instant, her friends surrounded them. Esán embraced her, grinning his delight and relief.

Thorlu became visible and, to his surprise, found himself welcomed with warm smiles from everyone. He looked around. "Are we in a time fold?"

Torgin, who had been studying him the whole time, glanced at Esán and Brie, then returned his attention to him. "We are. Thank you for helping us transfer you both into the fold."

Thorlu's brow arched in surprise. "What did I do?"

Esán released Brie. "Your invisibility cloak allowed us to move you unobserved by anyone watching the infirmary. We would have created a distraction if you hadn't been there. This way no one is the wiser." He put a protective arm around the twin. "We're sorry about Vygel, Thorlu."

Acceptance, something Thorlu had not experienced since before The MasTer's initial appearance, brought a series of emotions to the surface. Gratitude, a sense of inclusion, and a desire to live up to his past ideals made him slightly dizzy. He steadied himself and focused on the present. "We have things to discuss. Do you want to talk here?"

While Torgin, Brie, and Esán conferred, Gar gazed at him from behind black-rimmed spectacles and grinned. "You don't look mean anymore." He tipped his head. "Hey, guys, the Mocendi has really changed."

Brie put an arm around him and gazed up at Thorlu. "Chealim's faith in you is well-founded, Thorlu. We're glad to have you as an ally and friend. Let's get comfortable and talk here where we can monitor Dee and Vygel."

Torgin reclined in a chair by the instrument panel. Esán and Brie sat on the cot in one cubicle, while Gar pulled the curtain in the adjacent one, plopped down on the cot, and patted the spot next to him.

Thorlu sat down. Navigating through his response to their observation, he looked from one to the other. "What is your most pressing need?"

Brie spoke up. "Do you know where Skylyn is hidden?"

"I do. She's safe, for now." He gave a brief description of events on board the *Surgentin* since his return to the ship. "I have an important question to ask you, Brielle AsTar."

She responded by returning his steady gaze with one of her own. "I will do my best to answer it."

"Healer De Dilliére has put her genetic team on standby. They are ready to remove The MasTer's gene from your DNA."

Brie caught her breath. Her chestnut brown eyes widened. She glanced at Esán and back. "They can do that?"

"They can, but we must leave the time fold for them to accomplish it."

Torgin studied the instrument panel and glanced around the time fold's infirmary. "This ship is identical to the *Surgentin*. What do you all think about bringing Healer De Dilliére and her team here? They could do the removal, and then we can return them to their dimension."

Thorlu leaned forward. "Which brings me to another topic." He paused. "I would like Dee, Healer De Dilliére, to return to *El Aperdisa* with us. She will be in grave danger if we leave her here and—"

Gar grinned. "You love her."

Thorlu glanced down. The realization the young people were all smiling at him brought a slight blush. "I do love her." He smiled at Gar and at finally admitting his feelings. "You are a perceptive young man."

His grinned widened. "I like you, Thorlu."

A chuckle shook Thorlu's chest. "I like you, too, young Gar."

Torgin raised a hand for quiet. "Something's happening on board the ship."

Attention switched to activity in the infirmary below them. A med-tech ushered Callum into the area and pointed at the Head Healer. "She's the one who ordered him taken away." He shot a belligerent sneer in her direction. "She can tell you why."

Thorlu swore. "How did Callun escape from his quarters? I need to be there now. You can bring me back when things have calmed down."

The group huddled. The VarTerel's staff appeared. Esán withdrew Tumu Nnoci. "We'll keep track of you. You'll go back to the cubicle."

Thorlu had no time to think. Without seeming to move, he felt the brush of the curtain against his arm and heard the haughty voice of the med-tech.

H er mind racing, Brie hardly noticed Thorlu's departure. *They can remove The MasTer's gene. I'll be free to live without the constant fear of his anger overpowering me. My babies won't have to grow up with that haunting them. I can't*—Tears streamed down her cheeks.

Esán sat down and put an arm around her. "The potential removal of the gene must feel huge after everything you've experienced." He released her enough to see her face. "Brie, it may not happen, at least not right now. Skylyn and Thorlu need to be rescued and we have to escape the *Surgentin*. If we can find and bring the genetic team aboard, we will."

Hope fled. Pushing her emotions into the background, she wiped the tears away. "I understand." She hiccuped a breath. "Let's keep our eye on what's happening so we can be ready to bring Thorlu and Skylyn to us." A stray curl fell over her forehead. She smoothed it back from her face and sighed. "I'm certain Thorlu is correct in believing Dee will be in danger if we leave her behind." The desire for time alone overwhelmed her. "I need a moment."

She wandered into the passageway, found an empty cubicle, and sank into a chair.

E sán watched her go with a sense of desperation. *I love you, Brielle AsTar. We'll make it happen.*

He turned to find Torgin, eyes filled with sympathy, observing him. "We'll figure out a way to rid her of the gene, Esán, especially since we know it is medically possible. But now, we have things to accomplish. Look."

Below them, the SorTech snarled at the young healer who flinched and stepped from his line of vision. Narrowed hate-filled eyes swept back to Healer De Dilliére. "Where did you send Yencara?"

Dee gave him a calm, cold once-over that made her observers grin. "He threatened me, my assistant, and Mocendi Vintrusie. I had him removed. Ask the men who came to our assistance where to find him. Now if you will excuse me..." She faced her screen. The green light flashed.

Callum yanked her around to face him. "Do you know who I am? I can make you miserable for the rest of your life."

Thorlu stepped free of the cubicle. Mocendi purple flashed. "Release Healer De Dilliére, Callum."

The SorTech whipped her around with her back against his chest, a muscular arm encircling her ribs. "I suggest you back off, Thorlu Tangorra." He flashed a fierce scowl at the Mocendi. "You stole The Box—my box. Return it, or I will make your lover, here, suffer."

Thorlu glanced to the side, caught the Healer Adina's eye, and returned his attention to the SorTech. With placid amusement infusing his persona, he smiled a lazy smile. "I'm honored that you think Healer De Dilliére would consider me as a lover, but she is simply a professional charged with the care of my friend. Let her go, Callum. You and I will discover where Yencara is and discuss where The Box may have gone."

The med-tech, who had cornered Healer Adina, gave a surprised squawk and stumbled to his knees.

Callum's attention wavered. Thorlu gripped the wrist holding Dee, twisted it, and jerked his arm to the side. As Dee ducked free, he yanked again, dislocating the SorTech's shoulder as he twisted the arm behind his back. A pain-filled shriek left Callum gasping for breath.

Thorlu forced him to his knees. "You have a choice. I can leave you in pain for the rest of your turnings, or you can, like your pal, wake up with just a headache."

A whimpering Callum glared at the prostrate med-tech, struggled to free himself, winced, and grew still. "Give me the drug." He wiggled to glare at Thorlu. "I'll make you sorry you ever touched me." The drug took effect. He joined the med-tech on the infirmary floor.

A growing sense of unease made Torgin fidget with the compass. "Something is about to happen. Gar, go find Brie. Esán, prepare to use Tumu Nnoci."

Gar scurried from the time fold's infirmary in search of Brielle.

Esán withdrew the key. "Any idea what's alarming you?"

"It might be Yencara or Karlsut..." He shook his head. "They're both locked up, right?"

Brie preceded Gar through the hatch. She froze, her attention on Dee. "Something's wrong."

Gar's spectacles appeared, their rims like shimmering embers. He placed them on his nose. Fire opal eyes flashed to the scene below. "There beneath the instrument panel."

Tendrils of smoke writhed along the floor.

Brie's staff materialized. Her heart pounded. "We have to bring them into the time fold. Be ready."

"Thorlu, invisibility cloak now!" Her telepathic message triggered his immediate response.

Thorlu urging Dee and Healer Adina ahead of him into Vygel's cubicle, he pulled the curtain. A cloak of invisibility wrapped around them all as Yencara flashed into view, glanced at the prone SorTech, and scanned the space.

"I know you're here, Thorlu." He strode toward Vygel's cubicle.

Brie gave the signal. The curtain wafted. Yencara yelled, "No!"

The group materialized in the time fold. Dee moved to the side of the isolation pod and studied the information screen. She glanced back at Thorlu. "Is this the time fold?"

"It is. Why?"

"Thank goodness." She checked the instrument panel. "Vygel would not survive without the pod."

Gar pointed. "Look."

Smoke filled *Surgentin's* infirmary. Yencara staggered, gripped Callum by the armpits, and dragged him into the passageway. Flames engulfed the instrument panel. A hazard alarm sounded. Red lights flashed.

Two crewmen sprinted to the hatch. One grabbed a flame douser from the wall and worked on putting out the fire. The other dragged the med-tech out of danger, grabbed a second douser, and sprayed the smoking curtains.

Thorlu turned to Brie. "Now is the time to rescue Skylyn. The fire will keep them busy. It won't take Yencara long to realize she is next on our list. Can Dee and Marsili stay with Vygel?"

Torgin took charge. "They can stay here. We will go with you. Take us to her hideout in the fold and we'll bring her to us."

Thorlu regarded the group. "Is it safe to teleport in this dimension?"

Brie slipped a hand into Gar's and moved to the Mocendi's side. "It is."

A moment later, they stood gazing down at Skylyn. She stood, peered around the hidden cell, and frowned.

Torgin gathered his team. "Ready?"

Brie turned. "Will it hurt the babies to bring her into the fold?"

Thorlu shook his head. "I asked Dee. She said Skylyn and the babies will be fine. Hurry."

Tumu Nnoci's bow glowed. Gar held up the time crystal. The separation between the dimensions wavered. Skylyn arrived. A quick glance around and she grinned. "A time fold, right?"

Brie held out a hand. "Right. I am Brielle AsTar. You are carrying my babies."

Skylyn gave her a spontaneous hug, smiled up at Thorlu, and examined her other rescuers. Gar caught her attention first. "I love your glasses."

He offered a hand, palm up. "I'm Garon. Friends call me Gar."

She touched her palm to his, then touched her heart. "I am Skylyn. My friends call me Sky."

Torgin and Esán introduced themselves. Torgin motioned them all closer. "We need to get back to Dee and leave for *El Aperdisa*."

They arrived to find the healers waiting. "Yencara knows a bit about time folds. He is certain we are in one. I suggest we leave before he figures out anything that can create problems for us."

34

El Aperdisa

B rie felt her heart sink. The time to bring the genetic team to the fold had elapsed. Removing The MasTer's gene was no longer an option. She looked at the people surrounding her. *Because of me, you are in danger.* With a sigh, she tucked away her personal desires and held out a hand. Musette materialized. Her companions gave her their attention.

"Dee, Sky, and Marsili, prepare to enter the Land of All Time and No Time. You will experience some discomfort that will fade. Since no time passes in Mittkeer, Vygel will be safe in the pod. Stay close and follow my lead."

Torgin, Esán, and Gar prepared to do their part. Thorlu put shields around the entire group. Musette's crystal glow shimmered through the time fold. Mittkeer enclosed them in a star-sprinkled sphere of serene quiet.

Torgin ignored the upheaval in his stomach and held the compass in front of him. "Riffley."

The Firefly Constellation glowed on the chart floating above his hand.

Brie lifted her staff. Stars blurred, then refocused. The Firefly's wings sparkled overhead. The Land of Time withdrew, leaving them in *El Aperdisa*'s infirmary.

Brie introduced Dee and Marsili to the ship's Head Healer. While a med-tech settled Skylyn on a bed to observe her and the babies, a team prepared Vygel for a move to a more advanced isolation pod.

Esán touched her arm. "Let's leave them to it. You need to rest. I'll let Commander Odnamo know we're back aboard and ask him to have quarters prepared for Thorlu, Skylyn, and the healers. Torgin will take you to yours."

Brie glanced around. "Where is Gar?"

"He's gone to find Spyglass." Torgin linked arms with her. "I'm certain our friends will want to hear everything, so we'd better rest while we can."

Brie half expected to find Ari and Penee waiting for her in their shared suite. When she arrived to find it empty and quiet, she slipped into her sleeping cubicle and tried to nap. Sleep dodged, ducked, eluded her attempts to sink into its forgetfulness. On the verge of giving up, she stared at the ceiling. Thoughts came and went. Images fluttered into view and melted away. A yawn left her eyes teary. A sigh ushered her into dreamland.

S omeone sitting next to her brought her to the surface. Esán smiled down at her. "You've slept for the better part of a turning. How do you feel?"

She stretched and sat up, her thoughts making a swift dive into the loss of her option to live without The MasTer's intrusion into her life.

Esán regarded her with a look between sympathy and something she couldn't quite pin down. "Why don't we take a walk. Rethson and Elf are in flight training. Ari and Penee won't finish their work in DiMensionery for another chron-circle."

"Let me clean up a little. I'll join in the living space."

After he hugged her and left, Brie luxuriated in a shower cleanse, put on clean clothes, and brushed her long curls into a low ponytail. Refreshed and more relaxed, she joined him.

Their walk took them down a long corridor to a section of the ship she didn't recognize. Esán escorted her through a hatch that led to another short passage at the end of which Dee waited.

"I have a surprise for you, Brielle." She pulled a curtain aside.

Brie stared. Three people awaited them in an operating theatre. Info-screens, panels of lights, and sensors covered the walls. At the center was a table on a pedestal. Hope sparked. She turned to Esán. "Is this what I think it is?"

Dee answered. "If you think it's a genetic operating space, you are correct. *El Aperdisa* is better equipped to do a Somatic Gene removal than *Surgentin*. The team trained in the most advanced techniques in the Inner Universe. So my question, Brie, is do you give us permission to remove The MasTer's gene?"

The Star of Truth sent a wave of warmth through her. Deep in the recesses of her being, The MasTer stirred. Anger stabbed. She clenched her fists, set her jaw, and forced it to dissipate.

A short, sturdy man joined them. His intelligent eyes studied her.

Dee took her hand. "This is Geno-Tech Quinter. He heads the Genetic Team and has questions for you."

G-T Quinter glanced at the mini-screen in his hand. "We know you changed the genome from masculine to feminine. Is there anything else?"

Brie shivered. "A renegade personality has attached itself to the gene. Will you remove it, too? If not, what can I expect?"

Their expressions serious, Dee and Quinter conferred. Quinter nodded and returned to his team.

Dee faced her. "We aren't certain how the personality will react. G-T Quinter believes our best bet is to turn off the gene and observe you over the next few turnings. Once he and the team are clearer about the personality's attachment to the gene, they will decide the next step. If your decision is yes, you'll be helping yourself and others as well. Does that work for you?"

"May I have a minute to talk with Esán?"

"Of course, we'll be right here."

Brie drew Esán with her into the short passage. "You heard what they said. Should I do the procedure?"

"If you can help make things easier for you and your babies by assisting in the team's research, do it. What does the Star say?"

"It grew warm, a positive sign. Thank you." She hugged him. "It's the right thing to do."

He walked her back to the operating theatre. "I'll be right here when you're done."

His warm kiss gave her the confidence to walk over to Dee. "I'd like to help you figure out how to remove not only the gene but the personality."

G-T Quinter joined them. "Today's procedure won't take long. We'll use a focused white laser beam to pinpoint the gene. Once we know its position, we use a second laser to turn it off. It is what we call Light Surgery. It does not damage the tissues of the body, unless directed to do so. Healer De Dilliére will get you ready and explain the process."

ygel lay in the darkness of barely being. Years of hate and revenge, wound into a yarn-like ball, unraveled. Memories of Rayn, Rasiana, and Abarax stirred up feelings of jealousy. Because he loved The MasTer, they hated him. Thorlu's jealous desire to be The MasTer's personal Mocendi threaded his thoughts with resentment. Images of Thorlu's son flickered. *I erased Elf's memories and ordered his vocal cords cut.* A groan rattled in his throat. *How would I feel if he was my son?*

Air hissed from his lungs, leaving him gasping. Lids fluttered open. He cringed. Thorlu Tangorra's handsome face filled the oval window. *I remember.* A cough shook him. Self-hatred squeezed his heart. *I don't want to know who I am or what I've done.* Tremors of self-loathing hit one after the other until he turned his head away to avoid the sympathy on his fellow Mocendi's face.

Pain pierced his heart. His back arched. Lights in the pod flashed red. Med-Techs responded. The healer in charge called for the silver syringe. A sting in his neck sent him back into darkness.

The pain in his chest eased. His breathing stabilized. Nothingness so thick it smothered him left him wheezing. A slow emergence from the depth of his quiescent mindlessness brought him to the realization he wandered in desert-like grayness stretching in all directions. Detachment escorted him through a colorless plain. He looked behind him. No footsteps marked his journey. The pain of his life misted into nothing. He sought a sense of his physical body, failed to find it, and sighed. *I wonder if I am dead?*

"*Surazal.*" The word filled his knowing. "*Surazal, the land between life and death...*"

Thorlu sat next to the Isolation Ward, waiting for an update from Dee. Vygel's second heart attack had left him at death's door. Hands covering his face, he allowed his emotions to swim freely. *You took care of me when I was a child, Vygel Vintrusie. You fanned the positive in me, taught me to follow my instincts for good.* He lowered his hands. "The MasTer destroyed us both, and we did not know."

Dee hurried to into the small room. "Vygel is passing. It's time to say goodbye. Also, I encourage you to help him let go."

She led him to a curtain cubicle, where his boyhood friend lay pale and still.

Thorlu swallowed a lump in his throat. "I've watched others die but never felt like this."

Understanding glinted in Dee's eyes. "You've known each other for a long time. Sit with him, hold his hand, if you're comfortable doing so, and talk to him, Thorlu. The last of our senses to go at death is our hearing. Tell him stories. Remind him of your childhood together. Let him know he can let go of life. You will care for his son." She reached for the curtain. "I'll be right outside. Call if you need me."

Thorlu angled the chair to face his friend and sat down, his gaze fixed on the pale, lifeless face. "They tell me you are close to death, Vygel." He leaned closer. "Your recovery is unlikely, and yet I long for it." He squeezed the bridge of his nose. "If you recover, the removal of the gene from your son will enrage you. How will I help you understand how important your son's future is to the future of El Stroma?"

Vygel's hand twitched. Thorlu held it between his palms. "You may die in peace, my friend. I promise to care for your son like he is my own. Your body is ravaged, your memories are gone. Let death take you to the place of your longings."

A shiver ran through Vygel. His eyes fluttered open and focused on Thorlu's face. A soft exhale left his body empty of life.

Dee stepped into the cubicle, rested her hands on his shoulders, and whispered. "He's gone, Thorlu. When you are ready, I'll be outside."

Allowing his friend's passing to sink in, Thorlu rose, touched his heart, and bowed his head. As he refocused on his friend, a flash of purple caught his attention. *A Mocendi and his cape must not be parted at death.* The knowledge those aboard were unlikely to know the Mocendi Rules of Death prompted

Thorlu to fold Vygel's cape over his arm to return to him at his burial. He bid his friend a last farewell and stepped from death's empty quiet into the main infirmary.

Dee greeted him with a sympathetic smile. "You must allow yourself to grieve, Thorlu. When you are ready, we must discuss Vygel's funeral wishes."

"I believe it is best to discuss them now. Where can we talk in private?"

She led him to a small office cubicle. He sat down opposite and placed Vygel's folded cape on the desk.

"Vygel's desire has always been to join Rayn, The MasTer's carrier, in the TreBlayan Pit of Death. I prefer the funeral to be private unless the twins and their friends wish to attend." He took a breath and stood. "I'll speak with Commander Odnamo to arrange for taking Vygel's body down to Soasi, Vygel's home for most of his adult life." He stood. "Perhaps we could meet in the lounge later?"

Dee rose and came around the desk. "I have a meeting with the Head Medical Officer in a few minutes. I'll see you in the lounge when I'm done."

👁 👁

Brie walked from the Genetic Lab with a sense of wonder. The procedure to turn off The MasTer's gene had gone well. G-T Quinter had given her a list of things to watch for and sent her on her way.

Esán met her in the waiting area and gave her a gentle kiss. "How do you feel? You look great."

She touched her head where the light beam had entered. "It was amazing and so simple. Time will tell if Fisaco's personality is part of the gene or separate. Right now, I'm starving."

Esán laughed. "You sound like Gar. Come on."

They enter a private dining area where their friends gathered. Brie looked around the room. Ari and Elf sat together, talking in quiet voices. Den, who had arrived while she was with the Genetic Team, left Penee's side to give her a hug.

"It's great to see you, Brie. Penee and Rethson shared your adventures."

Brie smiled. "It's good to have you back with us, Den. Later, I'd love to hear about your adventures on RewFaar."

Gar came running up to them with Spyglass wagging his tail. "You should see what we're having to eat. They raise all the food on the ship, even the fish!" His specs appeared. He studied her through the thick lenses and grinned. "They did good, Brie. I don't sense The MasTer." He planted a quick kiss on her cheek and joined Torgin in the buffet line.

~ TreBlaya ~

Two turnings later, Thorlu surveyed TreBlaya's return to life from the balcony of Soasi. To his surprise, the young people chose to attend Vygel's funeral. Brie and Esán had helped to plan the service. Dee had accompanied them to the surface and stood by his side. Torgin played the piano and Gar the guitar as everyone filed into the garden. Penee and Ari sang the Song of Passing they learned on the Isle of Neul. Thorlu tucked the Mocendi's cape around his friend and, with the help of the young men, carried the woven basket containing Vygel's body to the edge of the fire pit, where an Astican picked it up, lifted into flight, and let it fall into the flickering flames.

After a farewell meal, the young people and Dee returned to the ship. He remained at Soasi for one last evening.

A noise behind him alerted him he was not alone. He turned to find Elf observing him from the double doors into the house. His son walked toward him and stopped a short distance away. "Brie shared what you did for her. She said I'm back from the depths of the fiord because of you."

The urge to hug his son made Thorlu's hand tremble. He made himself hold still. "I have changed since our last meeting, Troms el Shiv. Someday, I will share what turned me into a scoundrel."

Elf touched his throat. "It is so hard to forgive you when I've hated you for so long. I blamed you for everything bad that happened in my life." He lowered his gaze, swallowed, and looked up. "Do you think we can ever be father and son? Can you forgive me for what I did to you in Atkis?"

A rush of emotion forced Thorlu to concentrate on breathing. "There's nothing to forgive, Elf. We are father and son. As we understand and accept each other, we'll learn what that means. That you're here, and we're talking, is a first step. Thank for taking it."

Elf blinked back a tear and moved to stand beside him. They turned to stare at TreBlaya's healing landscape. Elf rested a hand on the balustrade next to his. The side of their hands touched. He noted a small smile curve his son's lips. Blinking away his own tears, he, too, smiled.

Revenge is a game, one of life's breaking,
That causes more pain, not a remaking.
Those who unwind in their devious brewing
Most often create their personal undoing.

Those who learn the art of forgiving
Discover that life is truly worth living.

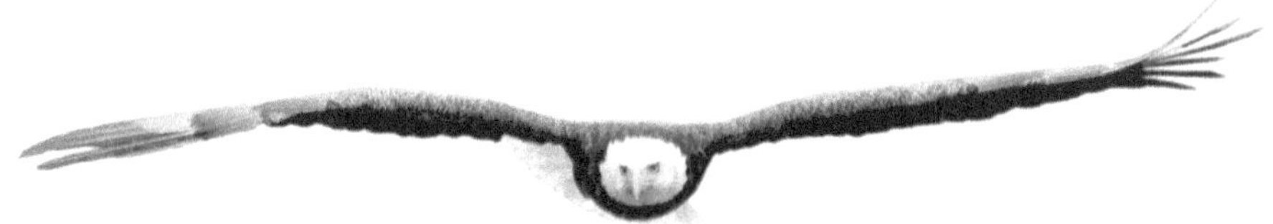

GLOSSARY LINK

A searchable glossary for the
VarTerels' Universe™ is available online at:

www.skrandolph.com/glossary

ACKNOWLEDGMENTS

I am extremely lucky to have a team of players who help to make my books the best that they can be. Critical eyes help to refine my writing and illustrations.

I acknowledge the following with gratitude:

A special thank you to Linda Lane, my editor and mentor. Her no-nonsense approach to both the storyline and any mistakes or errors I've made always makes my writing better. I can't imagine doing what I do without her.

Ann McEntire, my beta and proofreader, finds the little stuff better than anyone I know. I can't thank her enough for always taking the time to help me make my work better.

Leslie Randolph, whose keen eye for errors picks up the little things others miss, is my valued proof reader.

Tom Krantz, my partner in life and in all things regarding the book process, has a range of talents and experience that make him irreplaceable. A talented multitask master, he formats my books for paperback, hardback, and ebooks; manages my website and my newsletter; publishes my novels; and critiques my work, both written and graphic.

To Madison Stocker, Courtney Krantz, Jared Olmsted, Sean Krantz, Charles Lawrence, and Guy Molnar: A special thank you for allowing me to use their images to represent characters in my illustrations.

Although I prefer to use my own photography to create my digital art, I don't always have the breadth of material and visuals required. I thank all the talented artist who contribute to www.pixabay.com, www.stock.adobe.com, and nasa.gov for the supplemental photos that allow me to create detailed illustrations for my novels.

ABOUT THE AUTHOR
FROM DANCE STAGE TO WRITTEN PAGE

STORYTELLER

Dance, humanity's most ancient narrative art, captivated S.K. Randolph as a child living and dancing in the British Crown Colony of Bermuda. After graduating from the University of Utah with a BFA in Ballet, her dance career spanned four decades of performing, mentoring, teaching, choreographing, and directing. Over sixty of her original choreographic works were brought to life for theatre audiences around the globe, establishing her deep foundation in pacing, movement, and narrative structure. She was the Ballet Mistress of the Colorado Ballet and the Alberta Ballet as well as cofounder of the Bermuda Dance Theatre. For the last two decades of her dance career, she educated the next generation of creatives, as Director of Dance at Interlochen Center for the Arts, named the "#1 Best High School for the Arts in America", and at St. Paul's School.

S.K. at the helm of her forty-foot boat leaving Seattle, Washington on a transformative seventy-five day voyage up the Inside Passage to Sitka, Alaska. Then a decade writing while living afloat swinging on the anchor rode in one remote Alaskan cove or another. 2010

DIGITAL ARTIST

S.K., a pioneer in the digital art sphere, has been creating original digital art since 1997. Utilizing a unique, self-taught technique, she transforms photographs into vibrant, otherworldly masterpieces using Adobe Photoshop. Today, her VarTerels' Universe™ series features nearly 500 of these hand-crafted digital illustrations.

VOYAGE TO WRITING

In 2010, S.K. retired from the dance world to live with her partner on their boat in the world's largest temperate rainforest along the remote and rugged coast of Alaska. Isolated in nature, she spent a "gap decade" afloat honing her writing, refining her digital art style, and mastering shipboard skills (including catching dinner). It was during this creative voyage that she transitioned her storytelling from the dance stage to the written and illustrated page, self-publishing her first novel, *DiMensioner's Revenge*, in 2011.

TODAY

Now, in 2026, S.K. is currently writing the twenty-first installment of her saga. She and her partner reside in the lower-48 states, living on the side of the largest flat-top mountain in the world. From her mountain studio, she continues to cultivate her "Illustrated by the Author" Science Fantasy series, VarTerels' Universe™, dedicating her life to the timeless journey of a true storyteller.

S.K.'s website
www.skrandolph.com

Facebook
facebook.com/skrandolph11

Substack
skrandolph.substack.com

Destiny

VarTerels' Universe™ Book 17
Part II- CoaleScence
Novella
32 pages

Brielle AsTar, the youngest VarTerel in the Inner Universe, must hide her genetically engineered babies and their surrogate mother from ruthless spies while battling a dangerous gene threatening to resurrect an ancient evil.

Available in the paperback *Agothany 2* and as an individual eBook.

An epic science fantasy saga told through art and words
in companion shorts and illustrated novels,
available as paperbacks and eBooks.

Illustrated by the author, color in eBooks
and black and white in paperbacks.

Presented in suggested reading order.

DiMensioner's Revenge

Illustrated by the Author
VarTerels' Universe™ Book 1
Part I - UnFolding
Novel
642 pages, 73 illustrations

Four young people from a regimented city discover their destiny when they journey to Myrrh—the hidden remnant of Old Earth—only to find themselves hunted by a vengeful DiMensioner, his death shadow, and alien mercenaries determined to destroy everything they've come to cherish.

Available as a paperback with black & white illustrations and eBook with color illustrations.

Gifts

VarTerels' Universe™ Book 2
Part I - UnFolding
Novella
34 pages

A pregnant art student must deceive a ruthless surveillance state about her twin daughters' true father, the brother of a powerful Guardian, or become the perfect hostage in a deadly political game.

Available in the paperback *Agothany 1* and as an individual eBook.

Discovery

VarTerels' Universe™ Book 3
Part I - UnFolding
Novelette
32 pages

Fourteen-year-old Torgin must choose between protecting his passion for music and spying on the only friends who understand him in a dystopian city where the government controls every aspect of life.

Available in the paperback *Agothany 1* and as an individual eBook.

Rescue

VarTerels' Universe™ Book 4
Part I - UnFolding
Novella
31 pages

In a dystopian city where surveillance is constant and conformity is mandatory, twin sisters Ari and Brie must navigate secret portals and evade ruthless patrollers to rescue a lost boy and return him home before their forbidden act lands them all in the dreaded Five Towers.

Available in the paperback *Agothany 1* and as an individual eBook.

ConDra's Fire

Illustrated by the Author
VarTerels' Universe™ Book 5
Part I - UnFolding
Novel
504 pages, 59 illustrations

Kidnapped to a hostile desert planet, Esán must survive while his friends race to rescue him, unaware that their rescue mission will unleash ancient powers and reveal family secrets that could destroy three worlds.

Available as a paperback with black & white illustrations and eBook with color illustrations.

Encounters

VarTerels' Universe™ Book 6
Part I - UnFolding
Novella
29 pages

When a vengeful DiMensioner forms an unholy alliance with a death shadow to steal a legendary crystal and destroy the Guardian who banished him, he discovers that the children he saves along the way may hold the key to his own redemption—or his ultimate damnation.

Available in the paperback *Agothany 1* and as an individual eBook.

Metamorphosis

VarTerels' Universe™ Book 7
Part I - UnFolding
Novella
31 pages

Wrongfully banished from his home planet and left disfigured by a catastrophic magical accident, Laurent must shed his arrogance and accept his broken reflection before he can master the ancient art of dimensional magic and discover his true purpose.

Available in the paperback *Agothany 1* and as an individual eBook.

MasTer's Reach

Illustrated by the Author
VarTerels' Universe™ Book 8
Part I - UnFolding
Novel
686 pages, 60 illustrations

As the UnFolding reaches its climax, teenagers wielding legendary artifacts must evade deadly hunters across multiple worlds while uncovering shocking truths about The MasTer's identity and a centuries-old conflict that threatens to destroy the Eleo Preda people forever.

Available as a paperback with black & white illustrations and eBook with color illustrations.

Wanted

VarTerels' Universe™ Book 9
Part I - UnFolding
Novella
33 pages

A fugitive with a dark past escapes prison only to discover he's being hunted by a powerful mystical league that wants to control his untapped ability to bend reality itself.

Available in the paperback *Agothany 1* and as an individual eBook.

Jaradee's Legacy

Illustrated by the Author
VarTerels' Universe™ Book 10
Part I - UnFolding
Novel
336 pages, 51 illustrations

Separated as children during a brutal genocide, birth-mate twins Rayn and Rethdun must survive across galaxies while carrying the genetic legacy that could save their dying civilization or destroy them both.

Available as a paperback with black & white illustrations and eBook with color illustrations.

Agothany 1

An anthology of
the Companion Shorts
Gifts, Discovery, Rescue Encounters,
Metamorphosis, and *Collision*
in VarTerels' Universe™
Part I - UnFolding
256 pages

Available as a paperback.
Each Companion Short also
available as an individual eBook.

Incirrata Secret

Illustrated by the Author
VarTerels' Universe™ Book 11
Part II- CoaleScence
Novel
428 pages, 45 illustrations

Racing against ruthless enemies across mystical dimensions, the Universe's youngest VarTerel and a prophesied leader with legendary eyes must rescue kidnapped mentors from a cloud-shrouded island where a phantom octopus guards secrets that could reshape their world—or destroy it.

Available as a paperback with black & white illustrations and eBook with color illustrations.

Lessons

VarTerels' Universe™ Book 12
Part II- CoaleScence
Novella
26 pages

On the desert planet of DerTah, blind oracle WoNadahem Mardree must overcome devastating loss and her deepest fears when a mysterious shape-shifting DiMensioner arrives seeking knowledge, challenging everything she believes about fate, power, and love.

Available in the paperback *Agothany 2* and as an individual eBook.

Corps Stones

Illustrated by the Author
VarTerels' Universe™ Book 13
Part II- CoaleScence
Novel
438 pages, 52 illustrations

A young VarTerel and her friends journey to 1969 New York City to recover three stolen Corps Stones before their entire solar system collapses into chaos.

Available as a paperback with black & white illustrations and eBook with color illustrations.

Fishing

VarTerels' Universe™ Book 14
Part II- CoaleScence
Novella
30 pages

A twelve-year-old boy with extraordinary powers must survive slavery, betrayal, and the relentless pursuit of a deadly league that murdered his parents and will stop at nothing to control him.

Available in the paperback *Agothany 2* and as an individual eBook.

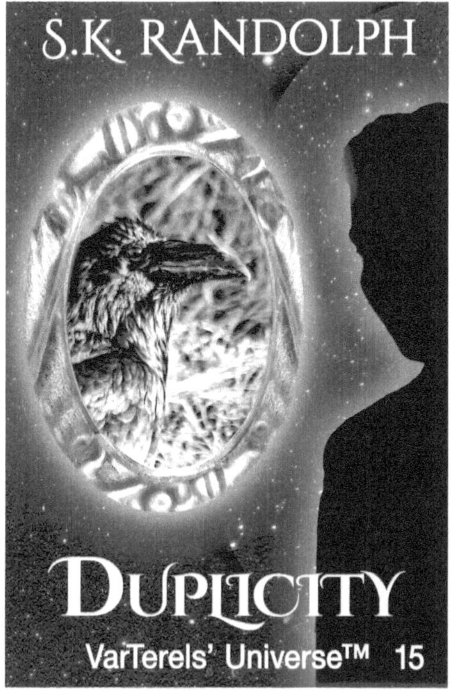

Duplicity

VarTerels' Universe™ Book 15
Part II- CoaleScence
Novella
30 pages

A sworn protector with shapeshifting abilities and a future Guardian destined to unite worlds must outwit a ruthless League of sorcerers determined to claim her before she can fulfill her destiny.

Available in the paperback *Agothany 2* and as an individual eBook.

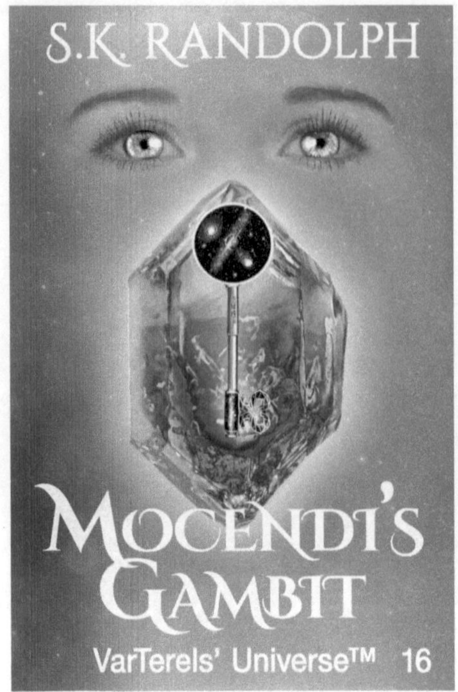

Mocendi's Gambit

Illustrated by the Author
VarTerels' Universe™ Book 16
Part II- CoaleScence
Novel
328 page, 35 illustrations

Stripped of her protective Star of Truth and held captive aboard an enemy ship young VarTerel Brielle AsTar must trust an unlikely ally—a former enemy seeking redemption—and escape through folded time before The MasTer's followers destroy everything she loves.

Available as a paperback with black & white illustrations and eBook with color illustrations.

Destiny

VarTerels' Universe™ Book 17
Part II- CoaleScence
Novella
32 pages

Brielle AsTar, the youngest VarTerel in the Inner Universe, must hide her genetically engineered babies and their surrogate mother from ruthless spies while battling a dangerous gene threatening to resurrect an ancient evil.

Available in the paperback *Agothany 2* and as an individual eBook.

Cimondeli

VarTerels' Universe™ Book 18
Part II- CoaleScence
Short Story
12 pages

Sixteen-year-old Desty has never seen the sky, but when she ventures beyond her underground refuge for the first time, she discovers her telepathic gifts, befriends a majestic flying lizard, and learns that healing a poisoned world may begin with bridging the divide between enemy tribes.

Available in the paperback *Agothany 2* and as an individual eBook.

Queen's Quest

Illustrated by the Author
VarTerels' Universe™ Book 19
Part II- CoaleScence
Novel
420 pages, 44 illustrations

A young VarTerel, a bearer of cosmic seeds, a musical genius, and a street-smart boy with magical spectacles must unite their extraordinary powers to shatter an impenetrable dome, defeat a rogue demi-god, and complete a universal cycle before time runs out.

Available as a paperback with black & white illustrations and eBook with color illustrations.

Collision

Prequel to VarTerels' Universe™
VarTerels' Universe™ Book 20
Part II- CoaleScence
Novella
64 pages, 14 illustrations

A genius physicist barely out of university must lead a team of Galactic Guardians wielding ancient instruments of power to rescue Earth from total annihilation, even as enemies from his past conspire to ensure the planet's destruction.

Available in the paperback *Agothany 2* with black & white illustrations and as an individual eBook with color illustrations.

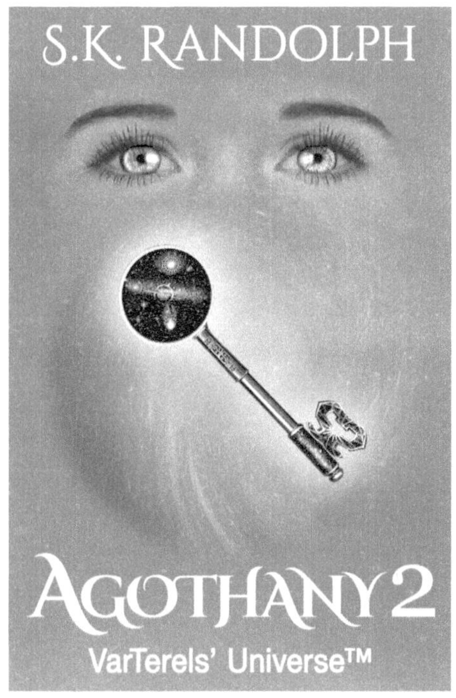

Agothany 2

An anthology of
the Companion Shorts
Lessons, Fishing, Duplicity
Destiny, Cimondeli, and *Collision*
in VarTerels' Universe™
Part II - CoaleScence
284 pages

Available as a paperback.
Each Companion Short also
available as an individual eBook.

Divided Destinies

Illustrated by the Author
VarTerels' Universe™ Book 21
Part III- QuicKening
Novel
a Work In Progress

Divided Destinies is a work in progress with a targeted release date of late 2026. An illustrated novel, it starts QuicKening, Part III of the VarTerels' Universe™.

See www.SKRandolph.com for current status and subscribe to S.K.'s newsletter to receive progress updates.